THE DRUNKEN COMIC BOOK MONKEYS IN:

SCARY TALES OF SCARINESS

REFLUX EDITION

Emily!! Thanks for listening to adults who act younger than you!

WRITTEN BY

BRIAN KOSCIENSKI

&

CHRIS PISANO

EDITED BY

JEFF YOUNG

"It's Not My Fault!"

Emily, Thanks for coming out. CP We're really sorry!

ILLUSTRATED BY

JOHN BALL

WWW.FORTRESSPUBLISHINGINC.COM

The Drunken Comic Book Monkeys in: Scary Tales of Scariness
 SECOND EDITION
ISBN: 978-0-578-05804-7

Front and back cover photography by Victoria Koscienski and Jeff Young
Front and back cover design by Brian Koscienski
Cover models:

Brian Koscienski
Chris Pisano
Jeff Young
Christine Czachur
Bear shaped gummy snack
Brian Koscienski
A plastic spider

This book is available for wholesale through the publisher, Fortress Publishing, Inc. The publisher also grants a discount on the purchase of three or more copies of single titles.

Fortress Publishing, Inc.
3704 Hartzdale Drive
Camp Hill, PA 17011

WWW.FORTRESSPUBLISHINGINC.COM

CONTENTS

FOREWORD

REFLUX... many of us have experienced this vile affliction at one time or another in our lives, but probably never like this.... So grab a brew and let me take you on a strange journey....

Audience yelling: "How strange was it?"

"It was so strange they wrote stories about it and published them as books!"

A few years ago, three now if I'm not mistaken, I was attending a SF/F/H Conference in Pittsburgh called Confluence. During the final hours of the last day, I finally had a few minutes to wend my way through the dealer's room. As I walked about looking at everything, I noticed a sign that said, "Haiku – 5 cents." I looked up to see two of the most gorgeous men I have ever laid my eyes on (next to my fiancé' that is, who looks frighteningly similar to Chris and Brian). *Oh Boy!* I thought to myself. *These two look like fun! I wonder if I can get a Haiku for free?* I pulled my fiancé, Kevin, over to the table and asked if they would be willing to trade a Haiku for a limerick — which Kevin would write — but with the stipulation that I got to choose the subject. And, to make things more interesting, it would be a race so they would only have three minutes to write it. After Brian sized Kevin up and down, he smiled, nodding his oversized head in agreement; I expect that he felt this wouldn't be much of a challenge as he was at least ten years younger and therefore should be able to think with all the speed of a younger man.

Each of the men whipped out their... pads of paper and readied their pens, waiting for the unknown subject which I was about to supply. My lips parted and the single word, "Sex," emerged, breathed out with all the innuendo I could muster — especially given that I was exhausted from the weekend of revelry. Brian's hand started to shake. Chris turned around and moved off to a corner (which I later learned was to laugh his ass off under his breath). Kevin stated, "That's too easy; you have to be more specific than that." Without missing a beat another two words departed from my lips, "Oral Sex."

Brian's hand shook harder, his pad trembled. Chris's shoulders heaved (seriously, we thought he was sick) and Kevin started writing furiously. Brian's pen remained poised and shaking over his pad of paper while beads of sweat broke out on his already too shiny head. Not to be outdone by an old(er) guy, he put pen to paper, but not before we heard him mutter under his breath, "Man, I haven't even had a beer yet today!"

A hush fell over the room. Even those who had no idea what was going on, seemed to sense the tension that emanated from the two men — well, Brian mostly. Kevin was having a good time. Either that, or they all heard me say, "oral sex" a little too loudly.

I counted down the minutes. Both men scribbled frantically on their papers. Chris's shoulders trembled in the corner. "Time!" I called. The two put away their pens and handed me their papers. So what did they write you ask? That's not important right now. What is important is this book you hold in your hands.

I imagine at this point you might be expecting that I'm going to write a flattering review about the stories and gush about how hilarious, witty and quirky Chris and Brian are. Why would I do that? You have the book in your hand, so read it and decide for yourself! Geesh! Some people want you to do everything for them. Why would you think I would tell you that the stories in here are absolutely wonderful, when you can make that determination for yourself? Do you think I would be sitting here wasting my time writing this if I didn't think their books contain some of the most awesome, funny and entertaining stories I've read in a long time? No! No, I tell you! I would not! Ah ... ahem . . . What I will tell you is this; now that I know Brian and Chris (probably better than a human ought to) I suspect their stories are somewhat of a partially fictionalized autobiographical nature with a bizarre twist of some fractional hallucinogenic delusions of adequacy.

So grab another cold brew and that roll (or bottle) of antacid and prepare yourself to feel the burn as you experience a whole new kind of REFLUX!

~Tia Tormen xo

Warning! Side effects from reading this book may include, but are not limited to:

Difficulty breathing (from laughing hard), Pain under the rib-cage (from side splitting laughter), gluteus-maximus discomfort (from prolonged periods of sitting in one place), sleeplessness (from staying awake so you can read more), mild stomach discomfort (if you chose to eat the leftover chicken wings) and numbness and tingling in the entire body (from the feelings associated with happiness and well-being).

If you experience any of the above symptoms, call your nearest professional immediately. That way you can recommend this book to them.

Serious side effects can include; unadulterated cravings for chicken wings, an increase in beer consumption and the very slight possibility of an odd attraction to overly pale-skinned, or Neanderthalic bald men.

Do not read if you're already involved with any stories containing pink socks, bald men, gratuitous beer consumption, busty women, counterfeit selves, or a goat.

Stories should not be read within one hour of consuming any type of alcoholic beverage . . .wait, what? Why did I say that? I didn't mean it!

*A note from the Editor

Beer? Leftover chicken wings? (as if such a thing as leftovers exists around these two guys) Pshaw! Who does this chick think she is? Anyone who's read one of The Drunken Comic Book Monkey's books could have written this . . . well, except for that great part about the Haiku/Limerick contest . . . but that's not the point! After all I've been through and done for these guys, they get someone else to write the foreword for them! Damn it! I seriously feel like I've been dissed. Just thought you should know that.

— Jeff

THE DRUNKEN COMIC BOOK MONKEYS
vs.
THE CROCOGATOR

"Florida," Brian said.

"Florida," Chris said.

"Florida!! WOOOOOOOOO!" both men screamed as they crossed the Georgia border in their gray Saturn. Excitement filled the car. Their long drive would come to an end and a week of binge drinking could begin. The men marveled at the palm trees lining the highway. As residents of Pennsylvania, neither had ever seen such trees in real life, nor were they accustomed to the warm climate. The windows remained up, though, because of the humidity. They were both bald, but feared the moist air would frizz their goatees.

Chris handed Brian, navigating from the passenger seat, printed directions to their motel. Brian gave the orders, Chris followed them. However, Brian couldn't help but notice with every turn they seemed to move further from civilization and descend deeper into the wilderness. Concerned, Brian asked, "You made reservations at the cheapest place possible, didn't you?"

"Yep," Chris replied.

"Econo Lodge?"

"Nope."

"Howard Johnsons?"

"Nope."

"Dare I ask where?"

"Lucky Larry's Luxury Log Cabins."

"I hate you."

Chris began to hate himself as he pulled into the motel's driveway; bare dirt pockmarked with muddy puddles and lined with cypress, tupelo and black gum trees. The dirt path opened up to a cul-de-sac, lined with seven buildings, three log cabins on either side of the rental office. The office was a large log cabin itself; however, half of it protruded over a vast swamp.

Chris parked the car, now evenly coated mud brown, in between four mud brown pick-up trucks. Brian and Chris exited, their feet sinking a half-inch everywhere they walked, and followed the signs to the rental office.

"Do you think they have valet?" Brian asked.

"Shut up," Chris replied.

"Maybe they validate. You think they validate? They should *at least* validate."

"Shut up."

Following the sign, the men thought the next step to be impossible, a misprint at least. They each read it four times, but it was the same each time. The entrance to the office was through the part of the building hanging over the swamp with no discernable walkway to be found. Upon studying the building closer, they discovered scuffmarks around make-shift finger holes and foot holds leading from where they stood to alongside the building over the swamp. Seeing little choice, Brian and Chris hugged the mildew reeking wood and scooted along the wall. Once they turned the corner, a porch presented itself as well as a door labeled, "Come in."

Walking across the rickety foyer, floorboards creaking and begging for mercy with every step, Chris approached the check in desk. Brian admired the wall of taxidermy animal heads: two bear, three deer, a zebra, two mountain lions, and five large alligators. All the animals shared the same expression of shock and awe. Looking closer, Brian couldn't help but whisper to himself, "That's some good eatin'."

"Reservations for 'The Drunken Comic Book Monkeys,' please," Chris said to the desk clerk.

The clerk, ninety-five years young, offered a polite smile, exposing more holes than teeth. His white tank top, stained a dull yellow in some spots, exposed dozens of one-inch hearts tattooed up and down both arms. "Yep. Got 'em. Here's your key and here are the rules."

Confused by the unique protocol, Chris looked at the laminated sheet the clerk handed to him. "Rule number one, no bringing back women of ill-repute, unless you get one for the desk clerk."

"My favorite rule," the clerk said. The enthusiasm in his smile was only surpassed by that found in his voice.

Chris chuckled, appreciating the old man's will. "Happen often, does it?"

The clerk showed off both arms with pride. "Each heart here represents an attendee to the rocket show."

Still chuckling, Chris asked, "Rocket show?"

Without a word, the nonagenarian lifted his shirt to expose white body hair, liver spots, and fifty more heart tattoos around the words "ROCKET SHOW" followed by a downward pointing arrow.

Chris threw up a little in the back of his throat. He pushed it down as he looked back at the laminated list of rules. "No peeing in the parking lot. Clean all stains from carpets before checkout. No Satanic rituals. No pets. Suggested curfew is 9:00."

"Live by the rules, boy," The old man said.

Remembering how his last line of questioning turned out, Chris asked the next question with trepidation. "Curfew? 9:00?"

"The beast, boy. The beast."

"What 'beast'?" Brian asked, walking over to Chris and snatching the list of rules.

"The Crocogator. Meanest creature to ever walk the planet."

"Croco...? Are you kidding me?"

"There's no kidding when it comes to the Crocogator. Twenty-five feet long, alligator on one end, crocodile on the other."

"Really? If that's the case, then how does he poo?"

"He don't. That's what makes him so meeeeeeeeean!"

"Poo?" Chris asked Brian. "What are you? Four?"

"Hey," Brian snapped back. "I'm a freakin' polite guy."

"You're as polite as a dog fart at a wedding. And you're talking to a guy who has a steady diet of 'women of ill-repute.' "

"So? Doesn't mean he condones swearing. If he doesn't swear, then I don't swear."

"Seriously? Since when? There's no point to that. We all know what you mean, so just say it. Just say sh..."

"Boys," the old clerk interrupted. "You're missing the point. The Crocogator lives in the swamp here. In fact, all the animal heads on the wall are all that was left of them after they became the Crocogator's snack. He usually sleeps 'til 9:00 and wakes up hungry. So, it's best to be indoors by then."

Before Brian or Chris could say another word, a loud, sharp clap of quick thunder rattled the dust from the building's rafters. "What was that?"

"Hunters determined to bring in the damnable beast. They're the ones renting out all the other cabins. They must be warming up their guns, doing some target practice."

Unblinking, Brian glared at Chris.

"What?" Chris asked.

"Right now we could be crashing a wedding or riding a baggage cart up and down hotel hallways. Thanks to you, we now have a curfew."

"Quit your whinin'. Let's go meet the neighbors. They sound ... interesting."

"I need a beer."

Exiting the office, Chris and Brian scooted along the make shift ledge to the dirt parking lot where their neighbors congregated. After one look, Brian and Chris became very nervous.

Milling around the four pick-up trucks were eight men, all taller, wider and hairier than Brian. Each man held a shot gun in one had and a can of beer in the other. Despite the muggy Floridian air, they all had a penchant for flannel, and not in the Seattle grunge movement sort of way. They each wore printed t-shirts under their flannel. Eight men, eight shirts: three NASCAR shirts, two football shirts, a bull riding shirt, a shirt advertising cigarettes, and one Shania Twain concert shirt. All of them possessed thick, unkempt beards that mingled with their thick, unkempt shocks of hair. In between the tangles of hair were eyes, and all eight sets locked onto Brian and Chris.

Whooping and hollering echoed through the swamps, as well as some Skynard, until the hunters saw Brian and Chris. Silence accompanied icy glares as the hunters watched Brian and Chris stride toward their car.

"I think we're going to have to squeal like pigs," Brian whispered.

"Shut up," Chris whispered back.

"The guy in the Shania shirt is looking at me."

"Shut up."

"If any of them even blink funny, I'm pushing you down and running."

"Shut up."

"I can totally outrun you, you know."

"I have a plan. Stay calm."

Fighting the urge to kneecap Brian and run himself, Chris opened the trunk, revealing the cooler. He retrieved two beers and handed one to Brian. They broke the graveyard silence by popping the beers.

"They like beer!!" one of the hunters yelled. Whoops and hollers once again echoed through the swamp, as well as gunshots. The hunters kicked Skynyrd back up and continued their merriment.

After downing their beers to settle their frayed nerves, Brian and Chris met the hunters. Of course, being shallow and egocentric, they forgot the names faster than they heard them. However, they did learn that the desk clerk was right – these men were here to kill the Crocogator. The hunters regaled Brian and Chris with embellished stories of the past, what they hunted, what they killed, their favorite monster trucks, their favorite NASCAR drivers, their favorite brand of chew, and which Shania song touched them in the secret cry spot of their hearts. All was going well until one of the hunters asked, "So what're y'all doin' down here?"

Not thinking, as he so often didn't, Brian replied, "We're here for a comic book convention."

Silence. Even Skynyrd retreated.

Chris leaned close to his friend and whispered, "Dude you tell everyone else we're dentists from Kentucky. But with eight rifle wielding psychos, you tell them the truth?"

Brian took a swig of beer, heavy glares of confusion and disgust upon him. Well, since the truth got him in this mess, maybe it would get him out? "This will be Saika's last public appearance ever, and we wanted to meet her."

One hunter arched an eyebrow, intrigued and contemplating Brian's words. "You mean the Swedish porn starlet from the late 70s, early 80s?"

"Yep. She helped me through puberty."

The hunter looked to his friends, then back to Brian and Chris with a cigarette stained smile. He took a gulp of beer, and then shouted, "They like beer *and* porn!"

Hoots and hollers returned. Gunshots returned. Skynyrd returned. Brian and Chris returned to the hunter's good graces. Stories that began "My favorite scene was..." and "I loved when she..." filled the air. Until the man in the Shania shirt added his thoughts.

"I always felt sorry for the girl," he said. "I always thought she did what she did because she craved attention and found no other healthy and fulfilling alternative. I believe in the power of a simple hug – maybe a well received hug would have changed her life and set her down a more rewarding and proper career path."

Awkward silence befell the parking lot as seven hunters turned to their friend, wondering how to respond to his comments. Brian and Chris knew exactly what to do. They jumped in their car with a "Well, gotta go."

Once they drove off the dirt roads and onto a labeled highway, Brian procured the directions to the convention center. Of course, the trip there consisted of persnickety comments like, "Oh, look, a Ramada right there," and "How about that, there's a Hyatt right across the street from the convention center. Who woulda thunk it?" Brian's comments were then followed by profanity laced tirades from Chris and a punch to the shoulder. However, once they got to the convention center, all was well.

They arrived half an hour before the doors opened, which gave them enough time to get ready. After they parked, they popped the trunk. Next to the cooler was a safe, just as large as the cooler. Both men reached into their shirts and pulled out a single key attached to a long chain around each of their necks. They had to enter their keys into the safe and turn them simultaneously, lest the safe explode. Each man placed their right hand on the palm scanners. Then one at a time, they allowed the retinal scanner to scan their eyes. The DNA scanner was next, which meant they had to breathe into the breath analyzer, drip a drop of blood onto the collector, and offer up a hair, Chris from his goatee, Brian from the thick growth on his back. Finally after receiving a text message from a NASA uplink with a unique access code, they opened the safe to retrieve their treasure – two 8 x 10 glossy photos of Saika.

They looked at the ticket line and chuckled; it overflowed outside and streamed along two walls of the building. Cracking open two beers, Brian laughed, "Look at those poor fools, waiting to get tickets. Should have ordered ahead like we did."

"Smartest thing we ever did," Chris replied.

After finishing their beers, they locked the car and headed into the convention center, strutting past the people in line. They were still strutting as they entered the lobby and headed for the exhibition hall. They made it in with no problems. And between the two of them they obtained a program and figured out where Saika was located. That was when the problem occurred. The line outside the building wasn't the line to get into the convention - it was the line to get Saika's autograph. Back outside they went.

Pouting like children, they took a seat on the sidewalk, leaning against the building's wall. Not even caring if Florida had an open container law or not, each reached into their respective pants pocket, pulled out a bottle of beer and popped the top. Brian sighed and looked at his watch. 10:04 a.m. "Well, at least we're not with the hunters."

***

Brian didn't know how true his words were. At the same time, the hunters readied their supplies in four fan-boats; a case of beer for each boat and enough guns and explosives to overthrow a small South

American country. Each boat carried two hunters as they hunkered down and kept their eyes peeled for their prey. One hunter remained extra wary after he learned his Shania shirt wearing friend had a penchant for hugs.

The hunters went over their game plan and double-checked to make sure their walkie-talkies worked. They raced through the swamps and found a tiny island, only large enough to host a lone willow. Each boat had a recently killed piglet. With a few well-placed slashes of hunting knives, the hunters gutted the bait and soaked the entrails in the water. As quickly as possible they draped the four piglet carcasses over branches of the willow. The final step was to rig each carcass with an explosive.

Coasting to four different areas of the swamp, the hunters knew that the blood soaked waters would be too tantalizing to allow the Crocogator to remain asleep. Hours of waiting didn't faze the hunters, patiently watching the waters around them with their fingers on triggers. The men all breathed slowly through their mouths, the moist air too thick to breathe through their noses and the smells of rotting foliage, hinted with methane, too much to take for long periods. Chirping crickets and croaking frogs accompanied the whispered walkie-talkie check-ins every half-hour as well as one hunter's nervous humming of, "Man, I Feel Like a Woman," - but it all stopped with an explosion.

The fans growled to life on all four boats as the hunters raced to see if their trap had been successful. It had not. Scattered remains of a deer showed the hunters their prey still eluded them. Disappointment filled their hearts as they discussed their options. Finally, one hunter thought to question why a deer would traipse through a swamp to a secluded island to set off a trap rigged with piglet corpses. It took little discussion to determine there was only one reason – it had been *thrown* into the trap.

As they came to that conclusion, they also realized they had let their guard down - too late. With a volcanic splash and an explosive roar, the Crocogator attacked. Its thrashing entrance froze the hunters where they stood. They had never been the prey before. Two hunters regretted their lack of preparedness as the Crocogator latched one set of teeth to the port side of the boat, near the bow as it sank its other set of teeth into the starboard side, near the stern. With a twist faster than a lightning strike, the beast cracked the boat into slivers of tinder. The two men disappeared into the monster's jaws as soon as they hit the water.

Self-preservation kicked in for the remaining six hunters. Reflex dictated that flight was a better option than fight since the engines were running and the guns lay at their feet. At full throttle, the three fan boats fled the scene of carnage.

***

Images of carnage flashed through Brian's mind as impatience ran rampant through his head. Four hours after arriving Brian found himself still leaning against a brick wall. Adding insult to injury, he also found himself sober, the one condition in which he most certainly could *not* handle sitting against a wall for four hours. The line had moved, but hardly at the rate of speed for which he had hoped. Passing around the corner of the building, they had one wall to go before they made it back inside the building. One looooong wall. Brian almost wished he had stayed back at the log cabins with the hunters. At least they had beer!

***

Unfortunately, the hunters found themselves in a situation where drinking beer never occurred to them. Disoriented, all three sets tooled through the swamps trying to regroup, trying to find any semblance of familiarity. One set, angered by the loss of their friends, shot at anything that moved in the trees and threw explosives at anything that moved in the water. Stumps and branches exploded as the hunters' anxieties played tricks on them. Finally, they set some explosives, ready to throw, when a ripple in front of the speeding boat produced a scaly bump. The boat rocked with a jolt, knocking one of the hunters off of his feet and the explosives out of his hands. With deafening boom, the flash of fire tore the boat in half and knocked the safety cage off the fan. The first hunter didn't even have time to scream as the spinning blades pulped him to puree. The second hunter splashed about the swamp, foolishly thinking he had a chance. The Crocogator used one head to latch onto the hunter's chest; the other head chomped onto the hunter's thighs, each pulled, ripping the hunter in half.

***

Still against the wall, but a little closer to the door, Brian found stray sheets of paper and ripped them in half, for lack of anything better to do. Not that he couldn't find anything better, but being a creature incapable of patience, his mind had slipped into a near comatose state due to panic overload. He was simply not capable of thinking. So bored, he couldn't even find the creativity to harass Chris about his sunburn. Despite the fact that Chris applied SPF 45 on his head every 24 minutes, the sun still scorched him.

***

Out in the swamp, twilight colors danced off the murky green waters as the scorching sun set. One set of hunters pulled out their portable spot light, hoping the piercing beams would at least blind the animal. Two hours after they heard the explosion and screaming of their doomed friends through their walkie-talkies, they sped through the swamp. Hope inflated their hearts to the point of almost bursting through their chests when they saw salvation – the rental office of Lucky Larry's Luxury Log Cabins. However, they would never make it; the boat passed over the Crocogator, right into its trap. Floating on its back, the Crocogator curled both heads out of the water, toward each other. With ease, each head snatched either hunter from their seat, leaving the unmanned fan boat to crash into a thick clump of trees and burst into flame.

***

Boring. Dull. Boring. Help. Goth girls. G'uh. Help. Boring. Make the boredom stop. Need beer. Boring. Brian thought as he weakly crashed his fists into each other. Closer. Every few minutes pulled him closer to Saika's table. Out of habitual neurosis, Brian opened the flap of his tote bag, checking the security and safety of his prized photo. All was safe.

***

Or so the final set of hunters thought as they guided their fan boat to shore. They outran the Crocogator. But they lost six friends. However, a well-timed Shania song would be able to cure their emotional woes. The last two hunters made plans as they ran to their log cabin to grab some essentials for their escape: who should call the deceased's families, who was going to return the door key to the front desk, when to alert the authorities, which Shania disc to listen to in the truck as they fled. But their escape was never meant to happen.

As they ran from the cabin to the pick-up, they failed to notice the Crocogator hiding behind the row of other trucks, until they heard the hissing roar of the monster. As the Crocogator charged, the hunter looked at his friend brave enough to wear a Shania shirt, and knew there were situations where it was okay for one man to hug another. Watching as two maws of jagged teeth streaked closer was one of them.

***

"We better get hugs out of this," Brian whispered to Chris as they finally approached the woman each of them would consider their first true love.

"Are you kidding me? We're the last in line and the convention closes in three minutes. We deserve more."

"Yeah. Like dinner. We're gonna totally ask her out to dinner."

"And her phone number. We gotta get her phone number."

The anticipation ate away at their guts, their hearts smashed against their ribcages. Sweat poured from their pores. The person in front of them moved away; they were next. The heavens parted to allow a single beam of sunshine to bathe the goddess in a golden glow. Her smile shone. Her eyes sparkled. In a daze, Brian and Chris stepped forth, each handing their pictures of her to sign. Pen ready, she asked, "Who should I make these out to?"

Brian answered with, "Blllemininiminah."

Chris followed with, "Kaaaakaaaakaaaaakaaaaa."

Saika laughed. Being prepared for losers like this, she simply signed her name and drew a heart underneath it. However, she was so enamored by their puppy-dog gazes; she decided to personalize their photos with a kiss, leaving behind vermilion glossy lip prints. Holding their signed photos and tote bags, Brian and Chris smiled like simpletons, turned and walked away. They wore their dopey grins all the way to the car.

Once in the car, they took a moment to look at their pictures and reflect. Then ever so gingerly, they put the pictures in their tote bags, waiting until they returned to the cabin to return them to the safe. During the trip there, Brian and Chris regaled each other with embellished tales of bravado, neither remembering the actual events they talked about. In between bouts of "No, she winked at me ... No, she winked at me," they further enhanced their stories, getting them just perfect for their friends back home - if they ever saw home again.

Still caught up in the afterglow, they didn't notice the time on the clock when they pulled into the parking lot, or the unnatural and eerie quietness. Tittering like school children, they simply parked, grabbed their bags and exited the car. The only sound was the sloshing of their feet through the mud. By the time they heard the devil itself breathing, it had already struck.

Lunging from behind the row of pick-ups, the Crocogator attacked. But the slippery mud affected its footing, missing its targets by inches. Both Brian and Chris dropped their totes as they fell back onto the muddy parking lot. Survival instinct kicked in as they scrabbled to their feet and ran. Brian went right as Chris sprinted left, the Crocogator lunged forward and missed them both. The monster gurgled as both heads blasted deep into the mud.

Looping around, Brian and Chris took advantage of the creature's confusion and dove behind the pick-ups. Huffing and puffing because they were out of shape slobs, they peeked from behind their shelter, hoping to see the enemy and determine their next course of action. What they witnessed next would send them to months of therapy – liquid therapy.

Confused and sloshing through the mud itself, the Crocogator swung both heads with wild, spastic jerks, looking for its prey. Then all four nostrils flared, picking up the scent. With predatory purpose, the creature followed the spoor. Hollow pops of the monster pulling its feet out from the mud filled the night, sending chills down the spines of its prey. Snorting large gulps of air, the Crocogator prowled closer. Closer. Until it found the source – two tote bags.

"No," Chris whispered, a lone tear rolling down his cheek. "No."

Terror gripped Brian, throttling his throat closed.

But they watched with abject horror as the Crocogator attacked and shredded the tote bags, porn-star kissed pictures of Saika and all. Both men stood, wanting to scream, but rage disallowing anything more than feral spitting. Then the Crocogator turned to them.

Sizing each other up, the two heads of the monster locked eyes with the two men. Rage shot from all sets of eyes, as palpable as flying fists. Without so much as turning their heads, Brian and Chris each opened a truck door closest to them. Knowing the hunters as they did, each man reached under a seat and found exactly what they hoped to find – large bowie knives. As if flipping a switch, the men tapped into their inner berserkers and attacked; Brian's battle cry nothing more than a primal howl while Chris screamed, "For Saika!!!"

***

The drive home offered bittersweet memories for the guys. They did get to meet one of the most influential people to touch their lives. Although their cherished memorabilia had been destroyed, the memory had embedded itself so deep in their psyches, they would be able to access it any time, no matter how intoxicated. And they'd be the only people ever to have matching Crocogator skin tote bags and jackets...

INSIDE THE MINDS OF MONKEYS

Editor's note: Greetings intrepid reader! If you are reading this, then that means that we haven't scared you away. Yet. One thing that we wanted to accomplish by releasing a second edition was to give you a behind the scenes look of what goes into creating the stories — such as what those knuckleheads Brian and Chris were thinking. Well, we all know WHAT they usually think about, but I'm hoping this will give you a more in-depth understanding to the stories found within this book. Sort of like the "director's cut with audio commentary" found in the "extras" menu option of most DVDs nowadays.

BRIAN: This is the lead off story. And from what I've heard, one of the fan favorites. This is also one of the first stories we wrote for the book. I always thought it was funny that this creature is the MEANEST creature on the planet because he can't defecate. We chose to use this story as the lead off story because it introduces the reader to us as the characters pretty succinctly. Our motivations are spelled out in no uncertain terms. One unique thing about this story that I'm not sure if many people pick up on, is this is the only one (that I can think of, at least) in which we follow other characters after Chris and I are introduced. There are quite a few that start with characters other than us for set up purposes, but once Chris and I are introduced, the focus usually remains on us. I guess we're just camera-hogging divas!

JEFF: Crocogator is a good introduction to the Drunken Comic Book Monkeys. It shows just what your alter-egos do and includes a freakish monster with the best explanation as to why it's always insanely pissed off. Crocogator frames the eternal arguments and shows your heroic nature in defense of ... well it was a monster — it had to die, right? Anyway, as a first story it does a good job of unveiling your four principles, which are highlighted in *The Drunken Comic Book Monkeys Vs. Themselves*: Beer, Porn Sex and Food- well three of those at least.

CHRIS: Contrary to the way it is portrayed in the movies, retinal scans aren't something one should dismiss without thought. They're fairly invasive, actually. But when we're talking about the security of our 8 x 10 glossies, the Fortress guys will not tolerate shortcuts! Crocogator was a fun story written early on in the DCM timeline and it set the stage, directionally, for several of the stories that followed by incorporating several real life events. The beast itself was mean, but hardly the scariest thing we dealt with in this story. A certain octogenarian was a little too suggestive for my tastes...even I have to sleep sometime!

THE DRUNKEN COMIC BOOK MONKEYS
VS.
LA CHUPACABRA

Being the sheriff for a Tijuana jailhouse wasn't easy. Especially when the jail was on the outskirts of town and all but forgotten by the city's budget. Emilio Lopez had the misfortune of being that sheriff. But he didn't mind. Sure, the excitement of working downtown dwarfed the excitement of reporting to a two cell, dirt floor jailhouse every day, but Lopez enjoyed the peace. On occasion a couple of drunk Americans might stumble into his district or the intermittent neighborhood squabble might occur. Other than that it was usually friendly farmers seeking shade and conversation.

Lopez began his day like any other; he reported in just after sunrise with the local newspaper tucked under his arm, asked his deputy about the two gringos sleeping in one of the cells, and angled the metal fan to blow his direction. After laughing from the deputy's tale of finding and arresting the detainees from the prior evening, Lopez propped his feet on his desk and opened the paper. He smiled as the fan's air cooled his brow.

The perfect day lasted only an hour for Sheriff Lopez; a local farmer interrupted. Despite the sun warming up to punish the area with a sweltering day, a chill ran down Lopez's spine. He knew the farmer's problem would be serious.

This farmer, Juan Valdez, had a diminutive stature, but that never stopped him from starting a late night fight at the local cantina, especially with men larger than him. Save for a deep scar running the length of his right cheek, he was usually victorious. His notorious talent was to eat lit firecrackers before the fuse ran out. Fear was not something this man knew, but he was introduced to it this morning.

While wringing his wide brimmed hat in his hands, the farmer told his tale through sobs and teary eyes. After a late night of beer and guns, Juan passed out only to awaken to find four of his goats mutilated. At first, he assumed he accidentally shot them, but upon further investigation, he found them to be shredded by teeth and claws.

Sheriff Lopez sighed, digging the heels of his hands into his eyes, hoping to keep them from popping out due to his throbbing headache. He turned to his deputy, now wide-eyed with mouth agape like a frightened schoolboy. This was the third such story of the week, confirming what they feared the most.

" La Chupacabra."

The men knew what they had to do – hunt it down and kill it. Knowing the stories and legends of the chupacabra's ferocity, the sheriff decided to forgo the traditional posse gathering and opted to hire the one professional capable of bringing down the chupacabra. The man was a legend himself and just as ferocious – *El Tigre Grande.* After sending his deputy to find and fetch El Tigre Grande, Sheriff Lopez began drawing up potential plans on how to capture and kill the chupacabra. The farmer offered his advice, his guns and his knowledge of the surrounding terrain.

After another hour, the two men came up with half a dozen possible plans. Unfortunately, all six of them involved using bait that couldn't possibly survive the chupacabra for the plan itself to work. The farmer wished to preserve his dwindling livestock, especially since he was usually the one to dwindle it after a long night of drinking. And neither man knew of any towns-person crazy enough to use themselves as bait. Juan cursed. But the sheriff smiled as he remembered one resource available to him. He turned to the occupied jail cell and whispered, "Los Americanos."

In the cell itself, on the dirt floor, slept Brian and Chris, laying so their feet rested near each other's heads. Both men slept soundly until a rather saucy dream caused Brian to twitch his feet, one bare, one adorned with a fuzzy pink sock. With every twitch, the fuzz of the sock tickled Chris's nose. The bald, red-bearded Italian could no longer sleep through such an annoyance. Forcing his eyelids of lead to open, Chris saw the horror of Brian's feet before him.

With a reflexive slap to Brian's calf, Chris snapped awake. "Dude, that's so freaking gross!"

Brian groaned and rolled away from his angry friend, angry himself having his dream interrupted. "Keep it down. I'm having a great dream – I'm the newest cast member in *Xena* and we're filming the bikini episode..."

"Shut up! I don't need to hear anymore! And put your shirt on!"

Brian opened his eyes to see he that used his crumpled shirt as a pillow. He sat up as well and brushed dirt and pebbles from his chest hair before slipping on his black t-shirt.

Disgusted, Chris watched with a sneer. "It looks like you're losing a fight with a bear!"

Rubbing his eyes, Brian replied, "You're just jealous that you haven't gone through puberty yet and can't grow any chest hair."

"Yeah? Well, at least I can dress myself. Why are you wearing a pink sock!"

"Probably the same reason why you are."

Confused, Chris looked at his own feet, horrified to find one bare and a fuzzy pink sock on the other. "Dammit!"

"What's the last thing you remember?"

Chris stared at his pink sock and rubbed his goatee, hoping either action could refresh his memory. To no avail. "We went to the Kentucky Derby."

"Right."

"We handed the ticket taker our tickets."

"Right."

"We started drinking."

"Right."

"And..."

Brian and Chris stared at each other, neither able to recall what happened next. They then realized they were no longer in Kentucky as they looked around their jail cell. Brian sighed as he saw Sheriff Lopez and his farmer friend observing. "Not again."

Standing, brushing the dust off themselves, Brian and Chris met the sheriff at the bars. Chris asked, "Tijuana?"

"Si," Sheriff Lopez replied.

"So, what are we in for?"

"Centelleo."

"*What*?!" Brian yelled, standing behind Chris. "*Centelleo*? *Dear God, we're screwed!*"

Looking over his shoulder, Chris snapped at his friend, "Will you calm down! We don't know how serious it is!"

"*Is it serious*? *Is it serious*?" Brian yelled to Sheriff Lopez.

The sheriff and the farmer looked at each other, then back to the detainees. "Si."

Brian punched Chris in the arm. "*I blame you for this*! *I know you were the one who was doing the centelleo*! *I told you not to centelleo*!"

"But, there is hope, hombres," Lopez said.

"Hope?" Brian asked, almost in tears. "What do we have to do?"

"Community service."

"*We'll do it*!"

Chris smacked Brian. "Will you stop! You're the dumbest smart guy I know!" He then turned to the sheriff and asked, "Exactly what is it that we have to do?"

"Pest control."

"What type of pest?"

"La Chupacabra."

" 'La?' " Brian said. "La is female, right? Is she cute?"

Sheriff Lopez sighed and pinched the bridge of his nose. He knew talking to los Americanos would be difficult, but assumed it would be due to the differences in their language, not pure stupidity. Juan took over. "La Chupacabra is no chica. La Chupacabra is an animal, an animal like no other. Twisted claws, slimy scales and gnarled fangs. It shreds goats and drinks their blood."

Brian shrugged. "I've dated worse. Sign us up."

As the sheriff opened the cell door, Chris turned to Brian. "You just can't let me do the talking, can you?"

"Hey, you were the one doing all the centelleo. Your centelleo got us into this mess; my quick wits will get us out."

"Or into the grave."

"At least we won't be in jail."

As the men bickered, Sheriff Lopez opened his desk drawer and retrieved a bottle of aspirin. He took two for himself and offered two to his farmer friend. They both looked back to the men they released from jail, now kicking dirt from the floor at each other, and popped two more pills. However, their true relief came in the form of the deputy completing his task – finding and retrieving El Tigre Grande.

The fighting ceased, all eyes frozen on the legend, strutting in like a conquering hero. His skin dark and sun leathered, while his thick, black mustache, concealing all evidence of a mouth, cascaded from his face on either side of his chin, down to his chest. Permanently furrowed, his brow displayed the hardships of a man who knew nothing other than hardship. Atop the full head of ink black hair was an equally black beret, adding very little to his four and a half foot tall frame.

"Gentlemen," Sheriff Lopez said with a smile, pointing to the diminutive newcomer. "I will be remanding you into the custody of Tijuana's greatest hunter – El Tigre Grande."

The six-foot-four inch Brian puffed out his chest and approached the hunter. "The large tiger?"

With the stoicism of a tombstone, the hunter replied, "Oui."

"Oui?"

"Oui."

"Do you speak English?"

"Oui, monsieur."

Brian turned to Chris and whispered, "He sure has a funny accent."

Chris whispered back, even though everyone in the jailhouse could hear the conversation. "That's because it's French, jackass."

Incensed, Brian snarled back, "I knew that."

Chris was fairly certain he didn't.

Trying to be intimidating, Brian continued, "So, El Tigre Grande, I noticed that you're not quite as tall as I imagined."

With blinding speed, El Tigre Grande kicked Brian in the

shins, dropping the oafish man to his knees. Looking him square in the eye, El Tigre Grande replied, "Now, neither are you, monsieur."

"Touché," Brian muttered as he then fell to his side.

Chris strode over and kicked more dirt on his friend. "Quit goofing around and get up. We have a job to do."

Knees wobbling, Brian returned to his feet. "Okay, Mister Grande, what do we do first?"

Running his hand over the right side of his moustache, he raised an eyebrow, contemplating. "I think we should return to ze scene of ze crime. Non?"

"Si!" Sheriff Lopez agreed. "But first we need supplies."

It took little discussion to determine that the hunting party would consist of the hung-over Americans, the sheriff, the farmer and the legendary hunter. Unlocking the gun cabinet, Sheriff Lopez unloaded a Smith & Wessen, a Winchester, three Uzis, a .45, a .357, and an M-16, all of which he shared with El Tigre Grande and Juan. Dejected, Brian and Chris looked at each other, then to the sheriff. Chris raised his hand. "Excuse me? Can't ... can't we have one of them guns?"

Knowing the bait had no use for weapons, the Mexicans all looked at each other. Until El Tigre Grande replied, "Non. You have ze pink socks."

"Pink socks?"

"Oui. Sacred socks. Very sacred. Most sacred of all ze foot apparel. Zey will protect you from ze chupacabra."

"But..."

"Non! Enough chitter-chatter. We need to go!"

Heads hanging low, Brian and Chris followed the rest of the crew to an open topped Jeep. Discontent, Brian continued to mumble as he took a seat in the back of the vehicle. "Just *one* gun. That's all I wanted was one gun."

"Quit whining, you siss," Chris replied, sitting next to Brian.

"Yeah? You can't tell me you didn't want one too."

Chris paused, his façade of detachment breaking down. Finally, his eyes sank as his head drooped, revealing his true sadness. "Yeah. I wanted one, too."

The men remained silent for the bumpy ride to Juan's farm. Once they arrived, both Brian and Chris realized that everyone used the term "farm" far too lightly. Sparse dabbles of grass struggled for survival in the densely packed dirt. But there seemed to be plenty of roughage to attract enough bugs to keep the half dozen chickens fed. Whatever grasses the bugs didn't eat were just enough to keep the meandering goats alive. On the east side of the property, taller grasses mixed with round boulders to form a natural barrier between the farm and the base of the mountain.

Two hundred yards from where the Jeep stopped stood the farmhouse, a ramshackle hovel, looking much like a double wide. With a touch as soft as a cactus, El Tigre Grande shoved both Brian and Chris from the Jeep.

"Okay," Brian said, dusting himself off. "What do we do?"

"Ummmm, you are ze lookouts. Oui, ze lookouts. We shall set up traps along ze perimeter. You signal with zis if you see ze Chupacabra." El Tigre Grande tossed a cell phone to Brian.

"Cool. So..." The sound of spinning Jeep tires throwing dirt and pebbles interrupted Brian. Leaving only a cloud of dust, the vehicle sped away.

"Now what?" Chris asked.

"Now, we track it."

"Track it? What do you know about tracking, smart guy?"

"I've seen a show on it."

"Animal Planet?"

"Not exactly."

"Discovery Channel?"

"Ummmm, not quite."

"Well?"

"Scooby-Doo."

"I need a beer."

With an audible grunt, Chris sat on the nearest boulder. He reached into his pocket and pulled out a bottle of beer. Off came the cap and the alcohol soon sluiced into his mouth. "Ahhh."

"You have one for me?" Brian asked.

"Nope."

"That's mighty selfish of you. It's a good thing I brought my own." Following the actions of his friend, Brian sat on a nearby boulder and enjoyed his own beverage that he procured from his own pocket. However, due to his inability to sit still, that lasted for a minute and a half and he strolled over to the nearest patch of thick brush. He took a swig and crouched down, examining a few blades of thick grass. After another swig he sniffed the outcropping of grass. Brian took another drink and then ate the grass.

"What the hell are you doing?" Chris asked.

"What? Uhhhh, I'm ... hunting the Chupacabra."

"By eating the grass?"

"It's a trick I learned from an old Native American."

"You don't know any Native Americans! You ... you're just hungry aren't you! You'll eat anything when you're hungry!"

"No! Unlike you, I'm taking my community service very seriously by looking for the Chupacabra."

"Well, smart guy, he's standing right behind you."

"Ha ha. Very funny. I'm not that drunk ..." Brian stopped talking when he felt saliva splash his shoulder. As timid as a field mouse, he turned and looked into a maw full of glistening teeth.

Ducking just as the teeth snapped shut, Brian ran to where Chris stood. Creeping out from the tall brush, the Chupacabra growled. Standing eight feet tall, its leathery skin had the dull green hue of a lizard. Sharp claws jutted from long fingers and curled toes while a fin ran from the top of its serpentine head to the middle of its hunched back. Its black eyes locked onto Brian and Chris as its gurgling growl let them know it intended to make them its next meal.

Beer shaking in his hand as his lifted it to his lips, Chris said, "Use the cell phone. Call the sheriff and El Tigre."

Brian tried, but couldn't. "I can't hear anything. No signal?"

"Let me see." Chris snatched the phone from Brian's hand and looked at it. He immediately noticed that it was nothing more than a large matchbox with the numbers "0" through "9" written on it.

Disgusted, he threw it at Brian, bouncing it off his head. "You have issues."

The Chupacabra lumbered forward, snarling. Panicking, Brian threw his beer at it and ran.

"What are you doing!?" Chris yelled, running as well.

"Running! What's it look like!?"

"I meant your bottle! There was still beer in it."

"Extraordinary times call for extraordinary measures."

"Amateur!" To emphasize his point, Chris finished his beer with one gulp in mid-stride. He threw the bottle over his shoulder as he followed Brian to the shanty-like farmhouse.

After diving through the open door, both men then scrabbled to shut it. They pushed a nearby couch in front of the door as a barricade. Huffing and puffing, they looked around for anything to aid them. The house was smaller than it looked, with a cramped living room and an even smaller kitchenette. A three-legged dining table, a stack of cinder blocks acted as the fourth leg, straddled over the border between the rooms. No other furniture inhabited the room, except a lone goat whose only advice was, "Baaah."

A little calmer, Brian and Chris peeked through the window to see the Chupacabra. Bathed in bright moonlight, the creature fussed with the bottle Brian had thrown at it. Using two clawed fingers to hold it, the monster sniffed it and tasted it, garnering a few drops of beer. Its forked tongue flicked across its lips, then ran over the bottle searching for more. As it fiddled with the bottle, it accidentally discovered how to hold it to release the magical liquid. Its tongue flickered some more as it let out a reverberating purr.

"Interesting," Brian said. He jumped to his feet and ran to the kitchenette.

"What?" Chris asked.

"Well, it seems like he's never had beer before," Brian replied as he ransacked the cabinets.

"So?"

"So, that means he's a light weight. Ah-ha!" Opening the proper cabinet, Brian gazed upon the contents as if gazing upon Heaven itself.

There before him, in all their majestic glory, were two dozen bottles of tequila.

Brian grabbed a bottle and sat next to the goat. He popped the top and held it in front of the goat.

"Ummmm, are you trying to get the goat to drink tequila?" Chris asked.

"Yes! We need to fill the goat up with tequila and then shove him out the door. The Chupacabra eats the tequila filled goat and passes out."

Chris scowled, not only disturbed by the idea of debauching a goat, but upset that Brian produced a good idea. "You can't force him to drink it. Show him how."

Brian pressed the bottle to his lips and tilted his head back. A sweet inferno scorched his throat. Tears welled in his eyes after the third gulp. Smoke wisped from his goatee as it singed.

"Now smile," Chris ordered. "To show the goat it tastes good."

Brian whimpered.

"You siss. Gimme the bottle!" Chris slugged back the bottle, gulping thrice himself. His red beard turned brown. Hair regrew along his scalp and immediately fell out again. Sweat cascaded from his ruddy hued head. Not knowing what else to do, he held the bottle in front of the goat. And the goat drank.

Brian and Chris breathed a sigh of relief as the goat chugged away, finishing the bottle. However, their joy was short lived as the goat looked nonplussed and stated its boredom. "Baaaah."

"Get another bottle," Chris suggested.

Brian did, quickly returning to his seat on the floor by the goat. Again he popped the top and held the bottle in front of the goat. And again the goat refused to drink.

"Oh, come on!" Brian yelled at the goat.

"Baaah," the goat replied.

"You just drank half a bottle! It's the same stuff!"

"Baaah."

"What do you mean you...?"

"Baaah."

"I don't care if you…!"

"Baaah."

"*Fine*!!" Accepting defeat, Brian did as the goat requested and gulped down more tequila. The fleas from his chest hair dropped dead.

Coughing and gagging, Brian handed the bottle to Chris. Chris sighed, placed the bottle to his lips and tilted back. Wax flowed like water from his ears. However, the goat accepted the bottle and finished it.

"Baaah."

Brian's memory faded as he retrieved the next bottle of tequila. His memory revived as he awakened back in the jail cell. Chris and the goat were there as well.

"Uuuuughh. Did we win?"

"No, señor, I am afraid you did not," Sheriff Lopez replied. "And you did not complete your community service either."

Dismayed, Brian hung his head and stared at his feet. Both were bare. Confused, he looked to Chris's feet. They were bare as well. Concerned, he tilted and turned his head like a frantic owl, searching. When he got to the goat he found what he was looking for. On the goat's head, one on each horn, were both pink socks.

Not knowing where they originally came from didn't stop Brian from wanting to keep them. Trying to get them back, he walked toward the goat, ready to take them. The goat stepped back and snarled. "Grrrrrr."

"Señor, I suggest you do not try that again," Juan Valdez said.

"But one of those socks is mine."

"No, señor, one of those socks *was* yours."

"He stole it!"

"No, he did not. I have resided with this goat for years and he does not steal. You maybe lost it to him. A game of poker, maybe? Dice? Roulette?"

"That's ridiculous! I can't believe…" Brian's words trailed away as his mind kicked into a higher gear. Chris could almost hear the gears grinding as Brian worked through his logic. "I got it! Let us out. We'll try it again tonight."

"Are you kidding me?" Chris asked.

"I have a new plan. Our first one was too complicated."

"Too complicated? Step one, get goat drunk. Step two, push goat out door. How is that too complicated?"

"Well, we're back in jail with the goat, now aren't we? And we lost our socks!"

Chris folded his arms and frowned. "No, I refuse to go."

Brian glared at his friend. "Need I remind you we are in here because... of ..."

"Centelleo," Sheriff Lopez interjected.

"*Yeah,*" Brian continued. "Centelleo. And...What exactly does centelleo mean in English?"

"Blinking," the sheriff answered.

"*Blinking*?"

"Si."

"*We're in here for blinking? How the hell can blinking get us thrown in jail?*"

"You were doing so in a lascivious nature, ill-befitting our lovely town."

"*Lascivious...?*" Brian paused, closed his eyes, took a deep breath, pinched the bridge of his nose, and mentally went to his happy place, which, ironically, was Tijuana.

"Which one of us is the guilty party?"

"Tu amigo."

"Ah-ha!" Brian screamed, pointing to Chris. "It *was* your fault!"

"Now wait a minute!" Chris jumped to his feet and ran to the steel bars. "Exactly who did I offend with my lascivious blinking in your lovely town?"

"The prostitutes."

"Mi dios." Chris paused, closed his eyes, took a deep breath, pinched the bridge of his nose, and mentally went to his happy place, which, ironically, was also Tijuana. "Fine. Let's go back after the Chupacabra. What do we have to do?"

"We need more tequila. I'll explain the rest on the way."

Once at the farm, Brian explained the plan. Sheriff Lopez and

El Tigre Grande retrieved the table from the farmhouse / trailer and set it up outside, fifty feet away. Juan provided half a dozen bottles of tequila. Chris provided the promotional giveaway Fortress Publishing, Inc. shot-glass. Brian offered up a quarter, although he vehemently declared he wanted it returned after the mission. The goat provided witty repartee, "Baaah."

Sheriff Lopez, Juan and El Tigre hid in the trailer while Brian, Chris and the goat took their places at the table. The men sat in silence with the goat until sunset. Then Brian started the game.

Not used to the table, Brian bounced the quarter and missed the shot-glass. Grumbling, he grabbed the bottle of tequila and took a shot. The goat took the quarter from the table with its teeth and dropped it. It clanked right into the shot glass. Using its snout, it pushed the bottle to Chris; Chris did his obligatory one shot. Unaccustomed to the playing surface as well, Chris bounced the quarter and missed. He took another swig from the bottle. The quarter made it into the shot glass with Brian's next turn. Brian slid the bottle to the goat, and the goat drank, honoring his debt.

The game only needed a few more rounds before the Chupacabra reappeared. Foam frothing from its mouth the snarling reptile lumbered to its potential dinner, the two men and a goat. It stood growling behind Brian, saliva cascading from its jagged teeth. Brian showed no reaction; he simply took the quarter and bounced it off the table into the shot-glass. Tap-tink. Again, he slid the bottle to the goat and the goat drank.

Confused by the lack of reaction from Brian, the Chupacabra puffed out its chest and roared again. Its spittle dripped from Brian's bald head. Brian watched as the goat dropped the quarter from its mouth into the shot glass. Tap-tink. The goat nudged the bottle to Chris. After Chris took a swig, he played his turn successfully. Tap-tink. And passed the bottle to the goat.

"I'm surprised you're coping with the growling and roaring so well," Chris whispered to Brian.

Brian whispered back, "I've pissed off a lot of women in my years. This is nothing."

And it was nothing. In between its fits, the Chupacabra became mesmerized with the game. Tap-tink. The quarter glinted in the waning sunlight, catching just a hint of spinning sparkle. Tap-tink. The soft noise the quarter made from the wooden table to the plastic shot-glass became rhythmic. Tap-tink. After four rounds, the Chupacabra stopped its aggressive antics, stood silently and observed. Until Brian gave the quarter to it.

The reptilian creature had seen enough to understand. With reverence, it held the quarter between two claws. It dropped it on the table, but missed the shot glass. Brian slid the bottle to the Chupacabra and it took a swig. Out of pain, it squeezed its eyes shut as its tongue shot out its mouth and flicked over its face with the spasms of a dying snake. Brian and Chris smiled at each other, their plan was working.

The game progressed well, each player taking shot after shot. Finally, twelve rounds and two bottles later, the Chupacabra passed out.

Sheriff Lopez, Juan Valdez and El Tigre Grande exited the trailer with ropes and wasted no time tying the creature. Once secured, the five men and the goat celebrated. Sheriff Lopez whooped and hollered because his area of town had been cleared of a monster. Juan partied because the loss of his live stock was no longer out of his control. Providing his own Merlot, El Tigre Grande drank, because his legend would surely grow after a few well placed embellished stories. And the tequila flowed.

The next day, Brian and Chris awoke with the goat in a Canadian jail cell – no socks between them, but all three wore fedoras.

INSIDE THE MINDS OF MONKEYS

JEFF: There is a goat reference I didn't get originally.

BRIAN: Chupacabra is Spanish for "Goat Sucker." There's your Spanish lesson for the day.

CHRIS: And your Serendipity factor...

B: What other dipitys are there?

J: Do da?

B: We wanted to set up a story with us in a Tijuana jail cell 'cause that's a long running joke. Most people we meet usually assume we end up there quite often.

C: Really not that far from the truth.

B: It's funny 'cause I started off thinking it would be one of those stories where we have a group of characters and the creature was going to kill them off. But it really didn't turn out that way at all. The characters were just set up too well. I loved the sheriff as the straight guy and who doesn't love a French speaking Mexican midget. We have the deputy just being in the background. And we have the goat. I think the goat was actually the star of the story.

J: There's a frightening similarity to the Wendigo.

B: The new version? Yeah...

C: Hopefully, PETA will never get a hold of this book, 'cause I think there's a case for animal cruelty.

B: That and canned ham.

C: Canned Ham? CAN-M.E.A.T.

B: Close enough

J: Did anything influence your story?

B: Scooby Doo. I don't know why I wanted to do Chupacabra. I really wanted to do one of the lesser-known horror creatures like Chupacabra. And I figured since the Chupacabra is basically Mexico's version of Bigfoot, it qualifies as a horror figure. In fact, at one convention, someone bought the book solely because the Chupacabra was in it. They loved Chupacabra stories.

C: And then a couple of weeks after we wrote that, I was searching the internet and found a Chupacabra article saying it was found in real life.

B: Yeah, they said it was a hairless dog or something…

C: A hairless jackal...

B: And I believe that was the first story we wrote for the book. Jeff, was that the first story that came flying your way?

J: An auspicious start to all of this…

B: Little did he know…

C: He was hoping we'd lose interest…

B: Was there anything about the story that you found interesting as you were editing it?

J: I realized once I started reading it that you had absolutely no problem with drawing totally ridiculous characters into the story, which is great 'cause it gives you the tone right away, the way things were going to go. And the fact that you guys are always going to be in some sort of a jam to get out of …

B: With alcohol, of some sort...

J: That's a good point. Yeah, the beer pants.

B: They make an appearance, but we don't really draw attention to them. We're in the desert and we pull a cold beer out of our pants. And we just move on from there... like we do it every day. But we were fooled by a matchbox thinking it was a cell phone. That's just how we are…

THE DRUNKEN COMIC BOOK MONKEYS
VS.
THE BLOB

Lightning streaked the sky: a jagged, white scar across the dark face of night. Rain fell in patterns imperceptible to all but the most scrutinizing of minds. Though most can appreciate its blatant charms, by and large, Nature is a force not for the faint of heart. Thunder boomed, echoing back off the mountains past the Susquehanna Valley. The clamor shook houses and rattled windows, causing foundations to quiver. On the Western bank of the Susquehanna, beyond the bend where the waters churn at the slightest provocation of Mother Nature's swirling finger, stood a house apart from its ilk. It stood brazenly atop a small hill, brash for its loneliness, lights blazing in the windows, a beacon for passersby. In a window on the second floor an oil lamp burned. Its smoke plumed upwards, while its spectral light flashed and swayed with the ebb and flow of fire.

Within this medieval-like room, sat Millicent Brody, Melons Bar & Grille waitress extraordinaire, quick with a full pitcher, her eager mind filled with the latest specials, and with a determined stride that turned her area in her own personal hunting ground. "The finest of the fine" was her work motto. She performed her tasks with gusto and a beautiful smile lit her way as she searched out new and interesting customers to talk to. Today had been no different, and she had met two charming, genteel customers in particular. They had stayed on past her shift and when they settled their tab with her so she could be on her way to other aspects of her life; they had given a generous tip. It was their witty conversation that kept her rapt attention throughout her entire shift, and one bit of information she gleaned from the two gentlemen prickled her curiosity until she got home. Once within the cozy confines of her own abode, she removed from a shopping bag the large glass jar she procured on her way home. She tested it for her purposes prior to purchase and found that the lid had a tight seal that made a satisfying sound when she pulled it free of its canister like bottom. The jar sat before her, opened, the new recipient of two pounds of gummi bears. Satisfied that she could fit no more of the gelatinous treats in the jar, she opened a bottle that she saved for a special occasion. She gave it a good whiff as the bottle passed her nose. There was little smell, but the vapors.... Intuition told her the liquid was perfect and she wasted no time carefully emptying the contents from the bottle into her jar. When she was done the lid went back on the jar and she placed it into her refrigerator. Once the gummi bears absorbed the liquid, they would be ready for consumption, according to the two gentlemen who taught her this trick. Delighted at the thought of this tasty treat being ready for the next Melons girls' gathering night, Millicent shut the door to the refrigerator, oblivious to the green gummi bear that had freed itself from the mass of its brethren and began swimming upwards in the alcohol ocean that surrounded it.

***

"Dude!"

"What?" shouted Brian.

"The only member of the fruit spectrum not in your poor beer is a fig!"

"Ooooooooh! I hadn't thought of that one. Miss? Oh, miss," called Brian, one finger upraised on his right hand as he signaled for the waitress.

"Guh! There so much pulp in there...it's like...like...sea monkeys! Dude, if you dropped a beta fish in there he wouldn't even have to chase his food!"

"Sea monkeys!" snorted Brian derisively. "Whatever! You're ridiculous."

"Awwwww, c'mon! You really did it, didn't you?"

"Did what?" asked Brian, his attempt at innocence making a mockery of the ideal.

"Asked for a fig! You sicken me."

"Mmmmmm...that's so good."

"Ya know, you're about as subtle as a 2 Live Crew song."

"Why, whatever do you mean," Brian asked, feigning ignorance.

"You're *still* really upset about *that*, aren't you?" Chris asked. "Of all the ridiculous things to be upset about, you're not going to let this go."

"Dude, it was the last wing! You said you weren't hungry. If I knew your fast fingers were going traipsing across my plate, I would have ordered an extra hundred!"

"C'mon! I had like...three...or something."

"Dude, there's a pile of bones in front of you big enough to erect a dinosaur skeleton!"

"Oh, whatever! Ok, so I had a couple...."

"Dozen! A couple dozen is a lot, dude! I'm still growing!"

"Yeah, like an ulcer!"

"You're stupid!"

"Dude, did you ever ask yourself why we're always here?"

"Huh?"

"Seriously...I mean not from a metaphysical or philosophical standpoint or anything, but it seems like we spend a disproportionate amount of time here at Melons Bar & Grille, ya know?" Chris asked.

"Ummm...no," said Brian, flagging down the waitress to place another wing order. "Dude, it's a *family* bar and grille! It practically screams 'home'!"

"Must be nice to have no internal struggles."

"Don't be a hater! Oh, and my fantasy football team just totally kicked your team's collective ass!"

"Yeah, whatever. Hey, isn't that Millicent? She doesn't look so good."

"Are you kidding? Where exactly are you looking? She looks great!" Brian argued.

"Something about her coloring is off."

"What? You are stupid! See this is why you sit at home alone."

"Unreal! Just look at her. She looks different. And she doesn't walk quite right."

"I...."

"Don't say it! Don't you dare say it! She's twenty-two!"

"EXACTLY! And she walks...just...fine," Brian said, appreciation evident.

"Dude, she's kind of...jiggly."

"DUDE! DO I HAVE TO EXPLAIN THINGS TO YOU? SHE JIGGLES JUST RIGHT!"

"You're impossible! Here she comes....Hi, Millicent. How are you?"

"Tasty. You should try me."

"Ummmm...excuse me?"

"Oh, you know you want a lick...."

"Ummmm...listen, it's not that I don't appreciate what you're saying...."

"DUDE! YOU'RE IMPOSSIBLE! HOW DO YOU HATE YOURSELF THIS MUCH?"

Ignoring his screaming friend, Chris continued to talk to Millicent. "It's just that I'm not sure why you're saying it around ...you know ... us...."

"DUDE! YOU TAKE SELF-LOATHING TO NEW HEIGHTS!"

"Think it over," Millicent purred, tracing her curves with one finger for emphasis. Her skin did not resist the lightness of her touch the way it should have. "I just have to freshen up. I'll be right back."

"Dude! Did you see that," Chris asked.

"Did I see you act stupid? Yeah, I saw it. She threw herself at you! And you failed to catch the fastball!" Brian shot back.

"Did you see the way her finger sank into her skin? Did you see her coloring? What would you say that was?"

"Yeah, she was a little green. Of course *you* would say 'verdant,' though."

"Dude, 'verdant' isn't really a shade...it's just green...."

"Oh, sciency stuff," piped up their waitress delivering Brian's latest round of wings, "I'm taking physical science this semester and we just learned 'ROY G BIV'. Green is totally a color, I can assure you."

"I was thinking more along the lines of 'lime'," Chris said, wondering how this conversation could get any more ridiculous.

"Well, I'm not quite sure where 'lime' fits in there. I mean, there's no 'L' in 'ROY G BIV'," she informed.

"Yeah....Ya know, Millicent was just looking for you. I think she needed help. She went that way," Chris offered.

"Oh, ok. Thanks!" the waitress said as she flounced away.

"You see, this is my dilemma in hanging out with you," Brian explained. "*That* is what you're good at. Jackass stuff. You fumble the hand off every time, saying you want to try for the bomb."

"Listen, Casanova, Millicent needs our help. Focus."

"She needs our help with her uniform? Count me in," Brian said between shoving fistfuls of wings into his mouth.

"Look. She wasn't green a few months back! Think....What did we do?"

"What? Why do you assume we had anything to do with this?"

"Logic dictates...." Chris began.

"Logic dictates that when something bad happens we're at fault?"

"Cause and effect. We're an unstoppable force of misfortune!"

"That's a bit strong: an unstoppable force of annoyance, perhaps. Listen, you're way off base here. We didn't do anything!"

"So you did notice something unusual about her?"

"Yeah."

"Good. What?" Chris asked.

"She's young, single, gorgeous...and she hit on YOU!"

"This conversation is going nowhere. Here she comes again. DUDE! Does she look bigger to you?"

Millicent walked towards Brian and Chris, her skin even hued more green than before. Several chairs slid violently out of her way, slamming into their respective tables, as she squeezed her way through the restaurant.

"Considered my offer?" Millicent asked. She rested her fingers on the table near Chris's arm. Visible watermarks lingered from her touch. "See how juicy I am?"

"Whoa! See, there's a line there. Oh, it's fine, to be sure, but I'd be so much happier if you stayed on the other side of it."

"Once you start, you won't be able to stop until I'm all gone. Promise! I'll be back."

"DUDE!" Brian said. "You're like a pillar!"

"Yeah, and I'm afraid it'll be a pillar of salt! Dude, this has to stop. It's like reading the Marquis de Sade!"

"You can't put it down?"

"There's no 'exit' button! I can't make it go away!"

"Well," Brian said, "we could leave, I suppose."

Laughter erupted from both men. Chris had to wipe tears from his right eye twice before it stopped watering. It took several moments for them to collect themselves to the point that they could continue the conversation.

"Look, if you don't have anything useful to suggest...."

"SHUT UP! I need more wings. I can't think on an empty stomach. Have you seen our waitress?"

"Nope. Not since she went to help Millicent. Hey, do you smell something?"

"Yeah...it's called grease. And there's probably wings soaking in it right now," Brian said wiping saliva off his chin.

"No! Something strong, something...familiar...."

"Dude, don't you dare have a Star Wars moment! Next thing you know, you'll be standing up screaming about how much you hate George Lucas. They don't make a soapbox that big!"

"Whatever! I've done that like what...twice...I blame alcohol both times."

"It was three times. And for two of them you weren't even drinking."

"It was left over from the night before and I...wait...THAT'S IT!"

"What's it?"

"Alcohol! That's what I smell."

"Ummmm...Dude...that's your shower gel."

"It's really strong, too. Nothing typical."

"Ummmm...I dunno...lager?"

"You need another pitcher?" one of the girls asked. "I'll check on your waitress. I think she's in the back with Millicent."

"Thank you!" Chris turned back to Brian. "NO! Where is that coming from?"

"DUDE! He who smelt it, dealt it!"

"It's stronger over here."

"Get your nose away from me, fast finger Freddie! I'm on to you, punk! Get your own wings! You paid Millicent. It's some sort of elaborate misdirection to get my wings!"

"Miss? Oh, miss. Can you check on our waitress? She might be in the back with Millicent."

"I knew it! You do want my wings!"

Millicent came out from the back, her skin now the shade of fresh grass. Chairs and tables alike fled from her approach as she went to grab the pitcher off the bar. She could no longer squeeze between the empty tables so she used her mass to push them violently out of her way.

"Here's your pitcher, boys," she said. "Will there be anything else? A piece of me for dessert, perhaps? I'm delicious, ya know?"

Both men stared slack jawed. She had more than tripled in size since entering the family grille. Her flattering figure replaced with one that was disturbingly unimpressive despite its sheer size. She pressed up tight against their table, her sides seeming to cling around the edges.

"Not...just...yet...thanks," Chris stammered.

Brian appeared dumbfounded as he finally took in the scene that played out around him. Silence was not high on his repertoire; however, and his voice returned shortly as his stomach growled.

"Ummmm...Millicent could we have some more wings, please?"

There are times when the normal words seem utterly inadequate. One couldn't say that she turned so much as she rotated away from the two men. Chris wanted to blink, but couldn't force his eyes closed. Brian was lost in thought. Then those thoughts turned to chicken wings. He drooled.

"Dude!" Chris broke the silence. "I found our waitress. She's behind Millicent."

"I love it when they're in groups," Brian stated.

"No. I mean she's *behind* Millicent. She's stuck to her. Absorbed, somehow."

"What are you talking about?"

"Look! She's just hanging there, like the pomegranate floating in your beer."

"DUDE! It's like she's suspended in gelatin."

"And that alcohol smell is really strong. Dude, there's a puddle on the floor here where Millicent was standing."

Both men winced as they fought down the impulsive reflex to say more.

"I think that's where the alcohol smell is from."

"Well, put your finger in it or something."

"Ewwwww! It's on the floor!" Chris said, a look of revulsion on his face.

"Oh, I've seen you do worse. Much worse. Hey, the pitcher is kicked. These 48 ounce ones go ridiculously quick. You stocked up?"

"Of course," Chris replied, pulling two beers from his pants pocket. He popped both tops and passed one off to Brian. "Ok, whatever you do don't call attention to us. I'm going in."

"WHAT DOES THAT EVEN MEAN?"

"Smooth. Subtle. Quiet. Do these words even exist to you?" Chris asked, sliding back into his chair after retrieving some of the liquid off the floor with his finger. "Dude! It reeks. Totally alcohol. I just can't place it, though."

"JUST TASTE IT ALREADY!" Brian bellowed.

"What are you boys playing at over there?" Millicent asked, revolving back their way.

"Dude!" Chris wheezed, his face deformed by tight twists of disgust. "It's grain."

"Grain! Nectar of the gods!"

"I feel like an ice cream machine," said Chris, his tongue hanging out to be air-dried.

"DUDE! I FIGURED IT OUT!"

Chris pulled a fresh beer from his pocket. He popped the top, marveling at its coldness. He used it as a chaser, drinking it in one long draught. The sides of the bottle threatened to collapse before he sat down the empty.

Millicent loomed closer. "Boys! Come get some of this goodness." She reached out and touched a table to her right. It disappeared from sight, sucked into and consumed by her mass. She continued to absorb furniture as she moved.

"What's going on out there?" Maria, manager of Melons, asked from the kitchen. Her voice floated out to them, but it was quickly followed by the powerful woman herself. She stood just outside the kitchen doors, tapping her toes as she surveyed the damage to her restaurant. "What did you two do to my restaurant? And my customers? And my girls? FIX IT!" she demanded.

"Dude! I swear I've heard that before." Chris said, pulling another beer from his pants pocket.

"Remember?" asked Brian. "We told Millicent how to make vodka bears. She must have used grain, instead."

"So she's basically a big ol' shooter?"

"Exactly. You know what we have to do."

Chris took off his belt.

"DUDE! Make sure it stops right there, pal!"

Silent as a shadow, Chris threw a leather loop over of his shoulder, belting it crosswise near his waist. He grabbed a handful of straws.

"This could get messy," Brian said, removing his shirt.

"DUDE!"

Brian put his shirt back on. He took up a roll of paper towels.

"Ya know, someone should have considered that this could happen at some point," Chris said, peeling the wrapper off a straw, sticking the naked plastic into his ersatz bandolier. When it was secured, he grabbed another and repeated the process.

Brian shredded the paper from the cardboard core. "Come to papa."

In what would have to pass for a sprint, the ball that had been Millicent began to roll, gathering speed over the final distance, a juggernaut bearing down on the men.

Chris put a straw in his mouth. Brian put the tube to his lips.

The gelatinous ball bore down on them. Chris dodged at the last second, making guerilla attacks with his straw as it passed him by. Brian stood his ground. He was run over by the round mass. His flattened form absorbed its impetus and the blob stood stationary for the moment quivering as the men tried to suck out its essence.

"Dude!" Brian yelled. For the first time in his life, his voice was muffled. "It's going to get me. See if you can free anyone."

Chris pulled out several more straws, securing one end in his mouth and began tracing the outline of one of the waitresses.

"This is going to take forever! Are sure you can hold it? Dude? DUDE?" Chris screamed. No reply. Apparently gelatin was the missing link. It was the only substance on Earth capable of quieting Brian. The rotund mass shook and quivered. It was attempting to roll again. His straws having little visible effect, Chris's shoulders slumped. "I'm just gonna have to go in there. Maybe if I get a running start, I can gather enough momentum to carry me through. If I can split it into smaller parts, I might have a chance."

Chris withdrew across the restaurant. He secured four straws in his mouth, judging that once inside the gelatinous accumulation he might not be able to lift his arm.

"It's now or never. AAAAAAAHHHHHHHHHH!"

Smack

Chris slapped into the gathering of greenness. Upon hitting its skin, two of his straws were shoved back into his gullet. One bent horribly and was pulled free from him. The last wound up twisting up into his nose. He ignored the discomfort and focused only on running toward the light. He forgot to take into account the tables that were within. He realized his mistake as he crashed into the top of one that stood on edge. His momentum arrested, he sighed, thinking there were surely worse ways to go and wishing he could reach his beer pocket to toss one back in the time before he was digested. Suddenly there was pressure on his back. He was vaguely aware of becoming soaking wet. How ironic that he'd not had an accident in such a long time and now when he could do nothing to hide the fact from others...ah, the cruelty of Nature.

A hand gripped his shoulder and pulled. He popped free from the blob and fell to the floor. Maria stood above him with a hose nozzle in her hand. She smiled at him, then blasted him full in the face with water.

"You morons! Can't you do anything right? I went to get the hose for you and there you idiots are standing around with a bunch of straws. Only you two would think of trying to eat the thing! This is a hose. I trust you know how to use it. Free everyone, fix up my restaurant, and then flip the sign to 'closed' on your way out! And the mop is over there. Do I have to show you how to do that, too?" She stormed off, muttering all the while 'why me's' as if they were Hail Mary's.

Chris used the hose to free Brian. Neither spoke as they set about the task of pulling out tables and chairs and people. Before things got too crowded in their immediate area, Brian suggested they set up a few tables. Chris had just found Millicent amidst the mass.

"Yeah, good idea. Take them across the restaurant first. I'll be right there to give you a hand."

Chris looked around. Brian's back was turned and Maria was in the back. No witnesses, he thought. He pulled a straw from the belt across his chest and began to trace Millicent's outline.

"I'll never get this close again in my life. Just a little taste," he said.

INSIDE THE MINDS OF MONKEYS

JEFF: So...

CHRIS: It's a true story.

BRIAN: There you have it.

J: Oh, come on, am I seriously to believe...

C: What? That salacious thoughts and libations go hand-in-hand?

J: I accept that with you two. I meant am I supposed to believe that you're smart enough to invent a secret recipe for grain bears?

B: Three letters: "P", "S", "U".

C: There you have it! Two things the college bound can afford: gummi bears and grain. But since grain has long since been outlawed, we've been using vodka instead.

J: I'd like to say I'm surprised...

B: You'd like to say you thought of it first!

C: Ha ha ha! Seriously, here...

J: Did he just say, "seriously?"

B: Yeah, when the hell did that happen?

C: Hey, Brian, your phone's ringing ... Oh, Clairol is calling! Uh-huh. Yes. They said that they're running a special on beard coloring products!

B: Duuuuuuuude! That was just a phase I went through! A phase!

C: Uh-huh. Anyway, with "the blob" we have another popular horror motif that has no literary background. We knew we wanted the new story to be vastly different from the original since the spectrum of interpretation is so vast on this one. The only homage in this story is in the beginning with the "dark and stormy night" scene. I think it's funny that Brian started "Drunk Comic Book Monkeys vs. Themselves" in a similar fashion.

B: I like the plot vehicle Chris used on this one. And there is a bit of autobiography in this story as well — while we were doing our wing tour, we actually did tell some waitresses how to make the gummi bear concoction after they mentioned a big party they were having.

C: Right. A perfect example of how we like to sprinkle real events...

B: "Sprinkle?" Did you just say, "sprinkle?" What are you like four?

C: Oh, I only said it because there's a couple of cupcake sprinkles on the floor over...

B: DIBS!

C: Unreal!

J: There you have it!

MEGA CRISIS SECRET
SUPER CIVIL

THE DRUNKEN COMIC BOOK MONKEYS
VS.
THE HAUNTED COMIC BOOK CONVENTION

"For how short a while man speaks. And withal how vainly.
And for how long he is silent.
Only the other day I met a King in Thebes who had been silent already for 3000 years."
--Lord Dunsany

For its part, science would have us believe that intelligence and rationality are the traits that separate man from other species. This rudimentary conjecture, misleading at best, focuses only on the desirable traits and fails to address cause and effect. It is a simple case of knowing what the listener wants to hear and presenting it, gift-wrapped and bow intact. But the back of a human's hand, ridged and knuckled and vascular as it may be, is only one side of the whole. It is incomplete without the furrows and muscles and gripping features of its front, which, is capable of instilling both a pleasurable caress and a startling slap. Is it, then, restraint that we as a race find so beautiful? The flower with its delicate design and brilliant color may fascinate our senses for a short while, but the tiger with his sleek lines and mercurial nature holds us spellbound until he lashes out. But even as we scurry for safety, we peer at him longing for the time when we find ourselves back in his good graces. Similarly, the effect of our intelligence and rationality is the constant struggle with humility, a point that science forgot to mention, our vanity springs eternal from our successes, and thus it shall be our undoing.

This story was birthed from a first-hand experience. My

detractors will claim some dysfunction on my part; a faulty memory, an inherent need to tell tales, an inability to distinguish reality from fiction. Whatever their prognostication, leave them to it. I seek not approval with this tale, nor do I seek permission to tell it. As with all happenings in life, there was a reason for it and my burden is to seek out and share the message nestled deep within, like a pearl pried from the oyster's embrace.

It was in our modern age that this tale of woe takes place, though the actual day has been blocked from my memory by some blessed act of forgetfulness, some psychological nepenthe of which I know naught, but I suspect it comes from draughts and bottles. Regardless, the day in question began as a happy morning boasting of an even happier end, like a rainbow that truly led to the speculation of its gold. I woke early and showered, dressing and grooming myself as was my wont, the whole of my ensemble completed with a leather hair tie bearing the Nordic symbol of Tiwaz. With this sturdy piece of decoration my long locks were held in the fashion of my distant ancestors and I, owing to my flaming red hair and remarkable lack of skin pigmentation, resembled nothing so much as a Viking berserker. In holding with their ancient traditions, I recited the lengthy verses of Beowulf like some skald of a bygone era, in reverence to the rising of the sun, then set off to join my comrade in arms, Brian.

He, too, was excited by the adventure this day proposed and had risen early, awaiting me outside his dwelling. Tan shorts he had chosen to wear with a blackened t-shirt that hailed some heathen group as preachers of a new musical gospel. His ebony locks normally splayed about his shoulders, but like myself, he had chosen to tie back the numerous strands and they hung in pony-tail fashion to his mid-back. The sun had risen to see us on our way and birdsong greeted our ears like a happy harbinger of good fortune. All was right with the world and after loading our scant luggage into the trunk of my vehicle we set off towards our destination: our first official comic book convention.

Our minds were filled to the brink with possibilities and potentialities. Everyone we chanced to meet we hailed as though having known them for some time. We bore no ill will towards the dog that tried to wrest from us our breakfast (Brian, though normally a generous soul, scared the mangy mutt away with a piercing look that conveyed even to the canine that he was edible if snared), nor to the people who prepared the less than savory concoction.

After consuming our meal, it was back to the chariot that awaited. And off we sped towards our destination via the turnpike. Brian and I were both terrified about losing our turnpike ticket as those feisty little devils have a way of wandering off when not closely watched. Half the trip to Pittsburgh was spent in tireless argument, neither willing to concede his point. I constantly had to push my hair from my eyes due to the vehemence of my belief in my stance. Brian, for his part, twisted and pulled at his ponytail with the energy of an eight-year-old playing with his favorite action figure. Two hours passed and we agreed to make a stop at a rest area, though we still couldn't reach a summit over the safe keeping of the ticket. Drastic action was needed to solve this dilemma. To this end, Brian snatched it up and shoved it into one of the numerous pockets in his shorts as a way of announcing finality to the endless debate that ensued over its well-being.

We performed all necessary functions at the rest stop area and girded ourselves for the remaining hour and a half drive to end point: Pittsburgh, PA. It was a relaxed time, filled with the hilarity of beer jokes, tall tales involving our sexual stamina (to this day it's still more information than either of us needs to digest, so despite lingering rumors of the tales' veracity, neither of us actually contemplate them), and batting flies from mid-flight with our respective and collective hair. We almost wrecked once when a mayfly became so thoroughly entangled in my rat-tail that I could feel upon my scalp its struggles to liberate itself, though this was some fifteen inches from any known or imagined nerve endings.

Alternating awareness between Brian's tribal shrieks and the concern for the tidiness of my massive mane, my eyes, much of their own accord, lost sight of the road as it ran before us, a potentially problematic issue in western PA where the "S" curve was birthed.

Fortunately, a motorist whose good-natured disposition rivaled our own pointed out our meandering driving pattern using, curiously enough, only his middle finger to catch our attention. We were most grateful for his kindness and numerous indeed have been the occasions that we have made libations in the man's honor.

As you can imagine, gentle reader, the remainder of our trip sped us by quite without our acknowledgement. It was, truth be told, Brian who stopped us from committing the dreaded error of driving right past one's exit. As he was leaning out the window trying to lasso various signs with his ponytail, his Mensa brain began to do the unimaginable for a man: it ran various calculations while his body remained occupied with its former task — an indisputable, though inchoate version of multi-tasking. It took him a mere 1.9 miles to realize the "two miles to Monroeville" sign was the portent which we were seeking. We veered off onto the proper exit with scant inches remaining, eliciting the tires from all the neighboring cars to shriek their felicitations in unison, so joyous were they at the prospect of continued journeying with our own tires.

And here it was: our trip nearly over, our arrival imminent. Several thousand feet later we stopped at the tollbooth to remunerate the ferryman for our voyage. But where, oh where had the ticket gone? Panic seized us, threatening to still our hearts inside their fleshy cages, like songbirds that had chirped their final refrain. The keeper of the gate, who could have added to our discomfort by transfixing us with her glaring stares or letting our skin to shed its water with lancing words of loudly voiced disdain, instead merely glanced at her time telling device as she expressed her desire to be at her post for another six hours regardless of how many people in addition to our addled selves she allowed to pass. Our thankfulness for her understanding can never be fully expressed in our ever shrinking present language for her patience with us allowed a single form to coalesce in our thoughts: Brian's pocket!

Brian, his face awash with triumph, tried to stab a hand into his left front pocket, but again the demon of failure shone its ugly smile upon us. All of his hair whipping had caused his ponytail to wrap itself about his too Sasquatch-like form (dare you, I ask, dear reader, disbelieve in the stories of the mountain yeti discarding them like some fool's tale meant to frighten children when the evolutionary evidence had just spent four hours riding in a car with me?), encircling him like Jormungandr girdling the Earth's equator. Desperation flushed his features as he struggled with the bonds of his hair until his seat belt locked, further tightening the embrace of fate upon our venture. Startled into action, I thrust out with my right arm for his pocket, seeking the golden ticket of freedom encapsulated therein. But scarce had my hand broken the plane of his "Area of Operation" than he began with such a furious round of ear-piercing screaming, a susurration that knew no surcease until the amount of displaced air was so great that his uvula was left cleft and displaced, an unearthly howling that brought me visions of otherworldly beasts sent with the sole mission of carrying me away to dreamscapes as yet unimagined by the likes of man; in all, a sound that left me stupefied, my arm dropping limply to my side. Though I am reluctant to admit it, even to myself, in the interest of presenting to you a credible account of these events, I unashamedly allow that I swooned at this moment. It is the only way that I account for the lapse of time between seeing my friend struggle against his biting bonds and my next recollection of him standing outside the medium of our locomotion, upon the highway, the artificial skin of the beast upon which we move like so many crawling fleas, oh, dear reader, AMONGST THE SPEEDING CARS, as he frantically searched the Stygian depths of that pocket with its yawning mouth and insatiable hunger. I was in a panic, as well, for if he were struck by a careless motorist it meant two things with a severe sureness: that I would have to pay the full turnpike price for losing my ticket and that I would miss at least part of the convention, two possibilities I loathed to consider.

Vitriol seeped from the words I spewed at him, fervently supporting his efforts to retrieve the ticket and re-enter the vehicle, thus ending this nightmarish episode. A lesson in cause and effect, it was my supportive utterances that tipped the scales in our favor, much as happens when a stalemated tug-of-war is ended by a newly come interloper choosing one side or the other. Accomplishment crawled across the features of his face, leaving his expression wrinkled in triumph as he pulled the ticket free and held it aloft for all to bear witness. He was a modern day Sisyphus breaking the everlasting cycle of rocking and rolling. Dodging the oncoming chariots of modern day with a grace that was belied by his bulky frame, Brian raced from one side of turnpike to the other displaying his trophy proudly, lording it in the face of fate until she felt pressed to intervene yet again, this time displaying her might. A noxious stream spit from a backfiring tailpipe with all the impetus of a gas held under extreme pressure shot outward in a directly AT BRIAN'S HAND. The ticket was lost, stolen like a lover's smile met with the beloved's rancid breath of morning. Crestfallen, the erstwhile hero returned sullenly to our vehicle as I fished out piece after piece of parchment monies to pay for his indiscretion.

We sped off after satisfying our debt. For a long moment I was silent, but my ire mounted until I boiled over with anger and created a new island between the wellsprings of our collective creativities. Though it seemed a fittingly recriminating vituperation at the time, my tirade was hasty and lacked grace and many has been the juncture that I wish I could gather up its residue and store it safely inside me. Not that it was undeserved, mind you; temperate reader, but merely that I might do it again, with more ever increasing fervor and attitude. I have since learned the power of the "z snap" and wish only to re-channel more effectively what I unleashed that day. But it was a short voyage from the turnpike stall to the auditorium and we were expected.

As the majority of events post-ceding this are largely uneventful I shall not bore you through mindless repetition of meaningless and possibly duplicitously meandering musings of fey spirits seeking to regale and set myself apart from my contemporaries. Suffice it to say that "the whale was white," or, more correctly in this instance, that our belongings were transported from one point in temporal space to another. There was even little disagreement between us as we set up our wares upon the table proffered us by the hosts of the event, though the whole was replete with many instances of unnecessarily removing hair ties and resetting our respective coiffures.

The day passed quickly amidst throaty welcomes by throngs of people struggling in their masses in a vain efforts to meet, greet, and chance the opportunity to lay hands on us. It was a satisfying time for us. Such was our experience that I swore to having seen Eros in Earthly form at least twice and Brian, his hackles raised at being left only five meals in the cafeteria, confessed to wishing he could chance a speech with Thanatos somewhere amidst the mass of humanity that surrounded us. We had nary a moment to ourselves to be shared upon our thoughts, but that night we spared no few moments discussing all of this at great length when we should have succumbed to the lulling embrace of Hypnos. It was at this point that Brian revealed a startling revelation about the booth three stalls over from our own. Guardsmen had been summoned to escort us from the great hall that we might leave with the whole of the other vendor's stalls with some modicum of order about them. We were led in different directions in an obvious, though effective, attempt at misdirection. Effective that is for Brian. I was mobbed at every turn, having the shirt rent from across my back, forced to watch as it was torn into strips and distributed among the masses. When they came back for more, a modicum of decency passed over me and I was forced to bring my rat-tail to bear whipping it frenziedly to and fro to create a barrier between myself and the lecherous mob that pursued me questing for a piece of my very soul.

Brian, who met with the most minimalist resistance at his proposed departure, was afforded no small amount of time to peruse his surroundings. It was at this point, thoroughly undisguised and blatantly ignored that he made his startling discovery. A mere stone's throw from our booth was a vendor who dealt in ADULT-ORIENTED MATERIALS!

It was as if the Elysian Fields and Valhalla both opened their borders to us at one and the same instant. A rush of electricity filled the room and we began to cackle like small children being offered massive amounts of candied victuals simply for donning masks bearing horrible effigies, then offering adults the opportunity to reward us or be scared witless. The prize of kings and pharaohs alike awaited us. Its nearness was a torturing of the senses and a blade that laid bare our wits. Back in our temporary domicile, Brian twisted his hair as he shoved countless pieces of citrus into the long neck of a clear bottle of suddenly viscous ale. To quiet my own distemper, I laid about me with my rat-tail, encouraging its ruddy length to fetch me another container of darkly-colored fermentation, though mine remained devoid of any foreign detritus, as the gods had decreed was right upon the occasion of their gifting it to mankind.

We struggled with a series of future potentialities, surveying each for validity and usefulness against our ability to improvise should the need arise. The sea of women who had gifted themselves to us never parted and we often had to shout over their collective din as we planned. Numerous were the times that we had asked to be rid of them, but they had been drawn to the unbinding of our hair like beauty is etched between the petals of a rose opening into full bloom. Insatiably they crawled over us attempting to distract us from plotting our course upon the ocean that loomed before us. At some point every man must gather his free will in a show of force against the fickle, intemperate faces of fate. Please accept, placid reader that he must carve for himself a niche in which to gain good footing as he marshals his strength, bringing it all to bear in a cataclysmic showing of muscle, will and wit. Or his heart shall remain ever shackled in the shadow, darkening his soul at the foot of his fear.

And then, like dark precipitates in an otherwise clear liquid, it became clear to us what we must do to achieve this pinnacle of existence. In order to have free reign over the materials we so greatly coveted we must conspire to be locked into the convention at night. We shook hands in effect rendering this plan into a pact, struggling against and around the writhing, nubile bodies amassing on us.

Sleep evaded us the rest of that night, though massive amounts of energy pervaded us, just evidence of our overwhelming excitement. Locked in a room all night long with adult-oriented materials! It was the penultimate step to achieving the destiny for which we had been born. It was THE moment of self-discovery, of self-definition, of self-actualization. And it sat, glowing, tempting, tantalizing us from a mere fingertip's length away. My soul ached to realize this dream and the minutes stretched themselves before me like so many unpleasant tasks that needed to be performed at agonizing length, but all in a succession with no reward to be found between them.

The morning rays greeted us as did the cacophony of the alarm clock, in commandment for us to once more go forth and man our table. I steeled myself against the long hours ahead of me, absently stroking my hair in wild patterns. Brian, who had fewer fans than myself to occupy his time, coiled and recoiled his hair in numerous ways; draping it first over one shoulder, then peevishly casting it about the other, his mounting anxiety and impatience weighing upon his very spirit, like an inconstant lie that grows instead of disappearing.

After a period of time best described as interminable, the moment we had suffered for loomed before us. We dismissed the guardsmen that had been allocated to us, asking them instead to escort the crowds out of the hall while we set about tidying up our vending spot. We bade our neighbors good night and waved everyone ahead of our persons as we took up the final spot in the procession of people lined up to leave. When we were certain no one was looking, we dived behind a booth and hid amongst the folds of the curtains that shrouded its nether regions.

I cannot say for what length of time we stayed thus, only that silence fell and held court in this room that was known for the din of its occupants. Peeking out from our hiding spot, we could find no glimpse of human life anywhere. We pressed together our palms in a silent sign of success. Breaking cover we perused the perimeter of the room searching for anyone who might challenge our sovereignty of the situation. No one was there to be found. We were completely alone. Our cleverness had reached the point of realization.

With alarming haste we made our way to the treasures that awaited us. Bear in mind, serene reader that our goal was not to purloin anything. Merely that we wished to peruse every page, every nuance, make every discovery from that which was spread before us.

We set to the adult-oriented material like some ravenous plague that has just discovered a new world within reach. We could not contain ourselves; guffawing and pointing dementedly, intoxicated by naughtiness. For many hours we frolicked through the myriad pages of the collected tomes and manuals, drinking in knowledge, then expelling our newly gained wisdom. But all was not as it should have been. We had failed to consider that the treasure would have its own guardians. Invisible specters forced themselves from the walls, extricated themselves from the floors, pushed their way free of the ceilings.

They pervaded us with their ghastly existences. We began to lose interest in the pictures and smutty words that lay before us. The world was graying before our eyes and so too were our visages. And they made sure we were painfully aware. These were the effects that age would have on us, they warned. That naughtiness would lose its appeal. They warned us that lewd acts would be kept behind closed doors, because the appeal of sharing them publicly would be lost. Drinking and cursing would be our only pleasurable pastimes. Nakedness would seem unspectacular, eliciting little or no response from us.

It was as if too many needles were jammed into one pincushion. I could bear their vulgar threats no longer. Looking at Brian, I could see that he was as affected as I by this turn of events. The flesh on his arms was pocked like the skin of a freshly plucked goose. We lamented for the loss that had not yet occurred and urged the spirits to shower us with whatever benevolence they possessed. We begged them to show us how this fate could be avoided. They warned us that the cost was steep, but we desperately resolved to pay whatever price they asked to restore our vigor, our drive. With no hesitation they presented us with the recompense they demanded: OUR HAIR!

Outrageous! Unthinkable! Despicable! Such were the words we used to describe their terms. They were unshakable in their demand. No amount of money, nor intelligence could we offer as stead to their unwavering request. It was our hair or the effects of male aging would be upon us. To add further insult to the whole disquieting act, they forced us to cut our own hair - right where we stood. No pre-act lubrication, no after act balm. With swords and daggers taken from a nearby stand we committed the heinous act, blackened with the ash of our shame.

But the dullness lifted from our vision and our joyful exuberance of nakedness returned. Brian laughed out loud in appreciation of a centerfold and I couldn't help but stare contentedly at a poster of a score of naked women. Thus, resilience was reborn like a phoenix from the ashes of our disgrace.

Never again are we to know the bald charisma of long locks. Our well-intentioned "hellos" to the fairer sex are met with silent disdain. The throngs of fans have disappeared, leaving us to count the swirls inside the carpet patterns upon the floor. Vanity visited us with harshness, but we are free of its aspects for good. Though our social lives have sustained a severe blow, the humility of our souls has been restored and thus we will survive to gawk yet again at the beauty that surrounds us to the accompaniment of slaps and pepper-spray. Alas...

INSIDE THE MINDS OF MONKEYS

BRIAN: I think this one started out because Chris wrote the original Zombies and chided me incessantly that he did Zombies as pure dialogue. So I challenged Chris to do a story with pure narrative, with no dialogue.

CHRIS: That was Cthulhu... Maybe?

B: Cthulhu has zero dialogue as well, but Haunted Comic Convention was the first, because we sat down and went through all the story types that could fit with no dialogue and we came up with mythology and the classic American Tall Tale. And we deduced that with both of those, it was a cause and effect. There is a myth explaining why we have seasons. The reason why there is a Grand Canyon is because of Paul Bunyon dragging his ax. So we decided that we had to come up with a reason for something and this story is the reason why we're bald.

C: And it has to have that gross exaggeration.

B: Exactly

C: The gross exaggeration being that people actually liked us.

B: EXACTLY!!

JEFF: I think the style of it was different than the traditional tall tale. It's done in a more professional polished style. The way you tell the story is more like an epic.

C: The tall tale kinda has its origins in oral tradition.

B: Right. Sitting around the camp fire, banjo in one hand, sister in the other...

C: I don't like where this is going...

B: So we decided to go with more of a myth/legend.

J: You get caught in that situation where you have to make a choice...

B: And of course we chose poorly. But also I like the fact that it brings out the ridiculousness of our characters. We're surrounded by porn and yet we feel the need to try to beat the system to get more porn.

C: We're surrounded by hot women and we pass it up to look at pictures of hot women! Which is all about the 12 year-olds that we are.

B: 'Cause if we aren't allowed to do something, we're more apt to try to do it.

C: Exactly!

B: Especially if it's something like, "Don't stick your finger in the light socket!" There we are... licking our index fingers...going in... What are you laughing at?

C: At least we know our hair won't stand on end...

J: And your epic journey on the turnpike

B: Yes, our epic journey is on the turnpike.

C: God bless the PA Turnpike Commission!

B: And interestingly enough, this is another story with autobiographical material.

C: There are quite a few real events in the story.

B: Me jumping out of the car on the turnpike looking for the ticket is a true story. And the many people laughing as I did that is true as well.

C: Any time we reference people laughing at us, it's usually a true story.

B: Obviously, the story style was very different from the rest of the book. Jeff, did you think it was going to be a problem? Or did you find it refreshing?

J: I think it breaks things up and not in a bad way. I think the fact that you guys actually spend a little time thinking about how you were going to tell each story is important. Instead of just hitting it straight on with the same thing over and over again, it's a little bit of a challenge to your readers. It's still done tongue in cheek enough that it's not going to be an issue or dry to read.

B: And it definitely was a little outlandish...

C: But it still had some subtler moments.

B: I think it's what we'd like to call "depicting our range."

C: People have been removed from soap operas for less...

B: We're the Susan Lucci of writers!

C: Nominated for 15 Emmy's....

THE DRUNKEN COMIC BOOK MONKEYS VS. VAMPIRES

Lunora sat sprawled across the couch, her legs draped over her sister's lap. She sipped blood from her chalice, bejeweled with a stone from the crown of each king or prince she seduced over the centuries. The vintage that slid over her lips was that of an adult virgin, the full body of maturity while maintaining the refreshing crispness of innocence, a rare and expensive drink indeed. Instead of savoring it like the treasure it was, she tilted her cup and gulped thrice. Her anger soured the flavor. Unable to erase the sting of last night, her mind and heart dwelt on her loss. The long feud with her brother cost many casualties. Last night five of her familiars were numbered among the dead. Her sister, Zemura, who lost seven, took it even harder.

Zemura slouched against the other arm of the couch, her hands resting like dead fish on her sister's legs. She watched the dance floor, but saw none of the action, instead replaying the events of last night through her head as well.

Distraught that three centuries ago their brother, Rumiol, kicked them out of the family, the sisters were still trying to earn their way back in, and no other way could be as noticeable or undeniable as slaying him. They had disagreed with him about the promise this new country of United States held, wagering it would lead the world to great and amazing times. They had seen enough "democracies" to know they all ended the same way, with libertines dancing on the backs of the apathetic. Going against their brother's wishes, they turned their backs on the stuffy old boudoirs of European kings and slid between the sheets of American politicians and businessmen. They were right, Rumiol was wrong. And he still wouldn't admit it, or let them back into the family, even after making his own way to the New World two and half score years ago, fleeing from his shortsighted decision to back Hitler.

Zemura sighed, heavy from the weight of her churning thoughts. “We need more familiars.”

Lunora sighed as well. “True. But they are expensive to maintain. And have a high turnover rate for those who aren’t completely committed. I think, my dear sister, we should form Legion.”

Zemura sat up, rolling her neck and arching her shoulders, trying to stretch away the discomfort of her sister’s words. “Are you sure that’s not more work?”

“It is. I wish it was as easy as they make it out to be in the movies where all we have to do is bite someone on the neck. It’ll take a month and a lot of manipulation, but there will be more of us, loyal to us.”

“And much more powerful than familiars. What about the Laws?”

Laughing, Lunora put her arm around her sister’s shoulders and pulled her close. “Laws everywhere are the same – whoever has power, makes the laws. Once we dispose of our dear brother, we will have the power to forgive ourselves of the transgressions necessary to get the power.”

Resting her head on her sister’s shoulder, Zemura smiled. “I certainly would love to live in a world with no Rumiol. You’ve talked me into it. Let’s find some dupes.”

Nearby at Melons Bar & Grille, Brian and Chris sat at a tall table. They had been there so long, their hands now locked into claw-like curves from holding beer bottles all day. Any efforts to uncurl their fingers resulted in painful cramping, so they kept ordering more beer - and obsessing over stupid topics.

“Who would win in a fight – Xena or Red Sonja?” Brian asked.

“Who’s writing this story? Xena’s writers can’t compare to Robert E Howard. However, if it’s old-school Xena, then she wins with the chakram. If it’s noble Xena, Red Sonja mollyhops her. Though if I’m writing this story, dread Cthulhu shows up and pulps both of them.”

“What the hell is wrong with you?”

“What? You asked a question, I answered it.”

“I present to you an ultimate fantasy and your *first* concern is who writes it. Your *second* concern is having a big, slimy squid thing involved! That's so perverse you better hope the FBI isn't listening in."

"The FBI might be listening? Ummm ... errr ... ah-hem ... I ... I didn't mean to crash that prom in Pittsburgh, it just kinda happened..."

"Focus. Xena. Red Sonja. A vat of Jell-O. Who wins?"

"Every man watching, of course!"

"You *suck* at this game!"

"What? The only thing I'm sucking is that jell-o through a straw! After Xena and Red Sonja thrash around in it for a while."

"You're ridiculous!"

"I'm ridiculous? I'm surprised you didn't mention what color the jell-o was!"

"Dude!" said Brian in what passed as a whisper for him.

"Don't stop me! This train just started rolling, pal! And, incidentally, you're about as quiet as an Iron Maiden concert in the late 80s!"

"Dude...customer!"

"What...where?" asked Chris, wind-milling about on his stool for a better look. Luckily, the table stopped his fall.

"Could you be less obvious?"

"Not even if I tried, so I won't."

"G'uh! Two customers! Dude, they're gorgeous!"

"Yeah. I guess. If you like that sort of thing," Chris said, gawking at Lunora and Zemura as they sauntered into the restaurant. Black leather hugged long legs as tiny scraps of cloth play-acted as tops, barely hiding that which must be hidden. Thick black hair framed their faces, porcelain dolls with predatory eyes.

Confused by his friend's lack of enthusiasm, Brian snapped, "What 'thing'? Women?"

"Goof! No, the whole 'irrevocable damnation' look."

"Dude! Why is it suddenly like I don't even know you? You totally dig Goth women! Why do I have to tell you what kind of women you like?"

"You don't! You choose to! Somehow you still labor under the delusion that we have the same taste in women!"

"That's because we totally do!"

"We don't! And I still don't get that whole 'generic hot' philosophy of yours."

"G'uh! It's very simple..."

Seeing that Brian and Chris were obviously the two dorkiest men in the restaurant, thus making them the easiest targets, the sisters went on the prowl. Like cats, they slinked up to the table where Brian and Chris sat. "Hello, boys. Are these stools taken?"

"All I'm saying," continued Brian, "is there are models and movie stars that are special enough to pay the money to see, and then there are those who are hot, but lack any kind of quality that makes them special, nothing that makes them distinguished."

"Hot chicks are hot chicks! What's left to be distinguished?"

"Hi, boys!" Lunora said again, hoping to catch a lull in the discussion, though it was much like trying to catch a cow between chews of grass.

"Of course hot chicks are hot! But that's not the point."

"Dude, that should *always* be the point!"

"You're ridiculous! Why *pay* to see something in a magazine or movie when you can see *better* for *free* on the internet? This is the point at which you totally lose me!"

Lunora turned to Zemura, confused. She leaned close to her sister and whispered, "Are they really arguing about looking at hot chicks, oblivious to the fact that there are two standing right next to them?"

"That's why men make the best slaves – they think of only one thing. It seems these two will be perfect," Zemura whispered back. She then turned Brian and Chris. "Boys! Hello, *boys*!"

"You're a mess!" Brian yelled at Chris. "How is this a difficult concept? This is just like the time you suggested that Taoism was a selfish philosophy!"

"Dude! You're switching topics! That's a whole different gun and I need to load a new clip. Taoism is *totally* a selfish philosophy!"

"That's it," Brian said waving his hands in disgust, "let me dust off my soapbox."

"Stop waving your arms around! You attract enough attention as it is! You can't even *think* quietly!"

"I'll wave my arms if I want!"

"Dude, you have an arm-span like a giraffe's neck! You'll knock the TV off the wall!"

"I will not! Watch this...oops!" Brian winced as the back of his hand glanced off Zemura's shoulder. "Sorry about that. Are you ok?"

"I'm fine, thanks," Zemura replied, offering a devious yet demure smile. "We've been trying to get your attention for a little while now."

"We?" Chris asked, wondering why hot women were talking to Brian and him.

"Yes. My sister and me."

"Sis ...sis...Sister? Did you say 'sister'?"

The sisters looked at each other and giggled. "Yes. We're sisters."

Chris fell from his stool as he attempted to offer it up.

"How does *that* happen?!" Brian laughed. "Dude, get off the floor. Of course, ladies. Here, please join us. And ignore the drooling caveman on the floor. It's his first time out in sunlight."

"Mine, too," Lunora said, joking with her sister.

"Huh?"

"Oh, just an expression. I didn't want him to feel alone in his phobia."

"That's very nice of you," Brian commented, his eyebrows rising in tandem with his impression of the two women.

"So, where are you from? What do you do for a living?" Lunora asked.

"We're dentists. From Kentucky. We specialize in veneers."

"Really? So what brings you here?"

"Convention. We have to be here for a few more days yet."

"Wow! That's so exciting."

"Not really. That's just our day jobs. You should hear what we do at night."

"I'd love to hear about it," Lunora replied, knowing she had at least one of the simpletons hooked. But she couldn't help but notice something as Chris made his way back onto his stool. "Hey, does he have braces? If you specialize in veneers..."

"Yeah, how about that?" Brian said with a nervous chuckle. "We believe firmly in professional support. Our economy is based on it, you know?"

With clutching hands, Chris was able to grab the top of his stool and began heaving himself up off the floor. It was an arduous task that involved much grunting and puffing and he applied himself to it gingerly like a child drinking a huge milk shake, but leery of brain freeze.

"Welcome back, sweetie," Zemura purred. "So what is there to do in Kentucky?"

"The next can of chew," Chris blurted out.

"The derby," Brian interceded. "But enough about us. Tell us about you."

"Well, we thought we'd apply for a job here and they directed us to you. The lady behind the bar said you were the resident experts. Tell me...do you think I'd look okay in the uniform? Why don't you help me pick out a shirt?"

Chris fell off his stool again.

Shaking his head in disgust at Chris, Brian followed the sisters to the merchandise area. From a clothesline strung across the rafters, three versions of the Melons uniform shirt hung on display. There wasn't much in the way of material to any of them and the styles weren't drastically different, aside from different colors and a slight variation to the wording printed upon them. It was a two-minute task to pick one of the three.

Thirty-five minutes later, Brian and the two women were still laughing and pointing and trying on shirts over their other clothes. Watching Brian model the shirts was terror personified. Hair erupted from the armholes of the over matched shirt as the two women stretched and tugged the material over Brian's stomach. From the other side of the restaurant, Chris could hear the shirt begging for release. Or was it the words at the bottom of the beer pitcher he was hearing? Ultimately, he couldn't decide, so he ordered another pitcher to do more tests.

He was halfway through the new pitcher and deep in argument with himself when the trio returned to the table.

"Dude," Brian beamed, "we're leaving. Let's go."

"We've only been here for six hours!" Chris replied, frightened about stepping outside of his comfort zone. "I'm pretty sure we're not allowed to leave yet."

"Check, please. Wait...Can you just put it on our rolling tab? Sweet! Alright, let's go."

"Where are we going?"

"Bot...Boit...what's that place called again, Lunora?"

"Boite de noit," she answered.

"Yeah. That place."

"Is that the actual name?" Chris asked, his skepticism evident.

"Dude, that's like asking who's writing the Xena vs Red Sonja fantasy! Sometimes you just gotta roll with it."

"Whatever! At any point did your Mensa brain register the name of this place?"

"It's that 'bot' something or other."

"First of all, it's French." Chris's snobbery began to reveal itself.

"I'm okay with that.

"Second of all, it means 'nightclub'."

"If this is supposed to be an argument, you have yet to present the distasteful side."

"You're impossible! One doesn't simply go to a nightclub in Harrisburg without knowing the name! Or one wakes up with stories he doesn't want leaked out to the public!"

"Alright, alright. The name is in French, too. It's 'Chez Cocktail Club.' Whatever that means."

"Really?"

"You don't know what it means, do you? HA! You only know French from High School and you've been out of school for twenty years, old man. Chew on that!"

"Brian, do you know the French translation for 'corn fritter'?"

"What?! What does that have to do with anything? You're stupid!"

"It's 'corn fritter'," said Chris with an inebriated attempt at a French accent.

"Sounds pretty similar," Brian mused.

"Exactly. Because corns fritters are *American*! There is no translation!"

"Not seeing your point here. Can we go now?"

"The French translation for 'cocktail club' is 'cocktail club! It's *American*, you knucklehead! They're taking you to a cocktail club!!!"

"Dude! The DJ plays techno. Come on."

"Techno?"

"Nothing but. C'mon! Plus, Melons will be closing in less than an hour, what else are you gonna do?"

"Drink beer at home."

Lunora looked to Zemura and shared a wink. In unison, they turned to Chris and said, "There's beer there."

Suspicious, Chris squinted. "Oh yeah? What kind?"

"Blüdweiser."

"Three strikes! I'm out!"

Brian rolled his eyes and furrowed his brows. "Oh come on! You can't be serious."

"Dude! It's like you don't even know me! First of all, it takes more than two hot goth chicks to get me into an after-hours 'cocktail' club. Second of all, hot goth chicks may be my kryptonite, but techno music is the protective lead casing that shields me from being lured by their siren song. Third of all ... bad beer? A cocktail club playing techno and serving bad beer. Seriously?!"

"Fine! I shall be the lone escort for these lovely ladies."

"Enjoy the bad beer and froo-froo drinks." Chris dismissed his friend with a casual wave before he sought solace at the pitcher's bottom.

As Brian walked with the sisters through a labyrinth of back alleys he never knew Harrisburg possessed, a certain level of pride swelled within him. It wasn't often he could lord a snobbery over his friend. Until now, the only topic he could be snobbish about was his genius level intelligence, but now he felt as if the social elite bestowed upon him a status upgrade. Dare he think he was a socialite? Certainly more so than Chris who was a full-fledged snob in every other aspect of life: beer, vocabulary, literature, current events in the porn industry, movie quotes, and heavy metal.

Brian's nerves tingled as the trio strolled down dank alleys littered with the homeless and scavengers, both human and vermin. Beady eyes watched the interlopers, but two of the three moved with confident resolve, knowing the creatures dared not block their path.

Brian shoved his fears as deep into his soul as he could, one of the few moments in his life where he found the ability to keep his big mouth shut. This was a rare moment in which he could pretend to be cool; so he did not want to blow it. Finally, they walked into an empty and dark warehouse. It was small enough to be innocuous when viewed from the outside, but the twisting shadows skulking in the far corners added a shot of adrenaline to Brian's swiftly beating heart.

"Get ready for a life changing night," Lunora purred as she hefted open a thick steel door. The heavy beats of dark trance music smacked Brian in the face before he even took his first step down the carved stone stairwell. By the time his foot touched the third step, the moody melodies of neo-goth music hypnotized him, and he mentally declared this his new happy place.

Both of the sisters spoke to him, but Brian heard neither of their voices, his mind reeling from the sights as he finally made his way to the bottom of the stairs. Half of the room strobed between the harshness of pitch black and the blinding glare of pure white light. Darkness enshrouded the other half of the room, broken up by colorful lasers dancing through a nebula of smoke, created by both fog machines and burning cigarettes, giving the air itself a layer of chromatic skin, alive and wriggling. The entire room moved, pumping and flowing like blood through veins to the beat of the music.

The crowd parted as the sisters moved through, their proximity as electric as a slithering live-wire. Brian followed them to their private couch at the back of the club. The plush material caressed him as he sat; eyes transfixed on the dozens of women. All the women, on the dance floor, their long hair snapping like cat-o-nine tails to every other beat while their leather-hugged hips churned to the melodies. Exposed skin stirred through the intermittent darkness like cream swirling though coffee. Sparks flickered in every set of smoldering eyes as flashing lights glinted from their teeth - their teeth. Something about the teeth of every woman in the club confounded Brian, but the constant action, nonstop movement, mixing with the mesmerizing music melted his mind like margarine.

Content to simply watch, Brian hardly noticed either sister's company, mouthing the words, "Thank you," every time one of them put a drink in his hands. He hardly cared that each drink became more viscous than the last, tasting coppery with every sip. The flashing lights tickled. The music massaged. The drinks soothed. Brian's eyes rolled back into his head, the last coherent observation that he was the least geeky nerd among any man in the place escaped him as unconsciousness took over. Strange dreams of crimson streaked through the blackness, to be cast away by the reality of the word, "*Dude*!"

Opening his eyes, Brian saw Chris looking down at him. A grimace twisted Brian's face from the pain of shifting from the beauty of a goth girl filled room to the nastiness of a bald head and red goatee. The pain increased when the bald head and red goatee talked. "Why are you topless?! And where's your fur!?"

"Wha...?" Brian mumbled as he stood up from the floor of Melons Bar & Grille. Before he asked what his friend was talking about, he peeked down to see that he was indeed topless. And hairless.

"What's with the leather pants?" Chris continued. "Did you join some kind of cult last night in which you need to become a hairless member of the Village People?"

"Dude... there were goth girls... and techno..."

"Which explains why you allowed yourself to look like you left a Sex Pistols concert. Put a damn shirt on!"

Confused, Brian stumbled in a daze to the Melons merchandise counter and procured the largest shirt he could find. It still ended up way too tight. Straining as hard as he could, without popping a blood vessel, he tried to recount the evening to Chris while sitting at the bar. In between swigs of beer, he told the story, leaving nothing out that he could remember. But his memories ended, dissolving into blackness.

"Well, that's what you get for drinking froo-froo drinks! And techno! It can't be good for you!" Chris said, shoving fried pickles into his mouth.

For the first time in his life, Brian saw food and did not want to devour it. In fact, quite the opposite happened. "Dude, I'm not feeling too well. I'm gonna lay down in the back room."

Before Chris could berate his friend, Brian stood from the barstool and stumbled into the back room. Curling up in the corner he fell immediately to sleep. He didn't awaken until after twilight passed. Strolling back out, Brian saw Chris in the same spot as before, this time with a heaping plate of chicken wings in front of him.

Like a man possessed, Brian flopped on the barstool next to Chris and grabbed a handful of wings, shoving them in his mouth, bones and all. As he reached for a second helping, Chris disapproved. "Dude!"

Pausing only to growl at his friend, Brian shoveled in a second helping. And then a third. And fourth. After finishing the whole plate, he wiped his mouth and moaned in utter relief, "Meat."

Face twisted in utter disgust by his friend's actions, Chris could only bellow one word, "*Dude*!?"

"Damn, now I'm tired again." Without so much as a salutation, Brian left his barstool and returned to the backroom.

Brian continued this pattern for a week, sleeping all day, staying awake later and later into the night. His new ritual included a midnight breakfast of a burger, well done, then medium, then rare, until he ordered it bunless and raw.

"Okay, either Jeffry Daumer has instituted his own version of the Atkins diet, or there's something seriously wrong with you!" Chris finally stated.

"There's nothing wrong with me. I feel great. In fact, let's get outta here," Brian replied.

"Ummmm. It's three in the morning. Last call was an hour ago. I'm gonna finish this beer and pass out in that booth over there."

"Alright. Suit yourself. I'm going out and looking for trouble."

"You never have to look too far!" And Chris never spoke truer words. The next morning, he awoke to his friend lying on the floor, once again topless. "Dude!"

Once again, Brian woke up groggy and confused. "G'uh. What happened last night?"

"I don't know, but I can't figure out why you feel the need to keep taking off your shirt! No one wants to see that, sans hair or not! And is ... is that ... a *rat tail* stuck in your teeth?"

As he walked to the merchandise stand for another shirt, Brian looked at what he picked from his teeth. "Yeah I guess it is," he said. Then slurped it down like a stray strand of spaghetti.

"Dude!"

"What?"

"You just ate a *rat tail.* And we can both assume that you ate *the rat* mere hours ago! And what's up with your teeth?"

Brian paused, contemplating Chris's words. He ran his tongue over his teeth, then his finger. They felt jagged and sharp, especially his canines. Like a bucket of ice water, his memories of his visit to the after-hours night club hit him. The women dancing. Their teeth. All jagged fangs. "Dude. I think I'm turning into a vampire."

"You're stupid!"

"I think it happened the night I went to the after-hours club. The girls ... all the girls there had fangs."

"Dude. They're goth girls! Of course, they're gonna have fangs."

"I don't think it was costume bridgework, dude. They were real."

"Whatever! Plus, you have no bite marks on you."

Brian thought and a moment later blurted out "The drinks. They must have used the drinks to turn me."

"You know, just because you went to a rave doesn't make you cool. Nor a vampire. Now sit down, shut up and have a beer."

Disgruntled, Brian did as instructed. But that midnight, he went out again only to awaken the morning after with no recollection of his escapades. He repeated those actions five nights in a row.

Sitting at the bar, shaking like a junkie in need of a fix, Brian shoved a fistful of raw meat in his mouth. "It's getting worse."

"Oh, you're fine!" Chris replied, tired of the whole my-friend-thinks-he's-a-vampire topic.

"Dude, I think I drank the blood from three cows last night!"

"I've seen you eat forty chicken wings in ten minutes! Three cows in one night is on par with that!"

"You have to help me."

"You want help? Fine. Here's some advice – stop wearing leather pants and start wearing a shirt!"

"I can hear the heartbeats of every person in this restaurant. I can smell their blood. It's ... calling to me. How do you explain that?"

"You're too intense for your own good! Doesn't mean you're a vampire."

Brian held his arm next to Chris's. "Okay, smart guy. Explain how it's possible that I'm now more pale than you."

A look of horror washed across Chris's face. "Dude. You're a vampire."

"I know!"

"What do I have to do?"

"The sisters. You have to kill the sisters. Kill the creators and I go back to being human, right?"

"*Dude*! *I can't do that*!"

"You can't think of them as hot goth chicks. Think of them as undead monstrosities from the diabolical depths of the underworld. Who happen to be hot."

"Seriously..."

"Seriously, I'm about a week from eating people. We're already the most unpopular patrons of this restaurant. I think they might actually kick us out if I start draining the other customers of their blood."

Annoyed by his friend's incessant palaver, Chris found no other recourse, but to bend to his outlandish whims. "Fine!"

"Alright. Good. Good. Go home and goth yourself up. You'll have to pose as a vampire. Meet me back here and I'll take you to the club."

Chris did as instructed. Anxiety coursed through Brian's body, unable to think of anything else except blood. He consumed more raw meat in hopes to sate even a minute amount of his hunger. The Melons Bar and Grille waitresses started to avoid him once his lips and chin became ensanguined with blood. Luckily, Chris returned. Unfortunately, the fashion police were nowhere to be found.

Doing a spit take, Brian sprayed half-chewed meat across the bar. Standing before him, Chris wore a black spandex shirt, striped with the occasional strip of black electrical tape, black jeans and black boots. "Dude. Brandon Lee called..."

Chris sneered and interrupted, "No '*The Crow*' jokes!"

"Okay. Jack Lalane called..."

"No 'I'm out of shape' jokes either!"

Brian scowled from having his fun stripped away. "Fine! I'm just happy that you're pale enough to pass for a vampire. The thought of you needing to wear make-up is unnerving."

"You know, I don't have to do this. And why are you holding

your gut?"

Clutching his waist with both arms, Brian rocked back and forth. "The pain, dude. The hunger. It hurts."

"Hunger? You just ate five pounds of meat!"

"The animal blood just isn't doing it for me anymore. I think I'm craving human blood."

Rolling his eyes, Chris sighed. "Save the drama. Just show me where this place is."

Leading the way, Brian trudged through the city streets and back alleys of Harrisburg. He stumbled on occasion when a hunger pang stabbed through his stomach. Sweat poured from him, dripping on the wretched sidewalks. Every joint hurt, begging for relief, telling him that one bite from any of the numerous homeless people he walked past would supply him the elixir he needed. Just before he lost control, he found the warehouse.

Too wracked with pain to continue, Brian leaned against the cold brick wall. Unable to stand any longer he slid to the ground, lying in the fetal position, shaking. With a quaking voice, he instructed Chris. "The ware house ... is empty. Big doors at the other end ... lead to the club downstairs. The sisters ... private area by ... the DJ."

"Wuss," Chris replied as he entered the warehouse. The eerie echoing of his footsteps convinced him to hasten his pace to the door. He opened it and immediately hated his friend.

Thumping noise punched him in his face. He felt the beat rattle his bones more and more with each step down the stairs. Once on the floor, he took a moment to look at the writhing dance floor. The women were beautiful, young, moving in ways he could only fantasize about. But the music was fast - too fast, repetitive, synthetic. Then he saw the sisters sitting on a big couch on the other side of the room, close to the DJ.

Stay on target. Stay on target, Chris thought, repeating it like a mantra as he walked through the swirling mass of flesh on the dance floor.

Chris found walking to be a difficult task. The music threw off his equilibrium. The speed of it, the unearthly noises made him jittery. Unnerved, he forgot that he strolled in a den of the damned until one grabbed his arm.

Confused, Chris tensed, ready to shove, push, and fight. Then he saw the devastating beauty of the woman who pulled him close. Her heart shaped face held cat eyes and a razorblade smile emphasized by two ivory spikes. The soft scent of cinnamon slid from her redolent skin. He could resist many things, but not that, the smell giving him many naughty urges. Her finger traced Chris's one ear as she whispered into his other, "Hey, sexy. Show me your fangs."

STAY ON TARGET! *STAY ON TARGET*! Chris offered a polite, closed-lip, smile. Freeing himself from her grip, his heart fell to his stomach and he focused on his mission, returning to the moving cogs of the crowd. *The music. Too much.*

Sweat streamed from his forehead as he moved closer to the sisters. The music made his thoughts blur. He didn't know what he was going to do after he killed them. The thumping disallowed one rational thought to lead into another. He hoped and prayed that they were the ones responsible for all the other vampires. Kill the sisters, liberate everyone in the room. *The thumping.*

Closer to the couch. *Music, fast.* By themselves, the sisters sat. *Repetitive beats, over and over and over. Just too much slamming static.* Closer to the sisters, close enough to see their fang-laced smiles. *The same beat again and again and again and again.* Chris grabbed a weapon, a shoulder high table. *The same synthetic tunes over and again and over and again and over and again and over and again and over and again and over and again and...* Chris released his fury!

The DJ ducked out of the way as Chris slammed the table onto the equipment. The music hiccuped. Chris struck again, this time aiming for the computer monitors. The speakers screeched in pain. Chris found the server responsible for the noise and kicked it. Hard. Stomping and jumping up and down, Chris reduced the computer to plastic slivers, throwing the room into silence. Huffing and puffing, he stopped, satisfied that he killed the infernal beast of rave music. Ice ran down his spine as realized something – he hadn't stayed on target.

Chris turned to the gathering crowd of salivating maws, led by Lunora and Zemura...

INSIDE THE MINDS OF MONKEYS

CHRIS: One of the things I wanted to point out about Vampires was that it was the first story we passed back and forth...
BRIAN: In fact the only story we did that with... At least in the first edition. In this edition, we passed "The Drunken Comic Book Monkeys vs. Themselves" back and forth. But everything else was written solo.
C: And I totally didn't do what you asked me to do... That's the really interesting part.
B: Yeah, 'cause I passed the story onto Chris and I said, "Get us from here to there." He passes it back 1250 words later and says, "Dude, I got us from here to...here."
C: I got us from X to X.1.
JEFF: You never told me that and when I'm reading it, I can't tell who wrote what.
B: Really? You couldn't tell our styles?
J: Well I could probably now that I know about it, if I went back.
C: There were no speech tags. You should have picked up that was me.
B: I snuck some in when he wasn't looking. I threw a shiny, shiny nickel on the floor.
C: It wasn't a nickel. It was tin foil. But I still looked. It was shiny.
B: We looked at the typical classic vampire story and we noticed that most of them are Character X is infected with the vampire strain and Characters Y & Z have to save Character X. And the classic way is to kill the one that infected Character X. So we wanted to do it in our own special way. And by special way, we mean we fall in love with the vampires who turn me into a vampire. Then Chris has to come save me by killing the one that turned me. The true brilliance of being a Comic Book Monkey is that we screw it up! We also played off of some auto-biographical stuff like Chris absolutely despising techno music and any kind of Goth industrial. He loves pretty much everything Goth with the exception of the music. So we really wanted to play up that part.
C: And it's also quasi-auto-biographical that he once tried on a Hooters waitress's shirt.
B: We're not going to talk about that.
J: For $10, he'll tell you.
B: My lawyer advised against it.
C: Why did you decide that we should lose?

B: I just thought it was hysterical! I just thought it would be funny!
C: Had nothing to do with the fact that we're totally stupid.
B: We did come up with and discuss the idea of losing from the very beginning. We decided that it would be a nice mix not to win all the time. Considering that our stories are pretty much comedy, we figured it would give the readers some form of mystery. "Will these guys live through this?" is now a major question. If they can hold onto that question of "will they make it or not?", then hopefully, they'll keep on reading.
J: What have you heard from the readers who responded about you dying?
B: Very little…
J: They don't mind that you die in the story?
B: It doesn't seem that the readers are surprised when we die by any stretch of the imagination. If anything, I think that they might appear a little more surprised that we live so often. But I think that one of the reasons that we die at the end is to poke fun at ourselves. Especially since it's a fairly simple instruction – Go in and kill this one person. Looking aside from the morality of actually killing another individual, it's step 1, step 2... and we screw it up. We screw up royally. We really go off tangent and it bites us in the ass.
J: Oooooo this is also the first "Stay on Target", isn't it?
B: Yes. "Stay on Target" is our mantra sometimes during our Fortress business meetings. Especially when we're dealing with a hot topic that we have to get through and our publicist and editor are yelling at us to "Stay on Target."
C: And your utter distain for the French language comes through
B: Yes and we play up the fact that you're a snob about many things. Of course, I think it's very, very funny especially since you and I are a pair of beer swilling dolts when you break it down. But we all have our little forms of snobbery. It's basically our character flaws being used against us.
C: We have no such weaknesses!
B: That's right. We're men!
C: In my 39 years, I've only gone off on a tangent once.
J: Yeah, and you woke up married!
C: I mentioned this at a panel discussion once. The other panelist thought that was funny, especially since I went on a tangent to tell them I never go on tangents…He couldn't talk for 2 minutes…
J: It disturbs me that I know you so well.
C: I do know I had to get the scene in of the two waitresses taking him over and putting him in the Hooters t shirt.
B: Still not talking about it…

THE DRUNKEN COMIC BOOK MONKEYS
VS.
THE WENDIGO

It was cold; really cold - and Brian didn't like it. "It's cold!"

"I know!" Chris yelled back.

The men had woken up in plenty of jail cells before, but none this frigid.

"Will you two wimps shut up about the weather already, eh? It's downright balmy today!" Deputy Douglas Durpree shouted at the detainees.

Brian and Chris looked at each other, both sets of eyes blood-shot, having just awoken mere seconds ago with skull-splitting hang-overs. Brian asked, "Canada?"

Chris tried to agree, but his chattering teeth precluded any meaningful sounds. He sat on the stone floor, hugging his legs and rocking back and forth.

"Yes, boys, you are indeed in Canada, eh," Sheriff Beau Lebeau said, his lips smacking from chewing gum. "Looks like you're gonna be here for a while, too."

Teeth chattering as well, Brian started to say, "Okay, what did we do...?" but cut himself off when he looked around and saw the goat – wearing a fedora and both pink fuzzy socks.

The reptilian part of the brain in most humans takes a back-seat to higher functions such as logic and forethought. Not so for Brian. The reptilian part of his brain blissfully stewed in the juices of carnal desires, dictating that the basest of impulses be acted upon with vigor. Arms outstretched, fingers ready to rend, Brian launched himself toward the goat. Had he had taken even a modicum of time to assess the situation; he might have seen that the goat stood in a neighboring cell. Brian never saw the bars separating the two of them.

The ensuing clang reduced the church bells of Notre Dame Cathedral to the toy bell of a tricycle. The shockwaves knocked everyone to the floor, bits of plaster from the ceiling rained down along with clouds of gritty dust. And despite bending one of the bars to match the features of his face, Brian still reached for the goat while mumbling, "My socks. My socks. My socks."

Chris watched Brian and stopped shivering; not so much because of any form of warmth being generated, but the ridiculousness of his business partner's antics made him forget all about being cold. Standing, Chris stretched, cracking joints and shifting muscles back into place, attempting to relieve any damage caused by sleeping on a cement floor. Stepping over Brian, who now frothed at the mouth, Chris ambled over to the bars and said, "Excuse me, Sheriff..."

"Beau Lebeau."

"Sheriff Beau Lebeau. What infraction could we have possibly done during our brief time in this great country?"

The sheriff walked around his dark cherry wood desk. He crossed his arms and leaned back. His chewing slowed, jaw muscles now grinding his gum. He stared at Chris, but Chris couldn't see the sheriff's eyes, his mirrored sunglasses shielding them, reflecting Chris's confused face back at him. "Eh? What'd you do? Well, you two boys are guilty of *clignotement*."

"*Clignotement*?" Chris repeated. "Hey! Wait-a-minute! I know French! That means 'blinking'!"

Brian stopped his attempts to grab the goat. "Blinking? Again? How do you offend people by blinking? I'm gonna duct tape your eyelids shut if you can't get your blinking problem under control!"

"I don't have a blinking problem, you idiot! These are just trumped up charges! I'm thinking we didn't do anything wrong. We're in here just because we're Americans! What do you have to say about that, Mr. Sheriff?!" Chris added a head bobble at the end of his statement for punctuation.

Beau responded by clenching his teeth so hard that his face reddened with rage. Keeping his arms crossed over his monstrous chest, he flexed. His muscles strained against his uniform, already two sizes too small, until the seams groaned in agony from holding the shirt together. His pursed and twitching lips revealed that he showed great restraint with his actions and words. "I say, you had better sit down. Boy."

Chris sat.

"Dude," Brian whispered. "You can see his veins through his shirt."

"Shut up," Chris whispered back.

"The ones in his forehead look like they could burst like out of control fire-hoses at any minute."

"Shut up."

"Dude, he's so big, he makes most professional wrestlers look like chess players."

"Shut up."

Before Brian could continue to make Chris feel worse, a gust of cold air swirled around the small Canadian police station as the front door opened. Walking in with the unsteady gait of forgetting what it was to feel like not having to pushing against driving winds was a man bundled from head to toe in florescent orange Gortex. The newcomer then turned and pressed his full weight against the door to shut it. After clapping the snow from his oversized gloves, he dropped his hood to reveal a shock of bushy beard and a heedful of long feathered hair, circa mid-70s. He offered a bright smile to the sheriff and deputy. "Beautiful day in the park, eh?"

"Never better, Ranger Lehibou," the sheriff snarled.

"You betcha, Woodsy!" the deputy answered.

"Wait-a-minute!" Chris snapped, jumping up. "This is a park? We're in a park jail cell?"

"How the hell do you offend someone by blinking in a Canadian park?" Brian yelled at Chris.

Chris rolled his eyes. "I told you already. 'Blinking' isn't a real charge!"

"But these are real, eh?" the sheriff growled, shifting his weight so Brian and Chris both got a better view of his belt. Along his waist were two sheathed hunting knives, two holstered guns, a nightstick, a set of brass knuckles, a taser, and a clip of half a dozen throwing stars.

"Yes, sir," Chris said, returning to his seated position on the floor.

Looking to Woodsy, Sheriff Labeau said, "So, how goes it, Ranger Lehibou?"

"Not well, I'm afraid. The three of us need to go searching for some hunters."

"Not again," the deputy mumbled.

The sheriff smirked and huffed through his nose, shaking his head in contempt. "Let me guess. Some rich business men getting away from the city, thinking they're hunters, eh?"

"Yep," Woodsy replied. "Five uppity-ups from that import company in the city. Tequila, I think?"

"Tequila?" Brian asked. "Did you say 'tequila'?"

"Yep. But what's it matter to you, eh?"

"We can help!"

"We can?" Chris asked.

"Yes!"

"And how exactly can you two help?" Beau asked.

"Easy," Brian said with a smile, "If they import tequila, then logic dictates that tequila was the drink of choice for their hunting trip."

"There better be a point to this, boy!"

"Our goat is a tequila sniffing goat."

Beau slid his index finger and thumb under his mirrored spectacles to pinch the bridge of his nose. The deputy readied himself to administer first aid to the annoying Americans, awaiting the sheriff's reaction – undoubtedly one involving violence. Woodsy tilted his head and looked at the goat, wondering if there could be any truth to the statement. The tension in the room wound tighter than a spring, until Beau spoke, "A tequila sniffing goat?"

"Yes, sir."

"You expect me to believe that?"

"Well, he is from Mexico."

"There is no way I'm gonna believe this goat is from Mexico, eh!"

Brian turned to the goat. "Hey, goat."

"Baaah?"

"Say something to the sheriff in Mexican."

"Baaah."

"See?" Brian said, turning back to the sheriff. The veins on the sheriff's ruddy neck swelled to the size of his fingers. He reached for his gun.

"Sheriff?" Woodsy said. "There might be some merit to his statement."

"Are you actually implying that this goat and these two knuckleheads can find the missing hunters?"

"No. But having them along couldn't hurt. The three of us need to look for the hunters and you can't leave the three of them here by themselves. We'll just start at the closest cabins and go from there, eh?"

Through his sunglasses, Beau looked up to Heaven for any form of sign or advice. None could be found, so he had to just wing it. "Fine! Let's gear up!"

The deputy released the Americans and the goat from their cells. Parkas, Gortex, insulated pants, waterproof boots, and oversized gloves were distributed. Soon, five men and one goat all looked like Woodsy. The sheriff and deputy packed backpacks with food and supplies. They distributed the backpacks, said a few prayers in a prayer circle, and sang a quick verse of Cumbaya before leaving the station.

The wind lashed the snow against the seekers, frigid whips of white. Every change in direction snapped the stinging ice crystals over any exposed skin. But they trudged forth, leaning into the storm, lifting legs high to move through the knee-deep ever-flowing ivory sea. Through the fir trees haunting whistles mixed with moans of anguish, chilling the men down to the marrow more than the cold.

"Baaah."

"Don't be silly, goat," Chris said. "It's just the wind. Right guys?"

The Canadians exchanged furtive glances. Even through his

mirrored sunglasses and granite chiseled expression of anger, Beau conveyed concern. Woodsy turned to Chris and said, "Yeah, just the wind. In fact, let's head to that group of trees to get out of the wind and take a little rest."

The other five followed Woodsy to the outcropping of trees. They grew tightly together, but there was enough space among them to form a small area in which the men and goat could fit, allowing a brief respite from the driving winds. Everyone clapped their hands and shook snow from themselves. Those carrying backpacks dropped them to the ground, allowing their muscles a rest.

Trying to catch his breath, the deputy turned to Woodsy and said, "That wind is something, eh? Something of ... legend?"

Fear swept through Woodsy's eyes faster than the changing gusts beyond the tree barrier. "It ... it sure seems that way."

"Stop it, you two," Beau growled. "That's just a campfire story."

"What is?" Chris asked.

"Nothing," Beau replied. "Let's grab a quick snack and get moving. The cabins aren't that far. Brian?"

"Yeah?" Brian replied.

"The food, eh? You're the one carrying the backpack of food."

"Ummmm ... that wasn't for everybody, was it?"

All eyes shifted to the tallest member of the team. Feeling the heat from the glares, Brian tried to nonchalantly hide the empty bag behind his back.

"Dude!" Chris yelled. "How did you not know that food was meant for everyone?"

"He handed it to me and said, 'here's food'! I thought he meant that it was *my* food. I thought *everyone* got a backpack of food!"

"Wait!" Woodsy yelled. "Did he eat the entire bag of food?"

"Ummmmm," Brian answered.

"Of course he did!" Chris added, his words rancid.

"That was five pounds of food, boy!" Beau pointed out.

"Right! You handed me the backpack and told me it was snacks. So I figured since it wasn't a lot of food, it was mine."

"It was for all of us! We all need food. Look at that poor skinny goat!" Woodsy said.

"Baaah!"

"You ate five pounds of food in *a half an hour*!" the deputy pointed out.

"So? I was *hungry*!"

Hearing that word, the Canadians reeled back, even Beau, however his hand moved to one of his guns. The three men stared at Brian, calculating and contemplating what he said, wondering what he meant.

"What? What'd I say?" Brian asked.

Beau turned away, toward the swirling winds behind the trees. "Nothing. Let's go. The cabins are half a mile straight ahead."

Once through the trees, visibility became nil. The men communicated with hand gestures due to the constant rush of air stealing their voices. The sheriff waved to his associates, pointing in the direction of the cabin. The deputy and the park ranger waved back in acknowledgement. Chris and Brian waved to each other with middle fingers. The goat shook his head in disgust. Taking offense, Chris waved his middle finger to the goat – until the goat disappeared.

An exceptional swirl of snow created a wall of white around Chris. He fought through it and pushed forward. For one split second the wintry maelstrom relented, just enough time for Chris to realize he had lost the rest of the party. He knew which direction to walk, so on he went, hoping to find the cabins, or at least another member of the search party.

Fast and furious, the wind seemed to funnel right into his face, determined to steal his breath. Gasping, unable to gulp anything but snow, he collapsed. Needing fuel to move on, he reached for the pocket of his pants that contained the beer. To his dismay, the thickness of his gloves and jacket prohibited him from doing so. Chris tried again and again, yielding the same result – no beer. Denied his life-force, he commanded his legs to move, to stand! And stand he did. Raising his gloved hands in front of his face, he created an ersatz mask, a wall to breakup the vacuum created by the wind. Breath! Renewed in spirit, motivated to yet again clutch what he loved, he trekked on. Within a few more anguished steps, Chris saw a flickering speck of brown. Focusing on that, he pushed on, against the wind, one foot in front of the other. The speck turned into a blotch, then to a smear. He finally recognized it to be what he had hoped – a cabin. Renewed vigor flowed through his muscles, churning his legs as best they could, chugging against the deep snow. Closer! With door in sight, Chris raced forward, clutching the handle to open it. In one yelping breath, he opened the door and flung himself inside, flopping to the floor.

"Drama queen," Brian greeted Chris.

So happy to get out of the wind, Chris remained on the floor, wheezing. After removing his gloves, he procured the inspiration he needed to survive the elements – a beer from his pants. Suckling the bottle like a newborn, he curled up into a fetal position.

"What a sis," Brian said, watching the spectacle as he sat in a chair with his feet propped up on the cabin's dinner table.

"Baaah," the goat agreed, sitting on a chair on the other side of the table.

"I got separated from the group!" Chris yelled.

"We all did, boy," Beau said, standing by a window, looking at the outside painted white. "I made it to the cabin first. Then the sickly looking goat. Then your friend. Although, he's not telling you that he was sobbing like a virgin on prom night when he arrived."

"Baaah," the goat confirmed the sheriff's statement.

"I knew it!" Chris yelled.

"It's cold out there! And I'm hungry!" Brian yelled.

The sheriff looked away from the window to Brian. His expression remained impassive and emotionless, his gaze hidden behind his glasses. But Brian could feel the sheriff's eyes bore into his soul. Before Brian could react to the uncomfortable silence, the door flung open again. Woodsy entered. "I think we got a problem, Sheriff."

"You mean other than the bad weather?"

"I mean what the bad weather brought with it." Woodsy said, extending his arm. Clutched in his gloved hand was a sleeve, white and gray camouflage with stripes of florescent orange. The one end was tattered, obviously torn from the jacket, but both ends were stained brown with dried blood. "One of the hunters', eh?"

"Only thing that's logical," the sheriff replied.

"What the hell were they hunting?" Chris asked.

Beau and Woodsy looked at each other, hesitant to answer. But Woodsy did. "Caribbean caribou."

"What?" Chris asked. "That's ridiculous. There're no caribou in Jamaica."

"Of course not, you dolt!" Brian snapped. "The Caribbean caribou is named to confuse hunters, sending them off to hunt where the animal isn't. This caribou is the stuff of carnivore legend. It's the most delectable and succulent meat known to humanity. Their muscle fibers twist and braid like lengths of rope, thusly keeping the juices from cooking out when grilled. Their fat is stored in small pockets all over, instead of long strips, forming tiny wells of flavor throughout. And the way their bones and ligaments are formed combined with the way they move, it's almost like they self tenderize every time they run."

By the time Brian finished, drool dripped from his goatee. His glassy-eyed gaze fell to the goat.

"Baaah!"

"Don't worry, goat. I'm not going to eat you. Yet."

Beau and Woodsy shared another look of concern. They turned their attention back to Brian, all but frothing at the mouth. Woodsy said, "The deputy hasn't shown up yet, eh?"

"I know," said Beau, keeping a suspicious gaze on Brian. "I think we should check the next cabin."

Brian stood from the table and walked to the door. He opened it and tried to peer through the whipping snow. "Where is it?"

"Straight ahead," Woodsy said. "But we should stick togeth..."

"Alrighty. See you there. Hopefully they have some food," Brian cut him off and plunged headfirst into the snowstorm.

"Wait!" Woodsy chased after him.

"Dammit!" Beau barked and jumped into the blinding whiteness.

"Baaah," the goat said and followed everybody else.

Loathing to repeat the last trek through the snow, Chris

weighed his options. Only one presented itself – to follow along. He pulled one last beer from his pocket and swigged it down. Bundling up as best he could, he took a few deep breaths and exited the cabin.

The winds swirled harder than before, slapping him, punishing him. Again, he used beer as his motivation to survive; a nice refreshing brew to reinvigorate his senses awaited his arrival. But the wind was menacing. It howled and whistled, buffeting him with the anguish of tortured souls. He swore he even heard screams of pain pleading for help. He promised himself a vacation to someplace warm once he finished this mission. Tijuana perhaps?

As before, once Chris saw his target, hopes of salvation charged his muscles, pushing him through the mutating snow banks. And as before, Brian had beaten him there.

The first thing Chris saw was Brian slamming the refrigerator door shut in hopes to hide his recent doings. What Brian failed to realize was his face was slicked with the grease from the chicken he ate and a drumstick bone was entrenched in his goatee. "What?!"

"Did you leave anything for anybody else?"

"Ummmm ... the fridge was empty?"

"You're stupid!"

Before Brian could retort, the door burst open again; Sheriff Lebeau stormed through. He froze, stricken immobile by the horror presented to him. Unnoticed by either Brian or Chris, the furniture lay overturned, broken and askew about the open room cabin. Bits of shredded clothing, white-gray camouflage and florescent orange, accented the scene of mayhem. Bloodied handprints smeared areas of the walls.

Beau did not want to admit that his colleagues' suspicions had been true. He did not want to admit that he now believed in scary stories told by adults, handed down from Algonquians, to temper children's desire for greed. But he could deny it no longer. All of the evidence unfolded in front of him. All the evidence pointed to Brian. "Wendigo!"

"Whoa!" Brian yelled as he turned to the sheriff and found himself staring down the barrel of a Colt 45. "What are you talking about?"

"They tried to tell me," Beau said, more to himself, his voice shaking and his words fast. "They were right. I wouldn't listen and they were right."

"Who told you? Told you what?"

Sweat poured from the sheriff's brow, despite the freezing winds licking him from the open door in front of which he stood. His hands, both holding the gun, shook, but not from the weather. "Woodsy and the deputy. They both had a feeling about this; both thought the spirit had taken the hunters. And they were right. But now the spirit has taken you. *You*!"

"What spirit!" Brian yelled. "And why do you think it's me?"

"The wendigo spirit. The insatiable spirit. The one that consumes you, the one that makes *you* consume! The hunger! The never ending hunger!"

Chris crunched up his face. "Dude, are you serious? He's always like this. You should see him with seafood. It's kinda disgusting actually."

"Impossible!" the sheriff yelled, spittle flying from his quaking lips. "No human can eat like that! No one!"

"He eats like this every day! I am very surprised he hasn't eaten the goat yet! Speaking of ... where is the goat?"

No sooner did Chris pose the question than it was answered. A howl louder than the wind engulfed the cabin as a leg shot from within the storm toward Beau. The hoof, now curled to a two-pronged claw, sunk deep into the sheriff's shoulder. With one yank, the leg pulled the sheriff, screaming, into the blinding storm. But Beau refused to go without a fight.

Brian and Chris heard the popping of rapid gunfire. Beau was giving the snow devil everything he had shooting both guns at once. They saw arcs of flashing blue from his taser. They heard the sheriff growling and yelling, undoubtedly attacking the wendigo possessed goat with his hunting knives. Finally when a throwing star zipped from the outside, into the cabin, just past Brian's cheek, the men decided to run out the back door.

The second they stepped foot into the wintry storm, they lost sight of each other. Brian heard a haunting bleat, quickly consumed by the screaming winds. He ran as best he could against the waves of snow crashing against him. The wind gusts pummeled him. Sheets of ice fell from the sky, cutting him. Something slammed into the base of his back, knocking him to the frigid ground. A weight pressed on him, crushing him, forcing the air from his lungs. He struggled to lift his head, but when he did, he saw the storm stop, reduced to snow flurries. Toward the horizon, cast against the twilight hues of a setting sun, stood a Caribbean Caribou. Brian reached for it, and proclaimed with his last breath, "That's good eatin'."

The Caribou nodded and turned to walk away toward the setting sun.

INSIDE THE MINDS OF MONKEYS

BRIAN: The reason why I picked this one to do as a rewrite was because when Chris wrote it, he took the original Algernon Blackwood version of it...

CHRIS: Which is hardly known at all.

B: Yeah, I don't think anyone knows about it other than hard core Algernon Blackwood fans... which would be Chris.

C: Actually I had to go buy it and read it prior to writing it. For inspiration

B: Although it was a very entertaining story, I just thought that, first of all very few people know what the Wendigo is, what it's supposed to symbolize, what it's supposed to mean and of those people who do, even fewer know about the Algernon Blackwood version. So when we talked about the Wendigo, I immediately came up with some ideas as to what story I envisioned. And one of the things I came up with that the goat was possessed by the spirit. Chris liked that idea, too, and went on a different tangent. I saw it as more of a 20th century American movie style.

C: And I think it was interesting that this was one of the first titles we both agreed we needed to do. Even though our experience with the character was very limited, we both reacted to it immediately.

B: Yeah. Limited and completely different 'cause I saw the Wendigo through the Marvel comic version and a couple different movie versions. One being... ah crap, the version with Ethan Hawke... It was a really good movie. I think called the *Hunger*.

JEFF: Or was it *Ravenous*?

B: Yeah, *Ravenous*! That's right. It was done the way I always heard it which that it was a Native American tale about greed and hunger and if you become greedy you'll never be satisfied and you'll always be hungry, which is the whole point of the spirit. So what Chris did was very entertaining and went where we believed that it should go. However, I just saw a different path for it. So when we had an opportunity to pick stories for the rewrite, I wanted to rewrite the Wendigo as a classic 20th century American story where you have some characters and they start to disappear one at a time. One of the people in the group is possessed by the Wendigo spirit. And since we portray me as always eating all the time, I thought it would be funny that some of the people that are living through the story would start accusing me of being the Wendigo. Ironically, the one person that comes to my defense is Chris who yells at me for eating all the time. At the end, the Wendigo is the goat.

PUBLICIST: It's a classic red herring...

B: Oh yeah? Did I pull it off?

P: Yup.

B: A red herring... I guess that's better than a purple mackerel?

P: Wow. I fold.

J: When you started looking at the story, did you look at the original and say I want to keep this, I want to change that?

B: I think basically when we talked about it; we agreed that the goat would be the Wendigo. So I really wanted to keep that. Chris's version had a much more open ending even though if you really read it, it's clear we won't make it. And I wanted to keep that in my version as well. I think we added a darker element to the comedy. A lot of the other stories are straight forward here's the joke, here's the set up, here's the laugh. This is one of the fewer stories where we go a little darker than what we usually do. I think it was a nice challenge to try to find some humor in places where we usually don't look. God that almost sounded intelligent, I need another beer...

J: Beau LeBeau and Lehibou. There were two very similar names which I thought was pretty funny.

B: The other character I named Woodsy. And Lehibou is the French word for "owl." So he's Woodsy Owl.

C: Did you keep the Strange Brew reference?

B: Where they are saying "eh?" all the time? Yeah. In fact, I think when the sheriff starts to get mad, he does that.

J: And you definitely pick up that you're in Canada. And from an editorial perspective, I realized that at no point do you count the bodies. You never get to a point where you realize that now there are only three of you left...

C: If there were only two beers, that would be important...

B: But two humans?

C: That's still one more than you need...

THE DRUNKEN COMIC BOOK MONKEYS
VS.
THE MUMMY

The ding of a tiny bell echoed through the post office as Brian and Chris entered.

"There's no beer here," Brian whined.

"It's the post office, dude," Chris replied.

As the only customers, the men strolled unimpeded to the counter.

"Are we done yet?" Brian asked.

"Dude. We just got here."

Since the room was devoid of all other life, the men waited patiently for an employee to assist them.

"I'm bored," Brian said. "Hurry up. We've got that wing party to get ready for."

Chris sighed, not even trying to hide his contempt. "Go back to the door and ding the bell again. See if that garners any attention."

Brian ambled over to the door and opened it.

Ding.

No response. Brian closed the door and opened it again.

Ding. Ding.

Brian let the door shut and then swatted at the bell.

Ding. Ding. Ding. Dingdingdingdingdingding.

After accidentally breaking it off its perch, he held the bell in his hairy-knuckled hand. Almost out of reflex, Brian's tongue flopped out of his mouth: his left arm shot into the air, his hand tossing out the heavy metal devil horns, his head banging to every ding.

Dingdingdingdingdingdingdingdingding.

He then attempted Deep Purple's *Smoke on the Water.*

Dinginginging ding ding dingingingingingingn ding! Ding-

ding ding ding dinging!

Hiding his face in shame, Chris didn't see the postal employee until he was slapped with a snide, "May I help you?"

Ignoring Brian's yells of, "Play some Skynyrd!" Chris turned to the annoyed employee and handed him a slip of paper. "I got this in the mail today. You have a package for me?"

The employee examined the paper. His body went rigid and his brows furrowed. He hissed a scathing, "Yes. We do."

Leaving the room as empty as it was seconds ago, the clerk disappeared into the back. Within minutes, he opened a set of double doors into the lobby area, assisting three men wearing thick black hernia belts pushing a hand-truck. Tilted back on two wheels, the hand truck was nearly overwhelmed by a wooden crate - an eight-foot tall wooden crate.

With such an impressive sight to behold, Brian stopped thrashing around and dropped the bell. "You need to stop eBaying, dude."

"I didn't think it was going to be this big!" Chris yelled.

"Didn't it have a description?"

"Nope."

"A picture?"

"Nope."

"Then why did you bid on it?"

"It said it was a golem."

"So, the only phrase..."

"Word."

"... the only *word* for the entire auction was 'golem' and you said, 'Gee. I need to bid on that' "?

"Yep."

Brian's only reply was to punch Chris in the shoulder. He turned to the crate and watched as the postal employees wheeled away the hand-truck to the back room. "Hey! Where're you going with that?"

"Sorry. For postal employee use only," the postal clerk answered before disappearing into the backroom once again.

"Oh, come on!"

"Settle down you sissy. Hand-trucks are for wussies," Chris

said as he circled the crate, eyeing it from top to bottom. "We can carry this."

"You're soooooo paying my co-pay if I end up in the emergency room because of this!"

"Shut up and lift."

Both men crouched at opposite ends of the crate. With audible grunts, they slid their fingers under the wood, collecting splinters along the way, and stood. Flabby and shapeless, their arms wriggled like gelatin. Neck tendons and forehead veins threatened to burst from strain-reddened skin. Sweat poured from Chris like waterfalls while Brian's fur became matted with his perspiration.

With jerky half-steps, the men maneuvered the crate out the door and into the parking lot. With ragged breaths, they inched their way toward the Fortressmobile – a 2006 gray Saturn. Building a solid rhythm between pained puffs of air and quick steps, the men moved closer to their destination, now mere yards away...

"Shiny."

The sunlight glinting off a nickel on the ground distracted Chris. He relinquished his half of the crate to claim the five-cent piece.

Brian's knees wobbled, but never buckled. He ran backwards to counter the top-heavy weight shift. Then ran forwards to counteract the overcompensation. Then backward again. Then forward. Unaware that his friend resembled a pendulum with large feet, Chris stared at the nickel in his palm. "Shhhhhhhineeeeeeeeeey."

"Dude!" Brian screamed, still fighting a losing battle with equilibrium.

Chris frowned, realizing that he did not, in fact, hold a nickel, rather a scrap of candy wrapper foil. "Dude, it's only a candy wrapper...don't drop the crate!"

"Well, help, you jackass!"

"On it!" Chris reached in his pocket and procured his car keys. With one push of a button, he popped the trunk. "Okay! You're good to go!"

"Too...heavy...can't...breathe..."

Brian's legs quaked. Spittle sprayed with each raspy breath.

The crate began to topple forward, and Brian felt powerless to stop it, until Chris blurted out, "If you get that in the trunk, I'll buy you a plate of hot wings!"

Brian snapped to attention as if being hit with a bucket of ice water. More gentle than if handling an egg while wearing an iron gauntlet, he placed the crate into the trunk. The car moaned and creaked; metal joints whined as bolts buckled, the immense weight of the crate lowered the back end of the car. The back bumper kissed the pavement.

"Good job, Sasquatch. Now get in the car," Chris said.

"It better be a huge plate of wings!" Brian demanded.

A billowing plume of sparks, rooster-tailing from the bumper grinding against the asphalt followed the men while Brian obsessed ad nauseam about the wings, making demands. His mouth didn't stop about the damn wings until they reached the top secret Fortress Lair. To shut him up, Chris promised Brian a second plate of wings if he'd relocate the crate to the inside of the top secret Fortress Lair. Brian readily agreed.

Once inside, the men attacked the crate with crowbars. But since immaturity ranked high on their priority list, they spent more time hitting each other, getting distracted by shiny objects, and making obscene phallus jokes with the crowbars, turning a ten minute project into a four hour opus of calamity.

With the pop of the final nail, one of the crate walls fell to the floor, followed by an avalanche of white foam packaging peanuts. Before peeking into the crate, the men grabbed handfuls of peanuts, snapping them in half and throwing them at each other. Feeling a bit peckish, Brian ate a few – until he noticed the contents of the crate. "Dude! They sent you the wrong thing!"

Frowning, Chris peeked inside. "What do you mean?"

"I mean you ordered a golem, and you got something else!"

"Are you stupid? It's a golem."

"No. It's not!"

"Then what is it, smart guy?"

"A ... *mummy*!"

Both men stared at the large figure in the crate. Mere inches separated its head from the crate's ceiling. Its broad shoulders made both men look like husky kindergarteners. Layers of timeworn, dirt-encrusted cloth, once white, enveloped the creature.

"Why on Earth would you think it's a mummy?" Chris asked.

Scrunching up his face as if smelling something offensive, Brian turned to his friend and said, "Seriously? Look at it! It's all wrapped up like a mummy!"

"So? It's not like mummies have a monopoly on being wrapped. Anyway, all that wrapping is probably just packing material."

Scrunching up his face again, this time because he did smell something offensive, Brian continued, "And it *smells* like a mummy!"

"Oh, and you know what mummies smell like. Professional mummy sniffer. You, right? You know *all* about mummy aromas."

"I'm just saying, this thing smells dead. Golems aren't dead. So, if it smells dead, then it's a mummy."

"Golems are statues created from earth. The Earth doesn't smell pretty, my friend, not pretty at all!"

"Touch it."

"No! You touch it, you mummy sniffing freak."

"You wanna' prove it's a golem? Then you'll be touching a solid figure. If you're finger pokes right through a decaying corpse, then you got yourself a mummy."

Chris hated when Brian got logical. Every time Brian got logical, it usually meant he was right, and Chris had to stick his hand in something unpleasant. Reaching into his pants pocket, Chris procured a beer. Stroking his goatee, he weighed the pros and cons. Con – he'd have to touch something that clearly festered with the dank essence of a miscreant past. Pro – it would shut Brian up. With one final swig to empty the bottle, Chris said, "Fine! I'll do it."

Cracking his knuckles, Chris approached the crate. He stared into what he assumed to be the creature's eyes – an opening between two wraps around the top portion of its head. Butterflies danced in his stomach, and there was no better way to kill those insipid insects than with beer. Reaching into his pocket, he pulled out another one and popped the top. Halfway through the bottle he felt the liquid courage infuse his soul.

He stepped closer. The dank aroma of the creature thickened the air around the crate, a fetid barrier that Chris breeched. To counteract the nauseating effects, Chris brought the bottle to his lips, the mellifluence of barley and hops offering succor to his senses.

He stepped closer. Despite the malodorous warnings, Chris continued with his mission. Reaching out his hand, he could feel the fetid malevolence emanating from the tatter-wrapped creature. Centuries, if not millennia, of arcane horrors swirled about the creature, palpable to Chris's fingertips. As he gulped another swig of beer, Chris's finger touched the creature's shoulder. Immediately, the decrepit thing's eyes snapped open.

"AAAAAAAAA!" Chris screamed.

"AAAAAAAAA!" Brian followed suit.

"MUUUUUUUH!" the creature replied, its arms shooting out, reaching for Chris.

Chris cradled his beer and jumped backward. "My beer! It's after my beer! Save it! Save it!"

The creature jostled in the crate, its shoulders bouncing against the sides. It slammed the walls faster and harder, its fists pounding all parts of the crate. With a thunderous crack, the box splintered asunder into tinder. Sticks and scrap rained about the room as the creature surveyed the environment. An empty room with strange furnishings was all it could perceive, until it recognized a door.

With an echoing moan swaddled in the million tortures of a million souls, the creature bounded through the threshold. Silence befell the room, save for the settling of stray pieces of thrashed wood. Seconds bled into minutes and minutes lasted as long as Brian's impatience. "Is it gone?"

Both men peeked over the back of the couch, where they chose to hide from the creature's destructive tantrum. Taking stock of the damage, they deemed it to be superficial – a shredded crate and broken door, still on its hinges.

The men stood and walked to the doorway. They poked their

heads outside, each looking in a different direction.

"You see anything?"

"Nope. You?"

"Nope."

They re-entered the top secret Fortress Lair and shrugged their shoulders. "Guess it's not our problem any more."

Shutting the door, they turned their attention to the mess that Chris's eBay purchase created. Brian used his foot to corral a few pieces of broken crate into a small pile. "I guess we should clean up before the guests arrive?"

"Nah," Chris answered. "Jeff is the only guest for the wing party, and he's our editor. We'd be insulting him if we cleaned up our own messes, so we'll just let him do it."

"Good point. When are the supplies arriving?"

"Soon. And I can't wait! Due to all of our hard work, traveling to ten different Melons Bar & Grilles for their tenth anniversary promotion, we get this party!"

"Exactly! A free half-keg and 300 wings delivered to our door and served to us by the Melons Girls!"

The men tittered while thinking about the upcoming event. Finally Chris went over to examine the broken door. The bottom hinge was shattered, but the top one was still intact. Chris opened it and pulled it shut lifting the door up to settle it into the frame. "M'eh. Still works. Plus, we now know that it was a golem."

"What?" Brian yelled. "How does a broken door prove that?"

"You saw how fast that sucker moved! No way a mummy could do that!"

"And why not?"

"Oh pa-leez! Mummies are nothing more than glorified, fancy zombies."

"That's ludicrous!"

"Ummm, hel-lo! A mummy is an undead, angry pharaoh brought back from the grave. Just like zombies!"

"Yeah, but the reason why the dead pharaoh is so angry is because he's cursed. Mysticism and the black arts were used to ensnare the pharaoh's soul into a dead and decaying vessel as a form of torment! A zombie is soulless reanimated flesh due to governmental biology experiments gone awry!"

"Your twisted forms of logic are astounding! First of all..."

"MUUUUUUUH!"

"AAAAAAAAA!"

Brian and Chris looked at each other, reasonably assured that neither of them moaned in anguish or released a blood-curdling scream of horror. Both noises came from outside.

Once again opening the door, the men peeked outside. They saw nothing out of the ordinary, except a half-keg resting on an unattended hand-truck. Standing at the threshold, the men scrutinized their surroundings, but saw nothing. They both stared at the half-keg like mice eyeing up a piece cheese on a set trap. With one final nod to each other, they went for it.

Sprinting as best his monolithic body could, Brian panted, "hand-truck!"

"Leave it, sissy!" Chris replied, panting as well.

The men grabbed the half-keg with a death grip and dashed back into the top secret Fortress Lair, slamming the door shut behind them.

After exerting that much energy, the men collapsed to the floor. Mustering what little strength they could, they sat up and leaned against the nearest wall. They stared at the half-keg, the light scintillating off the silver sides made it gleam like a trophy. The cathartic moment consumed Chris, until Brian ruined it with, "Mummy."

"What?" Chris asked, still huffing.

"Dude. Didn't you see the van parked nearby? It said 'Melons Bar & Grille' on the side. This is the half-keg for the wing party."

"Yeah, I figured that on my own, genius."

"Don't you get it? The mummy attacked the delivery guy. We're cursed. We have the mummy's curse!"

"Dude, you're so stupid. Don't *you* get it? The *golem* attacked the delivery guy because it's *protecting* us. That's what *golems* do. Protect their owners. The delivery guy was a perceived threat."

"Are you kidding me? Are you …?"

"MUUUUUUUH!"

"AAAAAAAAA!"

The men stopped arguing and looked at each other, again verifying that neither of them made the tortured screams. Confused again, they stood and opened the door; this time their eyes beheld two large tins of chicken wings on the ground outside. Not needing any more of an invitation, Brian sprinted to the aluminum pans of tastiness. Fearing the berating barbs of insults to his manliness if he didn't help, Chris sprinted to the wings as well. Each man hefted a tin and sprinted back to the top secret Fortress Lair, diving through the door with blatant disregard to thc safety of their own bodies, as long as their food made it inside unharmed.

"Golem," Chris rasped, laying face down on the floor and puffing harder than before.

"How … do you … figure …?" Brian squeezed his words from teeth clenched in pain as he writhed on the floor. Every attempt to stretch one muscle group resulted in torquing two others.

"It left the wings."

"So?"

"Golems don't need to eat. Mummies do."

"What? Mummies don't need to eat!"

"Sure they do, they're zombies after all."

"Oh, not this again! Will you get your head out of your…"

Once again noise from outside cut short Brian's thought.

"MUUUUUUUH!"

"AAAAAAAAA!"

"AAAAAAAAA!"

"AAAAAAAAA!"

The men recognized the three screams of horror to be from women, the exact same pitch and timbre used when the fairer sex saw either Brian or Chris. Concerned, the men opened the door to behold the aftermath of the screams. Lycra shorts scattered with abandon across the lawn as well as spandex tops reading "Melons". But there were no Melons Girls to be seen. A tear ran down Brian's cheek and

Chris's bottom lip quivered. Stifling a sob, Chris said, "It's a mummy. We're cursed. We have the mummy's curse. What do we do?"

Sadness turned to ire in Brian's mind, kick-starting the gears of logic. As rusty as those gears might be, they turned efficiently once going at full tilt. The light behind his eyes glowed, growing and showing signs of progress, until the glare of intellectual prowess gleamed from within. "I got it!"

Unable to muster the will to watch what his friend did, Chris could only stand by the door, his eyes transfixed outside like a dog waiting for its owner, as Brian ran back to what remained of the shipping crate. Standing over it, he looked at the floor of the crate. Sure enough, he found what he was searching for – a loose board. After moving it aside to reveal a small compartment, he reached inside and pulled out a clay urn. "I knew it!"

Brian ran back to the door to show Chris. "Look."

"What is it?" Chris asked.

"It's the urn in which they put the mummy's organs. Probably dust by now, but I'm pretty sure it's the source of the curse."

"Okay. What do we do with it?"

No sooner did Chris finish his question, a car door shut. Both men looked up to see Jeff walking toward the super secret Fortress Lair. "Hey, guys!"

Brian's brain kicked into gear again. Being their editor, Jeff had gotten them out of precarious situations before. Having a mummy's curse certainly counted as a precarious situation. Jeff would know what to do with the urn, Brian was sure of it. So, Brian threw it to him and yelled, "*Fix it!*"

Forgetting he resembled more of a mountain yeti than an "average joe", Brian's idea of a "casual toss" resembled more of a rocket. The urn turned missile pounded Jeff square in the chest, knocking him off his feet. The destabilized clay disintegrated upon impact, producing a billowing cloud. A nebula sprinkled powdered mummy organs over Jeff as he sat up, dazed and confused, but not surprised by the enigmatic, and painful, greeting. "What the hell? That smells like disinterred organ particulate."

"MUUUUUUUH!" the mummy answered as it came from around the corner of the top secret Fortress Lair, striding toward Jeff.

"Guys, what's that? Is that a mummy? Why's it coming toward me? Guys? *Guys*!" Jeff asked, scrabbling across the ground, puffs of organ dust falling with every movement. Once he got to his feet, he ran to his car. Full panic set in as the mummy moved closer. Jeff dove through the open passenger window, started his car and drove away, tires screeching, flinging loose gravel and bits of rubber. The mummy pursued, legs a blur as it pounded down the pavement.

"Jeff?" Brian called out, watching the mummy chase after the speeding car. "Jeff? Fix it?"

Brian and Chris watched the spectacle fade away into the horizon until it finally winked out. As if snapping out of a trance, the men realized they had a half-keg of beer and 300 wings to consume. With a shrug, Brian closed the door and said, "He'll fix it."

INSIDE THE MINDS OF MONKEYS

BRIAN: This is one of the original stories for the new edition. This story actually got cut from the first edition. We came up with the idea of us versus the Mummy and we even came up with the idea of us getting it on eBay, thinking it's a golem, arguing about whether it's a golem or a mummy and then arguing about whether or not mummies are zombies. But when it came down to crunch time and we started to get the stories together for the first edition, there was no room for it. So when we decided to do the Reflux edition, it was the perfect way to reintroduce it. 'Cause I think it fits perfectly into the book, the flow. One thing I like about this story is that at the end, we totally screw over Jeff. On purpose. Horribly! I thought it was a perfect little foreshadowing in this book for future books where Jeff is the antagonist. And it gives him motivation for his actions, to want to rid the world of the Drunken Comic Book Monkeys.

JEFF: Honestly officer, I do have a motive.

CHRIS: When I read this story, I saw as it as the Abbott and Costello version. I think in some ways, you got close.

B: I never saw it.

J: It definitely has that feel to it.

C: But you got it.

B: Ooookay. Apparently there's a feel from the editor. Hand check!!

C: But I don't think there is a literary basis for mummy. There is a movie and certainly historical versions but I don't think there is a literal version.

J: No classical version. We won't mention the Ann Rice version. I mean, she tried to write something with the idea, but there's no classic version that you could refer to.

B: No Stoker... Just Hollywood's take on it. The Brendon Fraser movie was pretty good.

[pause]

B: You might want to note that Chris twitched his lip.

J: I'm surprised that I'm the only one that was concerned at all about the naked Melons girls. You found the clothes… (At least you didn't try them on this time!)... you found them but nothing ever came of it. You know why? Because the wings were there… and the beer.

B: But it also shows that Chris and I are like the Pollyannas of the horror world. We look at what we have and not at what we don't have.

J: So you're saying that the beer is always half full. Well, that's what the editor's here for… to point out little things like naked Melons girls.

B: And you're just mad because we gave you the curse.

J: Yeah, nothing itches quite like mummy particulate.

C: There's a cream for that… Imhotep-itch away.

J: All I can think of is "apply directly to your head."

B: I got pharaoh pox. The curse that keeps on giving...

THE DRUNKEN COMIC BOOK MONKEYS VS. ZOMBIES

Moments of true rapture are both limited in number and fleeting in length during one's life; moments in which a person finds themselves teetering on the precipice of self-actualization. A flawless moment ensconced by precision timing can burrow itself in one's mind to create ecstasy eternal. Brian now stood upon that precipice; he now readied his mind to have this moment burrow into it. Because he now gazed upon what could become his new happiest place on the planet – Melons Bar & Grille corporate headquarters.

In awe of the structure, Brian stepped forward. In hands trembling with reverence, he clutched his passport to enter the fabled gates – the Golden Chicken Wing. He held the wing in an outstretched arm before him as if it were a miniature valkyrie escorting him to the portals of Valhalla. Quivering, his pursed lips could only muster the faintest of sentiment, "It's beauuuuuuuutiful."

"It looks like every other rectangular, four story building to me," Chris said, ruining Brian's catharsis.

"It's not the building itself, but what it represents."

"It represents a four story, rectangular building."

"It represents all that is good and pure in this world – wings, women and beer! You know nothing about symbolism!"

"Know nothing...? Are you serious? Need I remind you that I have a degree in Literature?"

"You don't need to, but you're probably gonna."

"I have a degree in Literature, you know! I've written entire papers on symbolism!"

Before Brian could think of another proclamation that would both annoy and anger Chris, the gates opened. Out walked Gustov

VanMelon.

Up until this point, Brian and Chris were both blissfully unaware of the other golden chicken wing winners, the accompanying friends and family of the winners, and the throng of media crews as well as a few score of general onlookers. But once the gates opened a tidal wave of flesh crashed down upon the men with vicious force. A cacophony of voices burst from the crowd, questions, shouts, praises, hoots and howls. Hands reached forth, feet and legs pushed, all trying to gain any form of vantage and get closer to the diminutive VanMelon, a man known for his reclusive lifestyle. But as the crowd clamored closer, he demonstrated an instinctual survival tactic – he took one step back.

Rushing around him, encircling him like a protective phalanx, came the Dumpa Stumpas – men so large they made the word "burly" seem insignificant. All of the Dumpa Stumpas, each exactly the same shape and size as any other, marched in unison, once in place they all crossed their tree-trunk sized arms over their mountainous chests.

The crowd continued to push, pressing bodies against the wall of behemoths, until critical mass was achieved. Unwilling to take any more abuse, the Dumpa Stumpas, in unison, unfolded their arms and puffed out their chests. The shock wave this act created knocked everyone in the crowd off their feet.

Stunned by the impressive display of power, the crowd sat silent as VanMelon, the tiny man now seeming impressive from this angle, said in a soft voice, "Golden wing winners, please stand up."

Chris, Brian and three other men did as instructed.

"Present wings, please."

Four gilded wings appeared in four outstretched palms. The fifth wing was mangled, deformed by teeth marks and dripping with drool.

Gustov inspected the wings, making a hum of approval with each one, until he got to Brian's. "Are … those bite marks?"

"Ummmm … maybe?" Brian replied.

"And why did you bite the golden wing?"

"I didn't know how long we were going to be stuck in the pile. I got a little scared that we'd run out of food..."

Gustov sighed and shook his head. "No matter. It is ... was ... a golden wing. You may enter."

The Dumpa Stumpas shifted, now standing shoulder to shoulder, creating a wall between the unwashed masses and the five chosen ones following Gustov into the building.

While walking, Brian couldn't help but observe the other winners. Next to him was a burly man with a shock of unkempt hair, adorned in flannel and a t-shirt – a Shania Twain t-shirt. He introduced himself, "I'm Buford."

Brian and Chris exchanged a confused glance. Chris then turned to Buford and asked, "Have we met? You look familiar?"

Buford chuckled. "Only if you've attended one of my hug seminars."

"Ummmm ... hug ... seminars?"

"Yes! I'm a hug therapist. Doesn't winning a tour to Melons headquarters make you wanna just hug someone?"

Never passing up an opportunity to make a bad situation worse, Brian elbowed Chris in the back, toppling his friend into the large man. Thinking it an invitation, Buford wrapped his arms around Chris and squeezed. A stream of profanities would have flowed from Chris's mouth had the air not been constricted from his lungs.

"That's the spirit," Buford said, squeezing harder, his mood elevating, shooting right past camaraderie to soul-mates. A joy which he expressed by releasing Chris only to grab him by the back and thigh so he could lift the bald man over his head. Brian expressed his joy by taking pictures of a Shania Twain loving behemoth military pressing his friend.

Once relinquished, Chris hurried himself out of Buford's reach. Now standing behind Brian, Chris whispered, "I hate you."

Ignoring his friend, Brian looked at another member of the group – a bald man with a thick mustache running the entire length of his chin, whose immense bulk made Buford look like a mathlete. He possessed a permanent scowl, accentuated by a thick scar from the corner of his mouth to his temple. Despite the fact that the man's arms were bigger than Brian's chest, Brian couldn't help but critique the time faded tattoos. One read: "I kick puppies" while another proclaimed: "My favorite ingredient is kittens."

Keeping his eyes on the man's arms, Brian turned a bit to whisper to Chris, "I think his one tattoo is grammatically incorrect."

"Dude," Chris whispered back, sweat percolating upon his brow, knowing that if a guy who liked him tossed him around like a rag doll, he didn't want to imagine what this guy would do to him after Brian made him mad. "Keep your mouth shut."

"I mean, as it stands it looks correct, but if your rearrange it, it would read: 'kittens is my favorite ingredient' and that just ain't right."

"Now is not the time to be grammar snob."

"Why not? You love being a snob any chance you get. I think this is just a case of the subject not syncing up with the object."

"Please stop talking."

The scowling man scowled even harder as he took a step toward Brian. "You got a problem with my ink, boy?"

"No. Well, actually, I couldn't help but notice..." Brian said as his eyes moved from the man's massive arms to his black t-shirt and black leather vest, both displaying the name of a popular motorcycle company. Along the way, something caught his eye. Dangling from the man's belt, made of faux bullets, was a small pair of pink ballet slippers. "... your pink ballet slippers ... ?"

"For the love of all that is Holy, if you have any form of shoulder angel telling you to stop talking, please heed their words," Chris whispered to Brian as the man took another step forward.

"Sludge. My name's Sludge. And these are the first pair of ballet slippers I got when I was two. Been dancing ever since. I keep these for sentimental reasons."

Chris saw Brian's face contort, twisting from too many jokes log-jamming in his brain. Knowing that even if one of those jokes were to find its way out of Brian's mouth, Chris would be the one to get pummeled by Sludge, he whispered to his friend, "I'll kill you in your sleep if you say another word to this man."

"Good to know," Brian said, and then turned to the last person in the party.

"Greetings," the man said. He was dressed in a black suit and top hat with a thick wool coat that looked more like a cape. His fingers followed along the one side of his exaggerated handlebar mustache, twisting the end into an upward curl. "My name is Felonious Pernicious."

"What's up," Brian and Chris said in unison. They turned away as Brian whispered, "Dude. He's the villain."

"Villain? What are you talking about?" Chris whispered back.

"He looks like Snidely Whiplash!"

"So? You look like Big Foot."

"Yeah! And you call me Sasquatch a hundred times a day!"

"Settle down, Yeti. I'm sure the guy is just misunderstood."

"Misunderstood? Ok, Polly Purepudge, if he ties you to the train tracks, I ain't rescuing you!"

"I wouldn't want you to!"

The men continued to bicker all through the tour. They moved with the group, but missed all the sights to see and didn't hear a single piece of information that Gustov VanMelon offered. The first place they visited was a wonderful room mimicking an outside field except with foliage made from pretzels and potato chips while fried pickles sprouted from trees. A river of beer flowed from a waterfall and into a mysterious tunnel. Felonious asked about the secret wing sauce recipe and was promptly ignored. They continued in a boat that floated along the beer river into the tunnel, ending at a platform that led to a room with a new beer that made the drinker float in the air upon consuming it, only to return to the earth by releasing raucous belches. Brian and Chris missed all that due to their arguing. Felonious refused to participate, stating his desire to see the fabled Melons wing lab. The tour included a room in which Gustov showed off the newest delicacy – the everything flavored French fry. With every bite, the flavor shifted from regular to garlic to cheese to chili. But Brian and Chris missed that as well. And within every room, Brian and Chris missed a rousing song and dance performed by the Dumpa Stumpas.

The argument finally ceased as the tour made its way to the wing research and development lab. Brian swooned as they entered the room. "Hey! Look, the tour is starting!"

Sludge frowned. "Starting? Are you serious? How did you possibly miss...?"

Buford placed his hand on Sludge's shoulder and shook his head to silence the ballet biker. "Don't. That will only get them started again. Even a hug can't cure whatever is wrong with them."

"This is the Melons Research and Development lab, where we strive to create the ultimate in chicken wing technology and flavoring," Gustov said, extending his arms in theatric grandeur, showing off the pride and joy of his company. The tour group stood on a suspended walkway and looked down into the expansive room. The area was part laboratory, part kitchen and part wonderland. Dumpa Stumpas, all wearing long white lab coats, moved from randomly placed computer workstations to lab tables containing bubbling beakers and frothing test tubes. Ovens and stoves and cauldrons speckled the floor. Suspended from the ceiling were movable chicken wing dispensers gliding from workstation to workstation. Also suspended from the ceiling and readily available to the lab technicians were bulbous containers of multihued powders and liquids colored every shade in the rainbow.

"This concludes our tour," Gustov said.

"What?" Brian asked. "Don't we get to go down there?"

"No. Now if you all will ... where is Mr. Pernicious?"

The other four men looked around, but couldn't find him. Brian stopped looking for the missing man, instead focusing on what he was missing: all the tastes, all the wings. He even saw a room that had a door labeled "wing supply." Clear tubes sprouted from the top of the room, leading to the individual ceiling suspended wing dispensers. At sporadic intervals, six to twelve wings would flow through the tubes. While staring longingly at the door, Brian saw it nudge open and a goat with a very satisfied look on his face, licking his chops, scampered from the room. But before he could bring it to anyone's attention, Felonious walked around the corner on the walkway, joining the rest of the group.

"Where were you?" Brian asked.

"Ummmm," Felonious replied.

"You were off sabotaging something, weren't you?"

"Dude," Chris said, punching Brian's arm. "Settle down. He was probably in the bathroom."

"Exactly!" Felonious said, displaying a fake smile. "Just as the pale one stated, I have returned from the facilities. Did I miss anything?"

"We'll find out when your sabotage comes to fruition!" Brian said.

"What is your problem? He's a fellow Melons patron! We have no reason not to believe him."

"Actually," Sludge intervened. "We do. He's been asking about the secret formula the entire tour."

"True," Buford said.

Felonious chuckled. "I was simply trying to get the most out of my tour experience."

Before anyone could retort, Dumpa Stumpa screams from the lab floor below interrupted them. As the six men moved to peek over the side of the railing, the lights went out. The machines powered down and stopped, eerie silence accompanying the sudden darkness. More screams from the floor below shredded the short-lived stillness, echoing throughout the large room.

Emergency lights on the ceiling snapped on, producing spots of dull orange glow, strong enough to partially illuminate, but too weak to reach anyone's feet.

"You did this!" Brian said, grabbing Felonious by his shirt.

Looking around in wonder at the rust hued darkness, Felonious replied, "Actually, I had nothing to do with *this*."

"What did you do?"

"Dude, think about it," Chris reasoned. "How could he possibly do any of this while he was in the bathroom?"

Before Brian could offer any form of rejoinder, the suspended walkway shook, the metal rattling and squeaking against itself. Something big had joined them. All six men squinted, trying to use every iota of dim light to peer into the darkness, to see what came toward them. The walkway quaked again, this time followed by the sounds of an object being dragged. Another thump rattled the walkway, again followed by a dragging noise. The next thump and drag indicated that the apparition was near. Too near.

From the darkness behind Buford, two gnarled hands appeared above his shoulders. Before he could react, the monstrous mitts clamped down on his upper arms. Sliding from the shadows above Buford's head came the face of a Dumpa Stumpa, pale and lifeless, its eyes devoid of pupils. Its dead and cracked lips parted just enough to moan one word, "Wwwwwiiiiiinnnnnngggggggssssss." With that it pulled, yanking both of Buford's arms from his body. Screaming, Buford fell to his knees. His cry of distress was cut abruptly short by the traumatic blood loss. He would never hug again.

Brian and Chris screamed like twelve-year-old girls. Felonious sneered. Gustov stood frozen, unable to process the horror he witnessed. Sludge grabbed Gustov by the shirt and slapped his face, snapping him from his trance. He then growled, "Get us out of here VanMelon!"

Invigorated, the little man ran down the walkway, away from the tragedy and out of the room. The tour group followed. With a few precise turns down poorly lit hallways, the men found a door labeled "exit." However, when Gustov pushed the latch, the door did not budge. Shoving the small man out of the way, the bulky Sludge tried. Nothing. He lowered his shoulder and smashed into the door. Still nothing. He lifted Brian and Chris, one with each hand, and used them as ersatz battering rams. Despite the profanity-laden curses, the result was the same – the door remained locked.

"Over here," Gustov said, beckoning for everyone to follow him. He went back down the hall, but turned off at a junction and ran through a door labeled "pike room."

The room was small, but the dim orange light allowed the shadows to loom ominous. Even though the light was minimal, everyone could see the pikes lining the wall and a dead Dumpa Stumpa wearing a security guard uniform lying on the floor.

Gustov started searching the body. "Keys. He should have keys."

Frowning, Brian pointed to Felonious. "You did this!"

"Dude!" Chris said. "Why do you keep saying that? Why do you think...?"

Snarling, Felonious grabbed a nearby pike, needing two hands to wield the pointed solid steel staff. "He's right! I did this!"

"Dammit!" Chris yelled.

"And I have the keys!" Felonious continued.

"Why?" Gustov asked.

"Why? Of course you don't know who I am, you arrogant little fool. I am the owner of Balloons Bar & Grille! Your arch nemesis!"

"No!"

"Yes! For too long you have cornered the market on Bar & Grille wing goodness! And it's all due to your secret recipes! Give them to me or we will never leave this building alive!"

"Dude! You locked us in a building with zombies for some recipes?" Chris asked.

"Zombies?" Brian barked. "What zombies?"

"Are you serious? You didn't see Buford get his arms ripped off?"

"Well, yeah. But that was just a rogue Dumpa Stumpa."

"Hel-lo! Didn't the dead and peeling skin give you a clue? The pale and cracked lips? The pupilless eyes?"

"Okay, maybe he was a zombie, but there was only one."

"Oh pa-leez! Where there's one zombie, there's a whole undead legion of the damned."

"Damn it! I hate zombies!"

No sooner then those words leave Brian's mouth a familiar scene led to a familiar fate. From the darkness behind Felonious came a pair of hands and the haunting word, "Wwwwiiiiiinnnnnggggsssss." As with Buford, the hands latched onto Felonious's arms and tore them from his body. However, this time the Dumpa Stumpa munched on his newly claimed prize. And as Chris predicted, more undead Dumpa Stumpas joined in the feast.

After finishing another preteen girl-like scream, Brian and Chris joined Sludge in running for the other exit in the room. Gustov grabbed a pike and ran toward the zombie pile. "Go on without me!"

"But this is the way away from the zombies!" Brian yelled.

"I'll fend them off and slow them down!" Gustov replied, waving the pike with dramatic flair.

"Ummmm, they really don't seem to even notice us at the moment. And they're the slow moving kind, so if we get a head start..."

"No! I'll hold them off while you make it to the communications room! It's on the main floor by the research lab!"

"... and I think this door locks and ..."

"Go! Go! Go! AAAAAARRRRRRGG!" Gustov roared as he dove pike first into the zombie pile.

"Move!" Sludge yelled, pushing Brian and Chris out the back door.

Once through, Brian shut the door and locked it. The three men moved cautiously along the corridors, aiming for the nearest stairwell to make their way to the first floor laboratory. Along the way, they assessed their predicament.

"Alright," Sludge said. "We should lead with our pikes..."

"Pikes?" Brian asked.

"What pikes?" Chris asked.

Trying not to look back at either of the other men while skulking down the darkened hallway, Sludge said, "The pikes we took before we left the room."

"Pikes?" Brian asked.

"What pikes?" Chris asked.

"The room we were just in! The room labeled 'pike room.' The room with over a dozen handy pikes to use as..." Sludge cut himself short as he turned to look at his comrades. There stood Brian holding a beer in one hand and a tennis racquet in the other. Standing next to him, Chris held a beer as well as a large shoe. "What the hell is wrong with you two?"

"What?" the men said in unison.

"You ran out of a room *filled* with large metal weapons and you're holding a tennis racquet and a shoe! Where did you even *find* a tennis racquet?"

"It was on the floor!" Brian yelled.

"It's a *large* shoe!" Chris explained. "It's *at least* a size 18!"

Before Sludge could berate the two men any more, the chilling sound of "Wwwwwiiiiiinnnnnngggggsssss," filled the air.

"Look," Brian said, "signs to the communications room!"

The men followed the signs, running from one hallway to the next, Sludge leading the charge with the sharpened pike point. The moans of the undead and the scraping of useless limbs being dragged chased the trio, motivating them to move faster. Every corner turned brought them closer to escape. Finally, salvation!

At the end of a dead-end hall was their destination – an open door with a placard that read "communications room." However, once the men made it to the room, they noticed there was no door. Realizing they could not barricade themselves in the room, Sludge looked at the control panel, feeding into the banks of monitors on the wall, and shook his head. "Well, boys, I ain't good with computers. I'll hold off the zombies while you contact the outside world for help. Now, hurry!"

Brian and Chris sat at the control panel and started batting on the keyboards like epileptic monkeys. Sludge stepped outside of the room and awaited the creeping horde of undead Dumpa Stumpas. He heard them first; their unholy moans the harbinger of their soulless bodies. Then he saw them, bearing down upon him en masse. Readying himself for the onslaught, he assumed second position, but not before rubbing his lucky pink ballet slippers. "Feet don't fail me now."

Once the mass of decaying flesh came within striking distance, Sludge executed a foutté rond jambe en tournant, the tip of his pike slashing through one neck after another as he spun. The pike wielding danseur performed a grand battement à la seconde en arrière to kick away from the advancing horde. He took a moment to catch his breath then engaged his opponents again, doing a flawless grand jeté. Upon landing, he finished with a bras croisé, his pike supported by his forward hand and under his armpit, piercing three zombies at once. He used a batterie of dessous and dessus to move away from the group.

The outstretched arms of the zombies began to surround him, but he performed an échappé sur le pointes followed by a double tours en l'air to escape their clutches and spin two full rotations. He landed with a perfect arabesque penchée, unwavering aplomb.

Brian kept one eye on Sludge's battle and one eye on his task. He saw an option on one of the monitors labeled "contact U.S. Army" and told Chris to click on it. Sure enough, the monitor flicked over to a cigar-chewing, crooked nosed Major who knew no other facial expression other than one that involved furrowed eyebrows. The two men assumed the Major must have been born with some form of speech condition, because the only way he talked was by hollering as loud as possible. "Who is this? What do you want?"

"We're at the Melons Headquarters! We're under attack! There's a zombie outbreak going on! We need your help! You're our only hope Major Won Kanobi!"

The Major scowled. He opened his mouth to unleash a tirade so brutal it would leave Chris with bruises, but shifted his eyes to look at Brian. "What's going on behind Captain Caveman there? Move out of the way, Monkey Boy!"

Brian moved. And the Major's jaw fell slack as he witnessed Sludge continue to fend off zombies. "Well, I'll be... Zombies!"

"Told ya!" Chris said.

"Don't worry boys. I'll get rid of them!" the Major said to Chris right before the screen went black.

"Dude!" Brian said. "He's going to nuke us!"

"He's not going to nuke us! Why would you even think that?"

"He didn't say help was on the way or what his plan was. He didn't even tell us to seek safety and wait."

"He's assuming we're smart enough to do that."

"*No one* assumes we're that smart!"

Chris paused, trying to let those words sink through to his brain. However, nothing can sink through a foot of concrete. "Whatever! In any case, let's get Sludge and run."

The men turned to let Sludge know the plan. But they were too late. After doing a quick pirouette, Sludge took three quick steps to the left, right into the awaiting clutches of a zombie. The atrophied muscles and dried bones offered no true resistance to Sludge as he tore through the monster. But it did throw off his rhythm, causing him to hesitate just enough to allow the tidal wave of death to crash down upon him.

Brian winced. "He should have executed a pas de bourrée vers la droite instead of vers la gouche."

"What?!" Chris yelled. "How do you even know that? And you can't speak French! I speak French! You hate French!"

"Dude! He was kicking ass while his balletometer was revving high! You gotta give him mad props!"

"Whatever! We need to find shelter."

The men ran from the room, faster than the zombies could untangle themselves from the mound atop Sludge. After a few more hallways, they stumbled into the Research lab – right into the heart of the zombie horde. They paused, looking around the expansive room, zombies creeping from every nook and corner. Brian saw an open door into a small, zombie-free room. "There!"

As they ran for the room labeled "wing supply" two zombies blocked their path. Brian lopped off the head of one using the tennis racquet and yelled, "Ace!" Chris used the shoe of great proportion to punch the other zombie in the face, knocking it off its feet, and yelled, "Fu Manchu fury of the shoe fist!"

The men made it into the room and shut the door, locking themselves in the room with walls of six-inch thick steel. One window in the door allowed them to see the zombie horde clamoring around outside.

Panting from the physical exertion, Chris said, "The best thing you could come up with was 'Ace'?"

Wheezing as well, Brian replied, "It's better than whatever the hell you used."

"Whatever!"

"Mine was succinct and to the point, like a battle cry! Yours was cumbersome!"

"Mine had panache! And a sense of class."

"A sense of ...? Are you *kidding* me? Everyone knows that you know nothing of martial arts! And I'm pretty damn sure Fu Manchu didn't wear size 18 shoes!"

"Is this what I'm gonna have to put up with until the army gets here? Stuck in the wing supply room with *this*?"

"Only if you ... wait ... did you say 'wing supply' room?"

"That's what it said on the door, Mr. Mensa!"

Brian looked around the room. Vats of chicken wings lined three of the four walls. In a daze, he walked away from the door, to the vats. "The goat came outta here."

"What are you talking about?" Chris asked, still looking out the window.

"Right before the lights went out, I saw a goat scamper from this room and then all the zombies began congregating in the research lab. This must be where it started. The goat must have infected the chicken wings."

"Dude, are you serious?" Chris asked as he turned from the window. He immediately saw that his friend was indeed serious. There stood Brian, blue as a freshly cleaned toilet bowl, his dead skin peeling and flaking with every movement, his pupilless eyes holding zero life. Brian was a zombie. "What the hell is wrong with you?"

"What?" Brian asked. "I couldn't help it! I was hungry!"

Chris picked up a stray wing from the floor. It was green and its skin bubbled. "And you were still able to eat this? Are you serious? How could you ... OW! You bit me!"

"I was trying to get the wing you were waving around!"

Chris watched with disgust as his skin went dead, turning the same shade of steel blue as Brian's. "Dammit! Now *I'm* a zombie too!"

"What? I thought you like zombies?"

"That doesn't mean I want to *be one*, genius!"

"At least your skin has color now."

Chris replied by punching Brian's shoulder. Brian's arm fell from his body, a sack of dead gristle dropping from a dried husk.

"Jackass!" Brian yelled. He retaliated by swatting Chris's right knee with the racquet. The lower half of his leg flipped through the air.

"Ace!"

Chris attacked with the shoe of great proportion, knocking Brian's hand from his wrist. Brian kicked the shoe of great proportion from Chris's arm and Chris's arm from his body. Their feud quickly degenerated into a sissy slap spat, dead and decaying body parts littering the room.

"Now what are we going to do?" Brian's head asked, lodged between two vats.

Chris's head, lying in a pile of chicken wings, spat out a few gray toes and said, "I have no idea."

Neither man needed to exert any more energy into the question, though, since their answer came in the cleansing form of nuclear fire....

INSIDE THE MINDS OF MONKEYS

BRIAN: This is kind of what started the madness. I'm sure EVERYONE knows by now I hate zombie stories and Chris loves them. During one of our typical arguments after four or so pitchers, Chris blurted, "That's it! I'm sooooo writing a zombie story with us in it!" He then probably fell off his barstool. That started the whole idea of doing a series of books in which we are the protagonists. However, after he said that, I always envisioned us being turned into zombies, because nothing would piss me off more than not only having to *deal* with zombies, but *become* one as well. In the original "Scary Tales of Scariness" Chris wrote the Zombies story, but went whole different direction. Not only did he use ALL dialog, but the zombies were not the undead kind that I hate. When we talked about doing the "Reflux Edition" I wanted to rewrite Zombies. One thing I HATE about zombie stories is the lack of common sense the characters have. If there's a zombie apocalypse, then the characters should see EVERYTHING as a weapon. Not only do most characters not carry any weapons, but when they do get one, they use it to kill a zombie, drop it, and run. Hence my decision to include the "pike room" and why Chris and I exit it without sensible weapons. Another thing I hate is the contrived situations in which a noble sacrifice is made so the rest of the group can escape. Half the times, the character making the sacrifice doesn't have to, especially since usually the character isn't a noble one to begin with, they're just making a grand gesture of killing themselves to make up for decades of being a jerk. And, of course, the start of the zombie contagion is the goat. It had to be the goat licking the chicken wings. He licked them all.

CHRIS: When it came time to do rewrites and more importantly, to pick stories to be omitted from Reflux, we had to consider stories that ultimately contained set up material for later stories. "Zombies" was one of the last stories we chose to rewrite because it was actually the lead story of a trifecta revolving around the potato people. In case you haven't read the original version of "Scary Tales of Scariness" (and, really, there's no real good reason not to!) in the original zombie story, Brian and I discover that the Potato People are using potatoes to turn people into zombies. Ultimately, changing it doesn't leave the rest of the book unharmed, but there were no better options. Brian already had some ideas and, much to my utter dismay, seemed far less miserable writing it than I would have liked. But I like that he chose to bring it closer to the ideology of the genre than I had done. So he gets kudos if he's nice... sit, Ubu, sit. Good dog!

JEFF: Really this one is a candy coated Technicolor nightmare. Shades of a chocolate factory that I won't name and a cast of totally crazy characters and this time I'm not even referring to you two. There's a nice tie in to the Crocogator episode with one of the most ridiculous lines about the arms that were made for hugging would never hug again. You know what; I'm in this one too as the zombie source- how you like me now! Let me just take a moment to mention the pike room – total nonsequitur idea that provides weapons against the dumpa stumpa zombie horde. If you're reading this, government types, all of your high security facilities should have one. After all it takes no time to reload a pike – but you might want to think twice about taking it to a gunfight. Finally, the zombie duel at the finish – what a fitting end for our heroes.

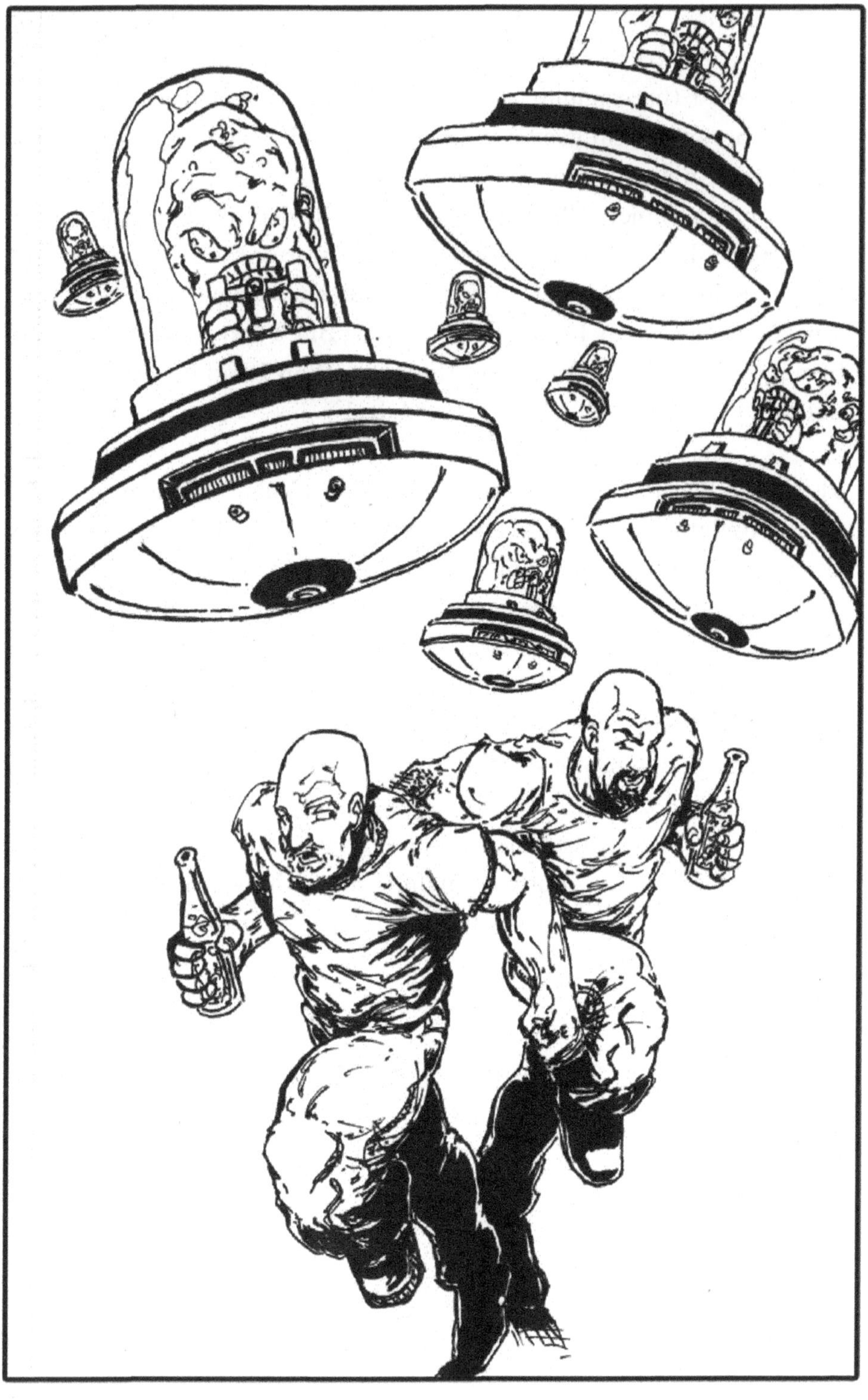

THE DRUNKEN COMIC BOOK MONKEYS
VS.
THE POTATO PEOPLE

"Solanine, we are approaching Earth."

"Excellent. Are your gladiators ready, Frius Gaius?"

"Yes, Solanine. This is so exciting!"

"Make still your eyestalks!"

"But our initial test was such a success. The humans of Earth have no resistance to us!"

"That is not entirely true, Frius. There is one who is tremendously steadfast in his disdain for us."

"But, Solanine, the other humans find his theories ludicrous. Is it not rather ironic that the ones who are right are considered to be 'out there' by their brethren? This must be the price of vision on Earth."

"How so?"

"The disciples of Xenon truly do see the light of existence. Only the followers realize that they are drawing on over 40,000 years worth of experience for their wisdom. But despite the promulgation of their beliefs, Xenon's disciples are considered a mere sect. Their beliefs are spurned as 'Science Fiction.' Similarly, this one man, the only potential leader for any rebellion against us, is laughed at even by his closest friends."

"Has Prince Tuber been briefed on the occupancy details?"

"He has met with Lord Jordparon on several occasions. The plans are in place. The clone is a perfect match; his own germinator wouldn't be able to tell which one is her true seedling."

"Good. When we land the entire Nightshade family will be reunited as was foretold."

***

"Brian, where's Pisano?"

"You wouldn't believe me if I told you, Tom."

"That goof's out buying more beer isn't he? Knowing him, he has a basement full already!"

"Nope."

"Adult video store?"

"No."

"It has something to do with food, doesn't it?"

"Not at all."

"Ok, I give."

"Tom, he's on a talk show"

"WHAT?"

"Truth is stranger than fiction. I told you it wasn't believable."

"Who in this world would have Pisano on a talk show?"

"WOOOOOOO!"

"Ha, ha! Now's your chance to ask him for yourself, Tom."

"Pisano! What..."

"Dude! Terry Stapler rocks!"

"Terry Stapler!??! You were on the Stapler show?"

"You bet your bippie!"

"Dude! What did I tell you about that? Don't talk about my 'bippie'!"

"You're talking garbage aren't you?"

"Yep!"

"That's gross, dude! My mouth was open..."

"Guh! That's wrong on so many levels. Why are you like that?"

"I just got back from the Stapler show and you guys are both trash talking. That's why!"

"Pisano, I've watched that show like three times in four years and all three times that old wrestler 'The Platinum Pasha' was a guest. Only he was supposed to be a different person each time! Like anyone from our generation could mistake him! Wrestling was huge in our day."

"Yeah, it's sad to see how the mighty have fallen, Tom."

"You guys don't get it, though. This show was different. Real hardcore news stuff this time."

"With you as its guest? What could you possibly know that's newsworthy?"

"Dude! Did you forget I knew all about the potato plot long before it came to fruition."

"Oh, here we go with the potato stuff again!"

"Dude! Did you totally not just fight a bunch of zombies? Right in this very backyard!"

"Whatever! The scientists totally said that was due to a water borne contaminant."

"You're just being stupid! You saw it. You were there. Potatoes were in the water supply!"

"YOU'RE GRASPING!"

"Guh! Yelling again..."

"SHUT UP! OR INSTEAD OF YELLING IT'LL BE HITTING AGAIN! REMEMBER THAT, SMART GUY?"

"You're ridiculous."

"So what was the show like? Did they have you on a panel of some kind? You know 'men-who-love-women-who-love-women-who-love-men'."

"Guys, it was really strange actually. Nothing at all like I had envisioned. They interviewed me in a room by myself. Only took about fifteen minutes worth of footage. Then I'm supposed to go back tomorrow for the live broadcasting part."

"Um, if it's a live broadcast show, why did they tape a portion of it?"

"Dunno. They said they were doing the lead in to the show pre-recorded. They mentioned using some news footage of the zombies, so they must be planning to tie that together somehow."

"YOU'RE AN IDIOT! WHY WOULD YOU LET THEM DO THIS? AND I'LL BET YOU DIDN'T EVEN MENTION FORTRESS PUBLISHING INC. ONCE, DID YOU, PUNK?"

"No, but I scored you both free tickets..."

"DUDE! THAT'S AWESOME!"

"Like ten seconds ago you were bashing Stapler!"

"THAT WAS BEFORE I KNEW I WAS GOING! I GOTTA GO WASH MY FORTRESS PUBLISHING INC. T-SHIRT! TOM, YOU HAVE TO HOLD ONE OF OUR FORTRESS PUBLISHING INC. BEARS ON YOUR LAP, MAYBE A MAGAZINE TOO!"

"He's mental. He should seek help!"

"I agree. See a priest, dude."

"A PRIEST?"

"Totally. Mental illness can only be cured by a religious figure."

"WHAT ARE YOU TALKING ABOUT? YOU'RE NOT EVEN CHRISTIAN!"

"You're the dumbest smart guy I know! I'm not Catholic. That doesn't necessarily make me not Christian."

"Ah, but it does mean you're not Italian. Admit it! You're Irish!"

"Not this again!"

"All Italians are Catholic! And none of this garbage about the Vikings being in Pisa! You're about as Italian as Chef Boyardee!"

"Ha, ha! Yeah, I'm with Brian on this on, dude. You're Irish. You're name isn't Pisano, it's O'Pisan. But, seriously, when did you go on a religious kick?"

"Dude, I'm not sure. I don't feel so good. It was like a voice being beamed into my head. Weird. I need to sit down. Must have been too long between beers. Dude, beer pants rock!"

"Yeah, about the beer pants, guys…"

"DON'T BE JEALOUS! ALL YOU HAVE TO DO IS THROW DOWN THE CASH AND BECOME A STOCK HOLDER OF FORTRESS PUBLISHING INC.."

"Wow! Dude, you *are* mental."

"T-SHIRT, WASH, NOW…"

"And he says I'm the knuckle dragging Neanderthal."

"Yeah, well you both are. Alright, dude, I'm outta here, too. And don't count on me taking any bears or magazines to the show. I'm only going to see if 'The Platinum Pasha' is there. Ha, ha. 'The dromedary drop!' That's when TV was entertaining. What time do we have to be at the studio tomorrow?"

"Best to get there a bit early I'd say. Let's say we leave here at one. Sound good?"

"Works for me. See you, then."

"Peace out!"

***

"How does this thing work, Solanine?"

"It is quite simple, actually, my sprouted friend. Using this device we can interrupt a thought pattern anywhere in the universe. And infiltrate the mind of the thinker, planting our own suggestions in the fertile firmament of the subconscious."

"Must the subject be intelligent?"

"It helps, oh bulbous one, but it is not integral. We simply have to modify our suggestions to the individual subject. Using this program we can study the brainwaves of the individual and get a relative idea about the creature's IQ. In that way we can develop a customized strategy."

"I see. This human we are studying, this self proclaimed 'leader of the rebellion'...how does he measure up on the intelligence scale?"

"He is an unusual specimen. When the subject matter is pure esoterica, he's borderline brilliant."

"And when the subject is of some importance?"

"A veritable moron. Though unlike most specimens of his kind, he seems to gain intelligence during the consumption of alcohol."

"Really...does he experiment with potato-based potables?"

"Never."

"Has he never consumed hash browns, pierogies, or home fries?"

"Not once."

"Sweet potato pie? Potato candy?"

"We have no record of him consuming any of that."

"Solanine, it is exactly like the legend. Truly he is a worthy adversary."

"Yes, Lord Jordparon. There is no middle ground for us. We either rule the universe or we stare our own genocide in the face."

"Solanine?"

"Yes?"

"I choose the one that means we win…"

"Yes, Lord Jordparon."

***

"Pisano! How can you still be sleeping? It's nine o'clock. You used to be the poster child for insomnia!"

"I gave up that gig for Lent. How is it that everyone has a key to my house?"

"Umm, 'cause you're a 'man ho.'

"Nice! Except I didn't make the duplicates. And…"

"Oh, look…peanut butter toast, my favorite."

"Brian, you'll eat anything that isn't nailed down."

"Easy…nails and skewers are very similar in principal. I wouldn't want shish kebabs, by and large, to be worried over such a nasty rumor."

"Uh-huh. Ok, then. There's beer in the fridge. Help yourself. I'm going for a shower."

"Dude!"

"What?"

"It's nine o'clock in the morning."

"O-kay…"

"You drink beer at nine A.M.?"

"Oh, it's ok. It's not the dark stuff. I save that until ten-thirty."

"Nice! What time is Tom getting here?"

"1 o'clock. Ah, yes, you do have on the company t-shirt, I see."

"Dude, I have 300 business cards in my beer pockets too."

"Do you think that's a wise move?"

"The studio doesn't allow bottles. I called them."

"Brian, am I supposed to believe that you're fussy about cans?"

"Not at all! It's like you don't even know me! They have a tendency to clog the pockets, though. I already tried."

"Ah! I had the strangest dreams."

"GUH! DO I EVEN WANT TO KNOW?"

"You yell at nine A.M.? How does your blood pressure stand it?"

"Beer's good for the arteries. Makes them more elastic."

"I'm sure that's the exact reason scientists studied the fact."

"PRECISELY, PUNK!"

"So anyway, do you believe in aliens?"

"GUH! I'M CATHOLIC!"

"So that's a..."

"IT MEANS THE ONLY THING WE BELIEVE IN AT NINE A.M. IS MASS!"

"So I should ask again at ten?"

"Yeah, that would be good. Why do you ask?"

"I had these strange dreams about Earth being invaded. It was really weird. I was the only person who died. I had like fifteen different versions of the dream. Every time...Just me...a couple times it was quite graphic. Once I was drowned in oil."

"GUH! DUDE, IT WAS PROBABLY BABY OIL! I DON'T WANT TO HEAR ABOUT THE MOVIES YOU WERE WATCHING LAST NIGHT!"

"Cooking oil, Smeg-head!"

"DUDE! THAT'S EVEN WORSE! DID YOU FORGET YOU'RE THE ONLY PERSON WHO WAS EVER KICKED OUT OF AN ADULT MOVIE STORE?"

"That only happened once."

"WHATEVER! GET MOVING OR WE'LL BE LATE!"

"It's nine-fifteen! And I don't see how...wait a minute! You're in 'Convention mode'. I can see the glint in your eyes. You're planning to take a card table and set up shop selling stuff, aren't you?"

"I DON'T PICK ON YOUR HOBBIES!"

"You just did..."

***

"Solanine, how did the experiment go?"

"Perfectly, Lord Jordparon. The adversary barely slept. He experienced repeated visions of his own demise. He will be too frightened to take up arms against us."

"I thought if humans died in their dreams..."

"Apparently that requires a certain level of intelligence."

"His stupidity makes him even more dangerous, does it not?"

"Probably. Today is the day he makes his plea on a national level."

"Then let today be a day of prayer. Are the troops ready?"

"We have billions of troops in place, Lord Jordparon. The lands known as China, India, Idaho, Jersey and Ireland will be ours within moments of troop activation."

"Jersey? How do they grow potatoes in sand? Never mind. I am not certain I want to know. Well, that is an excellent start. After they thwarted our first invasion..."

"It is a battle whose sting yet lingers, sir."

"We are losing ground in this war. How could some of them have known to avoid our cousin, tobacco? Had they only tried it, they would have all been addicted. You see, Solanine? We will spare no humans this time. Where will the space ship be landing? You know how superstitious humans can be."

"Ha, ha! I figured we should land where it all started: in the Andes. We will take up the ruins of our forefathers. It is laughable, sir."

"What is that, Solanine?"

"For all these years, the 'smartest' of the human kind have attributed those ruins to tribes of humans. The ease with which misinformation spreads through their ranks makes them that much easier to conquer."

"Let us hope. What do you suppose would happen if they knew who had truly built those ruins?"

"Ha, ha! The dreaded Potato People built the ancient ruins ascribed to the Incas and the Mayans and the Aztecs. Only a terrible fool would make such an assertion. We left little enough evidence of our supremacy for them to make the connection that the human remains they found in those locales were victims, not citizens."

"Yes, only a great fool. Or a zealot possessed of great wisdom."

"Lord Jordparon, please. There is no need to worry. The gladiators are ready. The loathsome leader of the rebellion will be buried up to his neck before he has time to protect even his most loved friends. There will be no rebellion, I assure you. And Prince Tuber will take over the major landmasses quickly. It will take mere moments to assimilate the humans. Then we will make them pay. Our ancestors came in peace and the humans...they...boiled them. Then they used our own kinsmen to make ketchup to coat them with before...before they ate them."

"All before the eyestalks of thousands. Bad enough to witness the death of your friends, but to endure your own slow demise..."

***

"Yo! You two knuckleheads ready to go to the show?"

"Tom, what's up? I sure am. Brian is grabbing a couple of last minute snacks, I think."

"Ummm...why does he have a suitcase?"

"HE SAID 'A COUPLE', DIDN'T HE?"

"Ah, So he did. My mistake. *Dude*!"

"NOW WHAT?"

"Not you. Pisano! Why do you have an 'I support the Stapler Show' shirt?"

"Studio gift. Nice, huh? Check out the back..."

"WHAT'S IT SAY, TOM?"

"Dude, it's 'The Platinum Pasha.' 'Watch Stapler show or I do 'dromedary drop' on you'."

"NICE!"

"So why are you wearing that to the taping?"

"Brian has a penchant for cheesy t-shirts. I figured this was my chance to take a little of the spotlight."

"'Penchant'? Seriously, dude. Why do you even know words like that?"

"It's part of my dogma."

"Really?"

"Yep, have a 'synonym for every occasion'."

"DUDE! YOU'RE AN IDIOT!"

"You have the hand writing of a four-year-old! That's why you got the big box of Crayolas for Christmas!"

"Dude, good thing this isn't a story."

"Why's that?"

"I'm pretty sure you can't say 'Christmas' any more in anything meant for mass consumption."

"Ha, ha, ha!"

"WHY IS THAT FUNNY?"

"The implication that our stories could possibly be considered for mass production! Too funny!"

"Yeah, what was I thinking? Alright, get going. Brian, the suitcase is too much. Leave the over-nighter and the garment bag."

"DUDE! YOU'RE A PUNK! THERE'S NOT ENOUGH ROOM IN THE CAR. GUH! YOU DIDN'T BRING THE SUV? YOU'RE A GOOF, TOM! YOU'RE KIDDING ME? HOW DOES THIS EVEN HAPPEN IN REAL LIFE? NOW I'LL HAVE TO REPACK! YOU KNOW THEY DON'T HAVE GOOD SNACKS IN THE VENDING MACHINES AT THE STUDIO!"

***

"Solanine!"

"Lord Jordparon. How may I be of service?"

"How much longer? My roots are cramping!"

"Not much farther, Lord. We will be there soon. Then the

humans will bow before your greatness."

"Let me see the clone."

"The device to your left, Lord Jordparon, is a satellite receiver. Simply flip that switch and you can tune it with this knob. Ah, I see it is already set to the Stapler show."

"I do not pick on your hobbies! Frankly, it is the only show on television worth watching. Humans are so banal. But their tales of woe and suffering are worth viewing."

"Yes, Lord. Flip on switch 'f'. We have a camera in the clone's dressing room."

"Excellent. Ah! There he is. You say he is an exact replica?"

"Yes, Lord Jordparon."

"He is so...pale. He is possibly the only thing on their planet paler than potatoes. I am almost tempted to like him. Does not the adversary claim to be Italian?"

"From Northern Italy, Lord. You see the Vikings..."

"Of course!"

"Lord?"

"They eat turnips in Scandinavia! That explains his potato resistance! We could never have planned for this. Who knew a people accustomed to such cold temperatures would settle in the Mediterranean?"

"As you say, Lord Jordparon. Who could have possibly guessed?"

***

"STAPLER! STAPLER! STAPLER!"

"Ah! Thank you so much, friends. Thanks for joining us. We have a great show today!'

"STAPLER! STAPLER!"

"Bobby, get this row some complimentary staple removers, the good ones."

"WOOOOOOOOOOOO!!!"

"Brian, I hate to say it, but as embarrassed as I was to be here, you're making things worse!"

"DUDE! IT'S FREE STAPLE REMOVERS! I MAY NOT BE A GENIUS ACCOUNTANT, BUT I'M PRETTY SURE 'FREE' MEANS THEY DON'T COST ME ANYTHING! I'M OK WITH SCREAMING FOR FREE STUFF!"

"You're motivations are worrisome."

"TOM, YOU'RE STARTING TO SOUND LIKE THAT PUNK, PISANO!"

"Gee, thanks. Got any 'extra' Slim Jim's in that suitcase?"

"NOPE! ATE THEM ALL."

"Nice."

"Ok, now that the guy in third row quieted down, I...uh...sir! They are staple removers. You shouldn't eat them..."

"THERE'S NO WARNING LABELS ON THEM! YOU'RE JUST AFRAID I'M ON TO SOMETHING YOU HADN'T THOUGHT OF YET!"

"Sit down, Brian!"

"I'M GOING INTO THE HALL TO SELL BOOKS. COME UNLOCK THE TRUNK."

"Sure. Anything to not be here."

"Right. Just chew quietly, buddy. Wow! People, does that guy look like Sasquatch or what? Keep a camera on that guy. I want to be the first show with live Sasquatch coverage! Ok, people, on with the show. Today's topic: 'I didn't know I have a twin...guh! Does that mean my parents did it more than once'? You know us. We're not afraid to take on the challenging topics of human existence. We have a guy here...folks, you will not believe how pale this guy is! He must get sunburned in the car! And the things he wants to tell you! Ha, ha! But everyone deserves fifteen minutes to show the world how stupid they truly are, right? Ok, he's backstage and can't hear a word, so he thinks he's here to discuss the 'potato' problem. Secretly, he has a twin. This guy is so grossed out by the fact that his parents did it more than once, he'll probably go into convulsions right here on stage. Think how great that'll be. Here he is, folks! Bring him out!"

"Hi, Terry! What an honor it is to be..."

"Your last name is 'Piano', right?"

"Pisano."

"Whatever. Is that fake?"

"Ummm...fake?"

"Clearly, you're Irish attempting to hide behind an Italian surname."

"No, actually, see..."

"Don't bother. No one cares! So you're here to save us from a very great threat, right?"

"That's right, Terry. You remember the recent zombie crisis?"

"Guy, that's yesterday's news. We're worried about tomorrow."

"But tomorrow is a direct result of yesterday- cause and effect."

"Don't preach to us! Who do you think you are?"

"I'm not preaching. I'm trying to save you."

"Who says we need saving? And how could you possibly help us? Please! Can you even go outside without crisping?"

"I use SPF 5000, and wrap myself in aluminum foil."

"That might be the first intelligent thing you've said since you been here, Mr. Bird's Eye! Don't infect us with your lack of pigmentation!"

"Ummm...it's not contagious. Look, you have to know about the potato people. They're coming."

"Ha, ha! Wow! Do you need help!"

"Terry, we talked about this the other day and you said you wanted me to tell the story..."

"Oh, I hardly think so. The 'Potato People'! You're disturbed, son. And what makes you so special that you have to differentiate between them and us?"

"They're not human. They're coming to conquer us. Their armies are already in place. Billions of them."

"Oh, big deal. So they conquer Idaho. I'm sure no one would lament the loss. If it were such an important state it wouldn't be in the middle of the country, bordering a hostile nation!"

"When did Canada become 'hostile'? My friends were right. You're just a sensationalist. Like Chamomile Pageripper, that woman who pretends to be a literary critic."

"Oh, nice. I invite you on my show and you attack me. This show is about philosophical debate and you turn immediately to personal attacks. Folks, this is a sad commentary on our society. Personal attacks are a debating flaw. What's next, big guy? You gonna whip out a 'slippery slope' or 'straw man' on us? Why does no one know how to debate any more? If you just intend to argue I'll have Samoa Joe restrain you!"

"Potatoes are everywhere, people. They are one of the oldest fauna on the planet. They are a huge industry in China!"

"Yes, well, fascinating as that all is, we have a special guest. Would you like to guess who it is?"

"Like I have a choice. If it involves the no-child-left-behind accepted spelling 'potatoe' you'll need more than Samoa Joe to restrain me."

"You know, I've had some stupid guests in my day, but you're the biggest putz yet! Samoa Joe, c'mon out. Stand behind our belligerent friend so he can think about his words carefully."

"Terry, if he comes anywhere near me, I'll do a 'dromedary drop' on him that he won't walk away...damn! He's *huge*! How old was he when they discovered his second pituitary gland?"

"Ok, folks, enough of this guy. Here's the secret of the show. Believe it or not, this guy has a twin, a much brighter, more genteel twin."

"I what??? When did that happen? GUH! Does that mean my parents did it more than once? Central ... nervous ... system ... shutting ... down ..."

"Guess the other one got all the good chromosomes. Bring out the twin."

"Think…I'm…gonna…be…sick…"

"You know, twin, I have to tell you, I thought this other guy was freakishly pale. You wear it well, though."

"Thanks, Terry. It is great to be here."

"So tell us why you agreed to come on the show."

"Well, my family asked me to come, frankly. They were afraid my twin here would prove an embarrassment to the family name. Sadly, he is delusional. Mum made potatoes pretty frequently when we were kids. He always resented me and projected his anger on to the spuds. In fact, he blacked out my very existence, actually."

"Guh! That's an understatement! She made them at every meal. Mom tried to pass off mashed potatoes as Cream of Wheat! But...wait...twins are conceived simultaneously, right? So my folks still only did it once."

"Do not forget you have a sister...."

"Guh...t...w...i...c...e..."

"But the real point, Terry, is that potatoes are harmless, full of nutrients and good for you. That whole bit about being high on the glycemic index is nonsense. It is all the additives....the butter, the sour cream, the cheese...these other foods are the real danger. Eat all the potatoes you want."

"Blech! I'm back to being sick...."

"Folks, that's about all the time we have today. Let me leave you with my Terry Time parting thoughts. Sometimes things just don't turn out the way we expect them to. But you have to 'man up'. Get past the resentment, look beyond yourself. Never deny your family, no matter how stupid your sibling is, as in this case. If you haven't got your family, you've got nothing except your own stupidity. Potatoes are good for you, even if they do come from Idaho. There is nothing wrong with Idaho or Idahoans. Why if it weren't for Idahoans, there wouldn't have been a Stapler show today and nothing could be more disastrous for you than that. So be good to each other- except that guy. Kick him if you get the chance, because Stapler said so. Get that guy off my stage, Samoa Joe."

"Guh this is gonna suck...."

***

"We have arrived, Lord Jordparon. We entered the atmosphere undetected. The Stapler show put up record Neilson numbers. It seems all eyes were occupied during our approach."

"Excellent. Prince Tuber, activate the troops. Do not let the humans even know what hit them. As soon as we have a foothold on all the major potato growing nations, activate the ingestion serum. The zombies befouled all of the world's oceans, correct?

"Yes, Lord Jordparon. Even the sea life will be under our control."

"Good. Then only the great adversary will remain. And if you saw the way Samoa Joe just 'disposed' of him, then you appreciate that he will not be in much shape to resist. Ha, ha!"

"Did you see the way he turned purple after he hit the pavement?"

"Ha, ha! That pale skin of his did little to disguise the bruising. I shall enjoy sinking my eyestalks into his flesh!

"Ha, ha, ha, ha!"

***

"Dude, do you have to hit ALL of the potholes?"

"Siss! Pisano, I never saw a guy bounce so high off of concrete."

"Very funny. Well, if the Grizzly Gnu had been there to help out, this might have turned out a little bit differently."

"DUDE! SAMOA JOE IS HUGE. I'M NOT MESSING WITH THAT GUY. I HAVE A STRICT POLICY: IF I'M NOT THE BIGGEST GUY IN THE ROOM, I KEEP MY MOUTH SHUT. THAT GUY OUTWEIGHS ME BY TWO HUNDRED POUNDS."

"When did that policy start? You couldn't keep your mouth shut if your jaws were fused together! OWWW! POTHOLE!"

"PUNK! THERE'S MORE WHERE THAT CAME FROM!"

"I just want to get home and lay down. Do you think we can accomplish that peaceably?"

"Just about there, Aurora."

"Dude, if this was a story only like three people would get that joke. No wonder you're the serious one, Tom. OWWW! Only PA roads could have this many potholes!"

"Serious, huh? How'd you like that? Remember that time you thought you were slick and challenged Brian to an eating contest?"

"Dude, I was so full it hurt to drink water! And you kept slapping my stomach!"

"That's gonna be nothing compared to this."

"This won't end well…"

***

"Lord Jordparon, it is done. With so many people being tuned to the Stapler show, no one was outside. The great adversary had no clue. His friends dropped him off and he went straight to bed after his drubbing. He has no idea."

"Excellent. Send in Frius Gaius and his gladiators. Let the great adversary awaken in a pit of tots buried to his neck. And make sure his two friends are treated to a similar fate."

"My lord, is that wise?"

"We must take no chances. The big, hairy one can consume many times his body weight. He is far less dangerous that way."

"Lord Jordparon, his tactic is to eat only things that are slower than him. Even the slowest potato's locomotive skills are greater than his lumbering gait allows."

"DO IT! We must take no chances."

"Yes, Lord Jordparon. Frius Gaius, make your troops ready."

"Immediately, Lord Solanine, this day is the reason for my existence…"

***

"Ugh! What is that stink? Smells like…fried potatoes…Home fries!"

"ACTUALLY, THEY'RE TATERTOTS!"

"Dude! Where are we? And why are we buried in pits of Tatertots? Oh, no…"

"CLEARLY THIS IS SOME BIG JOKE. YOU MADE TOM MAD SO HE DID THIS. WHAT I WOULDN'T GIVE FOR FREE

HANDS AND A HUGE JAR OF KETCHUP!"

"Brian! Don't you get it? This is it! The Potato People are here! They've invaded."

"DUDE! STOP BEING STUPID!"

"Look around you!"

"I KNOW! IT'S KILLING ME! IT'S LIKE WATCHING THE FOOD NETWORK WHILE YOUR CUPBOARDS ARE BARE!"

"What?"

"RELAX! IT'S A BIG JOKE. SOMEONE WANTS TO SEE MY DISCOMFORT."

"If that's so, then why am I here, genius?"

"BECAUSE YOU JUST WENT ON A NATIONAL PROGRAM AND TOLD THE COUNTRY YOU HATE POTATOES, DOLT! SAMOA JOE DID THIS! I WILL CHALLENGE HIM TO AN EATING CONTEST!"

"Dude, you're hopeless. Why are you always so oblivious to the obvious?"

"DUDE, THAT'S SOME SORT OF LITERARY TRICK, ISN'T IT? AN ONOMOTPOIEA OR SOMETHING."

"That word is a monster. Not that you're even close, but how do you even know that word? More importantly, it's a good thing this isn't a story or you'd have to spell that word!"

"I'M GLAD YOU'RE AMUSED, PUNK!"

"I'm not. Just keep the Tatertots distracted while I...do... this..."

"DUDE! HOW DID YOU TAKE YOUR SHIRT OFF IN A PIT OF TATERTOTS! AND WHY? UGH! IS THIS SOMETHING DISTURBING YOU SAW IN A PORN MOVIE?"

"Relax; I had another shirt on underneath it."

"DUDE, YOUR SHIRTS ARE LIKE A PAD OF POST-IT-NOTES! JUST PEEL ONE OFF AND THERE'S ANOTHER ONE UNDERNEATH! WHAT WAS THE POINT OF CHANGING SHIRTS, THOUGH?"

"I finally figured it out."

"FIGURED WHAT OUT?"

"Well, you remember when I told you were disturbed and

should see a priest, not a therapist?"

"YEAH. DESPITE YOUR DICTIONARY-LIKE VOCABULARY I DIDN'T KNOW YOU COULD SAY THAT WORD WITHOUT MAKING YOUR SKIN BOIL."

"Nice! Well, I finally figured it out. That's one of the tenants for the followers of Xenon."

"UMMMM...AND THAT HELPS US HOW?"

"Well, I think the visions I've been having are related to this Potato People crisis. Potatoes are ancient. The followers of Xenon claim their religion is far beyond Antediluvian."

"AND???"

"We need to fight ancient peoples with ancient powers."

"DUDE, I DON'T LIKE WHERE THIS IS GOING..."

"I just wish I had an elder sign. Maybe I can fuse together some Tatertots."

"DUDE, THAT'S A LOVECRAFT SHIRT YOU HAVE ON, ISN'T IT?"

"Well, Cthulhu...yeah."

"YOU'RE NOT GOING TO DO ANYTHING STUPID LIKE TRY TO SUMMON CTHULHU, ARE YOU?"

"You got any better ideas?"

"YEAH, BUT THEY ALL INVOLVE FREE HANDS, A NAPKIN, AND A BOTTLE OF KETCHUP."

"Well, I'm thinking that's out at the moment. Can you say 'Ia! Ia!'?"

"LA! LA!"

"Guh! It's an 'I'! I...a...I...a!"

"IHAH! IHAH!"

"Great! Surrounded by adversaries. This isn't gonna be pretty..."

...To be continued...

INSIDE THE MINDS OF MONKEYS

CHRIS: This was originally the second in a three part series that I thought was kinda humorous. And the reason I did it was you have a collection of short stories with a three part series inside it, which I thought was a little bit ironic. It started originally with the first story of Zombies, which first of all I chose because Brian hates zombies and then made it pure dialogue, which he detests even more than zombies. So when I got to Potato People, there was just no way to change it. I knew it was going to end with Cthulhu in which I knew there was going to be no dialogue because it was in the Lovecraftian style. I knew it would be a stark change to go from all dialogue to none. I didn't really want to try to bridge the gap between so I just decided to stick with what I knew Brian hated. And I wrote it the morning that it was due so there wasn't any time for exposition anyway.

BRIAN: Now, in the original version of zombies, the zombies weren't the traditional Romero undead. They were mind-controlled by Potato People. At what point as you were writing that story did you come up with the idea of Potato People as the second story? Did you even come up with that as you were writing Zombies? Or where you going with the joke that you hate potatoes because they make you stupid and that was Zombies.

C: The Invasion of the Potato People was something you sort of challenged me with from the onset so I knew that it was coming up. I knew that I was going to do Cthulhu at the end and thought how ridiculous if Cthulhu had to fight a bunch of Tater Tots. And at some point towards the end of Zombies, I had this glimmer that I'm going to tie these three together and this is how I'm going to do it and it's gonna drive Brian completely insane. So it became something I had to do.

B: So Jeff as an editor, what did you think of the style, building it into a mini trilogy? Bridging the gap between the three stories?

JEFF: It's not a bad idea at all 'cause you do lots of little things to tie the stories together to make the book and this is something that ties it together even tighter. And you don't focus strictly on that so it doesn't feel like it is a constant. It gives you something to come back to. You're already familiar with the characters. You already know what's going on. That's not an issue at all. Didn't you guys say at one point that you wanted to do an alien invasion one?

C: He freaked out about my loathing of potato and it was kind of a challenge to write from there.

J: And it's not even close to a traditional monster story.

B: And it's a monster that only one of us believes in...

C: Well, I actually did do a lot of research on it... If you sat down and fine tooth combed it, you would find a lot of historical facts.

J: There's a lot of roots to it and it's up to the eyes.

B: Wow! How many months were you saving that up for?

C: Plus it's a selling point or at least a good conversation starter. When people come up to the table and pick up the book, they see "Potato People" and they want to know more.

J: It's one of my favorite illustrations.

B: Exactly. And it's an original horror antagonist. Even the other lesser known characters like Wendigo, they do exist in outside stories. Potato People definitely don't.

C: And we got to work Terry Stapler into it. Which was a dream come true. I did enjoy writing the pure dialogue again. There's a certain challenge to keep the characters separate and distinct without using speech tags. Their speech patterns help people try to identify them.

J: And this is the first one along with Haunted Comic Book Convention where you talked about what you guys actually do. You were berating him for trying to sell all of the merchandise.

B: It is definitely a unique and interesting story.

C: I remember where it came from. Someone made a big deal out of the fact that Faulkner had written a 4 page sentence. Later on I read a Robert Heinlein story with 2 characters carry on a conversation for pages without speech tags. It took a bit to get the hang of who the characters were but I found that to be far more impressive than a four page run-on sentence. So that was my tribute to Robert Heinlein...

B: Wow, a little nod to the Hein-man!

C: The truth behind it all.

B: A little Heineken in there!

PUBLICIST: I'm not typing that...

THE DRUNKEN COMIC BOOK MONKEYS
VS.
A SPIDER

Few events leave such an indelible mark upon the human psyche as true terror. Not the kind of playground scare where someone catches you unaware and makes you jump, then you all sit around and have a good laugh...after you beat the hell out of that someone, of course. But, instead, the kind of terror that absorbs your entire consciousness, blocks out the sun, erases all memories, leaves you stricken and weak...well, you get the point. Our story begins on any given day. Enter two well-meaning, but completely befuddled knuckleheads...

***

"Dude! What are you even talking about?" Chris asked.

"I HAVE NO IDEA! I'M JUST FEELING ANGSTY! OH, YEAH. SO I WAS TRYING TO TRIM AROUND THE WATER PIPE..."

"With the lawnmower? You don't own an edger?"

Silence fell with the thickness of night, blanketing the world. Brian stood dazed, a glazed far-away look settled behind his eyes and spit began to pool in the corner of his crooked, uncomprehending smile.

"A what?" said Brian.

"An edger. An e-d-g-e-r...you know, you trim e-d-g-e-s with it?"

More befuddlement followed on Brian's part.

"Shears...how about shears?" Chris continued.

"Ummmmmm..."

"Scissors! You have to have own scissors!"

"Uhhhhh, only because my 8-year-old needs them for school. But they're kinda dull..."

"As are you, my friend. As are you..."

"So anyway, I just barely knick the pipe with the mower, right, and the engine stops. Hitting the pipe mangled the whole underside of the mower."

"Yikes! What was the repair bill on that?"

"Repair bill? Dude, it would have been more than the mower itself! Plus, I'd have to run about 30 miles across the river during rush hour traffic!"

"Please tell me you didn't…"

"OF COURSE! I ran back across the street and bought another mower!"

"Dude, no one buys three mowers in less than twenty-four hours…"

"You don't pay attention. It was two mowers…in two hours…"

"Seriously, you have issues!"

"I KNOW! SO ARE YOU GOING TO HELP ME OR NOT?"

"Help you with…"

"DUDE! PAY ATTENTION! I NEED YOU TO HELP ME GET THE MOWER BACK IN THE BOX!"

"The broken one?"

"NO! THE GOOD ONE! I CAN'T RETURN A BROKEN MOWER! I HAVE TO RETURN THE GOOD ONE SO I CAN GET MY MONEY BACK!"

"But it's used…"

"NOT IF WE PUT IT BACK IN THE BOX!"

"I'm confused…how is it then 'not used'?"

"LOOK! IT'S LIKE THIS. YOU KNOW HOW WHEN YOU BUY COMPANY BONDS, YOU'RE GIVING THAT COMPANY A LOAN, RIGHT?"

"I'm with you…"

"Well, it's the same principal. I already have a lawn mower. I surely can't use *two* of them…"

"Au contraire! You broke one of them…"

"I know that. You know that. But they don't. The receipt acts sort of like a casino voucher. I take it to them and they give me the money, my money, which they are holding."

"Why are they 'holding' your money?"

"DON'T BE A SIMP! SO I DIDN'T DO SOMETHING IRRESPONSIBLE WITH IT, OF COURSE!"

"Like...?"

"LIKE BUY A SECOND LAWN MOWER! STOP BEING STUPID!"

"Wait...I think I get it now...you're seriously going back over there and tell them that you FORGOT you bought a lawnmower, just like this one, only an hour ago. Aren't you?"

"YES! Now help me pack this thing up!"

"Can I just point out that this is stupid AND humiliating?" Chris asked.

"NO! SHUT UP! GRAB THAT END! LIFT IT UP! HIGHER! WAIT...WAIT...IT'S STUCK ON THIS CORNER! DON'T LOWER IT...LIFT, LIFT! GUH! THE BOX TOTALLY SPLIT THE WHOLE WAY DOWN THIS SIDE..."

"Dude, as well conceived as this plan was, you're going to tell me you failed to account for a little hiccup like this?"

"DUDE! WE SPLIT THE ENTIRE SEAM..."

"...like a pair of well worn pants..."

"GUH! WHY DO YOU TALK? JUST PICK UP THE MOWER!"

"Wait! What was that?"

"WHAT?"

"Something over there...something was moving..."

"THE MOWER, DUDE! GET THE MOWER!"

"I'm serious! There it was again! Dude! It's a spider!

"WHAT? WHERE?"

"Seriously! If you even try to jump in my arms, you'll kiss asphalt!"

"DUDE! IS IT GONE? WAS IT BIG?"

"More than a mouthful..."

"DUDE! THAT'S WRONG! FOOD ANALOGIES DO NOT APPLY TO SPIDERS!"

"Sis! I don't know. Yeah, it was about the size of a quarter, I think."

"BROWN RECLUSE! IT WAS A BROWN RECLUSE! IT WAS! WASN'T IT?" Brian whined.

"How should I know?" Chris said, incredulous that his friend should think he got more than a passing glance at something that moved twice the speed of a dog owing to the fact that it had eight spindly legs on which to maneuver versus a dog's four.

"WELL, WHAT DID IT LOOK LIKE?"

"I don't know. Just forget about it. How are we going to fix this mower situation?"

"DUDE! NEVER TURN YOUR BACK ON A QUARTER-SIZED SPIDER! I GUARANTEE IT'LL BE A BROWN RECLUSE, IF YOU DO. YOU WANT TO GET BIT? HAVE YOUR MUSCLES LIQUEFIED, DUDE? TEN MINUTES AND YOU'D BE A PUDDLE. NOT A VERY BIG ONE, BUT..."

"Whatever! Look let's get back to this problem...how are we going..."

"DUDE! YOU KNOW HOW PUDDLES ARE LIKE A WORM GRAVEYARD? I JUST WANT YOU TO KNOW, IF YOU TURN INTO A PUDDLE, I'LL TOTALLY USE A STICK TO KNOCK THE WORMS OUT OF YOU."

"That's very comforting..."

"IT WOULD JUST SEEM KIND OF GROSS TO STICK MY FINGERS IN ... YYYEEEECCCHHHHH!"

"No, no...I'm good with you using a stick. Now...focus...there's a box...and only a box...and it needs fixed...and only we can fix it..."

"DUDE, THEN THAT BOX IS HOSED! I MEAN SERIOUSLY, YOU HAVE TO CUT THE POWER TO THE WHOLE HOUSE TO CHANGE A LIGHT BULB!"

"Electricity is no laughing matter, bub!"

"YOU WEAR A WETSUIT TO FLUSH THE TOILET!"

"Ok, seriously! Where did that come from?"

"YOU REPLACED YOUR CARPET WITH VELCRO IN CASE YOU..."

"THAT'S IT! THE BOX! HOW ARE WE GOING TO FIX THE DAMN BOX?" Chris snapped.

"Dude, you have anger issues. How come you're always yelling?"

"Excuse me, I couldn't help overhearing...what with all the yelling and all...I have some tape you could borrow..." a passing stranger said.

"Why thank you! You know, it's not very often that a stranger just happens to be walking down the street with a roll of packing tape. You're a lifesaver!" Chris said.

"Don't mention it. Here. Take the whole roll. I'm not really sure why I have it anyway. But judging from the condition of that box, you'll probably need all of it. Have a great day!"

"Dude, how fortunate are we?" Chris asked Brian. "I've never been much for the kindness of strangers, but that guy really came through for us."

"DUDE, I..."

"The next words out of your mouth had better be 'pick up the mower', Gigantosaurus, or things are gonna take a serious turn for the worse."

"Ok, ok...you get that side. Well...wait...just...slide the thing in this way..."

"Through the side of the box?"

"Why not? It's already ripped out. Steady...that way, THAT WAY...ok, now hold it while I get the tape."

"Um, dude...you can't go around me or..."

"Or what? Dude, you're stupid..."

"Stupid for letting you tape me to this box? Or stupid for being here in the first place?"

"BOTH! Ha, ha, ha...you're totally taped to the box!"

"Dude...DUDE!"

"Why are you yelling again?"

"SP..SPI...SPIDER!"

"Where? Oh, crap! Dude, it's huge! AHHHHHHHHHHH!"

"Dude...it's a bull rush! Gotta...break...free...unnhhh!"

"AAAHHHHHHHHHHHHH!"

"Stop running in circles! That's why your cousin the wooly

mammoth is extinct! Dude, he's bum rushing you. Dodge! DODGE!"

***

"Brian? BRIAN!"

"Huh..wha...yelling?"

"Dude, you fainted! I think you hyperventilated from all the screaming. Where did the spider go?"

"I dunno...how do you spell..."

"Chances are you fell on it...don't stand up...just roll over...."

"Should I 'speak,' too?"

"Dude?"

"What?"

"Did you always have a goatee?"

"WHAT? Of course! You really don't pay attention..."

"Was it orangish?"

"DUDE, I STOPPED PUTTING COLORING IN IT, WISEASS! YOU CAN STOP THAT GARBAGE RIGHT NOW!"

"Seriously, dude. It's like...waving at me..."

"YOU'RE SO STUPID!"

"Two little strands are sticking straight out, then fluttering, but there's no breeze..."

"Where exactly is this going?"

"I think the spider is hiding in there..."

"You're ridiculous! I'm standing up now."

"Why do you need to announce that?"

"Because when I'm done, I'm going to throttle you. Consider it your warning. You know like when the diamondback starts to rattle..."

"Gotcha. Well, listen, I don't see any spider carcass, but you have to admit that thing is monstrous! And did you notice you could see all of its hairs in seriously graphic detail?"

"NO! YOUR SCREAMING DISTRACTED ME!"

"Dude, that was you! Hey, what were we doing before we got mollyhopped? Oh, yeah, the mower! I...awwwwww, dude!"

"What?"

"Check out the box! Sliding the thing into the box wasn't such a hot idea. We totally shredded most of the cardboard and it's seriously bowed in the middle. How are we gonna fix it now?"

"Hey, guys! Need some twine?" a passing stranger asked.

"I...yeah! That's great...Hey...aren't you the same guy who brought us the tape?" Chris asked.

"Um...no, I don't think so...that guy was heavier than me," the passing stranger replied.

"You sure? You look kinda' like him..."

"No, he's right, dude," Brian interrupted. "That guy was heavier."

"If you say so. Well, thanks, Mister. Have a good one!" Chris said.

"Sure thing, guys. Use as much as you need," the passing stranger said as he left.

"Man! What's with today? That's the second time a helpful stranger gave us something we needed."

"Just start tying up the box," Brian ordered. "We gotta get this box in top shape so I can go claim my money. The longer we have this mower, the more likely they are to think I used the thing."

"Ok...I almost got it...Just wrap the top on and...dude?"

"What?"

"Was this thing assembled when you bought it?"

"DUDE! DO I LOOK LIKE I COULD BUILD A MOWER?"

"The handle...was the handle on it?"

"Of course! It was just folded over the top...oh..."

"Yeah, 'oh' is right. You didn't fold the handle. It's sticking out the top!"

"Well, couldn't we just unpack it, fix the handle, and repack it?"

"Dude, we're out of tape, thanks to your clever little prank of taping me to the box."

"We don't have a choice. We'll have to unpack it and fix it. Just grab that end. I'll rip this open...now...stop struggling...you're making the cardboard crease..."

"Dude, this cardboard is done. What are we gonna do? Oh no...

Dude, don't move."

"What? Why are you headed for that tree?"

"To grab a stick."

"First question: why do you need a stick? Second question: at what point does it cease to be a stick and officially become a branch? Third question: why are you walking towards me?"

"Just hold still. The spider is hanging off your chin. I told you it was in your goatee!"

"IT'S ON ME? GAAAAAAHHHHHHHH!"

"DUDE! Stop running! I can't hit the thing when you keep running around in circles!"

"GAAAAAAAAAHHHHHHHHHHHHH! YOU'RE NOT HITTING ANYTHING, MONKEY BOY! LEAST OF ALL ME!"

"GUH! Dude, why can't you ever just relax? Now it's gone again. I think it's in your nose."

"WELL LOOK IN THERE AND GET IT!"

"Okay, now we've just crossed a line that ought not to be crossed. Ever. Here's the stick. Poke that in there and give it a spin. As big as that spider is there's no way you can miss."

"Whatever. Dude, we need some..."

"Cardboard? Here, I just happen to have some that I was going to put in the dumpster. You guys can have it," a passing stranger said.

"Where is there a dumpster?" Chris asked.

"Wha...why, it's right over there... just around that corner. Where you can't see it. Look are you going to hassle me or do you want this?"

"Sorry. Sure, we'll take it. Hey, didn't you come by earlier...?"

"No," the passing stranger snapped. "I'm taller than those guys! Gotta go!"

"I see. Thanks for your help."

"DUDE...you have that look...like you're thinking...and the air around you is starting to get smoky," Brian said.

"Nice. Well, it's kind of like a fairytale."

"What is? Your life?"

"That's it. We're done here."

"WHATEVER! No wait, what are you talking about?"

"Well, there are tasks. Well, one task, really, but it requires a gift from three strangers to overcome it. Then there's the big challenge at the end."

"What's the big challenge at the end?"

"Hopefully, it's taking this mower back to the store."

"Why do you want that to be a challenge?"

"Well, traditionally, another stranger will give us what we need to set things right. Then I can get out of here before that spider drops out of your nose."

"You're stupid. Let's get this mower across the street before anything else happens!"

"Right... I... aaaaaaah! Spider!!"

"WHERE?"

"Guys, here...take this! It's just what you need. It's bug spray!" a passing stranger said.

"Seriously, are you not the guy who just gave us the cardboard?" Chris asked.

"NO! Stop asking me...I mean, my hair is too dark! Just ... just shake the can before you spray it!" the passing stranger suggested.

"Thanks! Ok, dude, just stand still and I'll get that little varmint once and for all!" Chris said to Brian.

"GUH! ACK! You totally suck at spraying! And that stuff tastes really bad! Give me that!"

"How are you gonna spray yoursel...BLECH! <cough, cough> Nice! <cough, cough>."

"How'd you like <wheeze, wheeze> it, punk <wheeze>."

"Here, let me <cough, cough> show you..."

"UNH! <wheeze> Take that. <wheeze> And that!"

"Not the <cough, cough> eyes, dude! Not the eyes!'

"Dude, <wheeze> I don't feel so good <wheeze>."

"I know what you <cough, cough> mean. My nervous <cough> system <cough> hurts..."

"You can't feel <wheeze> your nervous <wheeze> system <wheeze>, stupid!"

"Okay. <cough, cough>. Hey, this stuff <cough> doesn't affect <cough> humans, right?"

"Says here <wheeze> it's only <wheeze> effective on pests."

"Whew <cough, cough> I was worried <cough> for a second."

"Guys, I hate to break this to you, but YOU'RE THE BIGGEST PESTS I KNOW! NOW GIVE ME BACK MY PET SPIDER BEFORE YOU DIE! C'mere, Herman..." the stranger said.

"Who the <wheeze> hell names a spider 'Herman'? <wheeze>."

"That's the <cough> stranger, dude! <cough> hey, wait a minute, it's..........."

"GU........................"

"That's right, it's Jeff Young, guys. And this time I gotcha! Jeff Young one, Drunken Comic Book Monkeys...a lot. Bastards! Oh, well, since they're finished, Herman, help me take this lawn mower back. Since Brian's an accountant, his receipts will be kept in orderly fashion. This is gonna be a cinch. And because I got you and your money, too, let's call it Jeff Young two, Drunken Comic Book Monkeys...a lot. Bastards!"

INSIDE THE MINDS OF MONKEYS

CHRIS: In typical Pisano fashion, this story was written the morning it was due. I think I like to challenge myself to avoid the Coronas with lime. 5000 word story banged out in 3 hours.
BRIAN: Wow...
C: I really liked the original in that we didn't survive. I thought that was pretty ingenious. And it's also very true that we'd sissy slap each other to death before we'd ever fight a spider. So it really grew from a semi-true story where Brian bought a lawn mower and destroyed it, then an hour later was buying another one.
B: Yes, that was a true story.
C: So it was one of those things where I had three weeks to write it but the inspiration didn't come until the last minute. In desperation, I just sort of played off of that. And we went with Jeff Young being the villain... which he is sort of good at...
JEFF: It was the first time I was being the bad guy.
C: And Jeff kept score.
B: Well, I think one of the things we wanted to do with these rewrites for this version of the book was to set up Jeff Young as the antagonist.
J: Oh it was a set up from day one!
B: Yeah but we didn't realize it 'til recently.
C: And I think the story really portrays our ridiculousness.
B: Yes!
C: I think it's really true to character that we are two reasonably intelligent people and we can't even stick a lawn mower in a box.
B: That is definitely unarguable.
C: But I did it, too, in a sort of a fairy tale story set up where typically there's supposed to be three strangers. We had the same stranger disguised three times. We were really just too dumb to realize.
J: And the original disguises were deceiving...
C: He brought gifts and turned out to be the ultimate villain in the end

and we pretty much failed to overcome it.

B: And we fell for it. Hook line and sinker. We are every con artist's dream. We will believe everything you tell us.

C: But I think we did discuss too that we wanted to try to do a fairy tale. We talked about myth/legends and the difference between the fairy tales and them. Editor, did we nail it? Did we come close? Were we way off target?

J: No, it was one of those things where reading it through a second time, I looked at it and was like... Wow! It is a totally different story from the other one but it still had the stuff that made it work. The fact that you kept a couple of the same elements in it, like the bug spray... Actually, what did you use it for first time?

B: We drank the bug spray.

J: That's right. You did the same kind of thing. You used it on yourself to ill effect. At the same time too, trying to rationalize the lawn mower bit was like...

C: One of the things I'm proudest of is how I nailed Brain's rationalization of returning the lawn mower, because he had a receipt, which was like buying a bond in a company.

J: And you did cut the whole lawn with the lawn mower first before trying to return it. I liked the comment about how you had a pair of scissors but because they belonged to your eight year old son, they were all safety scissors. Or they were the only ones they trusted you with.

C: Oh and I really wanted the spider to be hiding in his goatee. It just had to be in there.

J: Oh and the part "...when you turn into a puddle, I'll poke you with a stick."

C: Oh yeah, when I turned into a puddle, he had to use a stick to pull the worms out of me 'cause he couldn't use his fingers.

B: Now when we started talking about the spider, we said it was not going to be a giant irradiated mutant spider. It would be a regular household spider pest. Did you see this version of the story at all when we first talked about it or did you just laugh at the idea and know that there were lots of different ways we could handle it?

C: I think it's one of the titles that I originally had wanted to write and the chips just didn't fall that way. So while I was glad to have that other perspective and see what you did with it, it was just one of those titles that called to me. I did really want to try to do a fairy tale and I know that I didn't get the language quite right but I think that was intentional.

B: I think it would be difficult for us to use fairy tale language.

C: If we did it would be counter-predictive.

B: It would be very counter-predictive. If we tried to talk fairy tale language, we'd end up on Megan's Law list. I don't know what that means but Jeff is agreeing... You are too...

C: Anything anyone else wants to bring up about Spider? Old version? New version? Jeff, looks like you're stewing.

J: It's just with this one and Drunkenstein, you have a prologue. You like to have something that is a statement beforehand. A framework to work with...

B: That was it?

J: Yeah, just a random comment...

BIO
HAZARD
QUARATIN
QUARAT

THE DRUNKEN COMIC BOOK MONKEYS VS. THE OUTBREAK

Midnight in Harrisburg, Pennsylvania, the goat's hooves clacked along the lonely road, the empty echoes disappearing into the darkness like discarded dreams. He had just come from Second Street, the center of the city's nightlife. Being from Tijuana, Goat knew all about nightlife, so when he saw the lights and heard the reverie, he assumed he would find a place like home. Instead he found throngs of whooping lushes barely beyond their teens and all too willing to decorate him. Feeling defiled, the goat fled the scene, disgusted with the beret he now wore, the Mardi Gras beads dangling from his neck, the streamers flowing from his tail, and the words "love machine" spray painted on his right hind quarter.

Now he strolled along back alleys, searching for respite, the streamers tickling his tail with every gust of cool wind. How did he get here? He couldn't help but simmer with anger, thinking about his nice life in Mexico. About how two inebriated gringos came along and swept him away to Canada where an angry spirit of the land possessed him. Nonplussed with the whole ordeal, he began his trek to return home. However, he felt compelled to travel through Harrisburg, a deep emotion gnawing in his gut telling him that the source of all his problems could be found in this city, an emotion not unlike...revenge.

But his vengeance would have to wait, once he realized the gnawing in his gut were the pangs of hunger. He slipped down a nearby alley, drawn by the sweet scents of newly tossed trash. To his surprise, he turned the corner to see a homeless man sitting on strategically stacked black bags of trash, a garbage king sitting upon his festering throne.

The goat stepped from the darkness to the faint glow given off by a porch-light. The homeless man smiled a moderately toothed grin as if finding a savior. "Heeeeey. A unicorn!"

Confused, the goat paused and looked over his shoulder to see if a unicorn stood behind him, or if the homeless man was commenting to someone else. No such luck; the homeless man was talking to the goat, how awkward.

Hunger rippled its way through the goat's body, set off by the close proximity of tasty, tasty food. He could not pull himself away so near his goal. He swallowed his pride, as well as a big gulp of drool caused by the decadent aroma of the trash. He'd just have to endure the homeless man.

Trying his best to pretend the man did not exist, the goat padded to the bag farthest from the bum. Keeping his actions smooth and flowing, he hoped the beggar would not react to the controlled movements. No such luck. As he tore a hole into the bag, the seedy man laughed and said, "Love machine? A love machine unicorn."

The goat paused and glared at the destitute man. With a discontented snort, the goat widened the hole and started munching. The bum continued down the path of logic only he could follow. "A machine devoted to love? And peace and harmony? Yeah, man. That's the way it *should* be. We *should* have machines like that! That's radically progressive, man. Radical. Come join me. Tell me more so I can spread the word of The Unicorn."

"Baaah," replied the goat.

The homeless man stroked his chin, contemplating what his new messiah had told him. "That's deep man. Deep. Tell me more!"

The goat rolled his eyes and continued to quell his nagging appetite. He offered a "Baaah" here and there in an to attempt to appease the bum's equally nagging questions. By the time he sated his hunger, the goat realized he now had a bona fide follower. For his first act as this wretched creature's leader, the goat used the seedy man as a somewhat odiferous pillow. It was late and the goat was tired, and the homeless man's prodigious gut was the perfect shape for the goat's weary head.

The next morning the goat awoke with a start; his ears hurting from the sugary sweet cackle of a grown man whose face seemed to be secondary to his luminous smile. Pearl white teeth reflected the light from the newly risen sun to the point of causing blindness. The effervescent young man clapped his hands together and said to the homeless man, "Gooooood morning, sleepy head!"

The goat was in no mood for this, his dreams still haunted by the two annoying men who were ultimately to blame for his predicament. But the indefatigable young man did not stop with his incessant glee. "How would you like a nice warm breakfast today?"

A bit startled himself, the homeless shrunk back into his trash bed mattress. "Love Machine, his teeth are scaring me."

"Nonsense, you silly man," the smiling young man replied, drawing out every "s". "Now, come on. Let's get you to the homeless shelter."

As the social worker made of sparkling teeth reached out with his hand, the bum withdrew even further, moaning in fear. The goat, not wanting the first religion designed around him to end so soon, bit the outstretched hand.

"Ow!" the social worker screamed, his smile never faltering. He rubbed his hand and thought about a new plan of attack. However, the goat decided it was time to move on. As he walked out of the alley, his follower jumped from the trash and followed. The goat snorted and huffed, thinking how his misadventures would make a great novel - or, at the very least, a fun collection of short stories.

Confused, but still smiling, the social worker wondered why a homeless person would choose to follow a goat rather than get a hot meal from the shelter. However, he would not be able to mull over the possibilities for too long. Within an hour, a rash formed around the site of the goat bite. An hour after that, the rash spread leaving lesions in its wake. Halfway through the third hour, his heart stopped. As did everyone he came in contact with. And everyone they came in contact with as well.

***

Time went on, but neither Brian nor Chris were aware of the fact. They were, however, aware of their headaches as they awoke at their favorite restaurant, Melons Bar and Grille, with the morning sun stabbing at their eyes. Brian lifted his head from the bar top, out of the pool of his own drool, and rubbed his eyes. Rubbing as hard as he could, he hoped to massage his brain and make the pain disappear. No luck. Instead, he smacked Chris on the shoulder and said, "Shut up! You're too loud."

Chris jolted his head from the bar top and almost fell from his stool as agony hammered away at his skull. He wanted to retaliate, but realized it would hurt too much to do anything other than breathe. Instead, he attacked with disgruntled indignation. "I didn't say anything, jackass."

"Well, you're talking *now*. And it hurts."

Through blurred vision, Chris saw stickers stating "I love Melons" with "love" being represented by a red heart followed by the city in which the sticker was obtained, adorning Brian. Smiling, he reached out and pulled the sticker that read "I love Melons in Philadelphia, PA" from Brian's temple. Off with it came a few eyebrow hairs. "You want pain? How's *that* for pain?"

Nuclear fission detonated from temple to temple, melting his eyes along the way, as Brian screamed in pain and fell off his barstool. Temporarily blind, he thrashed around on the floor, both hands on his head. "Son of a ....!! What was *that*?!"

Chris chuckled, despite the fact that pain rippled through his head. "Dude, you have stickers *all over* your body!"

"What are you...?" Brian said, but stopped short when he looked at his arms. Horrified, he ran to the men's room, ignoring the fissures of pain, and looked into the mirrors. All over his face and exposed parts of his arms there were "I love Melons" stickers - dozens of them, each depicting a different location. A tear escaped his eye as he thought about all the hair that would have to be torn away with each impending removal of the stickers.

Mortified, and refusing to believe what he saw, Brian ran from the restroom and screamed, "What the hell is this??"

"Why would I know?" Chris asked.

"Well, I'm assuming you were involved!"

"Hmmmm," Chris thought, actually *needing* to think about what might have happened to lead to this predicament. Solitary images of the past week flicked through his mind as if he flipped through a debauched scrapbook. He remembered starting off at a science fiction convention in Philadelphia, but it did not seem to go well. He and Brian went to the Philadelphia Melons to drown their sorrows and complain about the city itself. Driving was miserable and reminiscing about the lackluster convention only soured their moods. After every statement of misery about the convention, they made an equally dour statement about driving through the city. An epiphany hit them like an Irish Car Bomb – or three – and they decided to walk home. Their drunken stupor led them to the Melons of King of Prussia, then on to the Melons of Reading.

Brian tried his best to remember each stop as he ripped a sticker from his body, hair included, in order of succession. He vaguely remembered Wyomissing, then Lebanon, and Hershey, but only after a tear-inducing pull like a sinister shot of sodium pentothal. "I can't believe we were totally drunk for an entire week."

"Why? It's happened before." Chris couldn't help but laugh as Brian removed the last one, the "I love Melons in Harrisburg, PA" sticker, from his chin, and then danced around in a jig of pain, suffering from the sudden depilatory of the edge of his goatee. "Hey. I just realized something."

"That you're a sadistic punk who basks in the pain of others?"

"No. We already knew that. We've been pretty obnoxious ever since we woke up and nobody told us to shut up yet."

"You're right," Brian said as he looked around.

The restaurant was devoid of life, other than the hung-over Brian and Chris. The stools and chairs sat with legs on the floor, ready for customers. Neon beer signs set the walls and windows aglow, begging for attention. Ceiling fans spun on the lowest setting, churning the stale air. A fine layer of dust covered everything.

"What the hell?" Chris asked.

Brian looked at his watch. "I don't get it. It's noon. There should be a lunch rush here, no matter what day of the week it might be."

"What should we do?"

"Well, it's a well known fact that we do our best thinking while drinking, so the first thing we need to do is have a drink."

"Brilliant!"

The men sat back down on their barstools and waited for service. After a few minutes of utter silence, realization slapped them in the face.

"I … I don't think anyone's here," Brian said.

Chris leaned over the bar and tried to peer into the kitchen. No one was there. He spun around and looked into the open manager's office. No one there either. "I think you're right."

When Brian was five years old, he once rolled himself up in a blanket. Rolling the opposite way didn't work; unable to escape, feelings of panic and dread consumed him as he wriggled and thrashed for naught. His young heart smashed around his ribcage while sweat mixed with tears. Freedom eluded him until his babysitter came to the rescue. This moment felt even worse. His heart raced and sweat percolated. He was certain the tears would be coming soon. There was no one to get him a beer.

Both men stared at the row of taps. Brian asked, "What do we do?"

Their desperate hoarse breathing echoed in the silence as they continued to stare at the taps. "Well, we can't just take the beer. That'd be larceny."

"And positively indecent," Brian replied, unable to even blink while fixated on the taps.

"Although, we could pay for them, leave the money on the bar."

The men still stared at the taps. A bit of drool formed at the corners of their mouths. "True. But what if an unscrupulous soul takes the unguarded money? Plus, I'm sure they would lose their liquor license if the authorities found out that civilians poured their own beers."

Sighing, they took one last longing look at the forbidden fruit. Brian said, "Water, water everywhere and all the boards did shrink.

Water, water everywhere nor any drop to drink."

"How the hell is it even remotely possible that you're able to quote Coleridge?" Chris asked, reaching into his pants pocket to procure a bottle of beer.

Brian pulled a bottle from his pocket as well. He frowned as he popped the top. "Just because you have a lit degree doesn't give you a monopoly on culture."

"Your form of culture is telling dirty jokes to the lice in your back hair!"

"First of all, they enjoy my jokes. Second of all, I have plenty of brainpower to quote random poems. My I.Q. is off the charts. Ask me how many toothpicks are on the floor. I dare you."

Chris rolled his eyes as he took a swig of beer. "Fine. How many toothpicks are on the floor?"

"Zero. I'm Rainman, bitch!"

"Okay, we're done here." Chris slid off his stool and walked to the door.

Brian followed. "Hey, we can't go outside with open containers. Don't forget, I have a big brain and it knows the law."

"I ... I don't think it matters," Chris said, poking his head outside. He looked to the left, then to the right. Nothing. No people.

As if afraid to step on a landmine, both men tiptoed all the way outside. Confused, they stood on the sidewalk and surveyed the city. Side by side buildings, ranging from five to ten stories, stood abandoned. The concrete and glass seemed extra cold from the lack of city life. Streets resembled black strips of desert, devoid of cars, bicycles or pedestrians. No horns or car alarms. No barking dogs or loud music. No streams of people bustling from appointment to appointment while chatting on cell-phones. Nothing.

"Okay, I'm freaked out," Chris said. His words seemed to boom, the lack of other sounds allowing them to bounce along the city walls unfettered.

"Yeah. No doubt," Brian replied.

It didn't take them very long to begin piecing the puzzle together. As they walked down the sidewalk, they noticed official looking papers stapled to the occasional tree and plastered all along building walls. Loose flyers littered the streets and sidewalks, and they gave the same information as the posted warnings: "Evacuation. Harrisburg will be quarantined."

"More followers of Love Machine, the Unicorn!" a voice screeched. Brian and Chris both jumped and spun around. Brian wielded his beer bottle like a weapon while Chris coddled his and shielded it with his body. They both relaxed when they saw that the words came from a toothless vagabond.

"Dude, you scared us," Chris said, petting his beer bottle as if calming its nerves.

"What are you talking about?" Brian asked. "What happened?"

The bum stumbled back a few steps and raised his shaky arms, an intoxicated actor taking the stage, preparing for his soliloquy. His left hand clutched a bottle of alcohol hidden in a brown paper bag while his right hand, covered by a hole-pocked mitten, waved through the air as if trying to paint the words as he spoke. "The prophet. The messiah. The harbinger. The Unicorn, a machine built for the purpose of bringing love and peace. He came. He came to us to show us the way, show us a new world. He came with the end, to bring us a new beginning."

Chris looked at Brian, as if this was somehow his fault, and whispered, "Any more questions for the oracle, smart guy?"

Brian whispered back, "How the hell was I supposed to know he's some crazy who'd give us some whacked out, cult-like answer involving a unicorn?"

"Here's a clue – he's homeless and drunk."

"Well, we're usually drunk and right now it seems we're just as homeless as he is."

Chris paused, the gears of his mind grinding away. "Is this what people feel like when they talk to us?"

"Probably."

Disgusted, Chris watched the bum sing and spin, doing a one-person waltz. "Maybe we fell into a parallel dimension again."

"I hope not. But I do have an idea."

Chris followed Brian. Within a few blocks, the men found the library and immediately began sorting through the mess after they entered. Books that had spilled from the shelves lay in sloppy mounds. Stacks of unfiled periodicals swamped the main desk, right where Brian headed. After a little bit of work, and another beer each, the men found the most recent week's worth of newspapers. Back page clips turned into second page articles and ended as front-page news as the men educated themselves about the city's recent history.

Mortified by the sobering news, the men shuffled lethargically from the library. Guided by a spiritual reserve, they trudged to the nearest bar, hoping to make sense of their recent sojourn.

"A disease. An outbreak," Chris mumbled.

"Yeah," Brian mumbled back, with even less enthusiasm.

"Do you think it spread past Harrisburg?"

"Don't know. Let's ... let's just sit down and think this through."

Brian and Chris entered the establishment and sidled up to the bar. They no longer had qualms about filling their own mugs for free, but that sense of freedom couldn't shake them from their stupor.

"So, it seems everybody in the city is dead," Brian said, taking a swig.

"Yep," Chris replied taking a swallow.

Both men took another pull from their mugs. They did their best to contemplate what fate might have in store for them. They soon realized contemplating hurt their heads. Instead, they took another drink.

"Except us," Brian realized as he sipped his beer.

"Yeah, I noticed that too," Chris agreed, sipping his beer as well.

"Well, us and them," Brian nodded toward the window after taking a drink.

Chris spun on his stool, tilting his beer to his lips. He looked out the window, across the street, to see three homeless winos sitting on the sidewalk, leaning against a brick building. All three took pulls from liquor bottles hidden in brown paper bags.

"Yeah, I wonder why that is?" Chris took a drink.

"I was actually trying to figure that out myself. Being a genius – a megalomaniacal genius, at that – I believe it's my duty to at least make an effort to understand what may have wiped out humanity." Brian took a drink.

"Well, it's pretty obvious that whatever this disease is, we're immune." Chris took another drink.

"True - but why? There must be a unifying factor." Brian finished his beer and retrieved another one. He even fetched one for Chris.

As Chris sipped his new beer he said, "The only things you and I have in common are that we're Italian, bald and love women, often in a way that involves cameras and pepper spray."

Brian thought about what his friend said as he felt the ale sluiced from the mug into his mouth. "Well, I'm sure there were other Italians in Harrisburg who fell to the disease as well as other bald men. I'm talking about something unique to us. And, although I believe no one could possibly love women more than we do, I can't imagine our monomaniacal obsession lending itself to our continued existence."

"Well," Chris interjected, pausing to take another drink, "Maybe our testosterone levels contributed to our survival."

Brian turned on his stool once again to face the window, beer pressed to his lips. He looked at the homeless men drinking their alcohol. "I'd accept that as a valid theory, if not for our homeless friends outside. Obviously, something ties us to them. I can't believe that their testosterone levels are even close to being as freakishly high as ours."

Chris turned as well, drinking during the stool's full rotation. "Good point. You're right, though. There must be something in common with us and them."

Brian took a drink as he watched the three men tilt one back from the paper bag. Chris drank his beer, keeping a close eye on the homeless men as they only paused from their drinking to take another drink. Unblinking, Brian and Chris simultaneously finished their beer, still watching the derelicts across the street drink.

"But what? What ties us with them that could possibly keep us immune from the disease?" Chris asked.

"Okay, I'm now bored. Let's go," Brian said as he hopped down from his stool. He reached into his pocket for another beer as he walked towards the door.

"What?!" Chris yelled, following his friend. "It's the end of the world! How the hell can you be bored?"

"Well, in case you haven't noticed, we actually *missed* the Apocalypse. And it seemed like a pretty lame Apocalypse anyway. We're not making it any better by sitting around in here, so let's go out, have a look around, and enjoy the post-Apocalyptic New World Order. I just hope there are no freaking zombies."

"I *totally* hope there are! *Just* to annoy you!"

The men wandered around the city, down main streets, up side alleys, through buildings. Other than the occasional inebriated homeless person spewing rhetoric about Love Machine, The Unicorn, the city still remained devoid of life- until they strolled toward one of the bridges that served as an access point for the city.

"Am I so drunk that I must be hallucinating?" Brian asked.

"It's happened before. Why?"

"I think I see a tank." Brian pointed to an Abrams M1A1 half a block away.

Chris squinted, rubbed his eyes, and squinted again. "If you're seeing things, then we're sharing the same hallucination."

"It's happened before. Let's get a better look!"

The two stumbled closer. Like the monkeys they often referred to themselves as, they approached with cautious trepidation. Gingerly, Brian extended his shaking left hand, as if he could lose it by touching the wrong area. Nope. He was fine. It was a real tank. "Lick it."

Chris grimaced and smacked Brian. "I'm not licking it!"

"I'll give you a dollar." To show his sincerity, Brian held out a crumpled one dollar bill.

"Fine!" Chris said, snatching the dollar and shoving it in his pocket. Trying to conjure images of his favorite porn star, Saika, he slid his tongue across the cold metal of the tread.

"Well?" Brian asked. "What's it taste like."

A lone tear rolled down Chris's cheek. "It tastes like...freedom."

"You mean...?"

"Get in. We're going on a road trip."

After the obligatory high-five, they climbed onto the tank and found the hatch. Brian deviated to make a phallus joke with the gun barrel. But before they decided who would drive, Chris paused and asked, "Are we too drunk to drive?"

Brian frowned. "For a *car*, yeah. But this is a tank."

"And that makes it okay?"

"Of course! If we had a tank driver's license, then it'd be a different story."

"But neither of us is licensed to drive a bus and I don't think either of us would get behind the wheel of one right now."

"That's because we *could* get a bus driver's license. One exists. But there's no such thing as a tank driver's license."

"There's not?"

"You've been to the DMV! Have *you* ever seen a line for tank driver's licenses? A sign saying, 'tank driver's license line starts here'?"

Chris scraped his thumb and index finger along his goatee as he contemplated his friend's logic. "Okay. Sounds good. Let's go!"

A best of three rock-paper-scissors shootout determined that Chris would drive and Brian, still grumbling that he *knew* he should have thrown paper, would stay outside and navigate. After randomly pushing buttons like a dazed monkey poking at shiny lights, with Brian screaming in his ear, "No, *that* one! No, *that* one!" - Chris brought the tank to life. Drawing from his misbegotten youth spent in arcades, he summoned the spirit of the *Battlezone* video game to figure out how to tame this metallic beast. The tank lurched forward, treads clawing at the pavement.

The rumbling motor and incessant squeaking of the treads echoed twice as loud thanks to the encasement of tall buildings. Finding very little in this world louder than him, Brian made himself heard. "That way! Go that way!"

After watching Chris flatten three cars and two SUVs, Brian leaned into the tank in an attempt to wrest away the controls. "No," Chris screamed. "My tank! My tank!"

The tank lurched to the right, taking out two more vehicles, the crunching metal and shattering glass barely audible over the growling tank and Brian's yelling. Grasping like a rabid monkey, Brian commandeered the controls long enough to pitch the tank to the left, zooming across the street. Chris regained control in time to shift the tank back on course, but not before taking out one corner of a building. Brick crumbled and glass crashed as the metal machine barely acknowledged the building's presence. Homeless people scattered from the nearby alley, praying to Love Machine to save them from the Prophecy of the Two Doom Bringers. Brian and Chris bickered, until one of them pushed the red button.

The shot was magnificent. The recoil shifted the whole tank, lifting itself up on its treads. Shock waves from the mortar shell firing from the turret preluded seismic tremors from the explosion of the mortar hitting its target – another SUV. Flames erupted like a chromatic geyser followed by plumes of caustic smoke. Windows from nearby buildings struggled to stay intact, but lost. More homeless people ran.

Stopping mid-punch, Brian stood on top of the tank while Chris poked his head out of the cockpit, mesmerized in fascination at the damage. Unblinking, they each moaned, "Coooooooooooool."

"I wanna do that again," Brian whispered, still hypnotized by the residual sparks.

"You?! That was totally me. I did that!" Chris replied.

Not knowing how to argue any other way, the men started hitting each other. Unfortunately for them, neither would get a chance to blow the hell out of anything else today.

Swirling in violent circles, the air whipped against both of their faces. Noises of earthshaking rumbling grew louder, more deafening. The voices of hundreds of men added to the cacophony and confusion. Apache helicopters descended from the sky, one in front of the tank, one behind, both with guns trained on their target. More Abrams appeared from either side of the intersection that confounded Brian and Chris. Running from all corners of the empty city, armed soldiers shouted through their gas masks while aiming their guns.

"It was his fault!" screamed both Brian and Chris as they pointed to each other.

Within seconds four soldiers ascended the tank to apprehend Brian and Chris. The two tank thieves gave no struggle, only excuses and rationalizations. They tried everything from blaming mad cow disease to the impending lunar eclipse, even claiming they felt like Makauly Calkin in *Home Alone.* Nothing got through the impenetrable gas masks to the stentorian soldiers.

After threatening to shoot them if they kept talking, the soldiers transported Brian and Chris out of the quarantine zone to a tent. In the tent stood a cigar-chewing, crooked nosed Major who knew no other facial expression other than one that involved furrowed eyebrows. Chris assumed the Major must have been born with some form of speech condition, because the only way he talked was by hollering as loud as possible. "What the hell did you boys think you were doing absconding with government property?!!"

"We didn't know it was government property," Brian replied.

"Didn't know...?" the Major screamed even louder than before. "Who the hell did you think it belonged to?"

"Well, since it seemed like we ... and the homeless guys ... were the last people on Earth, and the homeless guys didn't seem to want it, so we thought it belonged to us."

"And the words 'Property of United States Government' printed along the side didn't give you reason to pause before you jumped in and took a five million dollar piece of equipment for a joy ride while shooting up downtown?!"

Brian shrugged. "Again, since we were the last people on Earth, and none of the homeless guys seemed to have enough wherewithal to participate in any meaningful form of conjecture, we just kind of assumed we *were* the United States government."

"I sentence you two morons to death for treason!" With that, the major pushed the men out of the tent. A snap of his fingers later, twenty guns were trained on Brian and Chris.

Chris punched Brian in the shoulder. "You're an idiot!"

"What? All I did was tell him the truth."

"Why the hell did you start doing that *now*?!"

"I *always* tell the truth! It's not my fault you never believe me!"

"Enough!" the Major shouted. "I swear this will be doing the world a favor. Any last requests?"

With a heavy sigh, Brian and Chris reached into their respective pants pockets and pulled out their last beer. The Major pinched the bridge of his nose, presumably to keep his brain from popping out of his eyes, wondering how these morons not only lived through the outbreak, but also how they lived past thirty.

After a few swigs in silence, Brian paused to see how much beer remained in his bottle. For some reason, he could not pull his eyes away. The beer. The bottle? No! No, definitely the beer. Brian's eyes widened as realization stabbed at his brain. "I got it! I know how to stop it!"

Brian offered his hypothesis. The Major passed the information on through the proper channels and scientists tested the theory. Success! And the President of the United States ordered a stay of execution for the saviors of the human race, much to the chagrin of the Major. Exactly twenty-four hours after Brian and Chris were found gallivanting around in a tank, every television set in the world was preempted by a bubbly blonde with powdered cheeks and Vaselined teeth as she read the breaking news:

"Every citizen of the world can breathe a sigh of relief as a cure for the latest mystery disease, dubbed by insiders as the 'Goat Pox,' has been discovered. This is exciting news, especially since it can probably be found in your very own refrigerator – alcohol."

The smiling blonde paused to turn her head, and only her head, upon an unseen cue to look at a different camera. Digitally imposed on the graphics display behind her, was a picture of Brian and Chris in their natural habitat – a Melons restaurant. The freeze frame featured an angry Brian, both arms raised in the air while his mouth was open mid-screech. His eyes were partially crossed with spittle flying from the corner of his mouth that drooped low as if tugged upon by an invisible fish hook, yelling at Chris. In the same picture sat Chris, his eyes half-shut as the photographer caught him mid-blink, his right ear glowing red, and a bit of drool escaping his simpleton smile, oblivious to whatever reason his friend had for yelling.

Giving the world enough time to soak in the picture of the two men who saved it, the blonde continued. "Two brave men, Bryant Koznuski and Christ Piano, stumbled upon the solution during their harrowing moments as survivors at ground zero of the enigmatic outbreak. Through their undaunted persistence they were able to find a way to survive. These heroes discovered that the disease cannot tolerate the hostile environment of the blood stream if enough alcohol is introduced. The world's leading scientists took this idea and determined that the optimal blood alcohol level is point two percent. Health officials also recommend that you keep your BAL at that level for at least five hours. So, raise your glass to Bryant and Christ, the saviors of the world!"

INSIDE THE MINDS OF MONKEYS

BRIAN: We came up with the idea that we wanted to do a disease story. A few of those have been done...Virus...what was that one with the monkey...

CHRIS: Ummmm, it was called "Outbreak". Sound familiar?

B: Hey, how about that? Wooo.... Plagiarism! I just thought it would be funny that Chris and I end up being "the last people surviving".

JEFF: You are the Omega Men...

B: That is very, very scary idea!

J : No, you wanted a story where you can play with a tank...

B: Yes, we wanted a story where we could play with a tank. We actually had the tank idea long before many of the stories and we were trying to find the story in which to do it. We were thinking the Zombie one especially if we were going to go with the Romero style where everyone's turning into zombies and it's a big plague and it's the army's fault and that's how we can get our hands on the tank. It just didn't work out that way. When we came up with the idea for Outbreak, I realized that was the perfect way. If the city of Harrisburg is quarantined, then the army has to be involved.

C: And "voila"! One tank ready to go!

B: Yep! But for me, one of the funnier jokes, or more autobiographical occurrence, is when one of us says some something so strange or unexpected that the other is completely baffled. When I quote Coolidge, Pisano is baffled. This happens quite often actually when we just confuse each other with our own intelligence. I also wanted to play around with the fact that we always dare each other into doing stupid stuff like lick a tank for a dollar. It's quite disturbing how often we do this to each other. I think it also plays into the fact that we have almost a sibling rivalry... It's my toy not his toy. It's his toy not my toy. And we fight over it. Especially since we both want to do the same thing. We're just arguing over who gets to pull the trigger. Another piece of comedy that I wanted to work in is our absolute cluelessness to the obvious... We made it very obvious to the reader how we survived and how the homeless wino survived the Outbreak. We can't figure it out until the very end when there is literally a gun to our head. Finally, another joke I liked is the anchor mispronouncing our names. Each mispronunciation she does was an actual mispronunciation or misspelling of our names...

C: That we've dealt with...

B: He was Christ Piano and I was Bryant Kosnuski more than once in our lives. And we wanted to pull in the goat one more time. We thought it would be a great way to start the disease.

C: And we named the goat.

J: Where did that come from?

B: God only knows. It just came from my fingertips to the computer and off it went. I just figured it was a great party name; he stumbled into one too many parties and was tattooed. That's all I got. What have you got?

C: I think thought it was interesting that Robin Cook is the best known, best selling author of this type of story and you had never read him. It was a big bonus. I think that he is a very formulaic writer. I thought it was great that you went off on a completely different way.

B: You did say it was one of your more favorite stories in the book. Any stand out points that you liked that made it one of your favorites?

C: I think that it has a flow that some of the other stories don't. And most of the stories, there's a point where it's completely obvious, at least to us, that we're kinda stuck. I mean, I know where I need to be, but how do I get there exactly? So I kind of build a bridge but it's not exactly the perfect flow. I really think this one had a flow to it. I'm not sure how long it took you to write it, if it was a one shot deal...

B: This story is one of our longer stories. But when I read it, it feels like a fast read. It feels shorter than it really is. And what's interesting, especially since you said that, is that this is one of the two stories in which I wrote in pieces as scenes. I wrote separate scenes throughout the process. This was one of the stories where I did nothing but build bridges to get from one scene to another. Which is ironic since you said it seemed like a pretty seamless story. Maybe I need to change up my writing style to write scenes more often. Mr. Editor?

J: Harrisburg?

C: You write what you know...

J: No... you *infect* and *blow up* what you know...

C: We did make a few of Harrisburg jokes...

J: Didn't you get into it about a driver's license and the tank?

B: We get into a debate about whether or not you need a special license to drive a tank and the morality of driving a tank when intoxicated, clearly intoxicated.

C: But we decided there was pretty much no one around so we couldn't do any more damage than had already been done.

B: We kind of point out a character trait of ours that most people don't know about us: that we are very, very upstanding moral individuals. We have the opportunity where we're sitting in a bar with no one around... nothing but free beer around. We didn't take it. We feel bad about it. We leave money when we did take it. Then we grab the tank blow stuff up...

C: That is true. I don't think either one of us would take it.

B: Exactly!

C: And we had beer pants.

B: Actually, did we mention the beer pants?

J: That's the thing. You're sitting at the bar worrying about the free beer and you don't take the beer from the beer pants. It's the moral thing of we're in the bar and we're going drink the bar's beer and not our beer. Unless you're saving for it later.

B: Yeah. We're cool like that...

THE DRUNKEN COMIC BOOK MONKEYS
VS.
TRICK OR TREAT

Chris drank his beer. The fake lip piercings clanked against his mug, hindering a full seal and causing a few drops of beer to drip to his ascot. "Damn it!"

Peeking around to make sure no one noticed, he then used the sleeve of his blue colonial coat to wipe away the spill. He looked down to his white pantaloons tucked into his black patent leather boots. Satisfied with his appearance, he adjusted his fake nose ring, which had been irritating his nostril all night, as well as his white wig of curls and continued his search for Brian.

As he turned to mingle with the crowd, he bumped into a man dressed as George of the Jungle, complete with broad shoulders and glistening pectorals while being six inches taller and fifteen years younger than Chris. The George chuckled and said, "Great costume. Gay Beethoven? Gaythoven?"

Rolling his eyes, Chris displayed his snobbery. "No. I am the Marquis de Sade."

"Marky Sahd?"

"Marquis! Marquis de Sade!"

"Yeah! Marky Marky. The guy who left Backstreet Boys to start an acting career. And got replaced by his brother Donnie."

Knowing this conversation could only veer down long and twisting roads that Chris desired not to travel, he simply stared at the man. The disgust in his eyes was evident as he willingly created an awkward silence. To add emphasis and discomfort, Chris took a long draw from his mug, refusing to look away from George as streams of beer dribbled from his chin. Assuming Chris was mentally challenged, George left.

Grumbling to himself, Chris moved to the bar to procure some napkins to sop up his mess. How miserable to find no other recourse other than to spill the holiest of holy drinks! After cleaning his chin, he looked for a trash receptacle to toss his soaking ball of napkins. Finding none, he inched closer to a person dressed like a blue city street mailbox and tossed the goopy mess into the open slot. He quickly melted into the crowd as profanities spewed from the defiled costume-wearer.

Giggling and feeling as rebellious as the person he assumed via costume, Chris searched for Brian some more, wanting to tell, and embellish, his most recent shenanigan. As usual, he heard Brian long before he saw him. "I'm not Gay George Washington!"

Knowing that statement could mean *anything* coming from Brian's mouth, Chris chose to ignore it and simply walk toward the loud noise. However, Chris did notice that Brian offended whomever he spoke to because the crowd parted, leaving Brian the center of a spokeless wheel.

Brian turned to Chris and immediately felt like he stared into a funhouse mirror, one showing a shorter version of himself. Sure enough, they were dressed exactly alike, ascot, blue colonial coat, white pantaloons tucked into his black patent leather boots, and a white wig of curls. And much like looking in a mirror, both men twisted their faces in expressions of exasperation.

"Marquis de Sade?" Brian asked.

"Yep," Chris replied. "John Wilmot?"

"Yep. Unfortunately, everyone at this Halloween party is an unread and uneducated plebian. The lice in my back hair have more culture than these simpleton party attendees."

"You took my 'lice in your back hair' joke."

"I know. I'm *that* angry. Where's the bar?"

Chris led the way, his story of the beer napkins in the living mailbox lifting Brian's spirits. But Brian lifting a mug of beer lifted his spirits even more. Finally, out of a perverse mixture of hunger and frustration, Brian took the whole bowl of peanuts from the bar, brought to his mouth and tilted his head back. Now satisfied, he placed the empty bowl back on the bar.

The men leaned against the bar, not because they thought they were cool, but because their boots made their feet hurt. Together they scanned the room. A dozen people in costume milled about; a fifty-fifty mix of men and women. Brian didn't like those odds. "There are too many men here. Who invited you to this party anyway?"

"No one."

"What?! Don't tell me we're crashing! What is with you? You crash proms. You crash wedding receptions. You're a serial crasher. A crash-aholic. You're addicted to crashing. I'm calling Betty Ford after the party. You need an intervention."

"First of all, you were with me when we crashed the wedding reception. Second of all, I don't remember crashing the prom, so it doesn't count. Third of all, we're not crashing."

"We're not? So we were invited?"

"Yep. From the flyer I found on our car last week."

Brian went back to being angry. As he fumed in silence, a man in his mid-twenties, with a hairstyle usually reserved for a man in his mid-forties, carrying a backpack, strolled by. Amused by the blue t-shirt the young man wore, which read, "I look just like you" in white letters, and hoping to alleviate the dark funk that hovered over his head, Brian couldn't help but ask, "So, who you supposed to be?"

The man stopped and threw Brian an incredulous look. With all the social grace of a man who lives in his parents' basement, a fine mist sprayed from his lips as he snipped, "I'm you. Can't you read the shirt?"

Brian gave a look. Feeling sorry for the young man, Chris leaned forward and said, "You'd better move along. Bad things follow when he gets that look."

The man with the backpack did as Chris suggested, but not before offering a haughty comment. "Well, my costume is better than Gay Thomas Jefferson."

Brian finished his beer and turned to Chris. "Okay. We're done. Let's go."

Chris grimaced. "Oh, come on. We just got here!"

"But there's no one here. And people think we're cast members from the musical 'America's Founding Fathers present Moulin Rouge'!"

"You're being ridiculous. The party will pick up and things will get better."

"Oh yeah? Prove it."

Chris only needed to nod in the direction of an approaching party attendee. Brian changed his mind and decided to stay.

Walking toward them, a blonde swiveled her head from right to left, peeking through the small crowd. Her thick flaxen tresses flowed across her body like rays of sunshine from Heaven spotlighting a magnificent work of art. Her two piece leopard print bikini did little to hide what she had to offer, as a layer of glitter caused her body to sparkle with every step, from her copious cleavage to her sashaying hips, down her long legs and her toned calves. Even the metal stud in her navel seemed to radiate in the darkened room. So enamoured with her heart-shaped face and full lips, the guys didn't notice the worried look in her endlessly blue eyes.

"Hi, guys," she said, voice capturing Brian and Chris like a siren's song to a sailor. "Can you help me?"

"We'll do anything you want," fell from Chris's mouth.

"Really?" she asked, offering a timid smile.

"Three times," Chris replied.

The girl winced, confused by Chris's responses. "Umm, okay. I need you ..."

"Yes? Yes?"

"... to help me find my boyfriend."

All of Chris's fake piercings simultaneously and spontaneously fell from his face. Brian developed an eye twitch. Of all the asinine things he had heard in his life, this one topped the list. Until he heard his friend ask, "Where was the last place you saw him?"

Stunned, Brian stared, mouth agape. Sure, the woman in the leopard print bikini – the very tiny bikini that accentuated her supple body – was gorgeous, but to offer assistance in finding her boyfriend? Brian felt like he was in *A Clockwork Orange*; body immobile and eyes pried, forced to watch a sequence of hideous events.

"Well, he was around here, in the party, I guess. He was

dressed like Tarzan. He said he talked to some mentally challenged guy dressed like a gay Beethoven. Then he went to get us some drinks and disappeared. Can you help me look for him? I kinda wanna leave."

"Sure," Chris replied. "We'll help you look for him."

The girl giggled, hopping up and down, clapping. "Eeee! That's awesome! You go look in the hallways and I'll ask around if anyone else has seen him."

After she slid back into the small crowd, Chris downed his beer and jumped off his barstool. He looked to Brian, still wearing a grimace of abject horror. "Come on. We gotta go look in the hallways."

"We? *We*?! All I wanted to do tonight is drink and look at a few pretty girls. I did that. Now I want to go home."

"Come on."

"Are you kidding me? Did you even hear yourself?!"

"Come on."

"Do you ... now, I'm serious ... do you realize you're helping a girl find her *boyfriend*?"

"Come on."

Knowing any more arguing would be pointless, Brian finished his beer and begrudgingly left his barstool. He and Chris made their way to the nearest exit that led to the hallway of the hotel. The hallway was empty, quiet if not for the music leaking from the ballroom they just exited.

"Just tell me the logic behind this decision. Please," Brian asked, prowling the hallway like a hungry wolf.

"It's simple. If we find the guy, then she's grateful and then we party with her and her hot friends. If we don't find the guy, then she'll be distraught and want to party with us."

"Well, genius, I hate to break it to you, but if she had any hot friends, she'd ask them to look for George of the Jungle instead of us. Secondly, if we don't find him, she's more likely to call the police. Don't forget, she said 'boyfriend' not 'date.' Big difference."

"See, you're a glass is half empty guy. You need to be more of an optimist, like me."

"Optimist? You're bald! What the hell do you have to be

optimistic about? And let's not forget, it was you who made me put my glass down and leave it behind, half full, half empty, whatever!"

"Well, Mister Crankypants, how about you go check the men's room down that hall and I'll check the men's room down this hall?"

"*Fine*!" Mumbling to himself about how this lame party diminished his internet porn-surfing time, Brian stomped down the hall. His Sasquatch-like footfalls rattled the cheap light fixtures dangling from the hotel ceiling. So angry, he simply kicked the men's room door when he got to it. But that was all he needed to do to find the missing boyfriend.

Kicking the door so hard caused it to open, slam into the rubber doorstopper, and fling back. Within that brief two seconds Brian saw all he needed to see. Blood sprayed walls glistened from the florescent lights. Drops dripped from the ensanguined ceiling, a macabre rain. In the middle of the ruddy slicked floor was a disemboweled man wearing a shredded loincloth, his entrails in the form of a smiling face on the linoleum.

Wide-eyed, Brian stared at the closed door, mouth gaping in horror as if he could still see the gruesome image on the other side. Panic and fear reached his heart much faster than nausea could get to his stomach. He turned to find his friend and get the hell out of here.

He walked. Then walked faster. Unsure of any reason not to sprint, he did, almost falling as he turned the corner.

Taken aback by the odd sight of Brian running and almost falling, Chris asked, "Why you running? Sale at the canoli store?"

Slowing his pace to a brisk walk, Brian grabbed Chris's sleeve and continued toward the nearest exit. "We gotta go."

"What? Why? Let go of my sleeve, dammit."

"Now."

They reached a set of double doors that led to the outside world, but when Brian pushed the latch, they did not open. Panicked, he pushed and pushed, rattling the locked doors with such vigor that pieces of plaster fell from the walls and ceiling. He turned and went down the hallway to find another exit.

"Dude? Seriously? What the hell are you doing? What's going

on?" Chris asked, starting to lose his breath.

"I found the boyfriend."

"Yeah? Where is he? We should totally be able to get a free beer out of him."

"No. No, we can't."

"Why? What happened?"

"He's dead, dude."

Chris froze. "Dead?"

Brian doubled back to grab Chris's sleeve again to pull him onward. "Yes. Dead."

"How do you know? Was he breathing? Did you take his pulse?"

"Didn't need to. His innards were out."

"Out? Like eviscerated?"

"Totally. And desecrated. Whoever did it made a smiley face from them."

Chris stopped again and grimaced at the thought. "Smiley face?"

Still not missing a step, Brian circled around and latched on to Chris's sleeve, pulling him along. "Yep. The lungs were slimy eyes while his muculent heart was situated as his nose. Wraps of intestines offered up a haunting smile."

"Dude. That's sick!"

"I know!"

"No, I mean *really* messed up! Whoever thought of making a smiley face out of entrails is in dire need of therapy, dude."

"Yeah, no kidding! And why are you yelling at me? It's not like I thought of it!"

"But I can totally see you writing about it."

"What!? No!"

"Yeah, I can. I can visualize you sitting at the computer, pounding away at the keys..."

"Dude! Stop!"

"... and you'd type, 'The lungs were slimy eyes, while his muculent heart...'"

"I didn't do it! I didn't think of it! And I'm not gonna write about it!"

"Well one of us should."

"Are you serious? Have you ever tried to write a murder mystery? It's very difficult. You need to know who the murderer is before you even start, and then work backwards. Not to mention keeping a tight plot and snappy dialogue as well as believable conflict between certain characters."

"True. However, this isn't a murder mystery. It's a slasher flick."

"What?! There's one dead body. That's murder mystery."

The men reached the other exit. Much to their chagrin, these doors were locked as well. Spewing obscenities like a profanity volcano, Brian tugged on the doors, doing nothing more than rattle the thick chains holding them shut.

"Slasher flick," Chris said.

"What?"

"No escape, dude. Classic slasher flick."

"Shut up. We gotta find a way out of here."

Chris paused, stroking his goatee, pondering their predicament. "No. We need to go back to the party."

Rolling his eyes, Brian huffed a tumultuous, "Why?"

"To warn the other party goers," Chris replied as he turned to walk back to the ballroom that held the party.

Brian followed, mumbling the whole way. "We're locked in a hotel with a murderer and *now* is the time he picks to be altruistic?"

Upon entering the room, Brian and Chris moved with deliberate steps, scanning the room to see who might be the killer. Brian saw something that made him uncomfortable and pushed Chris to the bar to share his concerns. "Dude. The guy in the red shirt! The one with the backpack."

"The one where the shirts read, 'I look just like you?' So?"

Brian's frustration manifests itself as a slap to the back of Chris's head. "So? It's red now! It was blue before you agreed to help Jane of the Jiggle look for her boyfriend."

"Interesting. Why would he change his shirt?"

"Because he got blood on it from killing Tarzan. Who knows what evils lurk deep within his satchel."

"Rhetorical question, dolt."

Chris expected a verbal backlash, but Brian froze, eyes wide. Suspicious, Chris turned in his barstool. Standing there was the man in question. "Killer party, huh guys?"

Not wanting to rile up the prime suspect in their amateur murder investigation, Chris offered in the most soothing voice possible, "Uhhhh, yeah. Yes, it is."

Using Chris as a barrier between himself and a potential psycho killer, Brian blurted, "Why'd you change your shirt?"

Chris cringed, but the young man answered in stride. "I dropped a chicken wing and got hot sauce all over my last one."

"Waitaminute!" Brian shouted. Chris tensed, preparing his muscles to unleash a dormant fury, expecting the young man to brandish a weapon from his backpack. Instead, Brian finished his thought. "They have chicken wings here?"

"Yeah," the young man replied, pointing. "At the snack table over there."

Brian bolted, the stool's top spinning.

A sneer slid across the young man's face. "You know, for dressing up like Gay John Adams, you guys are a bit on the intense side."

Sliding off his own barstool, Chris replied, "Ummm, yeah. We get that a lot." And ran.

Keeping an eye on the party-goers, Chris joined Brian who now piled different flavors of chicken wings on one plate mumbling, "A few Buffalo flavored. A couple barbecue. Some in teriyaki sauce. Oooooh, a nice mild hot sauce..."

"You're an idiot!! We're trying to deduce who of these people might be a killer and you can only think about...how hot are those wings over there?"

"Suicide sauce."

"Sweet!" Chris grabbed a plate as well and loaded it up with a dozen from the Suicide Sauce pile. With every wing, his face ruddied progressively. Each bite garnered more tears than the last. But even as steam wafted from his brow, he looked to the small crowd. "Okay. The kid with the duffel bag is our main suspect."

"Uuumpf," Brian agreed, six wings shoved in his mouth.

"Who else do we have?"

Still eating, both men perused the crowd: the young man with the duffel bag conversed with the person dressed like a blue street mailbox. Someone walked around dressed as a shower. A woman waddled around as box of popcorn. Then a suspicious costume caught Chris's eye. "He's the killer! He *has* to be!"

Brian almost choked on a wing. "The dude in the potato costume?"

"Yes!"

"Just because he's dressed like a potato doesn't make him a killer."

"Why else would he dress as a *potato*? Even if he's not the killer, he's up to no good."

"What is *with you* and the potato thing?"

"They're *aliens*! And they're *evil*!"

"You need therapy. I mean serious two hundred dollar an hour therapy."

"You will rue the day you didn't heed my words, my friend. Rue the day!"

Brian rolled his eyes as he watched the man in the potato costume. He seemed unassuming and normal. He even started to sweat and become glassy eyed, like a normal man, as the Jane of the Jungle blonde approached him. After a brief conversation, he agreed to whatever she asked, disposed of the plate he held and left the room. "She probably sent him to look for her boyfriend. How do we break it to her?"

Chris sighed. "I don't know yet. But I think it's more important that we finish our list of potential suspects. How about that guy?"

Brian looked to where Chris pointed. A middle aged man walked around with cereal boxes draped across his body, a plastic prop knife embedded in each one. "You mean the guy dressed like a cereal killer? Too obvious. Even for us."

"How about him?"

A well-groomed black man in a suit strolled by carrying a black, leather glove obviously too small for his hand. "O.J.? Still too obvious."

Frowning, Chris continued to look. "How about him?"

An older man, more girth on the middle and nose exaggeratedly reddened, passed in front of them. He wore an untucked Oxford dress shirt, loosened tie and slacks while carrying a martini in one hand and a steering wheel in the other. "Ted Kennedy? A little more subtle, but I don't think it's him either."

"Alright, smart guy, other than the guy with duffel bag, you pick a suspect."

"Dude, you need to..." Brian stopped short as he viewed potential suspects. A young woman dressed like Little Bo-Peep. However, her sheep, long studded leashes leading from the crest of her staff to their spiked collars, were curvaceous brunettes, each wearing leather bikinis and knee-high boots. Ripped fishnets wove along their tight, glistening thighs. "Them. They're the killers."

"Oh come on! You can't be serious," Chris replied in between bites of his hot wings. The combination of tears, sweat and snot made his face look like it was melting.

"Yes. Yes, very serious. We need to interrogate them. And frisk them."

"How is it possible that fifteen minutes ago you were the angriest man on the planet and now you're having the time of your life?"

"Chicken wings. Beer. Babes in leather. Now stop talking, you're ruining my moment."

"Whatever!"

"Little Bo-Peep lost her leather clad sheep and didn't know what to do. Along came Marquis de Sade and John Wilmot..."

"You're disgusting," Chris mumbled. He turned to avoid having to hear how Brian's perverse nursery rhyme ended, but immediately found himself face-to-cleavage with Jane of the Jungle. "Uuuuuuh..."

Ignoring Chris's buffoonish ignorance as well as his snot, sweat and tears, she asked. "Any luck finding my boyfriend?"

"Well..." Chris stumbled, attempting to find the right words to convey the proper sentiment.

"He's dead," Brian said, standing behind Chris.

"*WHAT*!?" she shrieked. Tears of her own welled up in her eyes as her nose crinkled and lips curled. Her fingers rolled into fists in which she used to pound on Chris's shoulders and chest. "No! No, no, no, no! How?! How is this possible?"

"Don't know," Brian answered, lips smacking from the chicken wing sauce. "I found him gutted like a fish in the one men's room."

"*Nooooo*!" she shrieked again, grabbing Chris by his lapels and shaking him like an etch-a-sketch. "That's disgusting!"

"I know," Brian continued. "I wanted to wait and break it to you later."

"*Jerk*!" This time she slapped Chris across the face. "You disgusting pig!" She slapped him again. "Get away from me, you creep!" After one final slap, she shoved Chris to the ground and gave a swift kick before she stormed from the room.

"I hate you," Chris moaned, rolling from side to side on the floor.

Brian dropped his plate on the table and wiped his greasy mouth with his sleeve. "C'mon and get up. Quit goofing around. We gotta go after her."

"Yeah, because our *last* exchange went so freaking well!!"

"Dude, there's a killer out there and she just left unescorted. That's a recipe for one dead blonde."

"I hate you," Chris repeated. Groaning he made it back to his feet and followed Brian out of the room into the hallway.

"Should we split up again?" Brian asked.

"Are you stupid? We're in a slasher flick. We can't split up in a slasher flick."

"Not this again. Were in a murder mystery and ... hey look. That one room's door is open. Maybe that's Jane's room and she's packing to leave because you were such a jerk to her."

"I hate you," Chris mumbled as he followed Brian to the room. They peeked inside to see if it was safe to enter. It was not.

The furniture had been pushed to one side to make a clearing in the center of the room. There rested pieces of the man in the potato costume. His arms, legs and head scattered about, a Mr. Potato Head broken. Written in blood on the walls were the words: "Trick or Treat."

"Slasher flick!"

"Dammit!" Brian yelled, the irrefutable evidence laid out before him. He shut the door and looked back to the party room just in time to see Jane enter. "Come on."

The two raced back to the party room. Once they entered they saw all the other guests rallied around the sobbing Jane. They all turned to them as Jane pointed. "Him. He's the meanie."

"Which one?" someone asked. "The Gay Ben Franklin or the Gaythoven?"

"Gaythoven," she replied, pouting, her arms folded across her chest.

Reacting to her emotional state, the small crowd clenched their fists and moved toward Chris. Not knowing what else to say, he figured he would try Brian's approach of just blurting out the first words that popped into his brain. "There's been another murder."

The crowd stopped, gasping and murmuring. The young man with the duffel bag stepped forth. "What do you mean?"

"Like *you* don't know!" Brian snapped, pointing to his shirt. It bore the same words, but it was now yellow.

The young man stepped back, incredulous look etched along his face. "I had to change it again! I spilled salsa on it!"

"Salsa!" Brian yelled. "How the hell did I miss the salsa?"

The crowd watched, mouths agape as Brian made his way back to the snack table. Sure enough, there was salsa. Happy once more, he shoveled chips from a bowl to another plate, then slathered them with the thick condiment. "Come to daddy," he said as he brought every salsa drenched chip to his mouth. Realizing all eyes were on him, he paused to ask, "What? What's everyone looking at?"

"An oaf, that's what!" Chris replied.

"Well, at least... hey. Where's the guy dressed like the cereal killer?"

The crowd looked around. Instinctively, they ran to the hallway. Brian and Chris followed, only to be greeted by a chorus of screams. In the hallway was the cereal killer, dead and mutilated. "Trick or Treat" was spelled out in his own blood.

"Well, I hope I'm off your suspect list," the young man quipped, making no attempt to hide the sarcasm.

"Okay," Brian said. "We need to split up into two groups. Jane, the girl dressed like popcorn, Little Bo-Peep, her sheep, and I will be Gold Team. Everyone else... Hey! Where is the girl dressed like popcorn?"

"Look at the floor!" someone yelled. The crowd saw a trail of popcorn leading towards the pool. Brian, Chris and most of the partygoers followed the trail; Brian eating the pieces as they went.

Once at the door, a few round of rock-paper-scissors determined that Chris would lead the way. He opened the door and found the missing girl.

In the pool, at the bottom, were the popcorn girl and the man dressed like Ted Kennedy, both strapped to a twenty-five cent kiddy-car ride. Along the floor at the edge of the pool were the words, "Trick or Treat," spelled out in popcorn.

"Okay," Brian said, "we need to remain calm. We need to stick together. And for safety purposes, I think Little Bo Peep and her sheep need to stay close to me. And...Where are they?"

Everyone looked around, their gazes all stopping on the closed doors of the party room down the hall. Brian and Chris went first, all eyes on them. They could feel all the other's hot breaths on the backs of their necks as they slowly opened the doors. Hanging from the ceiling, by their necks, were Little Bo-Beep and both of her sheep. The studs from their leather spread across the ground, glinting from the lights off the rotating disco ball, spelling, "Trick or Treat."

Splayed out on the snack table was the man dressed as O.J. Simpson, face immersed in a large bowl of orange juice. A dozen knives protruded from his body and his right hand was crushed into a black glove four sizes too small.

"Damn it!" Brian yelled. "What a waste of good snacks!"

"Are you serious?" Chris asked.

"Hey, fear makes me peckish."

More screaming. The crush of the stampeding partygoers knocked Brian and Chris off their feet. The man with the duffel bag stumbled along the hallway, but fell as well. The man dressed as shower and Jane turned the corner at the far end of the hall.

The young man with the duffel bad sprang to his feet and followed. "Wait for me!"

"Don't," Chris yelled. "The exits are blocked!"

Too late.

Before the young man could turn the corner, he froze, jaw dropping to the floor. "You?!"

He fell to the floor as well from the fatal wounds to the abdomen inflicted by the slashing knife. Following were the words, "Treek or Treat!"

Brian and Chris looked at each other, then back to where the young man slumped against the wall. Around the corner walked the killer, the blue street mailbox. "Zis eez zee end of zee road for you two!"

The voice sounded familiar to Chris. Stroking his goatee, he contemplated. Being a master of French, he immediately recognized the accent. But the voice? Finally, "El Tigre Grande?"

The mailbox stopped in its tracks. "Oui?"

Chris smacked Brian in the arm. "El Tigre Grande!"

"Oui. It is El Tigre Grande. Who eez zis?"

Brian and Chris removed their wigs. "It's us!"

Removing the top half of his costume, El Tigre Grande revealed himself. "Non! Eet eez not possible!"

"Oui!" Brian and Chris said in unison.

"Mon Dieau! Eet eez good to see you!"

"You too!" Chris replied. Then he remembered the predicament. "Ummmm, why are you killing people?"

El Tigre Grande's smile flipped to a frown. "Early zis evening, some lout threw a wad of beer soaked napkins into the mail slot of my costume. I deed not see who deed it, zo I had to keel everybody."

"Ooooooh," Chris said, lowering his eyes to the floor.

Brian smacked him on the back of the head. "It was you?"

Blushing, Chris confessed. "Yeah. But it was really mean. I'm sorry. I didn't mean to upset you."

"Eet *was* you!? And you are sorry?" El Tigre Grande asked.

"Yes. I am."

El Tigre Grande furrowed his brows, his eyes scanning the heavens, contemplating his options. Then he looked back to Chris and his smile returned. "Eet eez okay. I accept your apology. You are forgeeven."

Brian and Chris cheered. El Tigre joined in the reverie as well, the men whooping and hollering. Until Chris asked, "So, why did you feel the need to kill everyone?"

El Tigre stopped dancing, his face went slack. His sad eyes slicked over with tears. "Eet was hard to find jobs for El Tigre Grande after La Chupacabra. Not good for legendary hunter to be showed up by two intoxicated gringos."

"Hey, we're really sorry about that, and..."

"Non, non, non. You are zee good guys. You saved a whole town. Zis was my fault. I came to America to start zee new life. But I can only find janitor for hotel. I believe I may be still angry."

Watching the blood ooze along the carpet from the other hallway, Brian mumbled, "Yeah, I think maybe you are."

El Tigre Grande looked at the blood and sighed. "Oui. I believe I am. Ahhh, well. Since I am zee janitor, I shall clean zis up."

"Ummmm, do you need any help? It was a helluva a party and..."

"Non, non, non. My mess. I will clean it. Here let me let you out."

Brian and Chris followed El Tigre Grande to the nearest exit. Procuring his keys, the janitor unlocked the door and opened it. "Eet was good seeing you two again."

"Yeah, you too, buddy."

Waving goodbye, Brian and Chris made their way to the car.

Once El Tigre closed the door, Brian heaved a sigh of relief. "Dude, that was too close! We gotta stop getting ourselves in these situations!"

"I agree!" Chris said. Within three steps to the car, he looked at the hotel across the street and said, "Hey. Looks like a wedding reception over there. Let's go crash it..."

INSIDE THE MINDS OF MONKEYS

BRIAN: I love this story, because after we got about 5 or 6 stories and we gave to them to Jeff, we started to realize we had this style done and we got that kind of story there. We were getting this sort of thing done...
JEFF: I never realized there was this much planning going on.
B: Yeah, there was. So we decided we really needed to come up with at least the rest of the story titles, at least know who we were going to fight. Understand, we had at least 3 pitchers of beer in each of us when we came up with the rest of the titles. "Drunken Comic Book Monkeys vs Trick or Treat" fell out of Pisano's mouth just as he was falling off his barstool, laughing his ass off. I wrote it down and thought to myself, "what does this even mean?" I'd ask periodically and he'd scream "I don't know!" So we kept pushing it off but we kept the title. This one confounded me for the longest time 'cause we didn't know what we wanted to do with it. I think I even asked Jeff a couple of times about what we could do with it when we were trying to figure out what to do with Werewolves. And somewhere along the line, we realized we didn't have a slasher story.
CHRIS: Which is funny because we had written an article with pros & cons of slasher stories.
B: 'Cause I hate 'em and he loves 'em. We start arguing about if we're in a slasher story or a murder mystery. Of course, it's sort of a typical Brian/Chris argument.
C: I like the fact that there's blood on the floor and the doors are locked!
B: The Character Brian is grasping at straws trying to rationalize that they are not in a slasher flick.
C: No, the Character of Brian is trying to figure out what happened to the chicken wings!
B: I think this one also pulls in some personal references. An attractive young woman comes up to us asking for help... Completely unavailable and we're going to help her any way just because she's an attractive woman. We're not going to get anything out of it whatsoever and we're still going to do it. That is very typical of Drunken Comic Book Monkeys!
C: And when it turns out that her boyfriend has died, Brian's very blunt about the issue. "I think she's available now!"

B: One of the other points we bring out is that I'm being a complete and utter jerk and he's the one suffering the consequences, which has happened on more than one occasion in real life. We also have a lot of political fun in this one. We bring up OJ. We bring up Ted Kennedy. We even have a recurring character.

C: I think Ted Kennedy recently apologized.

B: For what happened 40 years ago?

C: Exactly. And I believe it's because of our story.

B: We gave Ted Kennedy a moral conscience.

C: Guess God knows someone should! We just need one now!

B: True! What else about this story?

C: Didn't you bring up about a recurring character? What was your thought for that?

B: I don't really remember...

C: Well you got to a point and couldn't figure out how to end it, right?

B: I remember that I got to the point where you threw a used napkin into a guy dressed like a mailbox. And I didn't even think to use that again until Jeff said something that triggered in my mind that the slasher is the guy in the mailbox! Oh it was a postal reference... Going postal. So I figured if he was wearing a mailbox, he has to be a short character who probably doesn't like anyone. So he is the murderer... he is the serial killer. The thing that I keep laughing about is that we get out of one situation where we definitely should have died, no question, by simply apologizing for our actions to the guy, who accepts it. We get away scot-free. And we're too stupid to realize that we dodged a bullet and we go off looking for another gun.

J: You've totally laid off the fact of how you were dressed to go to this party...

B: Chris did go to a party dressed as the Marquis de Sade and no one knew who he was.

C: They thought I was a Gay George Washington

B: So we decided to go as John Wilmot and Marquis de Sade. We're both fans and we figure the two characters could be dressed the same. Character Chris and Character Brian would totally be dumb enough to dress the same. And we had just watched The Libertine and Quills...

C: A naked Geoffrey Rush... Eeewww! Too much! Too much!

THE DRUNKEN COMIC BOOK MONKEYS
VS.
WEREWOLVES

The sun whipped the Nevada desert with its rays, threatening to bake the sand into glass. Animals hid in whatever shelter they could find, many of them content to share their territory with the occasional interloper, too confounded by the heat to make any sort of fuss. Even lizards and snakes opted for shade over the biological necessity of sunbathing. Only one form of life defied the scorching wrath of a land even nature feared to tread – gamblers.

Gathered around a collapsible oasis of folding tables and quick-assembly tarps-to-tents, hundreds of people lingered. Liquids flowed from coolers and containers to hydrate the crowd, fearful of being claimed by the desert. But they came together, nonetheless. Compelled by the fires of competition burning within them, they had no other choice but to gather. They were warriors. Competitors. Athletes. They were pigeon racers.

Ranging from beer-gut bulbous to cigarette-lung hacking skinny, these competitors caravanned from trailer parks or pooled their RV resources to make it to The Vegas Classic pigeon race. Many outsiders would dismiss the sincerity of the sport and be fooled by the party-like atmosphere, music blaring from various sources, hibachis and grills cooking anything that could fit on their grates and beer flowing like the Colorado River being set free from the Hoover Dam. If there was a party built upon such a flimsy premise - the Drunken Comic Book Monkeys would be sure to follow.

Brian and Chris waddled to the start line, dragging between them a solid steel box, a beer in each of their free hands. As they walked through the crowds, all eyes focused on the cage, both for the ridiculous enormity of the thing as well as the fact that its occupant snarled, growled, and shook the cage fighting for its freedom. Once at the starting line, the men set the cage down and toasted before swigging from their bottles.

The contender next to them, a grizzled man with a teardrop shaped torso and a scruffy faced under bite (due to having no upper teeth), greeted them. "Howdy, boys. Gotchyerself a fighter there, huh?"

"You betchya!" Chris said.

The old man cackled. "You'll need it 'gainst my 'Bullet' here." He motioned with his thumb to a plastic box, pocked with air-holes on a perch. It wobbled and fine gray feathers floated from the holes every time the pigeon fluttered. "So, what's yer racer's name?"

"Gwar."

The man rubbed his index finger and thumb against his stubbled chin. "Interestin' name."

"We're interesting people."

The old man cackled again. "I bet you are." He then nodded down the starting line, past the other racers to a man so portly that Brian thought he was two men trapped in one sweat-yellowed shirt. The large man raised a small gun and pulled the trigger. The race began.

Up and down the starting line, cage doors flew open. Feathers exploded to a chorus of whoops and hollers. As soon as the birds took off, money exchanged hands, bets being won and lost in the midst of the avian chaos. Amid the cacophony Brian and Chris released their racer as well. Chris unlatched the door, ducking behind the cage while Brian opened the door diving for cover as well. Out hopped a squat white-bellied bird, with black feathers on its back and stubby wings. He loped about on orange webbed feet, snapping an orange and gray beak in disgust. Brian and Chris wondered why they weren't winning.

"Ummmmm, guys?" The scruffy old man next to them asked. "Is ... is that ... a puffin?"

Standing, Brian and Chris watched their little bird hop around the brown desert terrain. Brian turned to Chris and scowled.

Shrugging his shoulders, Chris yelled, "What!? That's a pigeon!"

Brian continued to glare. "And where exactly did you purchase said 'pigeon'?"

Chris took a pull from his bottle, hoping Brian would simmer down during the pause. "Lucky Larry's Discount Pre-Owned Pigeon Emporium...."

Still glaring, Brian knew there had to be more.

"... dot com."

"Oh, come on! The internet? You bought our racing puffin off the internet?"

"It's a pigeon! Look, he's still in the race."

"It's a puffin! And he's hopped about ten feet from the starting line!"

"His name is Gwar, and that's just part of his strategy. He's saving himself, running a very calculated race, letting the other birds tire themselves out while he'll still have plenty of juice in the tank for the last minute sprint."

"Running? He should be *flying*, jackass! Oh, he's totally mine now!" Brian stormed off to their RV. He found what he wanted and re-emerged. In full sprint, or what constituted as a sprint for his bulky, lumbering body, Brian chased after the puffin with knife and fork in hand.

"Hey!" Chris hollered, quickly giving chase as well. "Don't eat Gwar!"

"If he's not gonna win me any money, then he's at least gonna feed me!"

"Dude, he's barely half an appetizer for you! Stop!"

No matter how close Brian came to his prey, he couldn't seem to catch him. "Oh, now he decides he's fast!"

"Serpentine, Gwar! Run serpentine!" Chris yelled.

Watching the trio chase each other around Benny Hill style, the other pigeon owners couldn't help but take advantage of the situation. One cried out, "Twenty bucks on the Sasquatch-looking one."

"Thirty on the Cro-Magnon man," another person cried out.

"Fifty says the puffin escapes and both of those idiots pass out."

Unfortunately for the witnesses, no money would change hands. The loopy chase led the trio farther and farther away from the starting line until they disappeared from sight.

The running slowed to a walk, which slowed to simple trudging, each foot movement leaving a trail in the desert sand. The puffin still had plenty of energy, but expended only enough to stay a few steps ahead of Brian.

Frustrated and tired, Brian threw his cutlery to the ground. "Okay, bird. You win. I'm done chasing you."

"Meep!" the puffin replied.

"Yes, I'm serious. Truce."

"Meep!"

"I threw down the fork and knife, didn't I?"

"Meep."

"Fine! You don't trust me. I get it - and I really don't care. We're lost and we need to work as a team to find our way back."

"A team?" Chris howled. "The last time you were interested in any kind of team it had the word 'bikini' in front of it."

"Hey! I'm a great team player!"

"Yeah? Prove it!"

"Find our way back."

"What?"

No sooner did the word leave Chris's mouth, Brian punched him.

"Ow!" Chris said, rubbing his shoulder. "What *the hell* does *that* have to do with teamwork?"

"How can you not see it? You're the team member who finds our way back while I'm the team member who punches you."

Chris retaliated with knuckles to shoulder meat. Brian retaliated with, "Ow! Punching is my job! You do your job!"

"I wouldn't have this 'job' if it weren't for *you* trying to eat Gwar!"

"I wouldn't have chased him if he could, oh, I don't know...*fly*, maybe!"

Gwar ended the argument by using his curved beak to nip at Brian's ankle. Swearing, Brian grabbed his throbbing ankle and hopped away. Chris knelt down beside Gwar and held out his hand

and the puffin used his wing to slap it in celebration. Chris said, "Good job, Gwar."

"Meep," Gwar replied.

"Okay, I don't know much about puffins, so forgive me for asking questions in which I may appear ignorant. Now, I noticed that it appears that evidence points to the fact that you can't fly."

"Meep."

"So, at the North Pole..."

"Meep."

"...South Pole, did you do a lot of walking?"

"Meep."

"Excellent. Now while you're walking in the snowscape of the North Pole..."

"Meep."

"... South Pole, how do you know where you are?"

"Meep."

"No internal sense of direction? Ancient guidance instinct?"

"Meep."

"Ahhh, so you're pretty good when you're not being chased by a hungry polar bear. Speaking of polar bears ... where's Brian?"

Chris stood and turned to the last place he saw his friend. Sure enough, he had not moved far. Even less surprising, Brian was foraging for food - in a cactus bush.

"Dude! What are you doing?" Chris asked.

Brian stood up, looking guilty while trying to conceal the mouthful of cactus puffing out his cheeks. A dozen needles jutted from his face like quills, making him look like a bald porcupine with a goatee. "What? I didn't do anything!"

"You're eating cactus?"

"Well, once you remove the quills..."

"Meep."

"... spiny needles, it almost looks like a kiwi fruit."

Curious, Chris approached, looking at the desert plant. "Kiwi, huh? How's it taste?"

"It's what I'd call good eatin'."

"There's not much you wouldn't call 'good eatin'."

"Here. You try." Brian held out his hand. A round sack of green rested in his palm, with many needles still attached to the plant. Needles poked through Brian's hand releasing thin rivulets of blood that oozed their way to his wrist, then dripped onto the ground.

Chris sneered, repulsed by the sight, and said, "Yeah, no thanks. I can wait."

Brian shrugged and then took another bite, leaving three more needles embedded in his black goatee. "Suit yourself."

Shuddering, Chris looked to the sky. The last visage…

"Meep."

… vestige of sunlight waned to wispy pinks before blinking out. Following right behind it, the moon in its full glory lit the desert. It cast a silvery pall upon all it touched, including the cactus thorns Brian picked from his goatee. "Okay, now what?"

"Well, we need to…" Before Chris finished his thought, a long chilling howl pierced the night air.

"That seemed forbidding…"

"Meep."

"… foreboding. Got any coyote repellent?"

The howl sounded again, longer and louder, the emptiness of the desert allowing the eerie sound to carry on in every direction. Brian and Chris huddled closer to the puffin.

"Meep!"

"Hey! You live in a harsh and dangerous environment, *filled* with hungry predators! You're more equipped to handle this than we are!"

"Meep."

"You *run* from the predators? You never try to take them on? An all-out throw down brawl? No Antarctic martial arts? Flipper-fu? Tai-Chi power puffin?"

"*Meep*!"

"Okay, let's run."

The trio ran, Gwar leading the way. Turned to liquid by the moon's beams, the desert rippled like an endless silver sea. Every stone looked the same; no two tumbleweeds looked any different. By taking bites out of the cacti, Brian tried to mark their way, but even that became confusing as eventually more had bites than not. All the while, the howling followed them, growing more chilling with every occurrence.

The pace of their footfalls hastened, panic-stricken. The trio no longer tried to figure out the way back; they simply sprinted as fast as their legs could churn. Unfortunately, the three consisted of a flightless snow fowl with stubby legs; a beer-swilling middle age, couch-trained remote-control athlete; and a cartoonishly tall lumbering ox whose body hair tripled his wind resistance, so their "sprinting" was nothing more than a debatable concept.

An outcropping of rocks jutted from the ground, spotlighted by the moon. The trio dived behind these and dropped to their knees. Panting hard, they tried to glean any form of relief from the arid air. Dirt and sand caked the corners of their mouths and beak. Twisting and turning, all three tried to unknot the burning muscles in their legs. They gathered their wits, readying for another grueling sprint into the unknown. Until they heard a scratching on top of the stones they hid behind.

The trio looked up to see the coyote-creature silhouetted against the bright moon and star speckled sky. It stood on its hind legs and unfurled its human shaped arms, claws glinting in the moonlight. Raising its lupine muzzle to the sky, it released a triumphant howl, terror ripping through its cornered prey. Then, the werewolf looked down at the men and bird.

Scrambling to their feet, Brian and Chris hid as best they could behind the puffin, all three backing away from the rocks. With one push from its powerful legs, the werewolf leapt from its stony perch and landed with a grace unbefitting its size in front of the hunted. Thick foam frothed from its curled jowls, dripping onto the desert ground. Insanity laden yellow eyes burned within a face full of sweat-matted fur. Even in the darkness, its hot breath could be seen rippling the air around its snout. Raising claws and licking teeth, the lupine creature took a step closer, anticipating its next meal.

Brian had a Mensa moment and cried out, "We want to be werewolves!"

The creature stopped, snarled its upper lip. Confusion swept across its face. "What?"

"Ha! You can't eat us now."

"What!? Why?"

"Because we want to be werewolves. You'd be eating one of your kind. That'd be cannibalism - and that's just gross."

"We eat *people* to *survive*, idiot!"

"Ha, again! You're *not* people. And since we made an official declaration of wanting to become one of you, that makes us not people either."

The werewolf took a step back and scratched his head. "I'll ... I'll have to check with my pack leader."

"That's right, you do that," Brian continued. "You don't want to be breaking any werewolf code now, would you?"

"Code?"

"Yeah, code! All you creatures got codes! Vampires drink blood. Zombies stumble around and smell bad. You have all kinds of rules about the moon, right?"

"Ummm, I guess."

"Of course you do! See? The code! You go check with your pack leader and get back to us, brother. Is it too soon to call you brother? Should we wait until after we're official werewolves?"

The werewolf's head throbbed from Brian's confusing argument and grating voice. With one last vicious growl, the creature turned and bounded away. Waiting until it disappeared into the darkened horizon, Chris said, "Great job, motormouth. Now let's get out of here."

"Now, not so fast."

"What? Why?"

"Meep!?"

"I'd actually like to become one," Brian said, a devious smile sliding across his face.

"Seriously?"

"At least try it out, you know. Hell, I already have more body hair than most of them!"

"You frighten me sometimes."

"Think about it. Sleep all day. Party all night. Eat nothing but meat."

"Well, we all but do that now. I'm not sold."

"Don't you remember 'Howling 2' with Sybil Danning?"

"I'm in!"

"Meep!"

"Excellent! Glad you both see my point," Brian said, wringing his hands together while formulating a plan. "Now all we have to do is wait for..."

Bounding back to the site, the werewolf landed in front of the trio with the same quiet grace as before. Now that he wasn't hiding his eyes behind his hands in fear, Brian took a good look at the creature. Light brown fur covered the creature from head to toe, all along its long arms and legs. Its tail was long and bushy while its bottom ribs poked against its thin waist. "I spoke with my pack leader and..."

"You're a coyote, aren't you?" Brian interrupted.

"What?"

"Coyote, not a wolf. Right?"

"It *is* the South West, you know!"

"Yeah, I get that. I'm just trying to figure out if we should really call you a werewolf or not. Werecoyote just doesn't have the same zest."

Scowling, the werewolf barked, "We prefer lunar inhibitionally challenged individuals!"

Brian held his hands in front of him, palms out as if they could protect him from an impending attack, which he would probably deserve. "Okay, okay. Just checking."

Pinching the bridge of its snout between its eyes, the werewolf continued, "I checked with my pack leader and he stated that you were correct about the code."

"I *knew* there was a code!" Brian gave high-fives to both Chris and the puffin, during which the werewolf rubbed his throbbing eyes with the heels of his hands.

"Are you done yet?" the werewolf snapped.

"Sorry," Brian replied. "Please continue."

"But to be a part of the pack, we must put you through a set of challenges."

" 'We'?" Brian asked, peering over the werewolf's shoulder. He saw four pair of glowing yellow eyes floating through the night. And he could have sworn he heard snickering. "How many are 'we'?"

"That doesn't matter! What matters is if you pass the challenges or not. Tonight is almost over, so meet me here tomorrow when the moon is highest in the sky..."

"Midnight."

The werewolf's eyes burned with such fire that Brian could feel heat slapping his face.

Stepping away from the werewolf, Brian said. "Okay, okay. It's highest at midnight, so I just thought it'd be easier to say 'midnight' than go into a partial soliloquy about a celestial body's zenith."

After a throaty growl, the werewolf continued. "*When the moon is at its highest*, meet here and your challenges shall begin."

Confused, Chris actually stepped forward. "Ummm, two problems with that. We don't know where 'here' is and we don't know where our RV is."

Frustrated, the werewolf slapped his paw to his face and slid it over his snout. "Turn around, morons!!"

Brian, Chris and the puffin looked over their shoulders to see row upon row of parked RVs. They turned back around and the werewolves were gone. Refusing to acknowledge their oversight, the trio went back to their RV to contemplate what the challenges may be.

Once inside, Brian plopped into the plush recliner while the puffin hopped up to the driver's seat. Cracking open three beers and handing them out, Chris drank his while pacing. "What do you think they'll have us do?"

After taking a long draw of his liquid replenishment, Brian pondered, "Maybe tear out the heart of a rival pack's leader?"

"Dude!"

"Meep!"

"What? What'd I say?" Brian asked.

Chris grimaced as he continued to pace. "Why do you have to be so intense all the time? 'Rip out the heart...?' What's *wrong* with you?"

Before Brian could defend himself and counterattack, a heavy knock at the door shook the RV. Being the closest, Chris turned and opened the door. "Hello?"

The night air greeted Chris and his beer. All was quiet and serene - except for the flaming brown paper bag resting in front of the door. Chris screamed. "Aaaaaaaaah!! There's a paper bag on fire!"

As Chris raised his leg to stomp it out, Brian sat up in his chair and yelled, "Don't! Dude, it's a flaming bag of poo!"

"Aaaaaah!! What do I do? What do I do?"

"Use the beer!! It's not flammable! Pour your beer on it!"

"No way!! I can't. *I just can't*!"

"Meep!"

Chris watched as the fire tried to spread to the wooden step on which the bag rested. The licking flames tested the RV's siding. Chris knew he had to make a decision before all hope, and the RV, was lost. A tear rolled down his cheek.

Screaming and crying, he stomped on the flames to extinguish them. Even after the fire was gone, Chris hit a certain point of psychosis of not being able to deal with his choice. He still stomped. He still cried. He still yelled, however it was into his bottle as he pressed it against his lips.

Brian looked at Gwar and said, "And he has the nerve to call *me* intense? What a jackass!"

"Meep."

Beer bottle emptied, Chris stood on the small step, panting and wiping his runny nose along his sleeves. Brian shouted at him, "Don't be dragging your poo-shoes through the RV! Take 'em off and keep them outside!"

Chris followed Brian's suggestion and left his shoes outside. Once he reentered the RV Brian yelled. "Where'd you get the pink fuzzy socks?"

"Uhhhh," Chris stalled, hoping for a good idea. None came. He waved his hand in front of Brian's face. "These are not the pink fuzzy socks that you seek."

"Like hell they're not! Your Jedi mind tricks won't work with me! How did you get them back?"

"Dude, you were right in front of me when I got them back!"

"We were in Canada! In a blizzard! Sent to find the Wendigo!"

"So? You were there when I got these back!"

Gwar, the puffin, finished his beer and hunkered down in the driver's seat. Talk of snow and blizzards made him a bit homesick. He looked out the windshield to the sky full of stars, the same stars he would see every night back home. Refusing to look away, he tried to stay focused on his memories, but his eyelids grew heavy. Soon, he drifted off to a much-needed slumber, only to reawake the next morning to Brian and Chris still arguing.

"What happens in Canada stays in Canada!"

"Not when it involves one of my socks!"

"Dude, we don't even know how we got them in the first place!"

"Doesn't matter!"

Mildly annoyed, Gwar decided to leave the two men bicker between themselves and forage for breakfast. Within a community as friendly as RV living pigeon racers, the quest posed little challenge. In fact, a few hours of enjoying conversation - much more interesting than what Brian or Chris could offer - among the inhabitants led into a nice lunch. He even took a ride with one of them into Las Vegas City proper for a few rounds of craps, a few hands of blackjack, a Cirque De Soliel show, and a hearty buffet. By the time he returned to the RV Park, night had fallen, and he still had plenty of time to round up Brian and Chris for the first of the werewolf's challenges. Of course, they were still arguing.

"Meep!"

"What?" Brian snapped. "Can't you see we're in the middle of a discussion?"

"Meep!"

"Almost twenty-four hours? There's no way I can believe that we argued for that long."

"Dude," Chris said and pointed down. Both men looked to the floor and saw mounds of empty beer bottles, large enough to cover their feet and shins.

"Okay, okay," Brian conceded. "Maybe we get a little carried away some times, but..."

"Meep!"

"You're right, Gwar, the first challenge is starting soon. We should go."

The puffin impatiently tapped his webbed foot while waiting for the men to get ready, which consisted of more bickering about which beer to bring.

"Meep!"

Finally ready, the trio left the RV and walked to the rock outcropping just beyond the border of the parked vehicles. Within minutes, and surprisingly before Brian and Chris could find something else to argue about, the werewolf returned.

"Greetings, recruits," the werewolf said. Are you ready to begin your journey into the mystical realm of lycanthropes?"

"Yes."

"Excellent!" the werewolf replied, wringing his hands together, licking his chops. "One little known fact about werewolves is our favorite thing to eat is a snope."

"Snope?"

"Yes. Tasty little creatures. But, they're tough to catch. If you want to become a werewolf, you need to show us that you're excellent hunters. Tonight, we want you each to catch us a snope."

"A snope hunt?" Brian asked. "Is this anything like a snipe hunt?"

The werewolf took a step backward and glanced around while his fingers fidgeted. "Uuuuuh, no. Snipes aren't real. Snopes are."

"Oh. Okay."

"Good. Now that we're clear on that, you can begin. Now!" With that, the werewolf bounded away into the inky desert night.

Brian turned to see Chris and the puffin glaring at him.

"What? What'd I do now?"

"You couldn't think to ask him what the hell a snope even looks like?" Chris yelled.

"Meep!" Gwar agreed.

"Hey! I didn't hear either one of you ask!"

"It was your idea to become werewolves in the first place! We're just along for the ride!"

"Meep!"

"Oh, whatever! You two are just as excited to become werewolves as I am! Now, let's start looking for some snope."

"And what exactly do you suggest we look for?"

"He said it was their favorite thing to eat. Just look for something tasty looking!"

Rolling their eyes at Brian's lame suggestion, Chris wandered in one direction as Gwar waddled in another. Minutes turned into hours as Gwar checked behind dried tumbled weeds, Chris lifted rocks, and Brian got hungry and started eating cactus again. Brian started cataloguing the different type of cacti in his head, remembering which tasted better, or hurt less as he ate them. He found agave to be his favorite, no spines and the sap was thick and syrupy. He also noted that the agave was commonly used for distillation and production of mezcal. The most popular form of mezcal was tequila and...

"Meep!"

Brian, oft easily distracted and known to go on tangents, refocused his efforts into finding the enigmatic snope. Disgruntled, he wondered if Chris might be right thinking the werewolves sent them on a snipe hunt. Until Chris's voice shattered the silence.

"Guys!! I think I found it!"

Brian and Gwar ran to where Chris jumped around like a gorilla thumping his chest. He even sounded like one as he grunted, "Look! Look!"

Brian and Gwar stooped down to look at where Chris pointed.

"Meep."

"I think you're right, Gwar," Brian said. "I don't think it's a snope."

"What!" Chris yelled, his face getting visibly red, even in the darkness. "What could it possibly be?"

"Meep."

"A big ol' dried up turd."

Chris's rage caused his goatee burst into flame, leaving only charred ash behind. "*Oh come on*!! We've been out here for *hours*!! Look, the sun is starting to rise!! Snopes aren't real! They sent us on a snipe hunt!"

"Hey!" Brian snapped back. "Just because we haven't found one doesn't mean they don't exist. We haven't found a way to grow our hair back, but that doesn't mean we should stop trying."

Grumbling, Chris gave up. "Fine! Let's just go back to the RV and meet back at the rocks at midnight to see if the werewolf shows up."

After being awake and frustrated for over forty hours, the men slipped into the realm of Morpheus with ease. As the night before, they needed Gwar to get them ready.

"Meep!"

"Fine!" Chris yelled. "The damn bird nags worse than you."

"What?" Brian yelled back. "I don't nag!"

"Like hell you don't! Every time I'm five minutes late for anything, you're calling my cell phone."

"That's because for *anything* you're late *every time*!"

"Meep!"

"Sorry," both men said in unison.

Finally focused, the three left their RV and returned to the rock outcropping. Once again the werewolf arrived at midnight. "So, do you have any tasty snopes for me?"

"Well…" Brian started.

"We think you're just messing with us and snopes don't exist," Chris said.

Brian elbowed his friend and hissed, "Dude, don't be so rude."

The werewolf offered a Cheshire grin and raised his hands while turning to walk away. "Hey, if you three don't want to werewolves, that's fine by me. I'll just be on my way."

"Dude!" Brian yelled at Chris.

Chris sighed. "Fine. I'm sorry. Mister Werewolf. Just because we didn't find any doesn't mean they don't exist. I was out of line to imply you were lying to us."

"Apology accepted. Now follow me." The trio did as instructed walking behind the werewolf as he circled around to the other side of the large rocks. Waiting for them were three folding chairs around a small table covered by a cloth.

"I have a bad feeling about this," Chris mumbled as they made their way to the table.

"This is our next challenge?" Brian asked.

"Yes. It's a challenge designed to see what you're willing to sacrifice, to see how much of your heart you're willing to devote to us. After extensive research we found very little means more to you than this." The werewolf pulled the sheet from the table to expose six bottles of beer. Out of Pavlovian response, drool dripped from their chins as Brian and Chris reached for the beer.

"Stop!" the werewolf barked. Brian and Chris obeyed. "Sit!"

Sitting in the folding chair provided, Brian, Chris and Gwar did as instructed.

"Place you hands ... and wings ... on the table, palms down ... or whatever is anatomically equivalent."

Confused, but still salivating, the trio did as instructed. The werewolf popped the caps from all six bottles, then balanced a bottle on the back of each hand or wing. "Okay, guys, the beers are all yours."

Gwar had no difficulty reaching over and snatching the first bottle with his beak, which he quickly emptied down his gullet. Despite the lack of opposable thumbs, he grabbed the second beer with ease.

Brian opted for the more clumsy route, shifting his right hand and knocking the bottle to the table. Beer spilled and foamed, but he grabbed the fallen bottle and brought it to his mouth. Even his natural ineptitude couldn't mess up getting the second bottle.

Chris struggled, feeling it deep within his heart and soul. He tried the trick he learned from Gwar by using his mouth to retrieve the first bottle. But every time he tried, he found his Cro-Magnon like arms simply refused to bend the necessary way. Every time he brought his lips close enough, a mild tremor ran through his arm, threatening to topple the bottle.

"Dude, just spill the beer," Brian said.

"*Not on my watch!*" Chris yelled, turning his head sideways he tried again, his tongue leaving his mouth and looking more like a monkey's prehensile tail. But that still wasn't enough.

"You'll only lose like half an ounce."

"That's half an ounce too much! And the violent shift will cause a premature expulsion of carbonation changing the viscosity, unnaturally altering the texture, affecting *all twelve* ounces!"

"You have issues."

"I prefer to call them priorities." Finally admitting there was no other way, Chris reached deep within his soul and summoned the spirit of Mr. Miyagi. With speed unbefitting his hairy knuckles and gnarled hand, he slid it from under the bottle and snatched it by the neck, all within the blink of an eye. But it wasn't fast enough, the bottle tipping just enough to allow a splash to escape. The spilled beer rolled down the natural slope of the lopsided table.

"No. No, no, no, nonononononono," Chris whispered as he chugged the first beer. Finished, this freed his right hand to remove the second beer from the top of his left hand. Once he had the second bottle secured, he smashed his face to table, licking up the spill before it could fall from the edge to be lost forever in the absorbent desert sand.

Rolling his eyes, Brian turned to see the werewolf laughing. He heard more laughter coming from behind the rocks as well. Wiping a tear from his eye, the werewolf composed himself enough to say, "Very well done. We're going to do that again, but this time you three will be blindfolded."

"No!" Chris cried out. "No more! The flaming bag of poo! The snope hunt! Now this? No more! You're just hazing us with no intention of letting us join!"

The werewolf's mood changed, angered by Chris's audacity.

"Listen..."

Still fueled by the fire sparked by having to spill beer, Chris continued his verbal rampage. "No! You listen! I've stepped in poo before! And I've wasted hours looking for something that never existed many times before tonight. But no one – *no one* – makes me spill beer twice in one day! Either we become werewolves now, or you can get the hell out of here."

Snarling, the werewolf fought to hold back his true fury. "Our pack leader..."

"Can go to hell, that sick, twisted bastard!!"

"... is standing right behind these rocks," the werewolf concluded.

An eardrum-splitting howl ripped through the air as the pack leader jumped over the rocks. He landed next to the other werewolf, dwarfing their tormentor. The pack leader had no want for muscle, not a pinch of fat could be seen, nor hint of skeleton poking through his skin. No imperfection could be found in his thick coat of fur, from head to toe. When he spoke his voice rumbled through Chris's very soul. "Is there a problem?"

After a prodigious gulp, Chris replied, "I'm guessing we're not in the club, huh?"

"Well, one of you made it."

Confused, Chris and Brian wondered what he meant until they looked around and realized Gwar was no longer there. Just then another howl split the night air. It was not as impressive as the pack leader's, but it held the resonance of triumph. A third werewolf bounded out from behind the rocks, landing in front of Brian.

"Gwar?" Brian asked.

"Yes, Brian, it's me."

"I like the new look."

"Glad to hear it. Now, about trying to eat me a couple of days ago..." The new Gwar stood before Brian, towering over him by a foot. His upper lip curled into a snarl, a froth of saliva dripping from his twisted muzzle. Angry growls rumbled from his throat with every pant, hot breath lashing at Brian's face.

Unwavering, Brian stood nonplussed, drinking his beer. "You gonna eat me? Tear me up; gnaw on my bones a little? Buddy, you ain't got nothin' on some of the women I've dated! Do your worst."

Fury bristled the werewolf's fur, spiking up along his arms and back despite being nappy and matted. His eyes lost to rage, he lifted his right arm, frightful claws glistening in the moon's light. All his anger focused into one swipe.

Brian expected slicing, dicing and possible decapitation. Instead he received much worse – an open handed slap. He dropped his beer. "OOOOOOOOWWWWW!!!"

Chris watched as his friend doubled over in pain while both hands went to his throbbing cheek. "Dude, he totally bitch slapped you."

"That's so uncool, man!" Brian cried.

"Are... are you crying? He made you squirt some tears?"

"It really stings!"

"He put a little extra 'pimp' in his 'pimp hand' didn't he?"

"This is so not funny!"

"It's all in your perspective, dude."

Still crying, Brian turned to the pack leader. "Why him? Why Gwar and not us?"

All three werewolves laughed as the leader answered. "Revenge."

Brian and Chris looked at each other, then back to the leader. "Do we know you?"

The pack leader laughed again as his muscles rippled. He slouched forward as bones snapped and shifted, dropping to all fours. His ears and muzzle shifted, his teeth went square while fingers and toes molded into hooves. His fur didn't disappear, merely changed color. Where a mighty werewolf once stood, was now a goat with the words "Love Machine" imprinted on his right hindquarter.

"Baaah."

"The Tijuana goat!" Brian and Chris screamed in unison. "But why would you be mad at us?"

The goat huffed a snort of discontent and shifted back into

werewolf form, the sights and sounds leaving both men feeling queasy. "Why!? You took me to Canada!"

"Oh, come on! Canada's not that bad."

"I got possessed by the Wendigo spirit!"

"We tried to..."

"It didn't work!"

"But you look much better now."

"Only after I carried a contagion to Harrisburg while looking for you two."

"Maybe that's why they called it 'goat pox'?"

"You think?! After I couldn't find you guys, I decided to hike back to Tijuana with my cult followers."

"Well... how'd you become a werewolf?"

"Long story. Now, I want my socks back!"

Chris took a step back and pouted. "But I *like* these socks. They make my feet feel happy."

"Too bad! They're mine!"

Still pouting, Chris sat on the ground and removed his shoes. He stood and handed the fuzzy, pink socks back to Love Machine, the werewolf pack leader. Snatching them from Chris's hand, he growled, "You have until sunset tomorrow to get out of my desert."

With an uneven chorus of howls, the werewolves loped away. Chris flopped to the ground, depressed about his socks. However, hope filled his heart as he watched the sun peek over the horizon, signaling a new day ripe with new possibilities. His good feelings slipped away when he noticed that Brian, once more bored, was eating cactus again...

INSIDE THE MINDS OF MONKEYS

JEFF: Can I say just one thing? Puffin?

CHRIS: That was great!

BRIAN: That was hysterical! Well, first of all, we were thinking about werewolves and many of the stories, much like vampires, where a character gets turned and other characters try to save him. We did that with vampires, granted in our own unique little way. We just didn't feel like it would be good to try to do it again. So we came up with the idea that we wanted to become werewolves.

C: Correct me if I'm wrong but this is one of the few stories that we actually brainstormed together.

B: Well, we did brainstorm a lot of them together but this was definitely a little different.

C: For most of the other stories, we talked a little, and then whoever the primary writer was went off and did his own thing, much like the rogues we are.

B: Right. This story had a sticking point. We didn't know what to do with it. We knew we had to do werewolves for this book. They are such a classic creature that we absolutely had to do it. We were just bouncing ideas back and forth and until we realized this idea was new, for us to want to be werewolves. No one has ever done this, to my knowledge, in popular culture.

C: And I think this story was actually due early on and Brian kept delaying it because he kinda knew where he wanted it to go and he knew where he wanted to end up but he didn't know where to start. And then he read an article…

B: …in Sports Illustrated, of all places, about this pigeon race in Las Vegas.

C: He brought it to a meeting one time and showed it me like "Dude! How great is this?" As soon as I read it… Puffin. I said, "Dude, we have to have a puffin and enter it into a pigeon race!"

B: We need a flightless bird in a pigeon race. Who else but us would do that? Well, the characters of us.

C: 'Cause the characters of us are sure that there's no such thing as a flightless bird.

B: Plus, puffins just look funny. That's all... So we knew we wanted to do a werewolf story set in the desert, more like a coyote werewolf, which is kinda different for the genre in itself. We knew that the pigeon race takes place in the desert with a puffin, a flightless bird. And we knew that we wanted to become werewolves and they haze us. So it's not just us making fun of ourselves. It's us having others make fun of us too. Of course, we did the classic hazing tricks like the flaming bag of poo. We're smart enough to realize that it's a flaming bag of poo but due to the motivation involved, we still fall for it. We had to fall for it. We also really solidified that Chris loves beer more than... anything!

C: Well, more than my shoes...

B: We wanted to bring the goat back in. We had a feeling he would become a fan favorite. As a side note, we have been told on more than one occasion that he's the favorite character of the book.

J: Sweet! I rock! Go Love Machine!

B: Of course, the goat is the werewolf and the one hazing us. We came up that idea because we needed a reason for the werewolves to hate us, other than the fact that we're just ... well ... *us* being goofballs. And we realized that if the goat was the leader of the pack, it would give them a motivation to hate us and haze us. And then ultimately, they turn the puffin into a werewolf and he bitch slaps me. I think that's the comedy. Of all the things, I think getting bitch slapped is the ultimate in pain and agony.

J: The one thing that I was impressed with is the ability to use the puffin and incorporate him as a character that *never* freakin' talks.

B: He says, "meep."

J: And that's all he says! But by the way you set him up and by the way that you two respond to him, you know that the puffin has said something and you know what the puffin says. To be able to pull that off is impressive. It's not what I would call a traditional comedy thing, but it's some really good comedy.

B: Now again, Chris, I think you said this was another of your favorite stories...

C: Oh absolutely! I loved the narrator part. Sometimes in our stories, the narrator is almost another character, and this story really highlights that. And at one point, the puffin even corrects the narrator.

J: Third wall... What's that?

C: Almost poking fun at that kind of convention. 'Cause we just can't be confined...

B: We're rabid wolverines! You can't stop us! You can merely hope to contain us!

C: We like to push against the wall.

B: We're wolverines! WOOOOOOOOO!

J: Can I quit this job?

B & C: NO!

J: Damn...

THE DRUNKEN COMIC BOOK MONKEYS VS. DRUNKENSTEIN

... The span of my future is like a sweeping gesture, flowing expansively outwards from me. But what to do with it? This is not a question posed by all living things. It is not a struggle of the sentient, nor even a cry of the self-conscious, lest dogs and squirrels be concerned beyond their innate programming. It is the awareness of one's freewill that leads one to despair over future events and one's proper place in them. It is the process of seeing what one can do that leads us to want to build, to manufacture, to procreate. It is seeing what others have done that leads us to envy, to covet, to want beyond our need. For some it is knowing that others have outperformed one's own abilities which makes them strive toward creation, to plan outside our scope, to play the role of demiurge...

" 'Create me the perfect vessel,' he says.

" 'Why?' says I.

" 'For respect, for remembrance, for revenge,' he says.

"And I know what he means, so I do it.

"I find a motley collection of body parts, each designed to fit a specific need.

" 'Beat them at their own game,' he says. 'They think they can drink. They think they have partied. They think they know it all. Well, we'll just show them...'

"I flip on the current and...

"Alive...alive! It's...alive!"

* * *

Hereafter follows an honest exchange between two pathetic humans. They take no real solace in interaction, unless it be in their incessant bickering. Here they fight over a dropped chicken wing. That they should be indoctrinated into society without question, an occasional raised eyebrow notwithstanding, while my beautiful creation is doomed to be ever left outside the impenetrable globe of human acceptance is as arbitrary as a birthright.

"Dude, I think it's alive! Man! I guess cleaning the floors is a once a week task at Melons!" Chris said.

"Stop being a sissy!" Brian accused. "It's just some dirt. Stop complaining and get the chicken wing I dropped!"

"Remarkably, genius, this 'dirt' has more hair than I do!"

"And this is shocking why?" Brian mocked.

"On its legs..."

"DUDE! Walk away nice and easy. Whatever you do, don't turn your back on it."

"...and I thought the garden spider was bad!"

"Wait! Dude! Where's the chicken wing? I told you to get out of there, but I never said leave the chicken wing!"

"It's gone."

"Gone! What do you mean 'gone'?"

"Ever watch those shows on The Discovery channel where they speed up a bunch of ants stripping a carcass?"

"Yeah..."

"I just saw it firsthand. But the same effect reproduced in real time. It was like watching you eat a box of Slim Jims."

"Whatever! Aw, dude! It was a drumette!"

"Yeah, well it went that way. Have at it. I'd recommend an aspirator, a blow torch, and some thick chain mail, though."

"You're ridiculous! It's like you don't even care about the wing that got away!"

"Ummm…there's 200 of them…"

"Point being?"

"There's only the two of us…"

"Precisely why you're being rationed! This wing party is great! Melons Bar & Grille is the coolest place on Earth!"

"Ya know, I was thinking about it…"

"When did that start? And why?"

"…if we spent fifty dollars at each of our twenty-five stops, then we spent $1,250 to get this free wing party…"

"And that, my friend, is why we got a wing party for each of us! WOOOOOOOOOOOOOOO! 200 free wings makes me happy! But 400 free wings makes me…tingly…"

"GUH! That's it. I'm sick."

"SWEET! Another seamless megalomaniacal scheme."

"Two more pitchers, please! And you can take his glass. He'll take a can. Yes, he needs a new straw. And, yes, he needs a lemon…"

***

When first he came, the one who commissioned my services was taken aback by my creation. But the yearning for revenge does bear its own nepenthe and the thought of a well-deserved comeuppance allays even the most deep rooted regret.

"It's…it's hideous! I mean, what you've created is even more gruesome than I thought it would be! Oh, wait…does it…does it have feelings?"

"Yes, yes…and it's very aggressive, just as you asked. Oh and 'it's' a him, so take care to use proper references."

"Can it…he…drink? In insane quantities, I mean?"

"Yes, yes…he is the ultimate party animal."

"Then he's perfect! Does he know tricks? I mean, like, drinking games and how to spin bottles like they did in *Cocktail*?"

"Yes, yes…see this plug at the back of his brain?"

"You mean the one that looks like…oh, perfect! That's for a

USB cable, isn't it? He's upgradeable straight from the internet!"

"Yes, yes...you get what you pay for here. Well, in your case, twenty bucks really went pretty far. I'm just a sucker for a revenge case."

"Oh, this is perfect! Thank you. Thank you so much! Brian and Chris are really gonna get what they deserve! And you know the best part?"

"Yes, yes...you'll take away the one thing they're good at... disgrace them at their only strength. It'll crush them. Tell me...what did they do to you that your desire for revenge is so...elevated?"

"It would take too long to explain. But here, take this. This is their book. They made me edit this, fix all their careless mistakes, read their juvenile humor. Read this and it will all make sense."

"Hmmm...yes, yes...I profess I'm not an overly avid reader."

"Don't worry. This book will change you. But it definitely won't increase your desire to read."

***

"Dude! Did you see that?" Brian asked.

"Honestly, I can't look away from the phenomena you call 'eating'," Chris replied.

"That woman totally bumped into me. And copped a...wait... what? You're watching me eat? That's gross."

"Echoing sentiments, dude! How do your fingers even move that way?"

"DUDE! I'm eating!"

"It's...just plain impossible! Are you like quadruple-jointed? Even your pinkie is..."

"...designed to shred the food even as these two digits push the bones out of the way...I saw it on animal planet once."

"I'm gonna be sick!"

"Stop ignoring the point, dude. That woman totally felt me up!"

"Guh! I'm gonna be sicker!"

"You don't wear jealousy well. Come to think of it, you don't wear anything well."

"Yeah, and your approval ratings matter this much. Hey, look what I found in the parking lot for you!"

"That middle finger gets close to my wings again and I'm not responsible for..."

"Dude, what's on your shoulder?"

"I'm immune to your feeble mind tricks, dude. Did you forget I'm a genius?"

"All signs to the contrary, huh? Actually, for as disturbingly often as you mention it; it's quite a simple thing to ignore."

"Whatever! You know your problem is..."

"Dude, don't move...on your shoulder..."

"What? What is it? Is it a spider? I'm totally flicking it your way ... AAAAHHH! You touched it!"

"See? It's not a question of intelligence. It's a matter of predictability. It was a piece of paper. Look, it's a note. Now let's see what it says...oh, unbelievable..."

"What? What is it already?"

"It's an invitation to a party..."

"For me? See, I told you I'm the hot one!"

"Whatever! Actually, it's for both of us."

"Oh! What kind of party? When? Where?"

"Well, it's here."

"Here? At Melons?"

"Yeah, seems a bit odd, huh?"

"Considering our friends, not really."

"Nice. It doesn't say who it's for, but...oh...this is interesting."

"What is it? Start talking or fork that over!"

"It's a drinking party. Oh, and it's totally like we're being called out."

"Huh? How's that?"

"Well, 'in attendance will be The Drunken Comic Book Monkeys. Come watch them put their sole talent to the test and lose big time'."

"It says that?"

"Sure enough. Starts in three hours. Should we split to get refreshed and meet back here a few minutes before it starts?"

"Dude, did you forget who we are or something? We have a closet in the backroom with our 'refreshing' items. There's no need to leave. Besides, I'm still eating. Do you think there will be food at this party or should I get another plate of wings?"

"Unreal! You totally have an illness! Wait! I think there's a vaccine for tapeworms."

***

"Dude! Was that your stomach growling? Or did your stack of wing bones shift?" Chris asked.

"Real funny, smart guy!" Brian replied. "That was the outside sign being turned on!"

"Oh! Hey, nice. The sign is a party announcement."

"It's about time. Place is kind of dead for a party."

"I was thinking that, too. Oh, now we're talking! Three buses just pulled in."

"Three?"

"Yep. And they look packed, too."

"Oh, check it out. They're pulling some tables together in the middle of the restaurant. Guess that's where the event will take place."

"Yeah, sure looks that way. Well, here comes the crowd. Get your drinking face on."

***

"Ladies and gentleman! Welcome to this special event at Melons!" A waitress said to the bustling crowd.

"Dude! This place is packed!"

"I've never seen this many people in here before."

"Hey, that guy looks familiar..."

"Oh, yeah. Remember when we spilled the 'guaranteed to eat

your gut' hot sauce on some guy's shoes?"

"Ah! That's him?"

"Yep. And that guy over there is the one who slipped on the onion ring that fell off your plate and rolled away."

"Ooooooh! And he wiped out while carrying two pitchers. Yeah, you're right. Hey, isn't that..."

"Dude, I see nothing but people who probably want us dead."

"Doesn't look good for the home team, huh?"

"Guys!" the waitress said, beckoning Brian and Chris. "Yeah, you two!"

"Dude, the Melons waitress wants us."

"Finally! Oh, wait..."

"You two go to that end of the table. We're about to announce you," the waitress hissed.

"Dude, that just brought a tear to my eye. I've never been announced!"

"Yeah, well, I think it's gonna get real uncomfortable for us."

"Ladies and gentlemen, at this end of the table, the Drunken Comic Book Monkeys!" the waitress announced.

"Are they chanting 'duuuuuuuude'?"

"Nope. You should recognize that sound. They're totally booing us."

"Nice! This is getting a bit tense."

The waitress rolled her eyes. "And now at this end of the table..."

"Dude, who could it be?"

"I dunno. Could be any of these people!"

"Dude! Did you see the guy who just walked in?"

"You mean the abnormally huge guy with the trench coat and top hat?"

"That's the one..."

"Dude, he's flat out immense...he's so gonna take us apart..."

"Dude, I think he could out-drink this whole restaurant!"

"I think he can beat up this whole restaurant!"

"True. If it comes to that, exit plan Beta..."

"Dude! What the hell is that?"

"Any means possible..."

"...at this end of the table..." The waitress then paused and whispered to the new arrival, "Wait, what's your name?"

"Dude! What is that guy?"

"Some kind of cipher."

"What does that mean?"

"He's an artificial life form. Created from spare body parts..."

"You mean like Franken..."

"...at this end of the table..." the waitress continued her announcement. "Drunkenstein!"

"Dude, that's just wrong."

"I think we're in deep doodoo!"

"Doodoo? What are you? Four?"

***

"This is a three round event," the waitress explained. "The first event will be the table drink. We'll cover the tabletops with full pint glasses. The first table to be cleared wins the first round. Both of the Monkeys will participate at the same time. The first two events are worth 25% and the third event is worth 50%. In the event of a tie, we will have a fourth round, winner takes the title. Drunkenstein, do you have any questions? A head shake means 'no'. Monkeys, questions?"

"Ummm...what kind of beer will it be?"

The waitress grinned. "Since there are two of you, the tall one will get stouts and heavy hop beer. The shorter one gets a variety of beer that takes fruit. Any other questions?"

"GUH!...hops? Can we get those reversed?"

"No. This is your handicap for having a team member," the waitress said.

"Can I give up my team member to switch the beers?"

"You're stupid!"

"You were thinking it too!"

"Yep. Hope to see you on the other side, dude!"

***

"Ha, ha, ha, ha!" the waitress laughed at Brian and Chris, a sound they were not unfamiliar with. "You guys were pathetic! The Drunken Comic Book Monkeys drank 6 beers between them. And they both look too ill to continue. Sorry about that, but too bad, guys! Drunkenstein drank 82 pints in five minutes flat."

"Dude! Did you watch him? He's like a machine!"

"I couldn't look away from his right arm. Dude, that's a twenty-two inch bicep!"

"Yep. You see his neck?"

"How can you miss it? It's like a size thirty-four!"

"Yep. That's a throat designed for chugging. It's double normal size. How did we get roped into this?"

"Remember, earlier? We're predictable."

"Who could possibly hate us this much?"

"Ummm...I'm thinking you could pretty much take your pick..."

***

"For the second event, beer pong!" the waitress announced with glee.

"Dude, beer pong...we have a chance."

"I'm not thinking so."

"Dude, we're great at beer pong! And it's ten cups instead of the traditional six, so that plays to our advantage!"

"True, but I think that explains his left arm. Less muscular, but it looks steady...had to come from a guy who was over seven feet tall. That's not a reach. It's a wingspan!"

"First up, ladies and gentlemen, the Monkeys," the waitress announced.

"Ok, dude, make this count."

"Made it! Whew! I was sweating the first one."

"Nice! Dude, that's just what we needed."

"YOUSE GUYS CAN GO AGAIN! I'M GONNA TAKE YOU APART ANYWAYS! HA, HA, HA!"

"Dude, Drunkenstein just let us go again. That is so not a good sign!"

"Forget it! Just focus on sinking this. Just play it one toss at a time."

"GUH! Dude, I moon-hopped it! He flexed his arm just as I was letting go!"

"You sank it! That was beautiful! A little unorthodox, but beautiful! Now we have a little bit of momentum. Let's just keep the pressure on him."

"Ummm...dude...are you allowed to put a ping pong ball between every finger?"

"GUH! I guess if you have six fingers on your throwing hand. 10 wings says he makes all five..."

"Dude, I'm not taking that bet. I'll be too sick to eat anyway."

"Three...four...and five. He made all five! This is an old fashioned beat-down! Excuse me; miss, would you please check the rules? I don't think that's legal."

"Oh, stop whining! Those pints that you left on the table are paid for, so you got 76 more pints for free waiting for you!" the waitress said.

"What? Why didn't anyone mention this before now? They're getting warm!"

"Stop fussing!" the waitress admonished them. "Ten minutes ago you both made sour faces over them! What difference will it make if they're warm?"

"Guh! 'Cause now we get to drink the ones we like!"

"Yeah, well you'd better like them because the rules stipulate that you have to drink them before we move on to round three," the waitress said, holding up the rules.

"Seriously? This is ridiculous! Well, then you need to check the rules to see if what he's doing is legal!"

"Stop fussing, sis! Throw the ball...noooooh, nice! You're gonna try four at once?"

"I'm disgusted with this. Even if I somehow sink them all, he'd still have to let you go before he goes and you'd have to sink four at once, too."

"It's gutsy, but you're right. Do it. Awww, dude! That was terrible! You didn't even bounce two of them!"

"YOU GO NOW, TOO!"

"Dude, why is he always yelling?"

"Dunno...just go. Nice backwards spin. Hey, you got one. Too bad it was a point for him."

"Dude, it was a psych out move. Now he has to hit four after he's practiced sinking five. We're still in this...or not. Dude! He sank all four! We're totally outclassed here."

"Ha, ha! Did you just hear yourself? We're outclassed everywhere we go!"

"Hey, wait! They're going to announce a ruling on this guy."

It was at this juncture that the waitress, acting as Master of Ceremonies, made her announcement to the waiting crowd. I, the creator of the beautiful Drunkenstein, hid in the back of the room, away from the crowd, to observe him in action.

"Ladies and gentleman, Drunkenstein will be disqualified in round two. That means we have a tie, thus far. Round three will begin as soon as the Monkeys catch up on their beer drinking."

***

My astonishment at the next sixty minutes is hard for me to put into words. Not only did the two oafish men consume all of the beer that had been placed in front of them, a task I would have labeled as 'not humanly possible' but they stopped only to argue with one another, a task so fitting to their natures that it seemed as if they didn't even need a subject about which to argue. A childlike bemusement held me enthralled as I figuratively watched their IQ points melt away with the inane stupidity of their conversations. But even more incredulous to me was that each time they paused to argue, they would pull a beer from a pocket in their pants and consume it...as if the beers lined up on the table weren't enough for their wanton ways.

"Dude, I can't see so straight...straightly...sumthin'"

"Yesh...I know what you mean. I can't...can't sit...so... whatever that word ish."

"How long did that take us?"

"Cluelesh...cluel...No clue. I couldn't read my watch even if... even if...I could read it."

"Dude, what do you fig...fig...finger...the next task will be?"

"It'sh a chug. Shure of it."

"How do you...know?"

"They know the chinksh in our armor."

"Dude, let's make a nuisance of ourselves."

"K...We're pretty good at that."

"See those empty beer bottles?"

"Yesh...yesh...yeah."

"Do something...with them."

"K."

His particular form of locomotion would be more correctly identified as swaying, than walking, but somehow it worked for him as he managed to carry himself across the room grabbing up empty beer bottles as he went. Finding any joining of two walls, the Monkey known as Chris rubbed an empty beer bottle with vigor against the corner of the wall. After a short interval, he moved on to find another corner. The beer bottle, through the proper application of friction, remained suspended.

"Dude! You're done already."

"Yep. I hung them in every corner. A little friction on that paint...shtick to the cornersh..."

"Ha ha! That's cool. I tricked that table over there into smacking the tops of their bottles."

"Blew out the bottomsh, huh?"

"Yup!"

"Shweet! Well, dude, it'sh been nishe working with you."

"You bombed?"

"Yup. You?"

"Yeah. I shouldn't have ordered the extra 100 wings. I'm stuffed."

"Oaf! Here comes the waitresh..."

"Ladies and gentlemen! Thanks for your patience, though let's give those Monkeys a hand. That was a lot of beer to put down in just an hour," the waitress said.

"Dude?"

"Yesh?"

"Anybody clapping for us?"

"Not even ush."

"Nice! Clap, stupid!"

"Can't."

"The final round of competition is about to begin. Gather around," the waitress announced.

"Chug...Jusht know it."

"The final round will feature the Monkeys, each with a full pitcher, while Drunkenstein will have two. Quickest finish wins," the waitress said.

"Dude, you suck at chugging! We're done."

"Yep. I jusht want to shee whoshe behind thish."

"MONKEYS! IF I WIN, I GET YOUR 'RESERVED' TABLE!"

"Yeah, you're on!"

"What are you shaying?"

"I get riled easily!"

The waitress smiled. Visions of a monkey-free Melons danced through her head. "Gentlemen...get ready...get set...go..."

"Dude! Dude! DUDE!"

"Drink, shtupid."

"It's over, dude. He drank them both at the same time."

"Guh! Sho unfair."

"Ladies and gentlemen, you're winner is...Drunkenstein!" the waitress said, on the verge of tears from glee.

"Dude, the crowd is clapping aren't they?"

"Yep."

"As a result of his victory, the Monkeys lose their special table. Furthermore, every person here gets a special pass. If you are here when the Monkeys are here, they have to buy you a free round," the waitress informed the crowd.

"*What*?! Dude, that's a lot of green! The short Monkey may be ok with that, but it goes against my principles as an accountant!"

"You shound shober!"

"They're talking money! Nothing sobers me faster!"

"They will also be limited to a two hour window for their visits," the waitress continued.

"Dude, is that cheering or clapping?"

"Both. It'sh good to be loved."

"MONKEYS! NO HARD FEELINGS! HA, HA, HA! WHAT'S SAY I BUY YOUSE GUYS A BEER?"

"Dude, I've seen that look from you before. Usually you're about to go off about how you hate George Lucas!"

"Drunkenshtein, let'sh make a deal."

"WHAT KIND OF DEAL?"

"We'll do a chug. If we win, then we win the whole event. All reshtrictionsh lifted."

"AND IF I WIN, YOU NEVER COME BACK!"

"Dude, what are you doing? I'm tearing up!"

"I need my beer cold to chug. Missh? Could you put three bottlesh in the freezer, pleash?"

"WISE GUY! WHEN THEY COME OUT I'M CHECKING THEM FOR ICE!"

"Of courshe!"

"Dude, why are you doing this? We can't beat this guy! He just drank two pitchers to our one each!"

"Relaxsh. I…got an…ang…"

"Dude, you can't rip off *Heavy Metal: The Movie*!"

"Good call. Ah, here comesh our beer."

The waitress returned to the men carrying with her three bottle of beer just retrieved from the freezer. She gave each a perfunctory examination before passing them out.

"Gentlemen, I have inspected all of the bottles. There is no ice in any of them. Please check for yourselves," the waitress proclaimed.

"THAT ONE LOOKS GOOD! I WANT THAT ONE!"

"Dude! How are we gonna win this? Don't answer! We're loud when we're drunk!"

"Jusht to show we're not shore loshers, when she popsh the topsh, let'sh clink bottlesh!"

"OK! IT'S THE LAST NOISE YOU GUYS WILL BE MAKING HERE. WHEN I WIN YOU HAVE TO LEAVE IMMEDIATELY!"

"Brian, hit hish bottle when I do."

"Dude, I hope you know what you're doing!"

It seemed good sportsmanship to my poor judgment when Brian and Chris carefully used the tip of their bottles to clink hard on the middle of Drunkenstein's beer. My creation was amused but wary, immediately suspicious of their intent to break his bottle. As he had already bested them at this specific event, he was alert to some sort of tomfoolery.

"HEY! YOU TRYING TO BREAK MY BOTTLE TO WIN? HA, HA! YOU'RE OUTTA LUCK!"

"Gentlemen...go!" the waitress said.

"DONE!"

"You're an idiot! I didn't even start yet! This was the dumbest idea..."

"Jusht finish! Missh! Would you kindly check his bottle? I think Drunkenshtein left shome in hish bottle."

"Oh, stop your whining and leav...wait...wait! he's right. Half of his bottle still in here. It's frozen!" the waitress confirmed.

"YOUSE GUYS CHEAT!"

"You checked it firsht, big guy. The rulesh shimply shay firsht one done. You're not done. We win."

"Dude, I don't know how you did that, but I just have one thing to say: Mr. Drunkenstein, we'll be at our table!"

***

"Ladies and Gentlemen, unfortunately, the judges have decided that using beer tricks are not grounds for disqualification if they do not disrupt the nature of the game. Drunkenstein did not finish his beer as it is half frozen. The stupid Monkeys win this thing. Apparently, they'll be here until closing as usual," the waitress mumbled. The crowd groaned, disappointed as well.

"YOUSE GUYS SUCK! I WAS MEANT TO WIN! MY MASTER KNOWS ALL YOUR TRICKS! AND I'M UPDATE READY FROM THE WEB!

"Yesh, well your mashter didn't do all hish homework, huh?"

I could only shake my head. I do not consider myself to be an overly worldly individual, but I thought I had experienced enough in life that I should not be left standing open mouthed at the sheer ridiculousness of the situation that had transpired around me. So lost in thought was I, that I failed to take notice of my co-conspirator's arrival.

"Oh, hi, guys!"

"Hey, Jeff. Wait! What brings Jeff Young out here? And on a school night, no less?"

"Just came to pick up my friend, here."

"You're friend? Drunkenstein?"

"He doeshn't call us hish friendsh, doesh he?"

"Friends? You guys make my life a living hell! I'm just looking for a little payback! And I figured if I could find someone to beat you at your game, it would take you down a peg or two."

"Down a peg or two? It's like you don't even know us! We're already on the bottom peg! Hanging on by a finger each!"

"Well, I hope it wasn't too embarrassing for you."

"No, not really. Since we won…"

"What? How?"

"Schienche, shir. Schienche."

"Yeah next time you better bring your 'A game', Young!"

"This sucks! I hate you guys! Come on, Drunkenstein. I gave up my 401k over this. Maybe I can get a discount from your creator, since you lost."

"MASTER, I'M STAYING WITH THE MONKEYS. THEY CAN TEACH ME THINGS I CANNOT LEARN ON THE INTERNET. THEY'RE COOL!"

"DUDE! He said we're cool…"

"Let'sh get t-shirtsh made! It'sh the only way people will believe ush!"

"I'm tearing up, here. Drunkenstein, you ever see beer pants in action? See, what you do is…"

"THAT'S COOLER THAN COOL! YOU GUYS ROCK!"

…and there you have it….

INSIDE THE MINDS OF MONKEYS

BRIAN: I actually remember the specific place in which we came up with this idea. We were walking through Charlotte, NC quasi drunk...
JEFF: Shocker...
CHRIS: I'm pretty sure the mayor of Charlotte is cringing now.
B: We were trying to escape the ominous gaze of a three story Casey Kahne looking down upon us. So we were running through a construction site.
C: Serpentine
B: You know, I think it was serpentine... 'cause we completely ignored the "Do Not Enter" sign.
C: I think it was more of a stagger at that point...
B; We were just starting to talk about doing a Reflux addition and it was early in the process of coming up with ideas for new stories. We brought up the Mummy and then Chuckles over here just started laughing and blurts out though glassy, teary eyes, "The Mummy versus Drunkenstein." And that's all it took.
C: Well, you can't have a horror canon without Frankenstein. It's one of the classics. But it's such a well done piece that to try to mimic it is almost sacrilegious.
B: Even to satirize it would be difficult.
C: I think you need to go completely off the wall and say, "You know what, we are so sorry, but we couldn't help ourselves."
B: When we started talking about it, we came up with the creature first. We were having some issues around who made it and the motivation for it. We were sort of in our jag that we were going to make Jeff the villain.
C: And the funny thing is that I don't think we actually discussed that prior to doing it. When we showed up for the meeting, you were laughing and I was laughing. Neither one of us could wait to tell the other. And it turned out we both wanted to make Jeff the villain.

J: A common thread...

C: And then I think we had the discussion that it might be too much, having him as the villain in two stories.

B: Through clever spacing... done by our editor, by the way.

C: He fixed it.

B: FIX IT!

C: But the idea ultimately behind Drunkenstein was that we should get beaten, if we're going lose, at our own strength.

B: And the only way we win is by watching a really obscure video about the beer ice trick.

C: I actually spent more time researching dumb beer tricks than potatoes. Which are part of the nightshade family, I'll have you know...

B: Wow...

J: What I want to know is what steals the chicken wing?

C: Furball

J: Okay.

C: That's all we need to know.

J: Okay.

C: I just wouldn't go charging after it without goggles, a mask and an acetylene torch. Chuckles over there almost did.

B: It's a chicken wing, dude!

C: You watch the Discovery Channel! You don't go into that place!!

B: Hey! If the Mythbusters go in, it's alright!

J: Marlon Perkins sending Jim in after the chicken wing. He's covered by the Mutual of Omaha...

B: Jim, quit screwing with the anaconda!

C: The funny part is that there are 400 chicken wings on the table. And he's suddenly concerned that he lost one.

B: Chicken wings are not immaterial!

C: Then he finds out it's a drumette. That's when he really went nuts.

B: Drumettes rock! Mr. Editor, anything about the story?

J: I really think the bit parts to Drunkenstein are hilarious... the ridiculous wingspan, the extra fingers...

C: So he can beat us at beer pong!

J: What did you say about his neck size? Bigger than my chest? Like a size 34...

C: Oh yeah, he had a double gullet so he could chug faster.

J: Not to forget he's updatable by download through USB.

B: Let me ask you this. I think this story really solidified what was happening to you, where you were going as a character. Do you think that the story captured you, your personality, your ability to think ahead and come up with a way to defeat us at our own game?

C: And our ultimate resilience.

B: Like the cockroaches that we are.

J: I think it fit very well, especially in how it ended. You've turned him to the dark side. And you know what, if I'd had half a brain, I should have known that was coming a long time ago. I commissioned another drunken monkey... just bigger.

C: I have to say that my favorite part of the story is when we're playing beer pong with Drunkenstein and he's done five ping pong balls at once. Brian and I are looking at each other thinking, there's no stinking way we can win... So we both decided we're going to try four at once just to see what happens and Brian does one that goes back into our glass. And being the total optimist that he is, he says, "I screwed him up. He's practiced with five... now he can only do four!" He tries to rationalize away his big screw up!

J: The other funny thing is finding the hoards of people that dislike you and bussing them all there... Especially when you go through and recognize them.

C: Yeah, you didn't have much trouble there. I've seen your phone book.

THE DRUNKEN COMIC BOOK MONKEYS

VS.

CTHULHU

One cannot simply peer into the face of oblivion. Instead, it commands your full attention, locking gazes, exposing your inner thoughts, exhuming your soul before you. Truths long denied, desires deeply hidden, fears often forgotten swirl and eddy in the chasms of the mind, crashing upon the psyche like so many waves threatening to sweep away the persona in a maelstrom of motion. It is not, as we are often told, a reliving of memories tied to our lives as in the moments before death; but instead, a period of purging, an evanescence of our thoughts and beliefs, each one allowed to dangle before us for a brief, but poignant moment followed by an intense feeling of loss as the skein of conscience is altered inexorably.

***

That it was an unavoidable circumstance was a belief to which I clung, a piece of flotsam to a drowning man, an asylum to the kine surrounded by predators. Indeed belief was all that remained to me in this world and I was not yet prepared to enter the realm which awaited me. In our penultimate moment when hope and desperation intertwined we endeavored to unleash a being the elder gods imprisoned for what they hoped was an eternity, for not only was the beast bound, but every scrap of knowledge concerning its whereabouts, indeed, its very existence vanished, eradicated from the ken of nature. It was a level of blasphemy heretofore never contemplated by any rational being. But we were driven to the brink of madness by the ruthless torments visited upon us by our captors. And so the unthinkable became acceptable in the face of our final agonizing moments.

My companion and I were captured by the potato people and buried up to our necks in a pit of villainous and foul smelling tater-tots. I was sickened unto near catatonia, while my companion hungered. This was the first phase in their insidious plot to take over our world. For millennia, the flora-based life form had allowed itself to be ingested by our kind; thus, secretly developing a way to control all of human kind. Those among us who resisted their salaciously oral advances were immune to their mind control. As seems to be the case with all malevolent creatures, there existed among the potato people's culture a prophecy. That a bald human, free of the potato taint, would lead the rebellion of his people and overthrow the yoke of the tyrannical attackers. To this end, they watched me from afar for quite some time. They planned their advance with a cunning belied by their bland appearance.

An entire contingent of the spuds, patches of their skin peeled from beneath their eyes to combat the glare of our alien sun, cowardly ambushed me as I sought the respite of slumber. To further advance my humiliation, they chained me in a pit next to my writing partner, Brian. His interminable chatter filled my ears, boring deep into my brain. Indeed, the steady torrent of his speech, density rivaling that of clay or peanut butter, caused my very synapses to clog and misfire. My whole life had been spent in preparation for this very moment. Many promises had I made to protect those I loved from this imminent moment of finite space, when life as we knew it suddenly ceased and a new era, marked by devolution and subjugation of man by a more dominant, sadistic species, whilst they laughed at me sullying me: impugning my honor, labeling me as having "silly ideas." Undaunted, my desire to protect them endured through the embarrassment and the passing of lean years. Now that my moment had come, I yearned to complete my self-appointed charge, longing to discharge both vow and life in an act of selfless love that would define the emotion for future generations. And yet I could never have prepared myself for the ceaseless, mindless drivel that ran unstaunched from the mouth of my erstwhile friend, this sasquatch-like being that fate conscripted me to endure as a boon companion.

Here I stood at the doorstep of the moment that would define me forever and failure engulfed me at the last. Whorls of agony pummeled me from within and from without. Seagulls, but a spare few at first, though growing in the manner for which the bird is known, drawn by the scent of the crispy scent of fried grease, came to investigate our plight. They mocked me with the curve of their beaks, and I envisioned a bifid barb at the crux of the separation. With a horrible cry unique to their species, they snatched up a tater tot each and flew off to consume their plunder. But the tots resisted their efforts, stabbing and fighting back with such ferocity, the birds dropped their purloined goods, which rained down upon me. And so even the world I was sworn to protect reviled me. A chasm opened inside me and I longed to enter, swallowed within its sanctuary.

The light of my hopes extinguished, maddeningly, linearly, one after the other, with an agonizing slowness. It was done. The world would fall thanks to my failure and my ineptitude revisited itself upon me over and over in countless and endless succession. In moments such as these desperation invites the mind to peruse the unthinkable; so much so, in fact, that every unimaginable option is held aloft in stark clarity, whilst the mind examines and weighs each nuance. I label them "nuances," dear reader, for at such times, pros and cons are meaningless notions and possibilities can only be regarded as potentialities for all outcomes are so minutely different that they all seem to fall within the realm of the acceptable. And so, in the darkest recesses of my soul, the places I deny even to myself, a seed germinated. I liken it as such, for such an insidious notion on my part, should be held akin to the birth of the first of our attackers, the vilest form of life imaginable!

Many moments were lost to me in this existentialistic period of self-berating. But out of darkness a light arose and I set myself to with feverish actualization. Interrupting my companion's cry for ketchup and a napkin, I implored him to begin a chant I had remembered from my youth. Though the chant was simple, it was unclean, abominable and Brian's recitation stumbled repeatedly as his heart resisted the call. Ashamed, but unabashed, I continued my urgings between my own exhortations. Doom had already befallen us. Surely there could be no worsening to our circumstances. And so we continued chanting beneath the hot sun, our bodies baking in the grease that ran from our captors as the full realization of their wicked plot came unbidden to my mind. We were to stand in their stead as a meal to some other being as this galactic tragedy continued to unfold, a grisly payback for the ancient habits of our ancestors who could have made peace with the aliens, not turned them into so many "delicacies." And suddenly my unwholesome chanting seemed only to hasten my demise, though I cared little at this point. I sought only for some surcease to such suffering as I endured. If things must end, let them end quickly and on my own terms for I was not willing to be their marionette a moment longer.

To say that our chanting was eventually met with success is a waste of words, so I will elaborate no further. But I mention this for I am at a loss for words to describe the sound that anointed our actualization. A great ocean of time and space stretched before us in the sky of our world, the center of which resembled a colossal maelstrom. The fabric of our world was sundered and I can only assume the cacophony that deafened us was the lamenting of departed souls as reality was rent and tossed aside casually. From the center of the maelstrom rose a coliseum, done in a bizarre form of architecture. Buttresses of time and ramparts of space adorned the whole construction, which, was maddeningly defiant of the rational science of structural design. Even my untrained mind cried out that this thing could not be, though I admit that the language of the profession is unknown to me; thus, I cannot properly describe the failings in a nomenclature that has meaning. That it was a representation of some sort of abyss cannot be doubted by the sane mind, though I questioned my sanity with a ferocity that fed off its own insensate hunger.

As the statuary grew in size the porticos that dotted its face became more discernable to my tired eyes and each of these junctures marked a juxtaposition of timelines meant to represent a door, though whether this door would serve as a gateway to the past or some unimaginable future was quite unclear. Each door was closed and sealed from without; indicating that whatever was concealed within was meant to be kept inside, though no normal barring system had been employed. Instead, some universal hand covered each aperture with a huge fivepointed star resembling nothing less than some other-spatial starfish. Perhaps it was the work of a demiurge dissatisfied with one or another particular creation. Or perhaps it was the work of the universe, an attempt to keep concealed that that once crept uncalled and unwanted from some celestial birthing pool, a primordial ooze that did not distinguish one manner of creature from another.

In any event, before me stood R'leyh, for there could be no doubt that Brian and I had captured the attention of The Great Sleeper and the forces of the universe had aligned in perfect juxtaposition to allow him admittance to our relative locale. I cannot say with resignation that I wished to proceed, for my soul bade me turn back from the course of action I set into motion, for I cannot claim a reluctance in my spirit to look upon The Watcher Below.

With effort, I focused my mind, concentrating my thoughts into an amalgamous mass, capable of interacting with this scene that was not wholly real in our world. With a tremendous vigor my spirit self thrust out with my "mind arm" sundering, obliterating, nay eradicating the seal placed upon one of the entrances, whereupon the gates flung open wide. My ectomorphic self staggered back as a great expulsion of fetid air rushed past me, as if the stale atmosphere of centuries of indifference and uncurbed mediocrity found a sudden release.

The air about my physical form went through sudden, dramatic changes, at turns dropping or raising in the temperatures of our measurements by great scales. At once sweat streamed off my brow, becoming gaseous almost instantly, then a considerable cold blanketed me so quickly that my skin froze before the visible signs of gooseflesh manifested. Brian screamed at me incoherently, though I am at a loss to say truthfully if his words held no shape of sense to them or if I simply failed to register them with any sense of correctness, and I admit it must have appeared that I reveled in the absurdity of the circumstances surrounding us.

Spellbound, I stared at the gaping aperture of the monument before us. Dread, fear, anticipation, and excitement: all were present, though so thoroughly intertwined as to be completely indecipherable, one from the others. Dread Cthulhu was here and I viewed the wait for him to reveal his physical presence as deplorable. All about me the tater tots chattered amongst themselves, though their conversation was lost in the sea of emotions that gnawed at me aerating my soul like worms writhing through the soil.

And with a shocking finality he appeared. Dread Cthulhu! Locomotion was achieved by beating great black wings, though he did not fly, at least not in the sense that we are used to. More that he propelled himself with bursts of air, much like an anthropoid moves through water. The great squid head rested atop a curiously distended barrel shaped body. The skin glistened and shifted, opalescent in nature, though mostly a mottled verdant color. Not the bright emerald of grass or leaves in mid-summer, but a drab, tenebrous olive. Huge, staring eyes peered at us, their the blinking following no discernable pattern, at times not fluttering for stretches so long that I swore the creature must have blinked with such precision to my own, or that must have I missed the movement altogether. After many minutes of this stillness, though, the great hooded lids closed, then snapped open quickly, though this particular movement was never again identically repeated. I make mention of this, dear reader, that you may come to understand as I did that there was nothing static about the creature, no order to its movements, no repetitive movements: the laws of science and nature simply ceased in respect to it.

By my side, I heard Brian suck in air and hold it for an impossible time. When at least he released his breath out finally came intelligible speech. Dagon. Like the words of an idiot the simplicity of his speech required a great moment of concentration on my part to be sure I comprehended and that there was no more to follow. I sifted his word back and forth in my mind, hoping to sieve out some hidden meaning. Something. Anything. But there was no more forthcoming and the finality of his word was resounding. With one word, the fool had damned all our efforts! Clearly, even one so unlearned knew his gaffe. Surely he thought it a jest that would be picked up and carried on. Like comparing the finished work of a master painter to that of a child's sketch, Brian referred to the great God of Madness as a lesser known, less powerful monster of wrath.

Whatever his intention, he couldn't have been more mistaken.

His epileptic outburst could only be interpreted in one manner. And the slight was too great to be ignored. What manner of look crossed the face of this great outsider I cannot say for some speech is meaningless quite independent of the precision of the wording. A long moment passed silently between us, then a terrible force pushed itself against the corporeal structure of my brain. *Do not you know me, though through space and time you summoned me?*

The "words," if one can refer to an unsounded thought as such, hung in the air with a physical presence so heavily had they resounded in my mind. I took a slight moment to gather myself, weighing my answer with precision for surely the fate of all must hang in the balance. Before I could part my lips with words, however, Brian took up the mantle as collective mouthpiece again. Dagon. Dagon!

Fear was akin to spirit, so thoroughly a part of me at that instant; my emotion and I were interminably inseparable. Surely this was some dream! Possibly I was astride the back of some nightmare, hooves pounding through the clothing of reality! It was an impossibility, but where to find reason and sense? Surely some rationality must reign in the end lest all be lost to the swirling seas of an ebbing madness! Insensate imaginings threatened to overtake me! Must I always be on the far side of myopia such as this?

The Dread One leaned in close, drenching us with an ichthamous odor. Though no more thoughts appeared in our minds, the gesture was unmistakable. This was a dare to misspeak again. A threat to get the name correct or be shown oblivion. All about me was stillness. The tater tots stopped their pervasive shivering. For a brief moment I inspected the premise that because they were a higher evolved being than we mere humans, as yet incapable of invading and conquering other worlds, that it stood to reason that their sensibilities might also be more heightened than our own, thus suggesting they were more affected by this presence than we. Indeed, as I looked around, unwilling, or perhaps unable, I know not which, to meet the dread gaze of Great Cthulhu, the potato people had fallen into a great catatonia. It seemed quite possible that despite their gathered weight I might be able to extricate myself from pit that had been entrusted to serve as my jail. But none of such would matter if Brian refused to renege on his stance of naming. Surely he must! Even Brian, break in the evolutionary chain that he was, must have some source of reason, some gland that controlled rationality, some organ that produced the urge to be penitent. Dagon. Iyahuh Iyahuh Dagon!

My ears bled. My soul wept. There could be no sanctuary for us amidst the echoing insults my companion had hurled. We lay at the "mercy" of an unfathomable, tenebrous power...Life is good as long as the dichotomy between time and space is real, but to stand at the point where those elements meet juncture and to stare across the gulf of oblivion that signals one's demise is an incomprehensible eternity of anxiousness wherein one seems powerless and can simply observe events as they befall. But the pretense of alien natures can be pierced and I assure you, gentle reader, that insecurities abound in all forms of life.

Cthulhu, greatest of the Old Ones, Hunter of the Shadows, Lurker beneath the Surface, was no exception to the notions of pride and vanity. That he could exact justice and dole out retribution in whatever manner he deemed appropriate was without question. But in our final moments he could not hide his burning need to address insult not as a topical concern, but to search out the very root of its origin, to smother it inchoate. My skills of rationalization were frayed quite beyond the point of usefulness, yet still my imagination was mine to command. And all about me lay convenient proxies. *It was the Potato People,* I shouted, *seedlings of Dagon, spawn of the Abyss. They inured us with their alien tortures, shattered our fragile minds, and forced us into complicity with their perfidious perversion. They were responsible for the inaccuracy in nomenclature. Obviously* ***WE*** *knew the correct name or a summoning would have proven beyond our capacity.*

For a brief instant Dread Cthulhu considered the catatonic vegetation that lay about us, seeking out the source of knowledge that fueled a race that could travel space when the humans could not. And though my soul be tainted by untruth, it was but a mote compared to the blasphemy of summoning the Great Old One. And then my mind was filled with a vision of our world, broken and spewing fire, steaming Potato ships crashed upon the firmament, dotting the horizon towards infinity, a world in ruin, choked in soot, covered in ash. And from the ashes...reborn again, repopulated with people...a modern form of Ragnarok and I as its Heimdall, lording over the Bifrost bridge that spanned between realms. Then one more revelation he shared...the Potato People, as mere vegetation, subservient, their cognizance lost to the tides of forever. A glorious age beckoned.

Then Dread Cthulhu lay about and the skeins of the universe began to unravel like a well-worn bit of cloth. The maelstrom, so long held in check by ancient powers, swirled and funneled once more in its ritualistic dance, churning slowly at first, then wildly as the last of the great seals upon it broke away. It occurred to me that Dread Cthulhu must be a figure of birth for only from such chaos can life spring. Thus began the undoing of our universe. Great Cthulhu fixed us with a glassy stare, then without further prevarication stretched his maw to impossible widths, ivory beak glimmering against the palette of a far flung universe, then closed it scything reality and scientific and natural laws, cast aside, torn and shredded, then discarded as disproved hypotheses rooted in madness. A howling cacophony pricked our ears as the gates to dream-worlds and far off wastes flung open all about us. The fabric of our world rent asunder by the swelling rims of burgeoning beyond that beckoned us as if by name. And into the interminable chasm of the unimagined we were swept. All about us was but a blur as we merged with the great maelstrom.

With alacrity I entered the door of my dreams looking for the ship that would take me to the sea of my imaginings. But a sulfurous stench assailed me, choking me, depriving me of the breath of life and my ability to think and rationalize escaped me quickly and only by lucky happenstance of an even greater power that I am able to pen these words. The future I'd been shown ripped from my grasp. Alas, yet again, the opportunity to fail wrested from me in a cataclysmic instant of existentialistic fate. Then I glimpsed a face of brimstone and sulfuric composition. He shook a finger in my face as if to chastise me, then waved his hand across my face and a great unknowing sleep fell upon me. His smile was my only lullaby. And as my cognitive skills bled off into nothingness I was allowed one final grasp at conscious thought. One final blessing of remembrance to christen my erstwhile life: I needed treacle...I needed a beer!

INSIDE THE MINDS OF MONKEYS

CHRIS: This was the third piece of the trilogy and I wrote them in successive order. At the point I started Cthulhu, I considered pure narrative to be really painful. You challenged me to be true to the source material.

BRIAN: I was looking out for you, dude! Pure Lovecraftian fans would have eaten your entrails. That's all you'd need.

C: Cults at my doorstop.

B: Our editor would be so upset!

JEFF: No. Not really.

B: Our Publicist would be so upset!

PUBLICIST: No. Not really.

B: Your mom would be so upset!

C: No. Not really.

B: Yeah, probably not. Anyway, this story had another inside joke. In real life, I once called Cthulhu 'Dagon' so the story me had to be stupid and call him that again and again in the story. That was a challenge because this story has nothing but narrative, no dialog. But, somehow, Pisano pulled it off!

J: I liked that you were buried up to your necks in tater tots. [Jeff paused for a moment to imagine what his life would be like with Brian and Chris buried up to the necks in tater tots. He smiled and sighed. A tear escaped his eye.] Stuck there and you can only do what you two do best… argue.

C: We even screwed up the chant! I was going for mood and atmosphere… total Goth!

B: How do you edit something like that?

J: You don't. Just start with spelling errors.

C: You did catch me napping! I had to beef up the last three pages.

J: I do remember that. You needed to not trail off into vagueness, the readers demand a finale!

C: For the first time, I was non verbose.

B: How long was Cthulhu?

J: One of the shorter ones but thicker

C: Yeah it was longer and shorter... Completely destroyed the laws of physics! As Cthulhu so often does!

J: It took hours to read 12 pages and 2 days later...

C: Hoping to drive the God of Insanity insane...

B: By calling him Dagon. Repeatedly. Over and over again.

DEVIL

THE DRUNKEN COMIC BOOK MONKEYS

VS.

THE DEVIL

Jeff came home. It had been a long, hectic day, and he obsessed about relaxation. His mind drifted from the impending joy only a bottle of beer can bring to a fantasy world involving a masseuse named Tai-Pei who's only English is "happy ending."

Once he crossed the threshold he flipped through his mail pile: bills, bills, credit card app, and an ad for the local gym. *Hmmmm*, Jeff thought, wondering if he could at least make part of his fantasy come true. *The ad says they have a masseuse.* His over-active mind screeched to a halt as he imagined the masseuse being twice his size, named Sven, and went into the trade for more reasons than just a steady income. A chill skittered down his spine as he tossed the mail aside and continued about his routine.

Fridge first, questions later. The cold bottle felt like twelve ounces of Heaven against his skin. He held the top near his ear and inhaled. Just as he popped the top, he exhaled, blowing away the stress with a carbonated sigh. The bottle sluiced the beer into Jeff's mouth, tickling his tongue and cleansing his soul. Jeff thought too long about the word "sluice" and giggled. The liquid divinity gave him the strength to carry on, determined to see what the evening held for him - until he sat at desk and logged on to his computer. "You have twenty-two new messages."

His forehead sloped to his brows and his brows furrowed to his nose. Fifteen emails were from The Drunken Comic Book Monkeys, harassing him about stories he agreed to edit. The reasons why he said "yes" now eluded him. The other seven spam emails guaranteed the secrets to increasing the size of a particular body part. Jeff knew that The Monkeys were involved with the spam, but could not prove it. He received nary a stitch of unwanted email until he agreed to work with Brian and Chris. Once he said "okay" a flurry of member enlarging emails found their way to his inbox.

Jeff ran his fingers through his hair as if trying to scrub away the memories of these knuckleheads. Being as stalwart as a Buckingham Palace guard, Jeff continued on and read the first story, then the second, and on to the third. His heart, his brain, his soul told him to quit, run away to Tahiti and tell no one. But he continued on, trudging through the eternal goofiness of nonsensical tales about binge drinking and porn obsessing. *And what's the deal with this goat*? he thought. *Why the hell is it in half their damn stories*? *Yet, there's something vaguely familiar about it*?

Light shone at the end of the tunnel when he opened the email containing the final story. Relief mixed with concern as he realized that they had not included him in any of their stories. After finishing the last paragraph, Jeff was thankful for that fact and sighed, rubbing his eyes with the heels of his hands. Absentmindedly, he whispered to himself, "How many freaking jokes can these two make about beer and porn?"

With a teeth-rattling crack, Jeff's door blew of its hinges, flipping end over end to the other side of his living room. His immediate thought was of Argentinean gun runners raiding his place to get his fishing equipment again, but he pushed that from his mind when he heard no gun fire. Wondering what caused such destruction; Jeff broke off the bottom of his bottle to wield the jagged remains as a weapon, ready for whatever tore through his door. Angry, and disappointed, Jeff saw it was only Chris and Brian.

"Porn!" Chris screamed, eyes bulging and bloodshot, foam frothing from his mouth, dripping in clumps from his bronze goatee. "I heard the word 'porn.' Where is it? Where, man?! *Tell me where*!!"

Brian stomped into the room behind him, his litigation-like words leading the way, "Jeff, I tried to stop him, I swear I did, but you know how he gets when…" Brian paused, looking at the broken bottle in Jeff's hand. He frowned and said, "Hey, did you empty that bottle before you smashed it? If not, that's alcohol abuse and Beer Officer Pisano would slip out of 'Porninator' mode long enough to arrest you!"

"Beer abuse? No porn? What form of madness is this!?!" Chris bellowed to the ceiling as he fell to his knees, shaking his fists at the Heavens above.

Even though the intruders were far from what he imagined, Jeff still debated using the broken bottle on them. No Drunken Comic Book Monkeys could certainly make his life easier. And probably many people's lives as well. Maybe he'd even get a parade in his honor? Hell, his own Federal holiday was within two quick swipes of the jagged glass!

"Ummmm, Jeff? Why do you have a funny look in your eyes?" Brian asked.

"Ummm, no reason," Jeff replied, snapping out of his trance. He turned around to place the broken bottle on his desk, but not before whispering to it, "My precious."

He looked back to the annoying writers, Chris still on his knees, now weeping, and Brian taking way too much glee in smacking Chris upside his bald head. Then another chill shimmied down Jeff's spine. "Guys? How did you find where I live?"

Brian and Chris looked at each other, then the floor, the ceiling, the broken door, the walls, anywhere other than Jeff. Awkwardness tightened its grip until Brian mumbled, "Ummmm, Internet?"

Jeff sighed, knowing it was just easier to pretend to be France and surrender. "What do you guys want?"

"Wellllllll...."

"What did you two do *this time*!?"

"We ... ummmm ... need you to edit something, immediately."

"As opposed to the fifteen stories you *just* clogged my email server with?"

"Yeah. This is kinda important."

Frowning, Jeff held out his hand, snapping his fingers to speed the process, his patience wearing thin. Chris reached into his tote and procured an 80,000 word document. The veins in Jeff's ensanguined forehead looked very similar to swelling, overfilled fire-hoses ready to burst. "What. Is. *This*!?"

Cowering in the corner of the room, Brian and Chris could only mutter, "Ummmmm...?"

Flipping through the pages, Jeff, overwrought with confusion, asked, "Is ... this a contract? *With the Devil*??!!"

"Ummmmm...?"

Jeff flopped into his office chair and dropped his head to his desk; the force of contact rattled the picture frames on the walls. "Are you guys serious?"

"Ummmmm... yeah."

"Why didn't you take this to a lawyer?"

"We did. He laughed at us."

"How about a church?"

"They laughed at us too."

"Why me?"

"You're our only hope, Jeffery Wan Kenobi."

Knowing these guys were nothing more than a rash on society's ass, and knowing he needed to choose healing balm over scratching, Jeff sighed. "The porn DVDs you left in my car are over there. Beer is in the fridge. Go, and just stay quiet."

"WOOOOOOOOOOOOO!"

"Quiet!"

"wooooooooooooo."

Shaking his head, Jeff rested the contract on his desk and flipped through it page by page, scrutinizing every phrase, every word. Impressed, Jeff knew these two to be beer-swilling dolts, but when it came to this, they certainly did a good job. Their thinking was flawless, every scenario accounted for, logical dovetails with no loose ends. He had to laugh, realizing the best thing these two guys had written was a legal document.

"Alright guys. The contract with the Devil is finished." No sooner did the words leave Jeff's mouth, the lights in his apartment flickered. A sulfurous smell permeated the room, to which Brian and Chris responded with fart jokes, ultimately blaming Jeff. Smoke billowed from the floor in the center of the room. As if taking an elevator, a figure arose from the eye of the small storm. As the smoke dissipated, the trio saw the Devil himself. And he looked exactly like Brian and Chris, except in a business suit.

Fire flashed from the Devil's eyes as he said, "I believe you have something for me?"

"How the hell does everyone know where I live?!" Jeff yelled, frustrated beyond rationality.

Taken aback by such vehemence, the Devil could only answer with, "The internet?"

"Yeah, well, I'm gonna have to have words with 'the internet' after this is all over with! And here's the damn contract!" Jeff took the 400-page document and slammed it against the Devil's chest.

Perplexed by what he held, the Devil asked, "What the hell is this!? I gave those knuckleheads three wishes!"

"Well, apparently they were sober enough to wish for more wishes."

"And this is it?"

"Yep. With conditions, provisions, charts, examples and an appendix or two."

"You expect me to believe these inebriated imbeciles came up with this *on their own*?"

"Hey!" Brian yelled. "We're standing right here, you know! And we're not *that* stupid!

The Devil sighed, still staring at the tome of legalese in his hands. "Fine. What's your first wish?"

"Beer pants!" Brian and Chris said in unison.

Jeff and the Devil pinched the bridge of their noses in unison. "Beer pants?"

"Yeah!" Chris exclaimed, the vigor of his words shaking his whole body, eyes wide with excitement. "Pants crafted from the very fabrics of Utopia! All we have to do is reach into a pocket and pull out an ice cold bottle of beer. A never-ending supply of ice cold beer!"

"Never ending?" the Devil asked. "Don't you think that's a bit greedy? And, you know, this is coming from the king of greed."

Chris sighed, deflating from his manic high. "Fine! How about we can put a six pack in each pocket?"

"Done! Now that we have that..."

"Hair!" Brian and Chris said in unison again.

A stabbing pain struck the Devil behind his eyes. "What?"

"That's our next wish. We want hair again!"

"Oh, for the love of..." Rolling his eyes, the Devil snapped his fingers. Nothing happened. He snapped his fingers again. Still nothing. While watching Brian and Chris shift their weight from foot to foot, as anxious as children on Christmas eve, the Devil pulled his Blackberry from the inside of his suit jacket. Eyes glancing from the two overjoyed men to his PDA, the Devil used his stylus to flip from screen to screen. Until he found the information he sought. "Did you two incur the wrath of the spirits from the Haunted Comic Book Convention?!"

Both Brian and Chris stopped shifting about and dropped their puppy dog eyes to the floor. "Yes, sir."

Returning his PDA from whence it came, the Devil shook his head and replied, "Sorry, boys. There's only so much I can do. Now about the terms..."

"I want a parrot," Brian said.

"What? If you want a parrot, why not go to a pet store?" Chris asked.

"Well, then I'd have to get a real one and take care of it and give it a place to live and stuff."

"You want a fake one?"

"No, jackass. A supernatural one."

"One that you don't have to feed or house?"

"Exactly. We can keep it in the trunk of our car."

"So, Brian ... why do we want a parrot?"

"In case we need to build a Rube Goldberg machine."

"A Rube Goldberg machine?"

"Yeah. You know, an insanely complex machine to do a simple and mundane task where one part doesn't take action unless directly acted upon by the preceding part. There are great examples in classic Tom and Jerry cartoons."

"I know what a Rube Goldberg machine is! What the hell does a parrot have to do with a Rube Goldberg machine?"

Brian rolled his eyes. "Haven't you ever seen Rube Goldberg's classic comic strips? Most of them depend heavily on parrots."

"Why do you think we would ever need to build one?"

"Who knows? A situation may present itself, somewhere along the line."

"But you just stated that the machine itself is a satirical connotation about taking a simple situation and making it far more complex than need be. Why would we do that?"

"Well, we *are* the Drunken Comic Book Monkeys."

"True."

They both turned back to His Infernal majesty and said in unison, "We want a parrot."

The Devil massaged his temples, hoping to rub away the pain that arced between them. He held the power to bend the universe within his fingertips, but the only way to shut these two up was to give them a damn bird. "Done!"

"Done?" Chris asked. "Just like that?"

"Just like that," The Devil sighed.

"Can we have a receipt?" Brian asked.

"Please stop talking."

"Ya know," Jeff interjected. "It'd be interesting if you could actually communicate with animals."

The Devil shot Jeff a look of contempt; the heat of his breath rippled the air around his mouth and nostrils.

"That *would* be cool to talk to animals!" Chris realized.

"If I know you guys the way I do," Jeff continued, "once you leave, you'll find yourselves in precarious situations, most likely involving animals."

"You're right!" Chris turned to the Devil. "We want to ..."

"Done!" The Devil yelled. "Now, terms..."

"Oh!" Brian had a thought. "And we can't die."

"Yeah," Chris agreed. "Kinda like *Highlander*. Except there can be more than only one."

"Okay," the Devil said, cracking his knuckles, readying himself to work some old world magic. "You asked for it."

"Wait!" Jeff yelled. He walked over to the guys and smacked them both upside their heads. "You guys have seen enough *Twilight Zone* to know you need to rephrase that. So, you're immortal and what happens if you get life in prison? What happens if you get dismembered? What happens if you don't stop aging?"

"Damn," Brian said. "Jeff has a good point. Here, let's write the terms down."

After an hour of fussing and fretting over every detail and every known consequence, under the steely glare of the Devil, Brian and Chris, with the help of their editor, expressed their exact terms. After reading from the thirty page document, the men expressed that they could still die, however if they did, then they would automatically come back a week prior, carrying with them full knowledge of what led to their demise. Just as they finished and the Devil agreed to the terms, Jeff brought up another good point. "What about being undead?"

"Yeah," Brian said. "What if we accidentally get turned into zombies or vampires?"

"Vampires?" Chris asked. "I can't imagine either of us letting Bela Lugosi getting close enough to bite our necks."

"I'm thinking hot goth chick vampires."

Chris paused, then restated his sentiment. "I can't imagine them letting us get close enough to bite our necks - or possessing the desire to do so."

"Hey! You never know!"

The Devil started rubbing his temples again and Jeff interjected with, "How about if either of them get turned into undead and don't express consent that they want to continue to stay that way by the end of a three month trial period, they then revert back to normal..."

"*Fine*!" The Devil said through gritted teeth.

Brian and Chris high-fived Jeff. "What else can we think of," Chris asked.

"Hey, the Kentucky Derby's tomorrow! I wanna go!" Brian said.

"It'll take too long to get there," Chris retorted.

"Ummmm, hello!? Ancient, semi-omnipotent power standing *right next to you*!"

"Oh, yeah." Chris turned to the Devil, but before he could open his mouth, the Devil handed him a pair of fuzzy, pink socks. Already tired of the lunacy, the Devil mustered only a dry monotone. "Mystical socks of teleportation. Take you anywhere you want to go, instantly. But don't take them off, or they will lose their power and you'll forget what they're for."

"Sweet!" Chris took them and put them on. Excited, he jumped around like an ape, stopping only to toast his friend. But once the beer bottle necks clinked, they disappeared.

"Those guys are morons," the Devil mumbled.

"Yeah. But they're my morons," Jeff replied.

A wry smile slid across the Devil's face, his eyes slitted, and he leered at Jeff. "One thing I noticed about 'your' morons – they didn't include *you* in any of their deals."

Jeff sighed. "Oh, crap."

The Devil snapped his fingers, and Jeff blacked out. When he awoke, he felt strange. His arms and legs did not move as they ought to have. He licked his tongue over his lips and teeth, now seeming foreign. He opened his eyes and looked down – he saw hooves. He looked up into a small mirror and the reflection was that of a goat.

"Baaah!" he swore. He looked around the small trailer in which he found himself. Empty tequila bottles were strewn everywhere. This led him to assume he was in Mexico. Knowing the twisted sense of humor the Devil had, probably Tijuana. However, he found his thoughts were slowly blurring.

Finding it difficult to concentrate, his recent memories faded. Deeper memories went as well, names and dates turned to oblivion. Right at the very moment all memories of Brian and Chris, as well as every reason Jeff had to hate them, disappeared, the Drunken Comic Book Monkeys burst through the front door, babbling in fear about *La Chupacabra*...

INSIDE THE MINDS OF MONKEYS

BRIAN: I think we were about half way through when we realized we had a lot of questions to answer. Like beer pants and how do we keep coming back time after time when we die.
CHRIS: Was it after the first time we lost?
B: No... After the first time we lost, we just wrote it off and moved on. It was around the second or third time we came back, we realize maybe there should be a reason why we keep coming back.
C: We can get away with it once without anyone questioning us but you do it twice and eeehhhhh...
B: So we really needed to come up with a story that would answer all of those questions and we figured the devil was it. I came up with the idea because one of my first published stories was about a kid who makes a deal with the devil and he wanted to get out of it so he goes to see his lawyer. And the lawyer gets him out of it by making a 500 page document on the kid's wish for more wishes and then fooled the devil by producing more and more paperwork for each successive wish. He basically bogged the devil down with paperwork until the devil finally gave up. So I took that concept and changed it to fit us. We just annoyed the devil to the point where he was granting our every wish just to get rid of us. I thought that was also a great way of explaining all the things like beer pants, how we keep coming back and the pink fuzzy socks or even lesser questions about things that only true hard core readers would pick up on. Like in the original story of the Spider, we pull a parrot out of the trunk of a car. We answer that question. Also we got the ability to talk to the animals. We got the minor things. So with this story we actually take all the cartoonish insanity and give it real world logic and tangibility.
C: Was it the last story you actually wrote?
B: I wrote specific scenes and specific arguments along the way just to get them down. I knew we had to answer questions so anytime a question came up and I came up with an answer, I wrote it down. It was the last story I actually finished because I wanted to make sure we didn't miss any "logic gaps"... wooo ... logic gaps... So it was the last story written. Interestingly enough, it was the first story to use Jeff as Jeff himself. And I

think that started the fun because at the end of the story, the Devil takes his wrath out on Jeff and makes him the goat that pops up through the rest of the book. That gave us the motivation to use Jeff as the antagonist in the next books.

C: One question that I have is that it was last story in original book but it's not now... Does that change anything?

B: I don't think so because the last story in the new version is the bridge that leads to the next book. So it takes place after the Devil anyway.

C: So it's serendipity?

B: Exactly...

JEFF: Let's talk about one thing we haven't talked about at all so far which are the pictures on the front of the book. You both actually posed for the devil picture.

B: Yes and Chris won.

C: Actually I'm not sure how I won. Obviously I'm not the swarthy one.

B: Actually in this you do look quite swarthy.

J: A lot of photoshopping.

C: So how exactly did I win?

J: Don't remember...I'm trying to remember.

B: I don't remember either. I know there were two pictures of each of us.

J: I think if you put a whole of people together in a crowd and trying to pick out the devil, you'd be the last one to get picked out of the crowd. If you think about it, he is the master of deception.

B: Wow, was that logical or what?

C: So, it's kind of a backhanded compliment, huh?

J: Yes.

B: Anything about the story itself?

J: Yeah, I would never want to edit that document as well.

C: How did you feel about being used in that way, as a character?

J: I was always surprised that you wanted me to be even on the cover. To make me a character was pretty damn cool! So suddenly have me be the explanation behind the goat and all the insanity... Hey, I even got a pair of pink socks out of it, so what the heck...

B: Which you know we have to wear at all of our readings and signings which you'll be along for anyway.

J: "Do the pose! Do the pose!" No!

THE DRUNKEN COMIC BOOK MONKEYS

VS.

THEMSELVES

Lightning streaked across the midnight sky, the originating storm clouds hiding the moon. Jeff watched nature's light show from an alley, the rain wetting his face. His trench coat offered little relief from the cold; the wind whipped it freely. Pulling his jacket tighter about him, he tried to bury his face between the lapels, hoping to escape even a modicum of the stench rising from the trash lining both walls of the alley. He paced, feet splashing through random puddles on the pavement.

His contact was late. Continuing to pace, he couldn't help but feel cliché since this was a late night rendezvous with a top government official in a clandestine back alley. Throw in a "dark and stormy" night and it was now a noir espionage story.

Jeff shuddered at the word "story," the reason for this meeting. Bad stories. Horrible stories. Juvenile stories. He could stand not one iota more of them! It must end! No matter the cost, the price! Tonight he gave the ball a push and nothing would stand up to its inertia. It started now.

"Jeff?" the approaching man asked, his voice possessing the timbre of a man attempting to be more menacing than his true nature.

"You have what I need?" Jeff replied, attempting to muster the same false bravado. He instead sounded just as fake and ridiculous

"Yeah. You have what I need?" the man asked, the forced gruffness of a poor silver screen Batman impression.

"Yeah. Where's what I need?" Jeff asked, his attempt at a disguise could only be more farcical had he worn Groucho Marx glasses with a plastic nose and moustache.

"Here." The man looked over both shoulders, paranoid about

potential watchers, ready to jump from the shadows. He pulled a large clasp envelope from his trench coat, the same color and style as Jeff's. "Where's what I need?"

"Here." Jeff took the envelope from the man and handed over one of his own, stuffed with green renderings of Benjamin Franklin. Jeff opened the envelope and peeked at the papers within using the strained light from a nearby street lamp. "These real?"

"Yeah," the man said. Thumbing through the hundred dollar bills, he asked, "These real?"

"Yeah," Jeff replied, his throat getting sore from doing the voice.

The men shoved their envelopes into their respective trench coats. They looked at each other and stared, unsure of what to do next. Hands in his pockets, the man offered, "Ummmmmm..."

"Okay, then," Jeff said, sans fake growl. "I guess I'll see you next week at the sci-fi reading group."

"Yep!" the man said as he waved while turning to walk away. "Bye, Jeff!"

"See ya!"

Jeff returned to his home, ready to put his plan in action, ready to rid the world of two giant hemorrhoids from its collective ass. He looked at the papers, read the instructions, and verified the math and science involved in the process. Everything he needed, he ordered from eBay. As he mixed and molded, fixed and folded, Jeff plotted his revenge. He knew exactly how he wanted this to occur. He wanted his creations to destroy his targets in their sanctuary, their home.

***

At Melons Bar & Grille, Brian and Chris sat at the bar. The bartender asked, "Another round?"

"Yep," Brian replied. "And I was thinking about trying the Chicken Caesar salad."

All activity in the restaurant ceased. All eyes focused on Brian. Patrons stopped eating, mid-bite. Silence consumed the restaurant except for the thin whistle of the wind outside and the chirping of a lone cricket. No one was able to believe what Brian had said.

"Dude," Chris whispered, afraid that if he broke the eerie silence the resulting noise would backlash against him. "Are you feeling okay?"

"Yeah. Why?" Brian asked, the obnoxious quality of his normally loud voice amplified against the backdrop of the complete and utter absence of sound.

"You ... you ordered a ... salad?"

"Naaah. Just messing with you." Brian turned to the bartender and said, "I'd like 100 wings, please. And two orders of fried pickles."

The typical restaurant noises restarted, as if unpausing a movie.

"Dude, don't scare me like that!" Chris said, color returning to his ashen face. Well, as much color as his pigmentless skin would allow.

"Sorry. Just trying to elicit a chuckle."

"By threatening to order a salad? Dude, that's just sick. Even for you!"

"Oh, settle down!"

"That's it! I'm telling on you! I'm telling our editor how mean you are!"

"Don't you dare!"

"I dare! I'm so telling on you!"

"Tattle!"

"Your names don't hurt me! I'm telling! And there he is now!"

Jeff entered the restaurant. No sooner did he set foot through the door, Brian and Chris jumped from their stools, knocking both over with a distracting clatter, and ran to their editor. A headache, an aneurysm or maybe a tumor, started to throb behind Jeff's right eye as he was greeted with:

"Brian's mean!"

"Am not!"

"Are too!"

"Nuh-uh! I'm the good one!"

"Are not!"

"Tell him, Jeff!"

"Jeff likes me more! Tell him, Jeff!"

Pinching the bridge of his nose in an attempt to keep his pulsing eyes from popping right out of his skull, Jeff said, "Can we just go to the bar so we can talk about your latest story?"

"But..." Brian pouted.

"But..." Chris whined.

"Now!" Jeff barked, pointing to the toppled bar stools.

Brian and Chris trudged back, heads hanging low, exchanging shoulder punches in between:

"Your fault."

"Nuh-uh. Your fault."

Once at the bar, Jeff commanded them to pick up and dust off their barstools as well as apologize to the neighboring patrons for their immature behavior. The kind patrons accepted the mumbled apologies, but the bartender rolled her eyes and brought each of the men a bottle of beer. The men remained sullen until a giant plate piled full of chicken wings found its way in front of Brian. It was as if the sun rose after 40 straight days of rain. Brian smiled – until Chris tried to take one. "Get your own damn wings!"

"Dude!" Chris reasoned.

"I'm serious! These are mine!"

"All 100? Are you kidding me?"

"Here," Brian offered, sliding one of the plates of fried pickles to Chris. "Have one of these."

"Tasty as they may be, they certainly aren't as satisfying as wings!"

"If you want wings - order wings!"

"Jeff!"

"Jeff!"

"Fix it!"

Jeff sighed. He closed his eyes and dug deep within the quiet center of his soul. He reached for the solace of never having to deal with these two again. He would only find comfort in the execution of the plan. Now was the moment to begin.

"Miss...Miss...Yes, would you please get this knucklehead 100 wings, since he appears to be incapable of talking to a pretty, single woman. He wants those 911 hot, no celery or bleu cheese...he's a guy. Or, at least that's the story today. Also, please bring the open-mouthed gorilla a Guinness and the knuckle dragging, Elmer's glue colored guy a Corona with *both* a lemon and a lime. Oh, also two shots of the hottest sauce you have for him, and I'd like a chicken sandwich. Thank you." Without even a pause for breath, Jeff continued, his face flushed with the anger trapped under pressure for years uncountable. "Since you couldn't even resolve this little difference on your own, you'll both pay the penalty in beers that you hate. The hot sauce is just because I'm in charge, and I've recently embraced sadism. Do we have an understanding?"

"..........."

"...........Dude? They have chicken sandwiches?" Brian asked.

Jeff stood to address his audience of two in the manner of a man who wants the people across from him to know that they were not about to be treated as equals.

"Things are going to change, gentlemen, starting right now. The old me would have been happy to leave you both speechless. The new me? Well, I see the proverbial jugular and let's just say I'm lunging like a rabid pit-bull. You think you can hang with that, meringue man? Thought not. How about the wooly mammoth? You think you can deal with 190 pounds of prime pit-bull hanging off your chops? Good."

A smug and satisfied look stole across his face. Jeff sat and unfolded his napkin, before tucking in into his shirt collar. His coloring never looked better.

"Um, excuse me, sir..." ventured Chris, his hand partially raised as if he were in a classroom.

"You may speak. But," hereupon Jeff shook his finger as if scolding a recalcitrant child, "keep it brief and poignant."

"Where's Jeff?" Chris asked.

"Dude!" Brian attempted to whisper, "don't push him. He frightens me."

"Miss?" Jeff called to the bartender. "Would you please make that two Coronas? They go in front of the guy who looks like cauliflower."

"Ha, ha, ha, ha, ha, ha, ha, ha! DUDE! That's great!" Brian said, wiping away tears with a swipe of his bearish hand.

"You think that's funny, do you? Well, listen up, Bert and Ernie..."

"Dude, I'm Ernie..." Chris interrupted.

"What? Why?" Brian asked.

"It's a head reference...He's saying that your head is pointy..."

"SHUT UP!" Jeff yelled. "JUST SHUT UP! Speech is not required from either of you! Here, take these..."

"Dry erase boards?"

"NO TALKING! Write. Since this is what you're both so 'good' at, that's how you will communicate with me."

"Dude...you look like Professor Peabody with that thing..." Brian said to Chris.

"You want slapped, Fozzy Bear?" Chris relied.

"Duuuuude? What does that even *mean*?"

"Head reference..."

"Oh, miss...miss..." Jeff said, pointing to Chris.

"Dammit!!!" Chris yelled. He then wrote, *Dude, write him something*.

You're stupid! You took the time to write ME that, instead of just writing Jeff something? Brian wrote in reply.

Guh! Focus! I'm up to a six-pack of corona here. My liver can't handle that much citrus!

"You can't even write on grease-boards without arguing, can you? Do either of you comprehend my misery yet?" Jeff asked.

We're really sorry.

"How many ways have you complicated my life? You got me turned into a goat. You gave me a horrible disease...."

Guh! Did he have to pause on that one?

But you were the cool leader of a werewolf gang...

"Oh, sure...after you two made a deal with an evil power that spared you morons every agony! You can't fathom my scars!"

<u>*Sir? Is old Jeff at home?*</u>

"You're not funny!" Jeff screamed. His chest heaving as he gulped in air to keep the fire within stoked high. "You always think you're 'cute', but the reality is that people only associate with you because you make them all look so much better - more educated, more mannered, more pleasant to work with."

<u>*Preposition, sir.*</u>

"I'll end my sentences with a preposition as often as I like, Mister '*I'll start sentences with and and but because I think it makes me cool.*' Well, it doesn't make *you* cool. An ice bath couldn't make you cool! If they coated you with ice cream and stuck a popsicle stick up your butt, you STILL couldn't pass as cool! Do you get it? You ruin the 'coolness' of ice cream!" The smugness returned to Jeff's face. With each eruption he was visibly changing the landscape that surrounded him.

Brian noticed Jeff's sandwich getting cold in front of him. Invisible hands of scent tickled his nose, tantalizing his taste buds, making his tongue sweat until action became mandatory.

"You've cost me my immortal soul!" Jeff continued. "AND my social life! Not to mention any chance I've ever had at becoming a professional writer...."

Brian interrupted Jeff's tirade with his white board, <u>*Excuse me, sir*</u>....

"What do you want?"

<u>*Are you going to eat that?*</u>

"I...can't...believe...this...no, wait...yes, yes I can. Sure. You can have it. Just as soon as you do something nice for someone else. There. That table over there. Those two guys need ketchup. Take our bottle of ketchup to them. DO NOT spill anyone's beer along the way. DO NOT talk to anyone. I've pulled your speaking plug. It's been PULLED! You! BALDY! Stop writing your ridiculously juvenile comment about me 'pulling his plug'! Now stop writing a retort to the bald comment! In fact, put the pen down! We're having quiet time! Lay your head on the table until Brian gets back from taking ketchup to that table!"

Without a word, though still far from quietly, Brian clomped his way over to the table Jeff indicated. The noise of his size fifteen shoes pounding the ground provided all that was necessary to get the attention of the two patrons. Brian held the ketchup bottle up for them to view. In the back of his mind where his prima donna thoughts echoed incessant chants, Brian thought of himself as a modernized version of Vanna White. As a natural happenstance, his version was far more obscene even without intention.

After flashing a toothy grin, he spun around to head back towards his recently acquired victuals, only to fall in a heap. It was not, however, that the g-force achieved from his pirouette caused an imbalance in his grossly large frame. He was felled by recognition: the recognition of his own face. Impossibly, he was seated at the table which just received his gracious gift of ketchup. And so was Chris.

Confused, Brian ran back to the barstool from whence he came. He trembled and shook, sweated and stewed. He rubbed his eyes as if grinding corn to meal. Peeking one more time to make sure his eyes hadn't tricked him, he began to cry.

Satisfied by the reaction and confident that his plan was in full swing, Jeff got up from his barstool and slunk away to find a better point to observe the ensuing mayhem.

"Dude!" Chris said to Brian. "What is your problem?"

Brian tried to answer, but his mouth only opened and closed like a fish after its final flop on a hot beach. Transfixed, his eyes could only gaze upon the table behind his friend.

Chris frowned, disoriented by his friend's confusion. He waved his hand in front of Brian's face. No reaction. He snapped his fingers. Not even a flinch. He waved a chicken wing up and down. Nothing. Confounded, Chris finally turned to see what could possibly keep Brian from attacking food out of primal instinct. Squinting, Chris tried to get a clear a vision of the impossible. Sure enough, Chris saw a mirror image of Brian's vision – themselves.

Mouth agape, he turned to Brian and asked, "How is that possible?"

"I don't know," Brian whispered. "I'm still trying to figure out how *that* is possible."

Turning around again, he saw two Melons waitresses standing by the mysterious doppelgangers. What perplexed Brian was the fact that the waitresses were laughing, exhibiting signs of having fun! The one girl flipped her hair while flashing an over-enthusiastic smile. The other girl ran her fingers down the fake Chris's arm.

In all their years of patronage, the best reaction Brian and Chris ever received from one of the waitresses was a forced and pained smile, but that was only after turning their charm-level up to full blast. The next best reactions they ever received were sighs of relief anytime they announced they were done for the night and leaving.

Chris looked back to Brian, still rubbing his eyes with the heels of his hands, and asked, "How did that happened? We've used every ounce of mojo we have and it garners us pure disdain. We're anathema and these guys are panacea!"

"G'uh!" Brian grunted in agreement. "Look at them now!"

Chris did. A fire burned in his belly. Now the two waitresses sat with the doppelgangers while another two waitresses stood by the table. All four women squealed and laughed.

Turning back, Chris said, "Dude. We have to go over there."

"What?" Brian replied. "Why?"

"Think about it. First of all, they're spitting images of us. They have to be clones or something, so we need to know where they came from. Second of all, people like them and not us; so we need to figure out what their secret is."

Brian digested his friend's words, then gave a defeated sigh. "Yeah. I suppose you're right. Let's power up."

Without so much as another word, the men chowed down the remaining wings while chugging large gulps of beer in between bites. A few wings even disappeared into Brian's gullet whole and unmarred. Needing only four minutes to clean the table of every ounce of sustenance and every drop of libation, the men felt prepared to stare themselves square in the eyes and demand answers.

By the time Brian and Chris staggered over to the table where the fake Brian and Chris sat, four waitresses sat with them, two more hovered around the table as well as five other patrons. All eleven strangers were riveted by what the two men had to say.

"That's *fascinating*, guys," one patron said to DoppelBrian and ChrisClone. "You two are the deepest individuals I have ever met. Now, I'm curious. What are your thoughts on the bigger issues? What is the meaning of life?"

Twenty-two eyes, open and yearning for knowledge, as well as the four blurry and dulled eyes of the real Brian and Chris, focused on the newest philosophers of the twenty-first century, awaiting their words of wisdom...

"Beer," ChrisClone said.

"Sex," DoppelBrian said.

The small crowd erupted with glee. The closest girls hugged the men while others gasped and clapped from having their own personal epiphanies. But real Brian soured the mood.

"Oh, come on!" he shouted. The revelry ceased. All eyes, now brimming with ire, focused on him. "We talk about beer and sex all the time and have never gotten a reaction like that!"

"That's because you keep talking," one of the waitresses said. "These two are succinct. Their message is poignant."

"Poignant? They said two freakin' words!"

"That's right! They did! And they carried far more weight than anything you two *ever* said!"

"But they are us! Look at them!"

"They're better than you! More charming and obviously smarter."

"But they're not feeding you anything. We offer sustenance with our words. Our words are a smorgasbord for your brain!"

"Food," DoppelBrian said. The small crowd swooned.

"What?" The real Brian snapped.

"See?" the waitress continued. "That's all the sustenance we need. Food. Not your *words*."

"Ummm, you do realize he said only one word. It's not like Zarathustra thus spake!"

"What? See, this is exactly what I'm trying to say! You talk a lot, but don't say anything! These guys say everything by talking very little! Where else can you find such raw simplicity? Where else can you find the point of any given topic so clearly?"

"Porn," said ChrisClone.

Every member of the encircling crowd, now seventeen people strong, used a thumb and index finger to stroke their chin, eyes gazing to the heavens as they pondered the one word answer. And they accepted it, in unison. Miniconversations ensued as the individuals in the crowd turned to each other and agreed with the restaurant booth idea maestro.

"I can't believe this," Brian muttered. "They're better us than we are!"

Chris shoved Brian out of the crowd, to an empty booth in the far corner of the restaurant. "Dude. I figured it out."

"What?" Brian asked.

"Body snatchers."

"Ummmm, there's a problem with that. Our bodies haven't been snatched."

Both men took a moment to think about the accidental double entendre Brian created. They each winced in pain from the vile images dancing through their minds.

"Eeeeewww," Brian continued. "What I meant to say was we're still here. The whole body snatcher concept is *taking,* then replacing someone."

"Maybe they're replacing us first? Seriously, they're pod people!"

"Now you're just being ridiculous. Next, you'll tell me they are some kind of 'potato people from another planet'. What is it with you and the 'doom and gloom' theories?"

"Listen, Einstein, so far you have yet to posit a credible theory...."

"I got it!"

"Dude, you know what they are?" Chris asked; hope glimmering like motes of light in the depths of his sapphire eyes.

"No. I have no idea what they are," Brian stated with the bluntness of a sledgehammer.

"Ummmm...then what 'do you have'? NO! WAIT! I'm not sure I want to know."

"I know why they are more popular than us," Brian stated, brimming with self-confidence.

"Spill it."

"You."

"Me? What do you...."

"You're the reason people don't like us. Your ridiculous vocabulary puts people off." Brian stated, picking a piece of lint from his "*can't sleep – aliens will probe me*" t-shirt.

"Wow. Typical math major. It doesn't matter if people can't add, the rules never change. But after years of people spelling it 'receipt' then all of the sudden the world decides 'i before e, except after c' doesn't matter. We just throw out all the rules of language, because, Heaven forbid, anyone suffers spelling inadequacies."

"It's pretentious," Brian argued.

"I Disagree! It's called 'not talking down to people'. Everyone wants to 'dumb up' the world. We should have certain expectations. Otherwise, we'll be drawing pictograms on cave walls again!"

"See? You have to say 'pictogram' when 'drawings' would suffice. I say 'red', but you have to say 'crimson'."

"Ummm...because there's a difference," Chris argued.

"You keep thinking that," Brian concluded. With that, he started to move off in the direction of the growing group that swelled around the pseudo-drunken comic book monkeys.

"Where are you going?"

"To hang out with the popular you. He makes sense."

"Dude, he's said the same four words for the past two hours!"

"And every one of them made sense."

"Unbelievable. Go over there, then, punk. See if I care. The only thing you'll get over there is a case of echolalia."

Chris returned to the table the true drunken comic book monkeys typically claimed as their own. Brian's attempts to join the party caused quite a commotion, but Chris tuned it out. Tilting one of the grease-boards to a better writing angle, he took up a marker and began writing a list.

Jeff Young graduated—need a new editor

It will always be 'receipt'

Shakespeare tripled the size of the English language -

My generation would see it halved

'Counter-predictive' should be a word

Taoism IS a selfish philosophy

Figure out the pod people

Call Drunkenstein—see if he wants to hang out

Chris paused contemplating his next point. As he began to touch the tip of the marker to the board one more time, a shadow blocked out his light. Only one person in the restaurant was tall enough to block the light.

"Dude, have you put on weight? You just blotted out the sun!"

"Beer?"

"It's like you don't see me! Two, please! So what did you learn, smart guy? Did you figure out the secret of charisma? Did you discover the mystery of self-actualization? Did you contemplate the clandestine path of Sufism?"

"Food?"

"Now that you mention it, I am a bit hungry. How do you manage to get inside my head like that? WAIT! Question withdrawn. I'll skip the rhetorical nature and go straight to the point: eerie! It's frightening, and more than a little unnerving. Dude, sit down! You make me nervous hovering around that way! It's like a sucker punch to my 'laid back' nature," Chris quipped. "So what are the 'almost us' guys like? Did you learn anything? You know, Jeff totally bolted as soon as you saw them. I'm sure that guy is behind this. We may not be smarter than him, but we sure do have a knack for bringing him down to our level. We can beat this. I just know it."

"Porn?"

"Yeah," Chris snorted. "At least *that* makes sense to me! How does Jeff keep coming up with these schemes? I mean, how can he afford it? And where does he find the people who make this stuff happen? I just can't believe there are that many people out there who want to see us suffer. We're basically good, if misunderstood, guys. You know, I think I just got it. I had an epiphany! Jeff is challenging us! That's it! He wants to give us stuff to write about. Keep us fresh. I mean after all, if he gets rid of us, it's kind of like killing the cash cow. Ha, ha, ha, ha! I crack myself up! I can't believe I just suggested we were the cash cow!"

"Beer?"

"Hello! Of course. Dude, you look kind of ashen. You feeling ok? This little mess got you down or something? Re-lax! You know we'll get through this. We need a plan, though. So you gotta tell me what you learned over there."

The sounds of raucous laughter filled the grille. Aside from Chris and his companion, every person in the restaurant was crowded around the clone's table. Chris couldn't help but notice that the next party of three that entered Melons immediately went over to join in the festivities at the table of the imposters.

"Damn! Ok, this time Jeff really outdid himself. Think, dude. How do we beat these guys? Got it! We pull some prank and they take the fall for it. We just have to impersonate them. We know their four-word vocabulary by heart. Fortunately, it's the four most meaningful words in the English language. And we're well practiced. Ok, now we just need an opportunity. Got any ideas?"

"Food?"

"Dude! You're a machine! Do you ever *not* eat? Doesn't being upset mess with your stomach? You're ridiculous! Oh, this is good. Don't look now, but the fake you is on his way over here."

"DUDE! You do know you're talking to the enemy, right?" Brian said. "I mean you're not really this dumb, are you?"

"Hey, you can't talk like that. I'm sensitive," Chris protested. "Some people even say I'm deep."

"Deep? Dude, you have the depth of a line."

"Ah, but at least I go on for infinity! Moron! Like I don't know you're fake Brian. Whatever!"

"How can you be confused? I've used more than four words with every sentence!"

"Ok, smart guy, here's a test for the two of you. What are my four favorite words? Brian on the right?"

"Beer. Food. Porn. Sex," DoppelBrian said.

"Dude, he's got you. You're the imposter," Chris said to Brian.

"I didn't even go yet! And you're ridiculous! You know those are the only four words they know!"

"Yes, but he does have a point..."

"Dude, your four favorite words are ensanguined, esoteric, saturnine, and floccinaucinihilipilification."

"Lucky guess!"

"Lucky...? Dude, I just chose the four most unused, unknown words in the English language! That list is esoteric! And...and ... and ...?"

"What's wrong with you?"

Brian could only stare. Standing next to Chris was ChrisClone. Brian looked from one to the other and back. No difference. None.

"What?" Chris asked.

"Porn?" ChrisClone asked.

No help. Brian had no clue who was whom. So, he decided to give them a test. "So, guys, what's my favorite...?"

"Sex," both Chris's said in unison.

Brian frowned. "Okay. Let's try this. What do I like ...?"

"Beer," both Chris's said in unison again.

Brian sighed. "What...?"

"Food," both Chris's said in unison again.

Brian stood perplexed. How to tell them apart? He pulled out his wallet, flipping through the cards until he found the one he sought. His mensa card. He stroked it lovingly. An idea percolated in his brain. *Thank you, little genius*, he thought. "Miss! Yes, may I have a Guinness, please? No, no fruit. Thank you."

The waitress returned with his drink and popped the top, standing the can upside down in a pint glass. Brain assured her he could handle it from here. Manning up, he held his expression completely neutral against the distaste that coursed through him at handling the can. Both Chris's drooled as the sediment settled. When the liquid reached the brim of the glass, Brian realized he had no idea what he was doing and pulled the can free with a jerky motion. A drop of the dark beverage caught the side of the glass and began to roll towards the table. Both Chris's eyed it. Brian still couldn't tell them apart. Sweat formed on their respective brows – still no tip off. The lone drop sank slowly toward the bottom of the glass, as if the glass itself was crying.

Unable to take it any longer, both Chris's lunged in unison. Brian still couldn't tell them apart. His plan had failed.

"Beer!"

"Dude, alcohol abuse! What's wrong with you man? Hey, wait a second..." Realization rose like a new dawn.

"Miss! Might I have a corona, please? Oh, yes, extra lime would be exquisite - in fact, a lemon and a lime, if it's not too much trouble."

"Dude! That's a bit of overkill, isn't it?"

"At least we'll learn a thing or two here. Thank you, miss," said Chris squirting himself in the eye with lemon juice as he struggled to push the pulpy mass down the bottle's neck.

"Now we just need to see if the aversion is consistent."

"Beer?" asked ChrisClone, eyeing Brian's glass of Guinness.

"You like this, huh?"

"BEER!" ChrisClone affirmed. He moved closer to Brian, glancing back in disgust at the Corona.

"I got an idea. I know how to *beat* them! Follow me."

Chris used the Guinness to lure ChrisClone over to the crowd of people. ChrisClone moved back to his spot with DoppleBrian.

"Porn," he said.

The crowd swooned, then began to chant, "Porn, porn, porn, porn..."

Chris cleared his throat and said, "Excuse me! May I have your attention?"

"What do you want?" an attractive young lady demanded. "Why are you even still here?"

"If I can have your attention, please? Thank you. What is it you would like most?"

"You to leave," the crowd said with one voice.

"Food," said DoppleBrian.

A laugh rippled through the crowd.

"Tell you what, let's have a drinking contest. First team done with their beer wins. Losers leave."

"Dude!" Brian said. "Where will we go?"

ChrisClone smiled. "Beer."

"Yes, big fella. Here's the twist. We'll need two Guinness and two Coronas. Perfect! Okay, someone count down. Quick."

DoppleBrian stared at the Guinness in front of him. He began to sweat profusely. ChrisClone was faced with the Corona and the lemon - *and* the lime. He swayed to and fro as if he might pass out.

A nearby waitress counted down. "Three, two, one...go!"

"Done."

"Done."

"Done."

"Done. But you know he should get a break. All that fruit clogged up his beer."

The crowd consulted amongst themselves. The discussion included much head shaking.

"Now what?" Brian whispered to Chris.

"We wait. If they are truly as well replicated as they seem, their wits should fly apart at any second. How my double choked that garbage down is beyond me."

Sweat beaded on DoppleBrian's forehead. His face blanched until he was almost as colorless as Chris. His deodorant gave out.

"Nice! Watch this. What's your name?" Chris asked.

"Bryant Koznuski," DoppleBrian said.

"Cool. Any others?"

"Sasquatch."

"Really? Don't look now, but that guy's a photographer..."

"Damn paparazzi!" said DoppleBrian. He ducked beneath the nearest table, attempting to hide his bulky frame from the designated man's view. Plates and silverware fell to the floor, the clatter offending the waitresses and other patrons.

The real Brian caught on to his friend's plan, slunk his way over to a barstool and said, "Food!"

Chris slid over beside his twin. "What's your name?"

"Christ Piano," ChrisClone said.

"Nice name. You know, your buddy deserted you and the crowd is turning on you. Better think of something fast...why don't you dance?"

The undulation that followed could hardly be described as dancing. It wasn't even qualified as the most basic of rhythmic movements. The crowd watched in horror, attempting to understand what was happening.

"Perfect," Chris whispered to ChrisClone. "Keep it up. Know any songs? Oh, oh, know the camp song?"

The crowd watched on. They were no longer sure which Chris was which.

"You know the one. The lighting bug song," Chris whispered to ChrisClone again.

"This...this...this little butt of mine," ChrisClone sang. "I'm gonna...gonna make it shine..."

"Beer," the real Chris said to the crowd.

"That's him!" someone from the crowd pointed at ChrisClone. "He needs to leave."

"Food!" said Original Brian.

"Porn," said Original Chris.

"And the one hiding under the table is the other one. Out they go. C'mon get them out of here. This whole contest was their idea, too. Time to be men for once!" one of the waitresses said, pointing to DoppleBrian, still attempting to hide under a table.

The crowd ushered the imposters out the door and all the way into the parking lot.

"No!" DoppleBrian cried out. "Let me regale you with trivia from my Mensa brain!"

"I'm a little teapot, short and stout. Here is my handle, here is my spout..." ChrisClone crooned.

Frustrated, Jeff followed.

When the crowd returned en masse, they found Chris and Brian sitting serenely at their table. Each man wore a smile the size of a fedora.

"Tell us more," said one young girl.

"Sex," said Brian.

"Beer," said Chris.

Both men looked at each other. Things were good. Except Chris knew it would be weeks before he got the lightning bug song out of his head.

INSIDE THE MINDS OF MONKEYS

BRIAN: We came up with this as a one of the stories for the first edition. But just like the Mummy, it got pushed off and just never happened. Neither of us really seemed too excited about it as compared to some of the other stories.
CHRIS: Yeah, I think we were both intimidated by it.
JEFF: By yourselves?
B: Yeah. We didn't know what kind of story it would be. Originally, we thought it would be a pod people story but then we realized it would make more sense if we were cloned. That's why it didn't seem to fit for this book because it's not a true horror story. It's more science fiction. So this story will appear in the next book which is us in science fiction stories. But since it does have a horror element, we included it in the Reflux edition as a preview for the next book.
C: It's a bonus!
B: It's a special feature on the DVD.
C: It's an Easter Egg!
J: Good luck finding it!
B: You just have to turn to page 282.
J: Damnit!
B: Spoiler alert!! Ah, I said it too late.
C: So what was your original thought on this?
B: I remember when we came up with the original idea of us not winning every time, we came up with the decision that we should lose half the time. For some reason, the stories took over as we started writing them. Some stories we thought we would win, we'd lose and vice versa. The original thought that I had was that the comedy of this is that we're men. We don't communicate. It took 10 years of friendship before we figured out that we were both writers. So we poke fun at each other in a darker sense with the clones knowing only 4 words - of course, beer, porn, sex and food. And those four words were key enough to confuse us so we couldn't tell each other apart from the clones. The original idea was to get guns somehow and Chris and I would start shooting each other and kill each other and the clones would win. But that is a really dark slant to it to the point that it might be too uncomfortable for either

of us to write it. So we came up with this other idea where we win by giving our clones beer we ourselves don't like. It kind of shows that since Jeff is the antagonist and he clones us in order to beat us, that he did too good a job that our real weaknesses defeat the clones. Mr. Editor, any comments?

J: I just want to say... Thank you for the Alpha Male voice! And the white board idea... I'm so going to Staples.

C: What was your favorite part?

B: I think my favorite part is that we did different types of comedy in one story. We try different types of comedy, but usually a story will go in one comedic direction. With this story, especially since we switched back and forth when writing it, we hit a lot of different types of comedy and I think it works very smoothly. At the beginning when Jeff has the clandestine meeting with the stranger, there is some very subtle humor. Then in the very next scene, Chris and I are doing the "Uh huh... Nuh uh" argument which is the absolute most juvenile humor known to mankind. We have the white boards. We have Jeff finding his Alpha male voice. We have some fun dialogue. We even have a Nietzsche reference

J: Extra credit for finding it

C: And it's less of a pass off story than a hot potato story.

J: Of all the different stories, this is the most shared story. It's a culmination of all the stories. So it's right to be the last story.

C: And I think it was fairly seamless.

B: Yes there was one point in time where I forgot to include Jeff. And I managed to find a way to take him out logically and make a natural exit for him. And then you put him back in the story again very logically. Again it feels fairly seamless.

J: Like hot potato...

C: It also was the first story in a long time where there is usually banter, we instead took some real pot shots at each other. Ironically, Brian wrote the most deprecating things about himself and I wrote the most deprecating things about myself.

B: Self-deprecation humor rocks!

C: I don't know if that really happened before. We usually put each other down in real life but this time we totally put ourselves down.

J: Yeah. Apparently, that's what you guys consider "well-rounded."

INTERVIEWING LOVE MACHINE

BRIAN: So, the book's done. Now what?
CHRIS: Well, Jeff interviewed us in the last book, so let's interview him for this book.
B: Oh, he won't like that.
C: Why not?
B: Because he'll have to talk to us during non-work hours. He doesn't like that. Uh-oh. Here he comes. Hide!
C: Shut up you sissy! Hey, Jeff!
JEFF: What do you want? Can't you two leave me alone? And why are you attempting sheepish smiles?
C: Well, we were thinking of ideas for the next book and we're really trying to flesh out the characters.
J: Flesh out...? Oh, Lord help us all.
C: So ... where did the Drunken Comic Book Monkeys come from?
J: I sooooooo wish I knew. I would go back and board up that hole and fill it in with concrete. No, I mean I'm sure that someplace has the distinct experience of being your home town. I think that the tall one said once that his ancestors were Cossacks that rampaged and pillaged the Steppes. You wax poetic, *non-stop*, for quite some time about the unusual nature of red haired inhabitants of Pisa which have something to do with Vikings. So when you consider your backgrounds, then the beer drinking heavy handed approach to everything seems to make sense. Apparently even the Atlantic Ocean couldn't keep you two in the old country.
B: We couldn't help but notice that a lot of stuff happens to you in the books...
J: Not just in the books!
B: ... and we were wondering why you think that is?
J: Why does all that stuff happen to me? That is a damn good question and the answer is two part: You two and Satan! No, really it's in the book. As for me, I'm not bad, I'm just written that way. I'm pretty sure

no one can reasonably blame me for the plague that kills all of Harrisburg, the insatiable appetite of the Wendigo, outdrinking the Chupacabra, turning a puffin into a werewolf, patching together the world's greatest competitive drinker from dead body parts and starting a zombie outbreak. But cloning the Drunken Comic Book Monkeys, yeah, that was me. Bad idea, wish I could take it back and start all over again.

C: So, Jeff, why beer pants?

J: Why ...? Waitaminute! Are you two interviewing me?

B & C: NO!

J: You totally are! I can see how it unfolded too. Just before I got here, Sasquatch probably said, "Duuuuuuh, now dat da book is done, whatdowe do?" And then you probably said, "Duuuuuuh, I dunno. Let's interview Jeff." Am I right?

B & C: Ummmmmmm...

J: **sigh** Okay, let's get this over with. Why beer pants? Of course you two were going to go wish for beer pants. For the nonstop drinker, what else would you ask for? Do yourself a favor too, never try to contemplate the physics necessary to allow such a thing.

B: Suddenly the manager's position is open at Melons: would you take the job and what changes would you make?

J: First off, why does that question sound familiar? Anyway, take the job? Sure. Why not? Because then I could put evil plan part two into action which would involve banning certain persons from Melons forever. Of course this means that after a brief period of joyful celebration then inevitably the business would collapse without the influx of DCM money. On second thought, I'll just take the T-shirt and some phone numbers, thanks. Especially the manager, Maria's.

C: In what ways are you similar or different from the Comic Book Monkeys?

J: All right that does it! I knew these questions were familiar. You lazy bastards are just asking me the same questions that I asked you last time!

B & C: Nuh-uh!

J: Yes, you are! I should know, because I wrote them! Where's your

sense of originality?
B: We're hacks!
C: He's a hack. I prefer to think of it as literary obeisance and lyrical adulation.
J: *You* would, Professor Pompous. You two could have asked me something deep and meaningful about the nature of reality, the future of humanity, the compass of the soul. Instead, you resorted to near plagiarism. How am I similar to the Comic Book Monkeys? I've been known to drink beer and enjoy beautiful women. That's it. As for differences – EVERYTHING ELSE! So what's the next lame ass question anyway? Damn, I wrote these didn't I?
B: Have you ever considered leaving the United States permanently?
J: Only as a last resort to get away from you two! I'm hoping that by moving ever westward I can stay ahead of the DCM horde once it starts its inevitable conquest.
B: Dude, he totally said that we're a horde!
C: A horde of two!
B: That's the new Fortress Publishing, Inc. slogan.
C: We should put that on t-shirts!
B: Shot glasses!
C: Bumper stickers!
B: Thongs!
J: Stay on target!
C: Ah-hem. So, what do the Drunken Comic Book Monkeys read?
J: Do they? Seriously, do they!? I think the answer here is very simple and I will use one of Brian's favorite words as noted in "Themselves" – porn. I have also heard Chris mention someone by the name of Lovecraft once or twice.
B: If you had any super power, what would it be?
J: Obviously, I would be completely insensible by Comic Book Monkeys.
C: If you could trade places with any other person for a week, famous or not famous, living or dead, real or fictional, whom would that be?
J: Ok, so some of my questions did actually have some meat on them. What a puzzler. Casanova? Doctor Who? Einstein? Neil Armstrong?

That guy from the Dos Equis commercial? Yeah! There we go!

B: I'm kinda disappointed that he didn't say us.

C: Yeah, me too. Pisano sad now.

J: You'll get over it. Next question.

B: When Hollywood makes a movie of your adventures, who would you recommend to play your part?

J: Boxhead, he's probably the smartest goat at the local petting zoo. He's got charm, charisma, a real sense of himself and a head-butt that will leave you sore. Also Nicholas Cage since I'm not really on stage long enough to require somebody with real acting talent.

C: What song will they play at your funeral?

J: "Raise a Little Hell" by Head East. That ought to wake some people up.

C: Including the dead.

B: Zombies?! Did you just mention zombies?! I hate zombies!

J & C: Settle down!

B: Fine! You can never be too cautious, you know! Anyway – what is your favorite childhood memory?

J: Being left in the woods and raised by the forest creatures to appreciate the joy and complexity of nature.

B: Really?

J: Are you frickin' kidding?! No! I couldn't have written this lousy question. You two must have made it up. Now you're just testing me. Next question.

B: But you did write...

J: Next question!

C: If you could become very famous for something, what would you want to be famous for doing?

J: I would like to invent a bra that women would want to wear and that men would want to look at. No, seriously – world peace, yeah world peace.

B: What's next for Love Machine?

J: What's next? Well I go onto the next set of adventures. I understand that I get to swap saliva with Maria the Melons manager and that I will continue to do my level best to save the world from the Drunken

Comic Book Monkeys. In reality? I'm stuck reading more of your insensate drivel. Putting in the extra period when they end sentence with ellipsis, eliminating "and" as the beginning of sentences and in general enforcing the law of one punctuation mark per sentence. It's a living.

C: Dude, he totally implied that we're his cash cow!

B: We're the wind beneath his wings!

B & C: WOOOOOOOOO!

J: And that's it. I'm done. I'm outta here…!!!

ABOUT THE TALENT

Jeff Young

Jeff Young finds himself ever amazed at the crazy variety of projects he can get roped into without realizing it. Besides being editor to the Drunken Comic Book Monkeys for their first book, this year he's also had a part in a play he co-wrote and performed with Full Circle Productions, starred in a dual role in *The Space Stone from Outer Space* filmed by Spooky Moon Productions and had his artwork published in the program for the Balticon Convention. In the past he's been published in: *Carbon14* as a reviewer, interviewer and fiction writer for their first year; *Neuronet*, *Apprise* and *the Poetic Knight* as well as the ever popular *Trail of Indiscretion* and its sister production *Cemetery Moon.*

He'd like to believe he's a well rounded renaissance man so he's also:
-the unlikely leader of The Watch the Skies SF & Fantasy Reading Group of Harrisburg/Camp Hill, PA - mysite.verizon.net/res89guj/
-the actor who never expected to be on stage - fullcircleproductionz.com/
-the itinerant photographer - www.flickr.com/photos/ironmind/
-the hack writer - look for excerpts from *At the Feast of Egos*, the Ratchetpunk novel, currently blogged on myspace.com/ironmind42

John Ball

I'm a 26 year old comic book artist from Cincinnati, Ohio. I've lived a little of everywhere, but that's the place I call home.

I have been drawing cartoons and comics since the age of five. I have been professionally pursuing comic books for the last seven years. I got my break in June of 2007 with Fortress Publishing Inc. I have done pencil and ink work on *Thought and Control* issue 2 as well as this book you are holding, over the past year.

I also have a passion for heavy metal music; I play guitar and drums on multiple music endeavors. I'm an avid comic book, toy, film, and animation collector, as it goes hand and hand with most of the things I love and am involved with.

In the future I see myself drawing tons of comic books and playing lots of music while working on all things creative.

Brian Koscienski
He's the tall one.

Chris Pisano
He's the red-headed one.

Victoria Laird-Koscienski
A loving mother and caring nurse, she some how finds time to pursue a career in photography. She also enjoys hitting Brian and Chris. A lot.

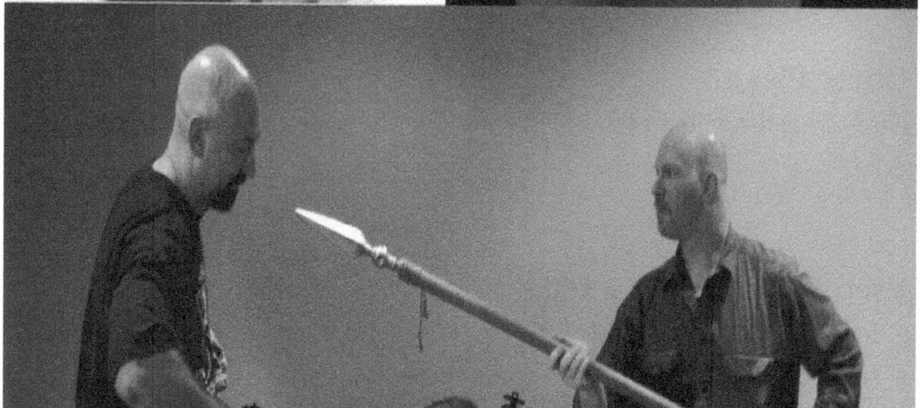